The Works of Lucian of Samosata - Volume III

Lucian of Samosata

Translated by F. G. Fowler and H. W. Fowler

THE WORKS OF LUCIAN OF SAMOSATA

Complete with exceptions specified in the preface

TRANSLATED BY

H. W. FOWLER AND F. G. FOWLER

VOLUME III

OF FOUR VOLUMES

What work nobler than transplanting foreign thought into the barren domestic soil? except indeed planting thought of your own, which the fewest are privileged to do. — *Sartor Resartus.*

At each flaw, be this your first thought: the author doubtless said something quite different, and much more to the point. And then you may hiss *me* off, if you will. —LUCIAN, *Nigrinus*, 9.

(LUCIAN) The last great master of Attic eloquence and Attic wit. — *Lord Macaulay.*

CONTENTS

LIFE OF DEMONAX

It was in the book of Fate that even this age of ours should not be destitute entirely of noteworthy and memorable men, but produce a body of extraordinary power, and a mind of surpassing wisdom. My allusions are to Sostratus the Boeotian, whom the Greeks called, and believed to be, Heracles; and more particularly to the philosopher Demonax. I saw and marvelled at both of them, and with the latter I long consorted. I have written of Sostratus elsewhere [Footnote: The life of Sostratus is not extant.], and described his stature and enormous strength, his open-air life on Parnassus, sleeping on the grass and eating what the mountain afforded, the exploits that bore out his surname—robbers exterminated, rough places made smooth, and deep waters bridged.

This time I am to write of Demonax, with two sufficient ends in view: first, to keep his memory green among good men, as far as in me lies; and secondly, to provide the most earnest of our rising generation, who aspire to philosophy, with a contemporary pattern, that they may not be forced back upon the ancients for worthy models, but imitate this best—if I am any judge—of all philosophers.

He came of a Cyprian family which enjoyed considerable property and political influence. But his views soared above such things as these; he claimed nothing less than the highest, and devoted himself to philosophy. This was not due to any exhortations of Agathobulus, his predecessor Demetrius, or Epictetus. He did indeed enjoy the converse of all these, as well as of Timocrates of Heraclea, that wise man whose gifts of expression and of understanding were equal. It was not, however, to the exhortations of any of these, but to a natural impulse towards the good, an innate yearning for philosophy which manifested itself in childish years, that he owed his superiority to all the things that ordinary men pursue. He took independence and candour for his guiding principles, lived himself an upright, wholesome, irreproachable life, and exhibited to all who saw or heard him the model of his own disposition and philosophic sincerity.

He was no half-baked enthusiast either; he had lived with the poets, and knew most of them by heart; he was a practised speaker; he had a knowledge of philosophic principles not of the superficial skin-deep order; he had developed and hardened his body by exercise

1

and toil, and, in short, had been at the pains to make himself every man's equal at every point. He was consistent enough, when he found that he could no longer suffice to himself, to depart voluntarily from life, leaving a great reputation behind him among the true nobility of Greece.

Instead of confining himself to a single philosophic school, he laid them all under contribution, without showing clearly which of them he preferred; but perhaps he was nearest akin to Socrates; for, though he had leanings as regards externals and plain living to Diogenes, he never studied effect or lived for the applause and admiration of the multitude; his ways were like other people's; he mounted no high horse; he was just a man and a citizen. He indulged in no Socratic irony; but his discourse was full of Attic grace; those who heard it went away neither disgusted by servility nor repelled by ill-tempered censure, but on the contrary lifted out of themselves by charity, and encouraged to more orderly, contented, hopeful lives.

He was never known to shout or be over vehement or angry, even when he had to correct; he touched offences, but pardoned offenders, saying that the doctors' was the right model, who treat sickness but are not angry with the sick. It is human, he thought, to err, but divine (whether in God or man) to put the error right.

A life of this sort left him without wants of his own; but he was always ready to render any proper service to his friends—including reminders to those among them who passed for fortunate, how brief was their tenure of what they so prided themselves upon. To all, on the other hand, who repined at poverty, resented exile, or complained of old age or bad health, he administered laughing consolation, and bade them not forget how soon their troubles would be over, the distinction between good and bad be obsolete, and long freedom succeed to short-lived distress.

He was fond of playing peace-maker between brothers at variance, or presiding over the restoration of marital harmony. He could say a word in season, too, before an agitated political assembly, which would turn the scale in favour of patriotic duty. Such was the temper that philosophy produced in him, kindly, mild, and cheerful.

Nothing ever grieved him except the illness or death of a friend, friendship being the one among blessings that he put highest; and indeed he was every man's friend, counting among his kindred whatever had human shape. Not that there were no degrees in the pleasure different people's society gave him; but he avoided none, except those who seemed so far astray that they could get no good from him. And every word or act in which these principles took shape might have been dictated by the Graces and Aphrodite; for 'on his lips Persuasion sat, ' as the play has it.

Accordingly he was regarded with reverence at Athens, both by the collective assembly and by the officials; he always continued to be a person of great consequence in their eyes. And this though most of them had been at first offended with him, and hated him as heartily as their ancestors had Socrates. Besides his candour and independence, there had been found Anytuses and Meletuses to repeat the historic charges: *he had never been known to sacrifice, and he made himself singular by avoiding initiation at Eleusis.* On this occasion he showed his courage by appearing in a garland and festal attire, and then pleading his cause before the people with a dash of unwonted asperity infused into his ordinary moderate tone. On the count of never having sacrificed to Athene, 'Men of Athens, ' he said, 'there is nothing wonderful in this; it was only that I gave the Goddess credit for being able to do very well without sacrifices from me. ' And in the matter of the Mysteries, his reason for not following the usual practice was this: if the Mysteries turned out to be bad, he would never be able to keep quiet about it to the uninitiated, but must dissuade them from the ceremony; while, if they were good, humanity would tempt him to divulge them. The Athenians, stone in hand already, were at once disarmed, and from that time onwards paid him honour and respect, which ultimately rose to reverence. Yet he had opened his case with a bitter enough reproof: 'Men of Athens, you see me ready garlanded; proceed to sacrifice me, then; your former offering [Footnote: i.e., Socrates.] was deficient in this formality. '

I will now give some specimens of his pointed and witty sayings, which may begin with his answers to Favorinus. The latter had heard that he made fun of his lectures, and in particular of the sentimental verses with which they were garnished, and which Demonax thought contemptible, womanish, and quite unsuited to philosophy. So he came and asked him: 'Who, pray, are you, that you should pour scorn upon me? ' 'I am the possessor of a critical pair of ears, ' was the answer. The sophist had not had enough; 'You are no infant, ' he went on, 'but a philosopher, it seems; may one ask what marks the transformation? ' 'The marks of manhood, ' said Demonax.

Another time the same person came up and asked him what school of philosophy he belonged to. 'Who told you I was a philosopher? ' was all he said. But as he left him, he had a good laugh to himself, which Favorinus observing, demanded what he was laughing at; 'I was only amused by your taking a man for a philosopher because he wears a beard, when you have none yourself. '

When Sidonius, who had a great reputation at Athens as a teacher, was boasting that he was conversant with all the philosophic systems—but I had better quote his words. 'Let Aristotle call, and I follow to the Lyceum; Plato, and I hurry to the Academy; Zeno, and I make my home in the Porch; Pythagoras, and I keep the rule of silence. ' Then rose Demonax from among the audience: 'Sidonius, Pythagoras calls. '

A pretty girlish young man called Python, son of some Macedonian grandee, once by way of quizzing him asked a riddling question and invited him to show his acumen over it. 'I only see one thing, dear child, ' he said, 'and that is, that you are a *fair* logician. ' The other lost his temper at this equivoque, and threatened him: 'You shall see in a minute what a man can do. ' 'Oh, you keep a man, do you? ' was Demonax's smiling retort.

He once, for daring to laugh at an athlete who displayed himself in gay clothes because he had won an Olympic victory, received a blow on the head with a stone, which drew blood. The bystanders were all as angry as if they had themselves been the victims, and set up a shout—'The Proconsul! the Proconsul! ' 'Thank you, gentlemen, ' said Demonax, 'but I should prefer the doctor. '

He once picked up a little gold charm in the road as he walked, and posted a notice in the market-place stating that the loser could recover his property, if he would call upon Demonax and give particulars of the weight, material, and workmanship. A handsome young exquisite came, professing to have lost it. The philosopher soon saw that it was a got-up story; 'Ah, my boy, ' he said, 'you will do very well, if you lose your other charms as little as you have lost this one. '

A Roman senator at Athens once presented his son, who had great beauty of a soft womanish type. 'My son salutes you, sir, ' he said. To which Demonax answered, 'A pretty lad, worthy of his father, and extremely like his mother. '

A cynic who emphasized his principles by wearing a bear's skin he insisted on addressing not by his name of Honoratus, but as Bruin.

Asked for a definition of Happiness, he said that only the free was happy. 'Well, ' said the questioner, 'there is no lack of free men. ' — 'I count no man free who is subject to hopes and fears. ' — 'You ask impossibilities; of these two we are all very much the slaves. ' 'Once grasp the nature of human affairs, ' said Demonax, 'and you will find that they justify neither hope nor fear, since both pain and pleasure are to have an end. '

Peregrine Proteus was shocked at his taking things so lightly, and treating mankind as a subject for humour: 'You have no teeth, Demonax. ' 'And you, Peregrine, have no bowels. '

A physical philosopher was discoursing about the antipodes; Demonax took his hand, and led him to a well, in which he showed him his own reflection: 'Do you want us to believe that the antipodes are like *that*? '

A man once boasted that he was a wizard, and possessed of mighty charms whereby he could get what he chose out of anybody. 'Will it surprise you to learn that I am a fellow-craftsman? ' asked Demonax; 'pray come with me to the baker's, and you shall see a single charm, just one wave of my magic wand, induce him to bestow several loaves upon me. ' Current coin, he meant, is as good a magician as most.

The great Herodes, mourning the untimely death of Pollux, used to have the carriage and horses got ready, and the place laid at table, as though the dead were going to drive and eat. To him came Demonax, saying that he brought a message from Pollux. Herodes, delighted with the idea that Demonax was humouring his whim like other people, asked what it was that Pollux required of him. 'He cannot think why you are so long coming to him. '

When another person kept himself shut up in the dark, mourning his son, Demonax represented himself to him as a magician: he would call up the son's ghost, the only condition being that he should be given the names of three people who had never had to mourn. The father hum'd and ha'd, unable, doubtless, to produce any such person, till Demonax broke in: 'And have you, then, a monopoly of the unendurable, when you cannot name a man who has not some grief to endure? '

He often ridiculed the people who use obsolete and uncommon words in their lectures. One of these produced a bit of Attic purism in answer to some question he had put. 'My dear sir, ' he said, 'the date of my question is to-day; that of your answer is *temp. Bell. Troj.* '

A friend asking him to come to the temple of Asclepius, there to make prayer for his son, 'Poor deaf Asclepius! ' he exclaimed; 'can he not hear at this distance? '

He once saw two philosophers engaged in a very unedifying game of cross questions and crooked answers. 'Gentlemen, ' said he, 'here is one man milking a billy-goat, and another catching the proceeds in a sieve. '

When Agathocles the Peripatetic vaunted himself as the first and only dialectician, he asked him how he could be the first, if he was the only, or the only, if he was the first.

The consular Cethegus, on his way to serve under his father in Asia, said and did many foolish things. A friend describing him as a great ass, 'Not even a *great* ass, ' said Demonax.

When Apollonius was appointed professor of philosophy in the Imperial household, Demonax witnessed his departure, attended by a great number of his pupils. 'Why, here is Apollonius with all his Argonauts, ' he cried.

Asked whether he held the soul to be immortal, 'Dear me, yes, ' he said; 'everything is. '

He remarked a propos of Herodes that Plato was quite right about our having more than one soul; the same soul could not possibly compose those splendid declamations, and have places laid for Regilla and Pollux after their death.

He was once bold enough to ask the assembled people, when he heard the sacred proclamation, why they excluded barbarians from the Mysteries, seeing that Eumolpus, the founder of them, was a barbarian from Thrace.

When he once had a winter voyage to make, a friend asked how he liked the thought of being capsized and becoming food for fishes. 'I should be very unreasonable to mind giving them a meal, considering how many they have given me. '

To a rhetorician who had given a very poor declamation he recommended constant practice. 'Why, I am always practising to myself, ' says the man. 'Ah, that accounts for it; you are accustomed to such a foolish audience. '

Observing a soothsayer one day officiating for pay, he said: 'I cannot see how you can ask pay. If it is because you can change the course of Fate, you cannot possibly put the figure high enough: if everything is settled by Heaven, and not by you, what is the good of your soothsaying? '

A hale old Roman once gave him a little exhibition of his skill in fence, taking a clothes-peg for his mark. 'What do you think of my play, Demonax? ' he said. 'Excellent, so long as you have a wooden man to play with. '

Even for questions meant to be insoluble he generally had a shrewd answer at command. Some one tried to make a fool of him by asking, If I burn a hundred pounds of wood, how many pounds of smoke shall I get? 'Weigh the ashes; the difference is all smoke. '

One Polybius, an uneducated man whose grammar was very defective, once informed him that he had received Roman citizenship from the Emperor. 'Why did he not make you a Greek instead? ' asked Demonax.

Seeing a decorated person very proud of his broad stripe, he whispered in his ear, while he took hold of and drew attention to the cloth, 'This attire did not make its original wearer anything but a sheep. '

Once at the bath the water was at boiling point, and some one called him a coward for hesitating to get in. 'What, ' said he, 'is my country expecting me to do my duty? '

Some one asked him what he took the next world to be like. 'Wait a bit, and I will send you the information. '

A minor poet called Admetus told him he had inserted a clause in his will for the inscribing on his tomb of a monostich, which I will give:

Admetus' husk earth holds, and Heaven himself.

'What a beautiful epitaph, Admetus! ' said Demonax, 'and what a pity it is not up yet! '

The shrunk shanks of old age are a commonplace; but when his reached this state, some one asked him what was the matter with them. 'Ah, ' he said with a smile, 'Charon has been having a bite at them. '

He interrupted a Spartan who was scourging his servant with, 'Why confer on your slave the privilege of Spartans [Footnote: See *Spartans* in Notes.] like yourself? ' He observed to one Danae, who was bringing a suit against her brother, 'Have the law of him by all means; it was another Danae whose father was called the Lawless. [Footnote: See *Danae* in Notes.]

He waged constant warfare against all whose philosophy was not practical, but for show. So when he saw a cynic, with threadbare cloak and wallet, but a braying-pestle instead of a staff, proclaiming himself loudly as a follower of Antisthenes, Crates, and Diogenes, he said: 'Tell us no lies; your master is the professor of braying. '

Noticing how foul play was growing among the athletes, who often supplemented the resources of boxing and wrestling with their teeth, he said it was no wonder that the champions' partisans had taken to describing them as lions.

There was both wit and sting in what he said to the proconsul. The latter was one of the people who take all the hair off their bodies with pitch-plaster. A cynic mounted a block of stone and cast this practice in his teeth, suggesting that it was for immoral purposes.

The proconsul in a rage had the man pulled down, and was on the point of condemning him to be beaten or banished, when Demonax, who was present, pleaded for him on the ground that he was only exercising the traditional cynic licence. 'Well, ' said the proconsul, 'I pardon him this time at your request; but if he offends again, what shall I do to him? ' 'Have him depilated, ' said Demonax.

Another person, entrusted by the Emperor with the command of legions and the charge of a great province, asked him what was the way to govern well. 'Keep your temper, say little, and hear much. '

Asked whether he ate honey-cakes, 'Do you suppose, ' he said, 'that bees only make honey for fools? '

Noticing near the Poecile a statue minus a hand, he said it had taken Athens a long time to get up a bronze to Cynaegirus.

Alluding to the lame Cyprian Rufinus, who was a Peripatetic and spent much time in the Lyceum walks, 'What presumption, ' he exclaimed, 'for a cripple to call himself a Walking Philosopher! '

Epictetus once urged him, with a touch of reproof, to take a wife and raise a family—for it beseemed a philosopher to leave some one to represent him after the flesh. But he received the home thrust: 'Very well, Epictetus; give me one of your daughters. '

His remark to Herminus the Aristotelian is equally worth recording. He was aware that this man's character was vile and his misdeeds innumerable, and yet his mouth was always full of Aristotle and his ten predicaments. 'Certainly, Herminus, ' he said, 'no predicament is too bad for you. '

When the Athenians were thinking, in their rivalry with Corinth, of starting gladiatorial shows, he came forward and said: 'Men of Athens, before you pass this motion, do not forget to destroy the altar of Pity. '

On the occasion of his visiting Olympia, the Eleans voted a bronze statue to him. But he remonstrated: 'It will imply a reproach to your ancestors, men of Elis, who set up no statue to Socrates or Diogenes. '

I once heard him observe to a learned lawyer that laws were not of much use, whether meant for the good or for the bad; the first do not need them, and upon the second they have no effect.

There was one line of Homer always on his tongue:

Idle or busy, death takes all alike.

He had a good word for Thersites, as a cynic and a leveller.

Asked which of the philosophers was most to his taste, he said: 'I admire them all; Socrates I revere, Diogenes I admire, Aristippus I love.'

He lived to nearly a hundred, free from disease and pain, burdening no man, asking no man's favour, serving his friends, and having no enemies. Not Athens only, but all Greece was so in love with him that as he passed the great would give him place and there would be a general hush. Towards the end of his long life he would go uninvited into the first house that offered, and there get his dinner and his bed, the household regarding it as the visit of some heavenly being which brought them a blessing. When they saw him go by, the baker-wives would contend for the honour of supplying him, and a happy woman was the actual donor. Children too used to call him father, and bring him offerings of fruit.

Party spirit was once running high at Athens; he came into the assembly, and his mere appearance was enough to still the storm. When he saw that they were ashamed, he departed again without having uttered a word.

When he found that he was no longer able to take care of himself, he repeated to his friends the tag with which the heralds close the festival:

The games are done,
The crowns all won;
No more delay,
But haste away,

and from that moment abstaining from food, left life as cheerfully as he had lived it.

When the end was near, he was asked his wishes about burial. 'Oh, do not trouble; scent will summon my undertakers. ' Well, but it would be indecent for the body of so great a man to feed birds and dogs. 'Oh, no harm in making oneself useful in death to anything that lives. '

However, the Athenians gave him a magnificent public funeral, long lamented him, worshipped and garlanded the stone seat on which he had been wont to rest when tired, accounting the mere stone sanctified by him who had sat upon it. No one would miss the funeral ceremony, least of all any of the philosophers. It was these who bore him to the grave.

I have made but a small selection of the material available; but it may serve to give readers some idea of this great man's character.

A PORTRAIT-STUDY

Lycinus. Polystratus

Ly. Polystratus, I know now what men must have felt like when they saw the Gorgon's head. I have just experienced the same sensation, at the sight of a most lovely woman. A little more, and I should have realized the legend, by being turned to stone; I am benumbed with admiration.

Poly. Wonderful indeed must have been the beauty, and terrible the power of the woman who could produce such an impression on Lycinus. Tell me of this petrifying Medusa. Who is she, and whence? I would see her myself. You will not grudge me that privilege? Your jealousy will not take alarm at the prospect of a rival petrifaction at your side?

Ly. Well, I give you fair warning: one distant glimpse of her, and you are speechless, motionless as any statue. Nay, that is a light affliction: the mortal wound is not dealt till *her* glance has fallen on *you*. What can save you then? She will lead you in chains, hither and thither, as the magnet draws the steel.

Poly. Enough! You would make her more than human. And now tell me who she is.

Ly. You think I am exaggerating: I fear you will have but a poor opinion of my eloquence when you see her as she is—so far above my praise. *Who* she is, I cannot say: but to judge from the splendour of her surroundings, her retinue, her host of eunuchs and maids, she must be of no ordinary rank.

Poly. And you never even asked her name?

Ly. Why no; but she is from Ionia; because, as she passed, I heard one of the bystanders speak aside to his neighbour: 'See, he exclaimed, 'what Smyrna can produce! And what wonder, if the fairest of Ionian cities has given birth to the fairest of women? ' I thought he must come from Smyrna himself, he was so proud of her.

Poly. There you acted your stony part to perfection. As you could neither follow her, nor make inquiries of the Smyrnaean, it only remains for you to describe her as best you can, on the chance of my recognizing her.

Ly. You know not what you ask. It is not in the power of words—certainly not of *my* words—to portray such wondrous beauty; scarcely could an Apelles, a Zeuxis, a Parrhasius, —a Phidias or an Alcamenes, do justice to it; as for my flimsy workmanship, it will but insult the original.

Poly. Well, never mind; what was she like? There can be no harm in trying your hand. What if the portrait be somewhat out of drawing? —the critic is your good friend.

Ly. I think my best way out of it will be to call in the aid of some of the old masters I have named: let them fashion the likeness for me.

Poly. Well, but—will they come? They have been dead so long.

Ly. That is easily managed: but you must not mind answering me a few questions.

Poly. You have but to ask.

Ly. Were you ever at Cnidus?

Poly. I was.

Ly. Then you have seen the *Aphrodite*, of course?

Poly. That masterpiece of Praxiteles's art! I have.

Ly. And heard the story they tell there, —of the man who fell in love with the statue, and contrived to get shut into the temple alone, and there enjoyed such favours as a statue is able to bestow. —But that is neither here nor there. —You have seen the Cnidian *Aphrodite*, anyhow; now I want to know whether you have also seen our own *Aphrodite of the Gardens*, —the Alcamenes.

Poly. I must be a dullard of dullards, if that most exquisite of Alcamenes's works had escaped my notice.

Ly. I forbear to ask whether in the course of your many visits to the Acropolis you ever observed the *Sosandra* of Calamis. [Footnote: This statue is usually identified with one of Aphrodite by the same sculptor, mentioned in Pausanias. Soteira ('saviour') is known as an epithet of Aphrodite: but Sosandra ('man-saving') is explained as a nickname of the particular statue, in playful allusion to Callias, the donor, who was apparently indebted to Aphrodite for his success with a certain Elpinice.]

Poly. Frequently.

Ly. That is really enough for my purpose. But I should just like to know what you consider to be Phidias's best work.

Poly. Can you ask? —The Lemnian *Athene*, which bears the artist's own signature; oh, and of course the *Amazon* leaning on her spear.

Ly. I approve your judgement. We shall have no need of other artists: I am now to cull from each of these its own peculiar beauty, and combine all in a single portrait.

Poly. And how are you going to do that?

Ly. It is quite simple. All we have to do is to hand over our several types to Reason, whose care it must be to unite them in the most harmonious fashion, with due regard to the consistency, as to the variety, of the result.

Poly. To be sure; let Reason take her materials and begin. What will she make of it, I wonder? Will she contrive to put all these different types together without their clashing?

Ly. Well, look; she is at work already. Observe her procedure. She begins with our Cnidian importation, from which she takes only the head; with the rest she is not concerned, as the statue is nude. The hair, the forehead, the exquisite eyebrows, she will keep as Praxiteles has rendered them; the eyes, too, those soft, yet bright-glancing eyes, she leaves unaltered. But the cheeks and the front of the face are taken from the 'Garden' Goddess; and so are the lines of the hands, the shapely wrists, the delicately-tapering fingers. Phidias and the Lemnian *Athene* will give the outline of the face, and the well-proportioned nose, and lend new softness to the cheeks; and the same artist may shape her neck and closed lips, to resemble those of his *Amazon*. Calamis adorns her with Sosandra's modesty, Sosandra's grave half- smile; the decent seemly dress is Sosandra's too, save that the head must not be veiled. For her stature, let it be that of Cnidian *Aphrodite*; once more we have recourse to Praxiteles.—What think you, Polystratus? Is it a lovely portrait?

Poly. Assuredly it will be, when it is perfected. At present, my paragon of sculptors, one element of loveliness has escaped your comprehensive grasp.

Ly. What is that?

Poly. A most important one. You will agree with me that colour and tone have a good deal to do with beauty? that black should *be* black, white be white, and red play its blushing part? It looks to me as if the most important thing of all were still lacking.

Ly. Well, how shall we manage? Call in the painters, perhaps, selecting those who were noted for their skill in mixing and laying on their colours? Be it so: we will have Polygnotus, Euphranor of course, Apelles and Aetion; they can divide the work between them. Euphranor shall colour the hair like his *Hera's*; Polygnotus the comely brow and faintly blushing cheek, after his *Cassandra* in the Assembly-room at Delphi. Polygnotus shall also paint her robe, —of the finest texture, part duly gathered in, but most of it floating in the breeze. For the flesh-tints, which must be neither too pale nor too high-coloured, Apelles shall copy his own *Campaspe*. And lastly, Aetion shall give her *Roxana's* lips. Nay, we can do better: have we not Homer, best of painters, though a Euphranor and an Apelles be present? Let him colour all like the limbs of Menelaus, which he says were 'ivory tinged with red. ' He too shall paint her calm 'ox- eyes, ' and the Theban poet shall help him to give them their 'violet' hue. Homer shall add her smile, her white arms, her rosy finger-tips, and so complete the resemblance to golden Aphrodite, to whom he has compared Brises' daughter with far less reason. So far we may trust our sculptors and painters and poets: but for her crowning glory, for the grace—nay, the choir of Graces and Loves that encircle her—who shall portray them?

Poly. This was no earthly vision, Lycinus; surely she must have dropped from the clouds. —And what was she doing?

Ly. In her hands was an open scroll; half read (so I surmised) and half to be read. As she passed, she was making some remark to one of her company; what it was I did not catch. But when she smiled, ah! then, Polystratus, I beheld teeth whose whiteness, whose unbroken regularity, who shall describe? Imagine a lovely necklace of gleaming pearls, all of a size; and imagine those dazzling rows set off by ruby lips. In that glimpse, I realized what Homer meant by his 'carven ivory.' Other women's teeth differ in size; or they project; or there are gaps: here, all was equality and evenness; pearl joined to pearl in unbroken line. Oh, 'twas a wondrous sight, of beauty more than human.

Poly. Stay. I know now whom you mean, as well from your description as from her nationality. You said that there were eunuchs in her train?

Ly. Yes; and soldiers too.

Poly. My simple friend, the lady you have been describing is a celebrity, and possesses the affections of an Emperor.

Ly. And her name?

Poly. Adds one more to the list of her charms; for it is the same as that of Abradatas's wife. [Footnote: See *Panthea* in Notes.] You know Xenophon's enthusiastic account of that beautiful and virtuous woman? —you have read it a dozen times.

Ly. Yes; and every time I read it, it is as if she stood before me. I almost hear her uttering the words the historian has put into her mouth, and see her arming her husband and sending him forth to battle.

Poly. Ah, my dear Lycinus, *this* lady has passed you but once, like a lightning flash; and your praises, I perceive, are all for those external charms that strike the eye. You are yet a stranger to her nobility of soul; you know not that higher, more god-like beauty. *I* am her fellow-countryman, I know her, and have conversed with her many times. You are aware that gentleness, humanity, magnanimity, modesty, culture, are things that I prize more than beauty-and rightly; to do otherwise would be as absurd as to value raiment above the body. Where physical perfection goes hand-in-hand with spiritual excellence, there alone (as I maintain) is true beauty. I could show you many a woman whose outward loveliness is marred by what is within; who has but to open her lips, and beauty stands confessed a faded, withered thing, the mean, unlovely handmaid of that odious mistress, her soul. Such women are like Egyptian temples: the shrine is fair and stately, wrought of costly marble, decked out with gilding and painting: but seek the God within, and you find an ape—an ibis—a goat—a cat. Of how many women is the same thing true! Beauty unadorned is not enough: and her true adornments are not purple and jewels, but those others that I have mentioned, modesty, courtesy, humanity, virtue and all that waits on virtue.

Ly. Why then, Polystratus, you shall give me story for story, good measure, shaken together, out of your abundance: paint me the portrait of her soul, that I may be no more her half-admirer.

Poly. This will be no light task, my friend. It is one thing to commend what all the world can see, and quite another to reveal what is hidden. I too shall want help with my portrait. Nor will sculptors and painters suffice me: I must have philosophers; it is by their canons that I must adjust the proportions of the figure, if I am to attain to the perfection of ancient models.

To begin then. Of her clear, liquid voice Homer might have said, with far more truth than of aged Nestor's, that

> honey from those lips distilled.

The pitch, exquisitely soft, as far removed from masculine bass as from ultra-feminine treble, is that of a boy before his voice breaks; sweet, seductive, suavely penetrating; it ceases, and still vibrating murmurs play, echo-like, about the listener's ears, and Persuasion leaves her honeyed track upon his mind. But oh! the joy, to hear her sing, and sing to the lyre's accompaniment. Let swans and halcyons and cicalas then be mute. There is no music like hers; Philomela's self, 'full-throated songstress' though she be, is all unskilled beside her. Methinks Orpheus and Amphion, whose spell drew even lifeless things to hear them, would have dropped their lyres and stood listening in silence to that voice. What should Thracian Orpheus, what should Amphion, whose days upon Cithaeron were divided betwixt his lyre and his herd, —what should they know of true concord, of accurate rhythm, of accentuation and time, of the harmonious adaptation of lyre and voice, of easy and graceful execution? Yes; once hear her sing, Lycinus, and you will know something of Sirens as well as of Gorgons: you have experienced petrifaction; you will next learn what it is to stand entranced, forgetting country and kindred. Wax will not avail you: her song will penetrate through all; for therein is every grace that Terpsichore, Melpomene, Calliope herself, could inspire. In a word, imagine that you hear such notes as should issue from those lips, those teeth that you have seen. Her perfect intonation, her pure Ionic accent, her ready Attic eloquence, need not surprise you; these are her birthright; for is not Smyrna Athens' daughter? And what more natural than that she should love poetry, and make it her chief study? Homer is her fellow citizen. —There you have my first portrait; the portrait of a sweet-voiced songstress, though it fall far short of its original. And now for others. For I do not propose to make one of many, as you did. I aim higher: the complex picture of so many beauties wrought into one, however artful be the composition, cannot escape inconsistency: with me, each separate virtue of her soul shall sit for its own portrait.

Ly. What a banquet awaits me! Here, assuredly, is good measure. Mete it out; I ask for nothing better.

Poly. I proceed then to the delineation of Culture, the confessed mistress of all mental excellences, particularly of all acquired ones: I must render her features in all their manifold variety; not even here shall my portraiture be inferior to your own. I paint her, then, with every grace that Helicon can give. Each of the Muses has but her single accomplishment, be it tragedy or history or hymn: all these Culture shall have, and with them the gifts of Hermes and of Apollo. The poet's graceful numbers, the orator's persuasive power, the historian's learning, the sage's counsel, all these shall be her adornments; the colours shall be imperishable, and laid on with no niggardly brush. It is not my fault, if I am unable to point to any classical model for the portrait: the records of antiquity afford no precedent for a culture so highly developed. —May I hang this beside the other? I think it is a passable likeness.

Ly. Passable! My dear Polystratus, it is sublime; exquisitely finished in every line.

Poly. Next I have to depict Wisdom; and here I shall have occasion for many models, most of them ancient; one comes, like the lady herself, from Ionia. The artists shall be Aeschines and Socrates his master, most realistic of painters, for their heart was in their work. We could choose no better model of wisdom than Milesian Aspasia, the admired of the admirable 'Olympian' [Footnote: See *Pericles* in

Notes.]; her political knowledge and insight, her shrewdness and penetration, shall all be transferred to our canvas in their perfect measure. Aspasia, however, is only preserved to us in miniature: *our* proportions must be those of a colossus.

Ly. Explain.

Poly. The portraits will be alike, but not on the same scale. There is a difference between the little republic of ancient Athens, and the Roman Empire of to-day; and there will be the same difference in *scale* (however close the resemblance in other respects) between our huge canvas and that miniature. A second and a third model may be found in Theano, and in the poetess of Lesbos; nay, we may add Diotima too. Theano shall give grandeur to the picture, Sappho elegance; and Diotima shall be represented as well by her wisdom and sagacity, as by the qualities for which Socrates commended her. The portrait is complete. Let it be hung.

Ly. 'Tis a fine piece of work. Proceed.

Poly. Courtesy, benevolence: that is now my subject. I have to show forth her gentle disposition, her graciousness to suppliants. She shall appear in the likeness of Theano—Antenor's Theano this time—, of Arete and her daughter Nausicaa, and of every other who in her high station has borne herself with constancy. Next comes constancy of another kind, —constancy in love; its original, the daughter of Icarius, 'constant' and 'wise, ' as Homer draws her; am I doing more than justice to his Penelope? And there is another: our lady's namesake, Abradatas's wife; of her we have already spoken.

Ly. Once more, noble work, Polystratus. And now your task must be drawing to a close: here is a whole soul depicted; its every virtue praised.

Poly. Not yet: the highest praise remains. Born to magnificence, she clothes not herself in the pride of wealth; listens not to Fortune's flattering tale, who tells her she is more than human; but walks upon the common ground, far removed from all thought of arrogance and ostentation. Every man is her equal; her greeting, her smile are for all who approach her; and how acceptable is the kindness of a superior, when it is free from every touch of condescension! When the power of the great turns not to insolence but to beneficence, we feel that Fortune has bestowed her gifts aright. Here alone Envy has no place.

For how should one man grudge another his prosperity when he sees him using it with moderation, not, like the Homeric Ate, an oppressor of the weak, trampling on men's necks? It is otherwise with those meaner souls—victims of their own ignoble vanity—, who, when Fortune has raised them suddenly beyond their hopes into her winged aerial car, know no rest, can never look behind them, but must ever press upwards. To such the end soon comes: Icarus-like, with melted wax and moulting feathers, they fall headlong into the billows, a derision to mankind. The Daedaluses use their waxen wings with moderation: they are but men; they husband their strength accordingly, and are content to fly a little higher than the waves, —so little that the sun never finds them dry; and that prudence is their salvation.

Therein lies this lady's highest praise. She has her reward: all men pray that her wings may never droop, and that blessings may increase upon her.

Ly. And may the prayer be granted! She deserves every blessing: she is not outwardly fair alone, like Helen, but has a soul within more fair, more lovely than her body. It is a fitting crown to the happiness of our benevolent and gracious Emperor, that in his day such a woman should be born; should be his, and her affections his. It is blessedness indeed, to possess one of whom we may say with Homer that she contends with golden Aphrodite in beauty, and in works is the equal of Athene. Who of womankind shall be compared to her

In comeliness, in wit, in goodly works?

Poly. Who indeed? —Lycinus, I have a proposal to make. Let us combine our portraits, yours of the body and mine of the soul, and throw them into a literary form, for the enjoyment of our generation and of all posterity. Such a work will be more enduring than those of Apelles and Parrhasius and Polygnotus; it will be far removed from creations of wood and wax and colour, being inspired by the Muses, in whom alone is that true portraiture that shows forth in one likeness a lovely body and a virtuous soul.

DEFENCE OF THE 'PORTRAIT-STUDY'

Polystratus. Lycinus

Poly. Well, here is the lady's comment. Your pages are most kind and complimentary, I am sure, Lycinus. No one would have so over-praised me who had not felt kindly towards me. But if you would know my real feeling, here it is. I never do much like the complaisant; they always strike me as insincere and wanting in frankness. But when it comes to a set panegyric, in which my much magnified virtues are painted in glaring colours, I blush and would fain stop my ears, and feel that I am rather being made fun of than commended.

Praise is tolerable up to the point at which the object of it can still believe in the existence of the qualities attributed to him; pass that point, and he is revolted and finds the flatterer out. Of course I know there are plenty of people who are glad enough to have non-existent qualities added to their praises; who do not mind being called young and lusty in their decline, or Nireuses and Phaons though they are hideous; who, Pelias-like, expect praise to metamorphose or rejuvenate them.

But they are mistaken. Praise would indeed be a most precious commodity if there were any way of converting its extravagances into solid fact. But there being none, they can only be compared to an ugly man on whom one should clap a beautiful mask, and who should then be proud of those looks that any one could take from him and break to pieces; revealed in his true likeness, he would be only the more ridiculous for the contrast between casket and treasure. Or, if you will, imagine a little man on stilts measuring heights with people who have eighteen inches the better of him in stocking feet.

And then she told this story. There was a noble lady, fair and comely in all respects except that she was short and ill-proportioned. A poet wrote an ode in her honour, and included among her beauties that of tallness; her slender height was illustrated from the poplar. She was in ecstasies, as though the verses were making her grow, and kept waving her hand. Which the poet seeing, and realizing her appetite for praise, recited the lines again and again, till at last one of the company whispered in his ear, 'Stop, my good man; you will be making her get up. '

She added a similar but still more absurd anecdote of Stratonice the wife of Seleucus, who offered a talent to the poet who should best celebrate her hair. As a matter of fact she was bald, with not a hair to call her own. But what matter what her head was like, or that every one knew how a long illness had treated her? she listened to these abandoned poets telling of hyacinthine locks, plaiting thick tresses, and making imaginary curls as crisp as parsley.

All such surrenders to flattery were laughed to scorn, with the addition that many people were just as fond of being flattered and fooled by portrait-painters as these by verbal artists. What these people look for in a painter (she said) is readiness to improve nature: Some of them insist upon the artist's taking a little off their noses, deepening the shade of their eyes, or otherwise idealizing them to order; it quite escapes them that the garlands they afterwards put on the picture are offered to another person who bears no relation to themselves.

And so she went on, finding much in your composition to approve, but displeased in particular with your likening her to Hera and Aphrodite. *Such comparisons are far too high for me*, she said, or indeed for any of womankind. Why, I would not have had you put me on a level with women of the Heroic Age, with a Penelope, an Arete, a Theano; how much less with the chief of the Goddesses. Where the Gods are concerned *(she continued; and mark her here)*, I am very apprehensive and timid. I fear that to accept a panegyric like this would be to make a Cassiopeia of myself; though indeed *she* only challenged the Nereids, and stopped short of Hera and Aphrodite.

So, Lycinus, she insisted that you must recast all this; otherwise she must call the Goddesses to witness that you had written against her wishes, and leave you to the knowledge that the piece would be an annoyance to her, if it circulated in its present shape, so lacking in reverence and piety. The outrage on reverence would be put down to her, if she allowed herself to be likened to her of Cnidus and her of the Garden. She would have you bear in mind the close of your discourse, where you spoke of the unassuming modesty that attempted no superhuman flights, but kept near the earth. It was inconsistent with that to take the same woman up to heaven and compare her with Goddesses.

She would like to be allowed as much sense as Alexander; he, when his architect proposed to transform Mount Athos into a vast image of the King with a pair of cities in his hands, shrank from the grandiose proposal; such presumption was beyond him; such patent megalomania must be suppressed; leave Athos alone, he said, and do not degrade a mighty mountain to the similitude of a poor human body. This only showed the greatness of Alexander, and itself constituted in the eyes of all future generations a monument higher than any Athos; to be able to scorn so extraordinary an honour was itself magnanimity.

So she commends your work of art, and your selective method, but cannot recognize the likeness. She does not come up to the description, nor near it, for indeed no woman could. Accordingly she sends you back your laudation, and pays homage to the originals from which you drew it. Confine your praises within the limits of humanity; if the shoe is too big, it may chance to trip her up. Then there was another point which I was to impress upon you.

I often hear, she said, —but whether it is true, you men know better than I—that at Olympia the victors are not allowed to have their statues set up larger than life; the Stewards see to it that no one transgresses this rule, examining the statues even more scrupulously than they did the competitor's qualification. Take care that we do not get convicted of false proportions, and find our statue thrown down by the Stewards.

And now I have given you her message. It is for you, Lycinus, to overhaul your work, and by removing these blemishes avoid the offence. They shocked and made her nervous as I read; she kept on addressing the Goddesses in propitiatory words; and such feelings may surely be permitted to her sex. For that matter, to be quite frank, I shared them to some extent. At the first hearing I found no offence; but as soon as she put her finger on the fault, I began to agree. You know what happens with visible objects; if we look at them at close quarters, just under our eyes, I mean, we distinguish nothing clearly; but stepping back to the right distance, we get a clear conception of what is right and what is wrong about them. That was my experience here.

After all, to compare a mortal to Hera and Aphrodite is cheapening the Goddesses, and nothing else. In such comparisons the small is not so much magnified as the great is diminished and reduced. If a giant and a dwarf were walking together, and their heights had to be equalized, no efforts of the dwarf could effect it, however much he stood on tiptoe; the giant must stoop and make himself out shorter than he is. So in this sort of portraiture: the human is not so much exalted by the similitude as the divine is belittled and pulled down. If indeed a lack of earthly beauties forced the artist upon scaling Heaven, he might perhaps be acquitted of blasphemy; but your enterprise was so needless; why Aphrodite and Hera, when you have all mortal beauty to choose from?

Prune and chasten, then, Lycinus. All this is not quite like you, who never used to be over-ready with your commendation; you seem to have gone now to the opposite extreme of prodigality, and developed from a niggard into a spendthrift of praise. Do not be ashamed to make alterations in what you have already published, either. They say Phidias did as much after finishing his Olympian Zeus. He stood behind the doors when he had opened them for the first time to let the work be seen, and listened to the comments favourable or the reverse. One found the nose too broad, another the face too long, and so on. When the company was gone, he shut himself up again to correct and adapt his statue to the prevailing taste. Advice so many-headed was not to be despised; the many must after all see further than the one, though that one be Phidias. There is the counsel of a friend and well-wisher to back up the lady's message.

Ly. Why, Polystratus, I never knew what an orator you were. After that eloquent close-packed indictment of my booklet, I almost despair of the defence. You and she were not quite judicial, though; you less than she, in condemning the accused when its counsel was not in court. It is always easy to win a walk-over, you know; so no wonder we were convicted, not being allowed to speak or given the ear of the court. But, still more monstrous, you were accusers and jury at once. Well, what am I to do? accept the verdict and hold my tongue? pen a palinode like Stesichorus? or will you grant an appeal?

Poly. Surely, if you have anything to say for yourself. For you will be heard not by opponents, as you say, but by friends. Indeed, my place is with you in the dock.

Ly. How I wish I could, have spoken in her own presence! that would have been far better; but I must do it by proxy. However, if you will report me to her as well as you did her to me, I will adventure.

Poly. Trust me to do justice to the defence; but put it shortly, in mercy to my memory.

Ly. So severe an indictment should by rights be met at length; but for your sake I will cut it short. Put these considerations before her from me, then.

Poly. No, not that way, please. Make your speech, just as though she were listening, and I will reproduce you to her.

Ly. Very well, then. She is here; she has just delivered the oration which you have described to me; it is now counsel's turn. And yet—I must confide my feelings to you—you have made my undertaking somehow more formidable; you see the beads gather on my brow; my courage goes; I seem to see her there; my situation bewilders me. Yet begin I will; how can I draw back when she is there?

Poly. Ah, but her face promises a kindly hearing; see how bright and gracious. Pluck up heart, man, and begin.

Ly. Most noble lady, in what you term the great and excessive praise that I bestowed upon you, I find no such high testimony to your merits as that which you have borne yourself by your surprise at the attribution of divinity. That one thing surpasses all that I have said of you, and my only excuse for not having added this trait to my portrait is that I was not aware of it; if I had been, no other should have had precedence of it. In this light I find myself, far from exaggerating, to have fallen much short of the truth. Consider the magnitude of this omission, the convincing demonstration of a sterling character and a right disposition which I lost; for those will be the best in human relations who are most earnest in their dealings with the divine. Why, were it decided that I must correct my words and retouch my statue, I should do it not by presuming to take away from it, but by adding this as its crowning grace. But from another point of view I have a great debt of gratitude to acknowledge. I commend your natural modesty, and your freedom from that vanity and pride which so exalted a position as yours might excuse. The best witness to my correctness is just the exception that you have taken to my words. That instead of receiving the praise I offered as your right you should be disturbed at it and call it excessive, is the proof of your unassuming modesty. Nevertheless, the more you reveal that this is your view of praise, the stronger proof you give of your own worthiness to be praised. You are an exact illustration of what Diogenes said when some one asked him how he might become famous: — 'by despising fame. ' So if I were asked who most deserve praise, I should answer, Those who refuse it.

But I am perhaps straying from the point. What I have to defend is the having likened you, in giving your outward form, to the Cnidian and the Garden *Aphrodite*, to *Hera* and *Athene*; such comparisons you find out of all proportion. I will deal directly with them, then. It has indeed been said long ago that poets and painters are irresponsible; that is still more true, I conceive, of panegyrists, even humble prose ones like myself who are not run away with by their metre. Panegyric is a chartered thing, with no standard quantitative measure to which it must conform; its one and only aim is to express deep admiration and set its object in the most enviable light. However, I do not intend to take that line of defence; you might think I did so because I had no other open.

But I have. I refer you to the proper formula of panegyric, which requires the author to introduce illustrations, and depends mainly on their goodness for success. Now this goodness is shown not when the illustration is just like the thing illustrated, nor yet when it is inferior, but when it is as high above it as may be. If in praising a dog one should remark that it was bigger than a fox or a cat, would you regard him as a skilful panegyrist? certainly not. Or if he calls it the equal of a wolf, he has not made very much of it so either. Where is the right thing to be found? why, in likening the dog's size and spirit to the lion's. So the poet who would praise Orion's dog called it the lion-queller. There you have the perfect panegyric of the dog. Or take Milo of Croton, Glaucus of Carystus, or Polydamas; to say of them by way of panegyric that each of them was stronger than a woman would be to make oneself a laughing-stock; one man instead of the woman would not much mend matters. But what, pray, does a famous poet make of Glaucus? —

> To match those hands not e'en the might
> Of Pollux' self had dared;
> Alcmena's son, that iron wight,
> Had shrunk—

See what Gods he equals him to, or rather what Gods he puts him above. And Glaucus took no exception to being praised at the expense of his art's patron deities; nor yet did they send any judgement on athlete or poet for irreverence; both continued to be honoured in Greece, one for his might, and the other for this even more than for his other odes. Do not be surprised, then, that when I wished to conform to the canons of my art and find an illustration, I took an exalted one, as reason was that I should.

You used the word flattery. To dislike those who practise it is only what you should do, and I honour you for it. But I would have you distinguish between panegyric proper and the flatterer's exaggeration of it. The flatterer praises for selfish ends, cares little for truth, and makes it his business to magnify indiscriminately; most of his effects consist in lying additions of his own; he thinks nothing of making Thersites handsomer than Achilles, or telling Nestor he is younger than any of the host; he will swear Croesus's son hears better than Melampus, and give Phineus better sight than Lynceus, if he sees his way to a profit on the lie. But the panegyrist pure and simple, instead of lying outright, or inventing a quality that does not exist, takes the virtues his subject really does possess, though possibly not in large measure, and makes the most of them. The horse is really distinguished among the animals we know for light-footed speed; well, in praising a horse, he will hazard:

The corn-stalks brake not 'neath his airy tread.

He will not be frightened of 'whirlwind-footed steeds. ' If his theme is a noble house, with everything handsome about it,

Zeus on Olympus dwells in such a home,

we shall be told. But your flatterer would use that line about the swineherd's hovel, if he saw a chance of getting anything out of the swineherd. Demetrius Poliorcetes had a flatterer called Cynaethus who, when he was gravelled for lack of matter, found some in a cough that troubled his patron—he cleared his throat so musically!

There you have one criterion: flatterers do not draw the line at a lie if it will please their patrons; panegyrists aim merely at bringing into relief what really exists. But there is another great difference: the flatterers exaggerate as much as ever they can; the panegyrists in the midst of exaggeration observe the limitations of decency. And now that you have one or two of the many tests for flattery and panegyric proper, I hope you will not treat all praise as suspect, but make distinctions and assign each specimen to its true class.

By your leave I will proceed to apply the two definitions to what I wrote; which of them fits it? If it had been an ugly woman that I likened to the Cnidian statue, I should deserve to be thought a toady, further gone in flattery than Cynaethus. But as it was one for whose charms I can call all men to witness, my shot was not so far out.

Now you will perhaps say—nay, you have said already—Praise my beauty, if you will; but the praise should not have been of that invidious kind which compares a woman to Goddesses. Well, I will keep truth at arm's length no longer; I did *not*, dear lady, compare you to Goddesses, but to the handiwork in marble and bronze and ivory of certain good artists. There is no impiety, surely, in illustrating mortal beauty by the work of mortal hands—unless you take the thing that Phidias fashioned to be indeed Athene, or Praxiteles's not much later work at Cnidus to be the heavenly Aphrodite. But would that be quite a worthy conception of divine beings? I take the real presentment of them to be beyond the reach of human imitation.

But granting even that it had been the actual Goddesses to whom I likened you, it would be no new track, of which I had been the pioneer; it had been trodden before by many a great poet, most of all by your fellow citizen Homer, who will kindly now come and share my defence, on pain of sharing my sentence. I will ask him, then—or rather you for him; for it is one of your merits to have all his finest passages by heart—what think you, then, of his saying about the captive Briseis that in her mourning for Patroclus she was 'Golden Aphrodite's peer'? A little further on, Aphrodite alone not meeting the case, it is:

So spake that weeping dame, a match for Goddesses.

When he talks like that, do you take offence and fling the book away, or has *he* your licence to expatiate in panegyric? Whether he has yours or not, he has that of all these centuries, wherein not a critic has found fault with him for it, not he that dared to scourge his statue [Footnote: Zoilus, called Homeromastix.], not he whose marginal pen [Footnote: Aristarclius.] bastarded so many of his verses. Now, shall he have leave to match with Golden Aphrodite a barbarian woman, and her in tears, while I, lest I should describe the beauty that you like not to hear of, am forbidden to compare certain images to a lady who is ever bright and smiling—that beauty which mortals share with Gods?

When he had Agamemnon in hand, he was most chary of divine similitudes, to be sure! what economy and moderation in his use of them! Let us see—eyes and head from Zeus, belt from Ares, chest from Posidon; why, he deals the man out piecemeal among the host of Heaven. Elsewhere, Agamemnon is 'like baleful Ares'; others have their heavenly models; Priam's son (a Phrygian, mark) is 'of form divine, ' the son of Peleus is again and again 'a match for Gods. ' But let us come back to the feminine instances You remember, of course,

> —a match
> For Artemis or golden Aphrodite;

and

> Like Artemis adown the mountain slope.

But he does not even limit himself to comparing the whole man to a God; Euphorbus's mere hair is called like the Graces—when it is dabbled with blood, too. In fact the practice is so universal that no branch of poetry can do without its ornaments from Heaven. Either let all these be blotted, or let me have the same licence. Moreover, illustration is so irresponsible that Homer allows himself to convey his compliments to Goddesses by using creatures inferior to them. Hera is ox-eyed. Another poet colours Aphrodite's eyes from the violet. As for fingers like the rose, it takes but little of Homer's society to bring us acquainted with them.

Still, so far we do not get beyond mere looks; a man is only called *like* a God. But think of the wholesale adaptation of their names, by Dionysiuses, Hephaestions, Zenos, Posidoniuses, Hermaeuses. Leto, wife of Evagoras, King of Cyprus, even dispensed with adaptation; but her divine namesake, who could have turned her into stone like Niobe, took no offence. What need to mention that the most religious race on earth, the Egyptian, never tires of divine names? most of those it uses hail from Heaven.

Consequently, there is not the smallest occasion for you to be nervous about the panegyric. If what I wrote contains anything offensive to the deity, you are not responsible, unless you consider we are responsible for all that goes in at our ears; no, I shall pay the penalty—as soon as the Gods have settled with Homer and the other poets. Ah, and they have not done so yet with the best of all philosophers [Footnote: Lucian's 'best of all philosophers' might be Plato, who is their spokesman in 'The Fisher' (see Sections 14, 22), or Epicurus, in the light of two passages in the 'Alexander' (Sections 47, 61) in which he almost declares himself an Epicurean. The exact words are not found in Plato, though several similar expressions are quoted; words of Epicurus appear to be translated in Cicero, *De nat. Deorum*, Book I, xviii s. f., hominis esse specie deos confitendum est: we must admit that the Gods are in the image of man.], for saying that man is a likeness of God. But now, though I could say much more, madam, I must have compassion upon Polystratus's memory, and cease.

Poly. I am not so sure I am equal to it, Lycinus, as it is. You have made it long, and exceeded your time limit. However, I will do my best. See, I scurry off with my fingers in my ears, that no alien sound may find its way in to disturb the arrangement; I do not want to be hissed by my audience.

Ly. Well, the responsibility for a correct report lies with you alone. And having now duly instructed you, I will retire for the present. But when the verdict is brought into court, I will be there to learn the result.

TOXARIS: A DIALOGUE OF FRIENDSHIP

Mnesippus. Toxaris

Mne. Now, Toxaris: do you mean to tell me that you people actually *sacrifice* to Orestes and Pylades? do you take them for Gods?

Tox. Sacrifice to them? of course we do. It does not follow that we think they are Gods: they were good men.

Mne. And in Scythia 'good men' receive sacrifice just the same as Gods?

Tox. Not only that, but we honour them with feasts and public gatherings.

Mne. But what do you expect from them? They are shades now, so their goodwill can be no object.

Tox. Why, as to that, I think it may be just as well to have a good understanding even with shades. But that is not all: in honouring the dead we consider that we are also doing the best we can for the living. Our idea is that by preserving the memory of the noblest of mankind, we induce many people to follow their example.

Mne. Ah, there you are right. But what could you find to admire in Orestes and Pylades, that you should exalt them to godhead? They were strangers to you: strangers, did I say? they were enemies! Why, when they were shipwrecked on your coast, and your ancestors laid hands on them, and took them off to be sacrificed to Artemis, they assaulted the gaolers, overpowered the garrison, slew the king, carried off the priestess, laid impious hands on the Goddess herself, and so took ship, snapping their fingers at Scythia and her laws. If you honour men for this kind of thing, there will be plenty of people to follow their example, and you will have your hands full. You may judge for yourselves, from ancient precedent, whether it will suit you to have so many Oresteses and Pyladeses putting into your ports. It seems to me that it will soon end in your having no religion left at all: God after God will be expatriated in the same manner, and then I suppose you will supply their place by deifying their kidnappers, thus rewarding sacrilege with sacrifice. If this is not your motive in honouring Orestes and Pylades, I shall be glad to know what other service they have rendered you, that you should change your minds about them, and admit them to divine honours. Your ancestors did their best to offer them up to Artemis: you offer up victims to them. It seems an absurd inconsistency.

Tox. Now, in the first place, the incident you refer to is very much to their credit. Think of those two entering on that vast undertaking by themselves: sailing away from their country to the distant Euxine [Footnote: See *Euxine* in Notes.]—that sea unknown in those days to the Greeks, or known only to the Argonauts—unmoved by the stories they heard of it, undeterred by the inhospitable name it then bore, which I suppose referred to the savage nations that dwelt upon its shores; think of their courageous bearing after they were captured; how escape alone would not serve them, but they must avenge their wrong upon the king, and carry Artemis away over the seas. Are not these admirable deeds, and shall not the doers be counted as Gods by all who esteem prowess? However, this is not our motive in giving them divine honours.

Mne. Proceed. What else of godlike and sublime was in their conduct? Because from the seafaring point of view, there are any number of merchants whose divinity I will maintain against theirs: the Phoenicians, in particular, have sailed to every port in Greek and foreign waters, let alone the Euxine, the Maeotian Lake and the Bosphorus; year after year they explore every coast, only returning home at the approach of winter. Hucksters though they be for the most part, and fishmongers, you must deify them all, to be consistent.

Tox. Now, now, Mnesippus, listen to me, and you shall see how much more candid we barbarians are in our valuation of good men than you Greeks. In Argos and Mycenae there is not so much as a respectable tomb raised to Orestes and Pylades: in Scythia, they have their temple, which is very appropriately dedicated to the two friends in common, their sacrifices, and every honour. The fact of their being foreigners does not prevent us from recognizing their virtues. We do not inquire into the nationality of noble souls: we can hear without envy of the illustrious deeds of our enemies; we do justice to their merits, and count them Scythians in deed if not in name. What particularly excites our reverent admiration in the present case is the unparalleled loyalty of the two friends; in them we have a model from which every man may learn how he must share good and evil fortune with his friends, if he would enjoy the esteem of all good Scythians. The sufferings they endured with and for one another our ancestors recorded on a brazen pillar in the Oresteum; and they made it law, that the education of their children should begin with committing to memory all that is inscribed thereon. More easily shall a child forget his own father's name than be at fault in the achievements of Orestes and Pylades. Again, in the temple corridor are pictures by the artists of old, illustrating the story set forth on the pillar. Orestes is first shown on shipboard, with his friend at his side. Next, the ship has gone to pieces on the rocks; Orestes is captured and bound; already Iphigenia prepares the two victims for sacrifice. But on the opposite wall we see that Orestes has broken free; he slays Thoas and many a Scythian; and the last scene shows them sailing away, with Iphigenia and the Goddess; the Scythians clutch vainly at the receding vessel; they cling to the rudder, they strive to clamber on board; at last, utterly baffled, they swim back to the shore, wounded or terrified. It is at this point in their conflict with the Scythians that the devotion of the friends is best illustrated: the painter makes each of them disregard his own enemies, and ward off his friend's assailants, seeking to intercept the arrows before they can reach him, and counting lightly of death, if he can save his friend, and receive in his own person the wounds that are meant for the other. Such devotion, such loyal and loving partnership in danger, such true and steadfast affection, we held to be more than human; it indicated a spirit not to be found in common men. While the gale is prosperous, we all take it very much amiss if our friends will not share equally with us: but let the wind shift ever so little, and we leave them to weather the storm by themselves. I must tell you that in Scythia no quality is more highly esteemed than this of friendship; there is nothing on which a Scythian prides himself so much as on sharing the toils and dangers of his friend; just as nothing is a greater reproach among us than treachery to a friend. We honour Orestes and Pylades, then, because they excelled in the Scythian virtue of loyalty, which we place above all others; and it is for this that we have bestowed on them the name of Coraci, which in our language means spirits of friendship.

Mne. Ah, Toxaris, so archery is not the only accomplishment of the Scythians, I find; they excel in rhetorical as well as in military skill. You have persuaded me already that you were right in deifying Orestes and Pylades, though I thought differently just now. I had no conception, either, what a painter you were. Your description of the pictures in the Oresteum was most vivid; —that battle-scene, and the way in which the two intercepted one another's wounds. Only I should never have thought that the Scythians would set such a high value on friendship: they are such a wild, inhospitable race; I should have said they had more to do with anger and hatred and enmity than with friendship, even for their nearest relations, judging by what one is told; it is said, for instance, that they devour their fathers' corpses.

Tox. Well, which of the two is the more dutiful and pious in general, Greek or Scythian, we will not discuss just now: but that we are more loyal friends than you, and that we treat friendship more seriously, is easily shown. Now please do not be angry with me, in the name of all your Gods: but I am going to mention a few points I have observed during my stay in this country. I can see that you are all admirably well qualified to talk about friendship: but when it comes to putting your words into practice, there is a considerable falling off; it is enough for you to have demonstrated what an excellent thing friendship is, and somehow or other, at the critical moment, you make off, and leave your fine words to look after themselves. Similarly, when your tragedians represent this subject on the stage, you are loud in your applause; the spectacle of one friend risking his life for another generally brings tears to your eyes: but you are quite incapable of rendering any such signal services yourselves; once let your friends get into difficulties, and all those tragic reminiscences take wing like so many dreams; you are then the very image of the silent mask which the actor has thrown aside: its mouth is open to its fullest extent, but not a syllable does it utter. It is the other way with us: we are as much superior to you in the practice of friendship, as we are inferior in expounding the theory of it.

Now, what do you say to this proposal? let us leave out of the question all the cases of ancient friendship that either of us might enumerate (there you would have the advantage of me: you could produce all the poets on your side, most credible of witnesses, with their Achilles and Patroclus, their Theseus and Pirithous, and others, all celebrated in the most charming verses); and instead let each of us advance a few instances of devotion that have occurred within his own experience, among our respective countrymen; these we will relate in detail, and whoever can show the best friendships is the winner, and announces his country as victorious. Mighty issues are at stake: I for my part would rather be worsted in single combat, and lose my right hand, as the Scythian custom is, than yield to any man on the question of friendship, above all to a Greek; for am I not a Scythian?

Mne. I have got my work cut out for me, if I am to engage an old soldier like Toxaris, with a whole arsenal of keen words at his command. Well, I am not such a craven as to decline the challenge, when my country's honour is at stake. Could those two overcome the host of Scythians represented in the legend, and in the ancient pictures you have just described so impressively, —and shall Greece, her peoples and her cities, be condemned for want of one to plead her cause? Strange indeed, if that were so; I should deserve to lose not my hand like you, but my tongue. Well now, is the number of friendships to be limited, or does wealth of instances itself constitute one claim to superiority?

Tox. Oh no; number counts for nothing, that must be understood. We have the same number, and it is simply a question whether yours are better and more pointed than mine; if they are, of course, the wounds you inflict will be the more deadly, and I shall be the first to succumb.

Mne. Very well. Let us fix the number: I say five each.

Tox. Five be it, and you begin. But you must be sworn first: because the subject naturally lends itself to fictitious treatment; there is no checking anything. When you have sworn, it would be impious to doubt your word.

Mne. Very well, if you think it necessary. Have you any preference among our Gods? How would the God of Friendship meet the case?

Tox. Excellently; and when my turn comes, I will employ the national oath of the Scythians.

Mne. Zeus the God of Friendship be my witness, that all I shall now relate is derived either from my own experience, or from such careful inquiry as I was able to make of others; and is free from all imaginative additions of my own. I will begin with, the friendship of Agathocles and Dinias. The story is well known in Ionia. This Agathocles was a native of Samos, and lived not many years ago. Though his conduct showed him to be the best of friends, he was of no better family and in no better circumstances than the generality of the Samians. From boyhood he had been the friend of Dinias, the son of Lyson, an Ephesian. Dinias, it seems, was enormously wealthy, and as his wealth was newly acquired, it is not to be wondered at that he had plenty of acquaintances besides Agathocles; persons who were quite qualified to share his pleasures, and to be his boon-companions, but who were very far indeed from being friends. For some time Agathocles—little as he cared for such a life—played his convivial part with the rest, Dinias making no distinction between him and the parasites. Finally, however, he took to finding fault with his friend's conduct, and gave great offence: his continual allusions to Dinias's ancestry, and his exhortations to him to husband the fortune which had cost his father such labour to acquire, seemed to his friend to be in indifferent taste. He gave up asking Agathocles to join in his revels, contented himself with the company of his parasites, and sought to elude his friend's observation. Well, the misguided youth was presently persuaded by his flatterers that he had made a conquest of Chariclea, the wife of Demonax, an eminent Ephesian, holding the highest office in that city. He was kept well supplied with billets-doux, half-faded flowers, bitten apples, and all the stock-in-trade of those intriguing dames whose business it is to fan an artificial passion that vanity has inspired. There is no more seductive bait to young men who value themselves on their personal attractions, than the belief that they have made an impression; they are sure to fall into the trap. Chariclea was a charming little woman, but sadly wanting in reserve: any one might enjoy her favours, and on the easiest of terms; the most casual glance was sure to meet with encouragement; there was never any fear of a repulse from Chariclea. With more than professional skill, she could draw on a hesitating lover till his subjugation was complete: then, when she was sure of him, she had a variety of devices for inflaming his passion: she could storm, and she could flatter; and flattery would be succeeded by contempt, or by a feigned preference for his rival; —in short, her resources were infinite; she was armed against her lovers at every point. This was the lady whom Dinias's parasites now associated with them; they played their subordinate part well, and between them fairly hustled the boy into a passion for Chariclea. Such a finished mistress of the art of perdition, who had ruined plenty of victims before, and acted love-scenes and swallowed fine fortunes without number, was not likely to let this simple inexperienced youth out of her clutches: she struck her talons into him on every side, and secured her quarry so effectually, that she was involved in his destruction, —to say nothing of the miseries of the hapless victim. She got to work at once with the billets-doux. Her maid was for ever coming with news of tears and sleepless nights: 'her poor mistress was ready to hang herself for love. ' The ingenuous youth was at length driven to conclude that his attractions were too much for the ladies of Ephesus; he yielded to the girl's entreaties, and waited upon her mistress. The rest, of course, was easy. How was he to resist this pretty woman, with her captivating manners, her well-timed tears, her parenthetic sighs? Lingering farewells, joyful welcomes, judicious airs and graces, song and lyre, —all were brought to bear upon him. Dinias was soon a lost man, over head and ears in love; and Chariclea prepared to give the finishing stroke. She informed him that he was about to become a father, which was enough in itself to inflame the amorous simpleton; and she discontinued her visits to him; her husband, she said, had discovered her passion, and was watching her. This was altogether too much for Dinias: he was inconsolable; wept, sent messages by his parasites, flung his arms about her statue—a marble one which he had had made—, shrieked forth her name in loud lamentation, and finally threw himself down upon the ground and rolled about in a positive frenzy. Her apples and her flowers drew forth presents which were on quite another scale of munificence: houses and farms, servants, exquisite fabrics, and gold to any extent. To make a long story short, the house of Lyson, which had the reputation of being the wealthiest in Ionia, was quite cleared out. No sooner was this the case, than Chariclea abandoned Dinias, and went off in pursuit of a certain golden youth of Crete, irresistible as he, and not less gullible. Deserted alike by her and by his parasites (who followed the chase of the fortunate Cretan), Dinias presented himself before Agathocles, who had long been aware of his friend's situation. He swallowed his first feelings of embarrassment, and made a clean breast of it all: his love, his ruin, his mistress's disdain, his Cretan rival; and ended by protesting that without Chariclea he could not live. Agathocles did not think it necessary to remind Dinias just then how he alone had been excluded from his friendship, and how parasites had been preferred to him: instead, he went off and sold his family residence in Samos—the only property he possessed—and brought him the proceeds, 750 pounds. Dinias had no sooner received the money, than it became evident that he had somehow recovered his good looks, in the opinion of Chariclea: once more the maid-servant and the notes, with reproaches for his long neglect; once more, too, the throng of parasites; they saw that there were still pickings to be had. Dinias arrived at her house, by agreement, at about bedtime, and was already inside, when Demonax—whether he had an understanding with his wife in the matter, as some say, or had got his information independently—sprang out from concealment, gave orders to his servants to make the door fast and to secure Dinias, and then drew his sword, breathing fire and flagellation against the paramour. Dinias, realizing his danger, caught up a heavy bar that lay near, and dispatched Demonax with a blow on the temple; then, turning to Chariclea, he dealt blow after blow with the same weapon, and finally plunged her husband's sword into her body. The domestics stood by, dumb with amazement and terror; and when at length they attempted to seize him, he rushed at them with the sword, put them to flight, and slipped away from the fatal scene. The rest of that night he and Agathocles spent at the latter's house, pondering on the deed and its probable consequences. The news soon spread, and in the morning officers came to arrest Dinias. He made no attempt to deny the murder, and was conducted into the presence of the then Prefect of Asia, who sent him up to the Emperor. He presently returned, under sentence of perpetual banishment to Gyarus, one of the Cyclades. All this time, Agathocles had never left his side: with unfaltering devotion, he accompanied him to Italy, and was the only friend who stood by him in his trial. And now even in his banishment he would not desert him, but condemned himself to share the sentence; and when the necessaries of life failed them, he hired himself out as a diver in the purple-fishery, and with the proceeds of his industry supported Dinias and tended him in his sickness till the end. Even when all was over, he would not return to his own home, but remained on the island, thinking it shame even in death to desert his friend. There you have the history of a Greek friendship, and one of recent date; I think it can scarcely be as much as five years ago that Agathocles died on Gyarus.

Tox. I wish I were at liberty to doubt the truth of your story: but alas! you speak under oath. Your Agathocles is a truly Scythian friend; I only hope there are no more of the same kind to come.

Mne. See what you think of the next—Euthydicus of Chalcidice. I heard his story from Simylus, a shipmaster of Megara, who vowed that he had been an eyewitness of what he related. He set sail from Italy about the setting of the Pleiads, bound for Athens, with a miscellaneous shipload of passengers, among whom were Euthydicus and his comrade Damon, also of Chalcidice. They were of about the same age. Euthydicus was a powerful man, in robust health; Damon was pale and weakly, and looked as if he were just recovering from a long illness. They had a good voyage as far as Sicily: but they had no sooner passed through the Straits into the Ionian Sea, than a tremendous storm overtook them. I need not detain you with descriptions of mountainous billows and whirlwinds and hail and the other adjuncts of a storm: suffice it to say, that they were compelled to take in all sail, and trail cables after them to break the force of the waves, and in this way made Zacynthus by about midnight. At this point Damon, being seasick, as was natural in such a heavy sea, was leaning over the side, when (as I suppose) an unusually violent lurch of the vessel in his direction, combining with the rush of water across the deck, hurled him headlong into the sea. The poor wretch was not even naked, or he might have had a chance of swimming: it was all he could do to keep himself above water, and get out a cry for help. Euthydicus was lying in his berth undressed. He heard the cry, flung himself into the sea, and succeeded in overtaking the exhausted Damon; and a powerful moonlight enabled those on deck to see him swimming at his side for a considerable distance, and supporting him. 'We all felt for them, ' said Simylus, 'and longed to give them some assistance, but the gale was too much for us: we did, however, throw out a number of corks and spars on the chance of their getting hold of some of them, and being carried to shore; and finally we threw over the gangway, which was of some size. '—Now only think: could any man give a surer proof of affection, than by throwing himself into a furious sea like that to share the death of his friend? Picture to yourself the surging billows, the roar of crashing waters, the hissing foam, the darkness, the hopeless prospect: look at Damon, —he is at his last gasp, he barely keeps himself up, he holds out his hands imploringly to his friend: and lastly look at Euthydicus, as he leaps into the water, and swims by his side, with only one thought in his mind, —Damon must not be the first to perish; —and you will see that Euthydicus too was no bad friend.

Tox. I tremble for their fate: were they drowned, or did some miraculous providence deliver them?

Mne. Oh, they were saved all right; and they are in Athens at this day, both of them, studying philosophy. Simylus's story closes with the events of the night: Damon has fallen overboard, Euthydicus has jumped in to his rescue, and the pair are left swimming about till they are lost in the darkness. Euthydicus himself tells the rest. It seems that first they came across some pieces of cork, which helped to support them; and they managed with much ado to keep afloat, till about dawn they saw the gangway, swam up to it, clambered on, and were carried to Zacynthus without further trouble. These, I think, are passable instances of friendship; and my third is no way inferior to them, as you shall hear.

Eudamidas of Corinth, though he was himself in very narrow circumstances, had two friends who were well-to-do, Aretaeus his fellow townsman, and Charixenus of Sicyon. When Eudamidas died, he left a will behind him which I dare say would excite most people's ridicule: but what the generous Toxaris, with his respect for friendship and his ambition to secure its highest honours for his country, may think of the matter, is another question. The terms of the will—but first I should explain that Eudamidas left behind him an aged mother and a daughter of marriageable years; —the will, then, was as follows: *To Aretaeus I bequeath my mother, to tend and to cherish in her old age: and to Charixenus my daughter, to give in marriage with such dowry as his circumstances will admit of: and should anything befall either of the legatees, then let his portion pass to the survivor.* The reading of this will caused some merriment among the hearers, who knew of Eudamidas's poverty, but did not know anything of the friendship existing between him and his heirs. They went off much tickled at the handsome legacy that Aretaeus and Charixenus (lucky dogs!) had come in for: 'Eudamidas, ' as they expressed it, 'was apparently to have a death- interest in the property of the legatees. ' However, the latter had no sooner heard the will read, than they proceeded to execute the testator's intentions. Charixenus only survived Eudamidas by five days: but Aretaeus, most generous of heirs, accepted the double bequest, is supporting the aged mother at this day, and has only lately given the daughter in marriage, allowing to her and to his own daughter portions of 500 pounds each, out of his whole property of 1,250 pounds; the two marriages were arranged to take place on the same day. What do you think of him, Toxaris? This is something like friendship, is it not, —to accept such a bequest as this, and to show such respect for a friend's last wishes? May we pass this as one of my five?

Tox. Excellent as was the behaviour of Aretaeus, I admire still more Eudamidas's confidence in his friends. It shows that he would have done as much for them; even if nothing had been said about it in their wills, he would have been the first to come forward and claim the inheritance as natural heir.

Mne. Very true. And now I come to Number Four—Zenothemis of Massilia, son of Charmoleos. He was pointed out to me when I was in Italy on public business: a fine, handsome man, and to all appearance well off. But by his side (he was just driving away on a journey) sat his wife, a woman of most repulsive appearance; all her right side was withered; she had lost one eye; in short, she was a positive fright. I expressed my surprise that a man in the prime of manly beauty should endure to have such a woman seated by him. My informant, who was a Massiliot himself, and knew how the marriage had come about, gave me all the particulars. 'The father of this unsightly woman, ' he said, 'was Menecrates; and he and Zenothemis were friends in days when both were men of wealth and rank. The property of Menecrates, however, was afterwards confiscated by the Six Hundred, and he himself disfranchised, on the ground that he had proposed an unconstitutional measure; this being the regular penalty in Massilia for such offences. The sentence was in itself a heavy blow to Menecrates, and it was aggravated by the sudden change from wealth to poverty and from honour to dishonour. But most of all he was troubled about this daughter: she was now eighteen years old, and it was time that he found her a husband; yet with her unfortunate appearance it was not probable that any one, however poor or obscure, would have taken her, even with all the wealth her father had possessed previous to his sentence; it was said, too, that she was subject to fits at every increase of the moon. He was bewailing his hard lot to Zenothemis, when the latter interrupted him: "Menecrates, " he said, "be sure that you shall want for nothing, and that your daughter shall find a match suitable to her rank. " So saying, he took his friend by the hand, brought him into his house, assigned him a share of his great wealth, and ordered a banquet to be prepared, at which he entertained Menecrates and his friends, giving the former to understand that he had prevailed upon one of his acquaintance to marry the girl. When dinner was over, and libations had been poured to the Gods, Zenothemis filled a goblet and passed it to Menecrates: "Accept, " he cried, "from your son-in-law the cup of friendship. This day I wed your daughter Cydimache. The dowry I have had long since; 60,000 pounds was the sum. " "*You?* " exclaimed Menecrates; "Heaven forbid that I should be so mad as to suffer you, in the pride of your youth, to be yoked to this unfortunate girl! " But even while he spoke, Zenothemis was conducting his bride to the marriage-chamber, and presently returned to announce that she was his wedded wife. Since that day, he has lived with her on the most affectionate terms; and you see for yourself that he takes her about with him wherever he goes. As to his being ashamed of his wife, one would rather 26 suppose that he was proud of her; and his conduct in this respect shows how lightly he esteems beauty and wealth and reputation, in comparison with friendship and his friend; for Menecrates is not less his friend because the Six Hundred have condemned him. To be sure, Fortune has already given him one compensation: his ugly wife has borne him a most beautiful child. Only a few days ago, he carried his child into the Senate-house, crowned with an olive-wreath, and dressed in black, to excite the pity of the senators on his grandfather's behalf: the babe smiled upon them, and clapped his little hands together, which so moved the senators that they repealed the sentence against Menecrates, who is now reinstated in his rights, thanks to the pleadings of his tiny advocate. '

Such was the Massiliot's story. As you see, it was no slight service that Zenothemis rendered to his friend; I fancy there are not many Scythians who would do the same; they are said to be very nice even in their selection of concubines.

I have still one friend to produce, and I think none is more worthy of remembrance than Demetrius of Sunium. He and Antiphilus of the deme of Alopece had been playmates in their childhood, and grown up side by side. They subsequently took ship for Egypt, and carried on their studies there together, Demetrius practising the Cynic philosophy under the famous sophist of Rhodes, while Antiphilus, it seems, was to be a doctor. Well, on one occasion Demetrius had gone up country to see the Pyramids, and the statue of Memnon. He had heard it said that the Pyramids in spite of their great height cast no shadow, and that a sound proceeded from the statue at sunrise: all this he wished to see and hear for himself, and he had now been away up the Nile six months. During his absence, Antiphilus, who had remained behind (not liking the idea of the heat and the long journey), became involved in troubles which required all the assistance that faithful friendship could have rendered. He had a Syrian slave, whose name was also Syrus. This man had made common cause with a number of temple-robbers, had forced his way with them into the temple of Anubis, and robbed the God of a pair of golden cups, a caduceus, also of gold, some silver images of Cynocephali and other treasures; all of which the rest entrusted to Syrus's charge. Later on they were caught trying to dispose of some of their booty, and were taken up; and being put on the rack, immediately confessed the whole truth. They were accordingly conducted to Antiphilus's house, where they produced the stolen treasure from a dark corner under a bed. Syrus was immediately arrested, and his master Antiphilus with him: the latter being dragged away from the very presence of his teacher during lecture-time. There was none to help him: his former acquaintances turned their backs on the desecrator of Anubis's temple, and made it a matter of conscience that they had ever sat at the same table with him. As to his other two servants, they got together all his belongings, and ran off.

Antiphilus had now lain long in captivity. He was looked upon as the vilest criminal of all in the prison; and the native gaoler, a superstitious man, considered that he was avenging the God's wrongs and securing his favour by harsh treatment of Antiphilus. His attempts to clear himself of the charge of sacrilege only served to set him in the light of a hardened offender, and materially to increase the detestation in which he was held. His health was beginning to give way under the strain, and no wonder: his bed was the bare ground, and all night he was unable so much as to stretch his legs, which were then secured in the stocks; in the daytime, the collar and one manacle sufficed, but at night he had to submit to being bound hand and foot. The stench, too, and the closeness of the dungeon, in which so many prisoners were huddled together gasping for breath, and the difficulty of getting any sleep, owing to the clanking of chains, —all combined to make the situation intolerable to one who was quite unaccustomed to endure such hardships. At last, when Antiphilus had given up all hope, and refused to take any nourishment, Demetrius arrived, ignorant of all that had passed in his absence. He no sooner learnt the truth, than he flew to the prison. It was now evening, and he was refused admittance, the gaoler having long since bolted the door and retired to rest, leaving his slaves to keep guard. Morning came, and after many entreaties he was allowed to enter. Suffering had altered Antiphilus beyond recognition, and for long Demetrius sought him in vain: like men who seek their slain relatives on the day after a battle, when death has already changed them, he went from prisoner to prisoner, examining each in turn; and had he not called on Antiphilus by name, it would have been long before he could have recognized him, so great was the change that misery had wrought. Antiphilus heard the voice, and uttered a cry; then, as his friend approached, he brushed the dry matted hair from his face, and revealed his identity. At the unexpected sight of one another, the two friends instantly fell down in a swoon. But presently Demetrius recovered, and raised Antiphilus from the ground: he obtained from him an exact account of all that had happened, and bade him be of good cheer; then, tearing his cloak in two, he threw one half over himself, and gave the other to his friend, first ripping off the squalid, threadbare rags in which he was clothed. From that hour, Demetrius was unfailing in his attendance. From early morning till noon, he hired himself out as a porter to the merchants in the harbour, and thus made a considerable wage. Returning to the prison when his work was over, he would give a part of his earnings to the gaoler, thus securing his obsequious goodwill, and the rest sufficed him amply for supplying his friend's needs. For the remainder of the day, he would stay by Antiphilus, administering consolation to him; and at nightfall made himself a litter of leaves near the prison door, and there took his rest. So things went on for some time, Demetrius having free entrance to the prison, and Antiphilus's misery being much alleviated thereby. But presently a certain robber died in the gaol, apparently from the effects of poison; a strict watch was kept, and admittance was refused to all applicants alike, to the great distress of Demetrius, who could think of no other means of obtaining access to his friend than by going to the Prefect and professing complicity in the temple robbery. As the result of this declaration, he was immediately led off to prison, and with great difficulty prevailed upon the gaoler after many entreaties to place him next to Antiphilus, and under the same collar. It was now that his devotion to his friend appeared in the strongest light. Ill though he was himself, he thought nothing of his own sufferings: his only care was to lighten the affliction of his friend, and to procure him as much rest as possible; and the companionship in misery certainly lightened their load. Finally an event happened which brought their misfortunes to an end. One of the prisoners had somehow got hold of a file. He took a number of the others into his confidence, filed through the chain which held them together by means of their collars, and set all at liberty. The guards being few were easily slain; and the prisoners burst out of the gaol *en masse*. They then scattered, and each took refuge for the moment where he could, most of them being subsequently recaptured. Demetrius and Antiphilus, however, remained in the prison, and even secured Syrus when he was about to escape. The next morning the Prefect, hearing what had happened, sent men in pursuit of the other prisoners, and Demetrius and Antiphilus, being summoned to his presence, were released from their fetters, and commended for not having run away like the rest. The friends, however, declined to accept their dismissal on such terms: Demetrius protested loudly against the injustice which would be done to them if they were to pass for criminals, who owed their discharge to mercy, or to their discretion in not having run away. They insisted that the judge should examine carefully into the facts of their case. He at length did so; and was convinced of their innocence, did justice to their characters, and, with a warm commendation of Demetrius's conduct, dismissed them; but not before he had expressed his regret at the unjust sentence under which they had suffered, and made each of them a present from his own purse, —400 pounds to Antiphilus, and twice that sum to Demetrius. Antiphilus is still in Egypt at the present time, but Demetrius went off to India to visit the Brahmins, leaving his 800 pounds with Antiphilus. He could now, he said, leave his friend with a clear conscience. His own wants were simple, and as long as they continued so, he had no need of money: on the other hand, Antiphilus, in his present easy circumstances, had as little need of a friend.

See, Toxaris, what a Greek friend can do! You were so hard just now upon our rhetorical vanity, that I forbear to give you the admirable pleadings of Demetrius in court: not one word did he say in his own behalf; all was for Antiphilus; he wept and implored, and sought to take all the guilt upon himself; till at last the confession of Syrus under torture cleared them both. These loyal friends whose stories I have related were the first that occurred to my memory; where I have given five instances, I might have given fifty. And now I am silent: it is your turn to speak. I need not tell you to make the most of your Scythians, and bring them out triumphant if you can: you will do that for your own sake, if you set any value on that right hand of yours. Quit you, then, like a man. You would look foolish if, after your truly professional panegyric of Orestes and Pylades, your art were to fail you in your country's need.

Tox. I honour you for your disinterested encouragement: apparently you are under no uneasiness as to the loss of your tongue, in the event of my winning. Well, I will begin: and you will get no flowery language from me; it is not our Scythian way, especially when the deeds we handle dwarf description. Be prepared for something very different from the subjects of your own eulogy: here will be no marryings of ugly and dowerless women, no five- hundred-pound-portionings of friends' daughters, nor even surrenderings of one's person to gaolers, with the certain prospect of a speedy release. These are very cheap manifestations; the lofty, the heroic, is altogether wanting. I have to speak of blood and war and death for friendship's sake; you will learn that all you have related is child's-play, when compared with the deeds of the Scythians. After all, it is natural enough: what should you do but admire these trifles? Living in the midst of peace, you have no scope for the exhibition of an exalted friendship, just as in a calm we cannot tell a good pilot from a bad; we must wait till a storm comes; then we know. We, on the contrary, live in a state of perpetual warfare, now invading, now receding, now contending for pasturage or booty. There is the true sphere of friendship; and there is the reason that its ties among us are drawn so close; friendship we hold to be the one invincible, irresistible weapon.

But before I begin, I should like to describe to you our manner of making friends. Friendships are not formed with us, as with you, over the wine-cups, nor are they determined by considerations of age or neighbourhood. We wait till we see a brave man, capable of valiant deeds, and to him we all turn our attention. Friendship with us is like courtship with you: rather than fail of our object, and undergo the disgrace of a rejection, we are content to urge our suit patiently, and to give our constant attendance. At length a friend is accepted, and the engagement is concluded with our most solemn oath: 'to live together and if need be to die for one another. ' That vow is faithfully kept: once let the friends draw blood from their fingers into a cup, dip the points of their swords therein, and drink of that draught together, and from that moment nothing can part them. Such a treaty of friendship may include three persons, but no more: a man of many friends we consider to be no better than a woman who is at the service of every lover; we feel no further security in a friendship that is divided between so many objects.

I will commence with the recent story of Dandamis. In our conflict with the Sauromatae, Dandamis's friend Amizoces had been taken captive, —oh, but first I must take the Scythian oath, as we agreed at the start. I swear by Wind and Scimetar that I will speak nothing but truth of the Scythian friendships.

Mne. You need not have troubled to swear, as far as I am concerned. However, you showed judgement in not swearing by a God.

Tox. What can you mean? Wind and Scimetar not Gods? Are you now to learn that life and death are the highest considerations among mankind? When we swear by Wind and Scimetar, we do so because Wind is the cause of life and Scimetar of death.

Mne. On that principle, you get a good many other Gods besides Scimetar, and as good as he: there is Arrow, and Spear, and Hemlock, and Halter, and so on. Death is a God who assumes many shapes; numberless are the roads that lead into his presence.

Tox. Now you are just trying to spoil my story with these quibbling objections. I gave *you* a fair hearing.

Mne. You are quite right, Toxaris; it shall not occur again, be easy on that score. I'll be so quiet, you would never know I was here at all.

Tox. Four days after Dandamis and Amizoces had shared the cup of blood, the Sauromatae invaded our territory with 10,000 horse, their infantry being estimated at three times that number. The invasion was unexpected, and we were completely routed; many of our warriors were slain, and the rest taken captive, with the exception of a few who managed to swim across to the opposite bank of the river, on which half our host was encamped, with a part of the waggons. The reason of this arrangement I do not know; but our leaders had seen good to divide our camp between the two banks of the Tanais. The enemy at once set to work to secure their booty and collect the captives; they plundered the camp, and took possession of the waggons, most of them with their occupants; and we had the mortification of seeing our wives and concubines mishandled before our very eyes. Amizoces was among the prisoners, and while he was being dragged along he called upon his friend by name, to witness his captivity and to remember the cup of blood. Dandamis heard him, and without a moment's delay plunged into the river in the sight of all, and swam across to the enemy. The Sauromatae rushed upon him, and were about to transfix him with their raised javelins, when he raised the cry of Zirin. The man who pronounces that word is safe from their weapons: it indicates that he is the bearer of ransom, and he is received accordingly. Being conducted into the presence of their chief, he demanded the liberation of Amizoces, and was told in reply, that his friend would only be released upon payment of a high ransom. 'All that was once mine, ' said Dandamis, 'has become your booty: but if one who is stripped of all can have anything yet left to give, it is at your disposal. Name your terms: take me, if you will, in his place, and use me as seems best to you. ' 'To detain the person of one who comes with the Zirin on his lips is out of the question: but you may take back your friend on paying me a part of your possessions. ' 'What will you have? ' asked Dandamis. 'Your eyes, ' was the reply. Dandamis submitted: his eyes were plucked out, and the Sauromatae had their ransom. He returned leaning on his friend, and they swam across together, and reached us in safety.

There was comfort for all of us in this act of Dandamis. Our defeat, it seemed, was no defeat, after all: our most precious possessions had escaped the hands of our enemies; loyal friendship, noble resolution, these were still our own. On the Sauromatae it had the contrary effect: they did not at all like the idea of engaging with such determined adversaries on equal terms; gaining an advantage of them by means of a surprise was quite another matter. The end of it was, that when night came on they left behind the greater part of the herds, burnt the waggons, and beat a hasty retreat. As for Amizoces, he could not endure to see, when Dandamis was blind: he blinded himself, and the two now sit at home, supported in all honour at the public expense.

Can you match that, friend? I think not, though I should give you ten new chances on the top of your five; ay, and release you from your oath, too, for that matter, leaving you free to exaggerate as much as you choose. Besides, I have given you just the bare facts. Now, if *you* had been telling Dandamis's story, what embroidery we should have had! The supplications of Dandamis, the blinding process, his remarks on the occasion, the circumstances of his return, the effusive greetings of the Scythians, and all the *ad captandum* artifices that you Greeks understand so well.

And now let me introduce you to another friend, not inferior to Dandamis, —a cousin of Amizoces, Belitta by name. Belitta was once hunting with his friend Basthes, when the latter was torn from his horse by a lion. Already the brute had fallen upon him, and was clutching him by the throat and beginning to tear him to pieces, when Belitta, leaping to earth, rushed upon him from behind, and attempted to drag him off, and to turn his rage upon himself, thrusting his hands into the brute's mouth, and doing his best to extricate Basthes from those teeth. He succeeded at last: the lion, abandoning his half dead prey, turned upon Belitta, grappled with him, and slew him; but not before Belitta had plunged a scimetar into his breast. Thus all three died together; and we buried them, the two friends in one grave, the lion in another close by.

For my third instance, I shall give you the friendship of Macentes, Lonchates, and Arsacomas. This Arsacomas had been on a visit to Leucanor, king of Bosphorus, in connexion with the tribute annually paid to us by that country, which tribute was then three months overdue; and while there he had fallen in love with Mazaea, the king's daughter. Mazaea was an extremely fine woman, and

Arsacomas, seeing her at the king's table, had been much smitten with her charms. The question of the tribute was at length settled, Arsacomas had his answer, and the king was now entertaining him prior to his departure. It is the custom for suitors in that country to make their proposals at table, stating at the same time their qualifications. Now in the present case there were a number of suitors—kings and sons of kings, among whom were Tigrapates the prince of the Lazi and Adyrmachus the chief of the Machlyans. What each suitor has to do is, first to declare his intentions, and quietly take his seat at table with the rest; then, when dinner is over, he calls for a goblet, pours libation upon the table, and makes his proposal for the lady's hand, saying whatever he can for himself in the way of birth, wealth, and dominion. Many suitors, then, had already preferred their request in due form, enumerating their realms and possessions, when at last Arsacomas called for a cup. He did not make a libation, because it is not the Scythian custom to do so; we should consider it an insult to Heaven to pour away good wine: instead, he drank it all off at one draught, and then addressed the king. 'Sire, ' he said, 'give *me* your daughter Mazaea to wife: if wealth and possessions count for anything, I am a fitter husband for her than these. ' Leucanor was surprised: he knew that Arsacomas was but a poor commoner among the Scythians. 'What herds, what waggons have you, Arsacomas? ' he asked; 'these are the wealth of your people. ' 'Waggons and herds I have none, ' was Arsacomas's reply: 'but I have two excellent friends, whose like you will not find in all Scythia. ' His answer only excited ridicule; it was attributed to drunkenness, and no further notice was taken of him. Adyrmachus was preferred to the other suitors, and was to take his bride away the next morning to his Maeotian home. Arsacomas on his return informed his friends of the slight that had been put upon him by the king, and of the ridicule to which he had been subjected on account of his supposed poverty. 'And yet, ' he added, 'I told him of my wealth: told him that I had the friendship of Lonchates and Macentes, a more precious and more lasting possession than his kingdom of Bosphorus. But he made light of it; he jeered at us; and gave his daughter to Adyrmachus the Machlyan, because he had ten golden cups, and eighty waggons of four seats, and a number of sheep and oxen. It seems that herds and lumbering waggons and superfluous beakers are to count for more than brave men. My friends, I am doubly wounded: I love Mazaea, and I cannot forget the humiliation which I have suffered before so many witnesses, and in which you are both equally involved. Ever since we were united in friendship, are we not one flesh? are not our joys and our sorrows the same? If this be so, each of us has his share in this disgrace. ' 'Not only so, ' rejoined Lonchates; 'each of us labours under the whole ignominy of the affront. ' 'And what is to be our course? ' asked Macentes. 'We will divide the work, ' replied the other. 'I for my part undertake to present Arsacomas with the head of Leucanor: you must bring him his bride. ' 'I agree. And you, Arsacomas, can stay at home; and as we are likely to want an army before we have done, you must be getting together horses and arms, and raise what men you can, A man like you will have no difficulty in getting plenty of people to join him, and there are all our relations; besides, you can sit on the ox-hide. ' This being settled, Lonchates set off just as he was for the Bosphorus, and Macentes for Machlyene, each on horseback; while Arsacomas remained behind, consulting with his acquaintance, raising forces from among the relations of the three, and, finally, taking his seat on the ox-hide.

Our custom of the hide is as follows. When a man has been injured by another, and desires vengeance, but feels that he is no match for his opponent, he sacrifices an ox, cuts up the flesh and cooks it, and spreads out the hide upon the ground. On this hide he takes his seat, holding his hands behind him, so as to suggest that his arms are tied in that position, this being the natural attitude of a suppliant among us. Meanwhile, the flesh of the ox has been laid out; and the man's relations and any others who feel so disposed come up and take a portion thereof, and, setting their right foot on the hide, promise whatever assistance is in their power: one will engage to furnish and maintain five horsemen, another ten, a third some larger number; while others, according to their ability, promise heavy or light-armed infantry, and the poorest, who have nothing else to give, offer their own personal services. The number of persons assembled on the hide is sometimes very considerable; nor could any troops be more reliable or more invincible than those which are collected in this manner, being as they are under a vow; for the act of stepping on to the hide constitutes an oath. By this means, then, Arsacomas raised something like 5,000 cavalry and 20,000 heavy and light armed.

Meanwhile, Lonchates arrived unknown in Bosphorus, and presented himself co the king, who was occupied at the moment in affairs of state. 'I come, ' he said, 'on public business from Scythia: but I have also a private communication of high import to make to your Majesty. ' The king bade him proceed. 'As to my public errand, it is the old story: we protest against your herdsmen's crossing the Rocks and encroaching on the plains. And with reference to the robbers of whom you complain, I am instructed to say that our government is not responsible for their incursions, which are the work of private individuals, actuated merely by the love of booty; accordingly, you are at liberty to punish as many of them as you can secure, And now for my own news. You will shortly be invaded by a large host under Arsacomas the son of Mariantas, who was lately at your court as an ambassador. I suppose the cause of his resentment is your refusing him your daughter's hand. He has now been on the ox-hide for seven days, and has got together a considerable force. ' 'I had heard, ' exclaimed Leucanor, 'that an army was being raised on the hide: but who was raising it, and what was its destination, I had no idea. ' 'You know now, ' said Lonchates. 'Arsacomas is a personal enemy of mine: the superior esteem in which I am held, and the preference shown for me by our elders, are things which he cannot forgive. Now promise me your other daughter Barcetis: apart from my present services, I shall be no discreditable son-in-law: promise me this, and in no long time I will return bringing you the head of Arsacomas. ' 'I promise, ' cried the king, in great perturbation; for he realized the provocation he had given to Arsacomas, and had a wholesome respect for the Scythians at all times. 'Swear, ' insisted Lonchates, 'that you will not go back from your promise. ' The king was already raising up his hand to Heaven, when the other interrupted him. 'Wait! ' he exclaimed; 'not here! these people must not know what is the subject of our oath. Let us go into the temple of Ares yonder, and swear with closed doors, where none may hear. If Arsacomas should get wind of this, I am likely to be offered up as a preliminary sacrifice; he has a good number of men already. ' 'To the temple, then, let us go, ' said the king; and he ordered the guards to remain aloof, and forbade any one to approach the temple unless summoned by him. As soon as they were inside, and the guards had withdrawn, Lonchates drew his sword, and putting his left hand on the king's mouth to prevent his crying out, plunged it into his breast; then, cutting off his head, he went out from the temple carrying it under his cloak; affecting all the time to be speaking to the king, and promising that he would not be long, as if the king had sent him on some errand. He thus succeeded in reaching the place where he had left his horse tethered, leapt on to his back, and rode off into Scythia. There was no pursuit: the people of Bosphorus took some time to discover what had happened; and then they were occupied with disputes as to the succession. Thus Lonchates fulfilled his promise, and handed the head of Leucanor to Arsacomas.

The news of this reached Macentes while he was on his way to Machlyene, and on his arrival there he was the first to announce the king's death. 'You, Adyrmachus, ' he added, 'are his son-in-law, and are now summoned to the throne. Ride on in advance, and establish your claim while all is still unsettled. Your bride can follow with the waggons; the presence of Leucanor's daughter will be of assistance to you in securing the support of the Bosphorans. I myself am an Alanian, and am related to this lady by the mother's side: Leucanor's wife, Mastira, was of my family. I now come to you from Mastira's brothers in Alania: they would have you make the best of your way to Bosphorus at once, or you will find your crown on the head of Eubiotus, Leucanor's bastard brother, who is a friend to Scythia, and detested by the Alanians. ' In language and dress, Macentes resembled an Alanian; for in these respects there is no difference between Scythians and Alanians, except that the Alanians do not wear such long hair as we do. Macentes had completed the resemblance by cropping his hair to the right shortness, and was thus enabled to pass for a kinsman of Mastira and Mazaea. 'And now, Adyrmachus, ' he concluded, 'I am ready to go with you to Bosphorus; or, if you prefer it, I will escort your bride. ' 'If you will do the latter, ' replied Adyrmachus, 'I shall be particularly obliged, since you are Mazaea's kinsman. If you go with us, it is but one horseman more; whereas no one could be such a suitable escort for my wife. ' And so it was settled: Adyrmachus rode off, and left Mazaea, who was still a maid, in the care of Macentes. During the day, Macentes accompanied Mazaea in the waggon: but at nightfall he placed her on horseback (he had taken care that there should be a horseman in attendance), and, mounting behind her, abandoned his former course along the Maeotian Lake, and struck off into the interior, keeping the Mitraean Mountains on his right. He allowed Mazaea some time for rest, and completed the whole journey from Machlyene to Scythia on the third day; his horse stood still for a few moments after arrival, and then dropped down dead. 'Behold, ' said Macentes, presenting Mazaea to Arsacomas, 'behold your promised bride. ' Arsacomas, amazed at so unexpected a sight, was beginning to express his gratitude: but Macentes bade him hold his peace. 'You speak, ' he exclaimed, 'as if you and I were different persons, when you thank me for what I have done. It is as if my left hand should say to my right: Thank you for tending my wound; thank you for your generous sympathy with my pain. That would be no more absurd than for us—who have long been united, and have become (so far as such a thing may be) one flesh—to make such ado because one part of us has done its duty by the whole; the limb is but serving its own interest in promoting the welfare of the body. ' And that was how Macentes received his friend's thanks.

Adyrmachus, on hearing of the trick that had been played upon him, did not pursue his journey to Bosphorus; indeed, Eubiotus was already on the throne, having been summoned thither from his home in Sarmatia. He therefore returned to his own country, collected a large army, and marched across the mountains into Scythia. He was presently followed by Eubiotus himself, at the head of a miscellaneous army of Greeks, together with 20,000 each of his Alanian and Sarmatian allies. The two joined forces, and the result was an army of 90,000 men, one third of whom were mounted bowmen. We Scythians (I say *we*, because I myself took part in this enterprise, and was maintaining a hundred horse on the hide)—we Scythians then, numbering in all not much less than 30,000 men, including cavalry, awaited their onset, under the command of Arsacomas. As soon as we saw them approaching, we too advanced, sending on our cavalry ahead. After a long and obstinate engagement, our lines were broken, and we began to give ground; and finally our whole army was cut clean in two. One half had not suffered a decisive defeat; with these it was rather a retreat than a flight, nor did the Alanians venture to follow up their advantage for any distance. But the other and smaller division was completely surrounded by the Alanians and Machlyans, and was being shot down on every side by the copious discharge of arrows and javelins; the position became intolerable, and most of our men were beginning to throw down their arms. In this latter division were Lonchates and Macentes. They had borne the brunt of the attack, and both were wounded: Lonchates had a spear-thrust in his thigh, and Macentes, besides a cut on the head from an axe, had had his shoulder damaged by a pike. Arsacomas, seeing their condition (he was with us in the other division), could not endure the thought of turning his back on his friends: plunging the spurs into his horse, and raising a shout, he rode through the midst of the enemy, with his scimetar raised on high. The Machlyans were unable to withstand the fury of his onset; their ranks divided, and made way for him to pass. Having rescued his friends from their danger, he rallied the rest of the troops; and charging upon Adyrmachus brought down the scimetar on his neck, and cleft him in two as far as the waist. Adyrmachus once slain, the whole of the Machlyans and Alanians soon scattered, and the Greeks followed their example. Thus did we turn defeat into victory; and had not night come to interrupt us, we should have pursued the fugitives for a considerable distance, slaying as we went. The next day came messengers from the enemy suing for reconciliation, the Bosphorans undertaking to double their tribute, and the Machlyans to leave hostages; whilst the Alanians promised to expiate their guilt by reducing the Sindians to submission, that tribe having been for some time in revolt against us. These terms we accepted, at the instance of Arsacomas and Lonchates, who conducted the negotiations and concluded the peace.

Such, Mnesippus, are the deeds that Scythians will do for friendship's sake.

Mne. Truly deeds of high emprise; quite a legendary look about them. With Wind's and Scimetar's good leave, I think a man might be excused for doubting their truth.

Tox. Now, honestly, Mnesippus, does not that doubt look a little like envy? However, doubt if you will: that shall not deter me from relating other Scythian exploits of the same kind which have happened within my experience.

Mne. Brevity, friend, is all I ask. Your story is apt to run away with you. Up hill and down dale you go, through Scythia and Machlyene, off again to Bosphorus, then back to Scythia, till my taciturnity is exhausted.

Tox. I am schooled. Brevity you shall have; I will not run you off your ears this time. My next story shall be of a service rendered to myself, by my friend Sisinnes. Induced by the desire for Greek culture, I had left my home and was on my way to Athens. The ship put in at Amastris, which comes in the natural route from Scythia, being on the shore of the Euxine, not far from Carambis. Sisinnes, who had been my friend from childhood, bore me company on this voyage. We had transferred all our belongings from the ship to an inn near the harbour; and whilst we were busy in the market, suspecting nothing wrong, some thieves had forced the door of our room and carried off everything, not leaving us even enough to go on with for that day. Well, when we got back and found what had happened, we thought it was no use trying to get legal redress from our landlord, or from the neighbours; there were too many of them; and if we *had* told our story, —how we had been robbed of four hundred darics and our clothes and rugs and everything, most people would only have thought we were making a fuss about a trifle. So we had to think what was to be done: here we were, absolutely destitute, in a foreign country. For my part, I thought I might as well put a sword through my ribs there and then, and have done with it, rather than endure the humiliation that might be forced upon us by hunger and thirst. Sisinnes took a more cheerful view, and implored me to do nothing of the kind: 'I shall think of something, ' he said, 'and we may do well yet. ' For the moment, he made enough to get us some food by carrying up timber from the harbour. The next morning, he took a walk in the market, where it seems he saw a company of fine likely young fellows, who as it turned out were hired as gladiators, and were to perform two days after. He found out all about them, and then came back to me. 'Toxaris, ' he exclaimed, 'consider your poverty at an end! In two days' time, I will make a rich man of you. ' We got through those two days somehow, and then came the show, in which we took our places as spectators, Sisinnes bidding me prepare myself for all the novel delights of a Greek amphitheatre. The first thing we saw on sitting down was a number of wild beasts: some of them were being assailed by javelins, others hunted by dogs, and others again were let loose upon certain men who were tied hand and foot, and whom we supposed to be criminals. The gladiators next made their appearance. The herald led forward a strapping young fellow, and announced that any one who was prepared to stand up against him might step into the arena and take his reward, which would be 400 pounds. Sisinnes rose from his seat, jumped down into the ring, expressed his willingness to fight, and demanded arms. He received the money, and brought it to me. 'If I win, ' he said, 'we will go off together, and are amply provided for: if I fall, you will bury me and return to Scythia. ' I was much moved.

He now received his arms, and put them on; with the exception, however, of the helmet, for he fought bareheaded. He was the first to be wounded, his adversary's curved sword drawing a stream of blood from his groin. I was half dead with fear. However, Sisinnes was biding his time: the other now assailed him with more confidence, and Sisinnes made a lunge at his breast, and drove the sword clean through, so that his adversary fell lifeless at his feet. He himself, exhausted by the loss of blood, sank down upon the corpse, and life almost deserted him; but I ran to his assistance, raised him up, and spoke words of comfort. The victory was won, and he was free to depart; I therefore picked him up and carried him home. My efforts were at last successful: he rallied, and is living in Scythia to this day, having married my sister. He is still lame, however, from his wound. Observe: this did not take place in Machlyene, nor yet in Alania; there is no lack of witnesses to the truth of the story this time; many an Amastrian here in Athens would remember the fight of Sisinnes.

One more story, that of Abauchas, and I have done. Abauchas once arrived in the capital of the Borysthenians, with his wife, of whom he was extremely fond, and two children; one, a boy, was still at the breast, the other was a girl of seven. With him also was his friend Gyndanes, who was still suffering from the effects of a wound he had received on the journey: they had been attacked by some robbers, and Gyndanes in resisting them had been stabbed in the thigh, and was still unable to stand on account of the pain. One night they were all asleep in the upper story, when a tremendous fire broke out; the whole building was wrapped in flames, and every means of exit blocked. Abauchas started up, and leaving his sobbing children, and shaking off his wife, who clung to him and implored him to save her, he caught up his friend in his arms, and just managed to force his way down without being utterly consumed by the flames. His wife followed, carrying the boy, and bade the girl come after her; but, scorched almost to a cinder, she was compelled to drop the child from her arms, and barely succeeded in leaping through the flames; the little girl too only just escaped with her life. Abauchas was afterwards reproached with having abandoned his own wife and children to rescue Gyndanes. 'I can beget other children easily enough, ' said he: 'nor was it certain how these would turn out: but it would be long before I got such another friend as Gyndanes; of his affection I have been abundantly satisfied by experience. '

There, Mnesippus, you have *my* little selection. The next thing is to settle whether my hand or your tongue is to be amputated. Who is umpire?

Mne. Umpire we have none; we forgot that. I tell you what: we have wasted our arrows this time, but some other day we will appoint an arbitrator, and submit other friendships to his judgement; and then off shall come your hand, or out shall come my tongue, as the case may be. Perhaps, though, this is rather a primitive way of doing things. As you seem to think a great deal of friendship, and as I consider it to be the highest blessing of humanity, what is there to prevent our vowing eternal friendship on the spot? We shall both have the satisfaction of winning then, and shall get a substantial prize into the bargain: two right hands each instead of one, two tongues, four eyes, four feet; —everything in duplicate. The union of two friends—or three, let us say—is like Geryon in the pictures: a six-handed, three-headed individual; my private opinion is, that there was not one Geryon, but three Geryons, all acting in concert, as friends should.

Tox. Done with you, then.

Mne. And, Toxaris, —we will dispense with the blood-and- scimetar ceremony. Our present conversation, and the similarity of our aims, are a much better security than that sanguinary cup of yours. Friendship, as I take it, should be voluntary, not compulsory.

Tox. Well said. From this day, I am your friend, you mine; I your guest here in Greece, you mine if ever you come to Scythia.

Mne. Scythia! I would go further than Scythia, to meet with such friends as Toxaris's narratives have shown him to be.

ZEUS CROSS-EXAMINED

Cyniscus. Zeus

Cyn. Zeus: I am not going to trouble you with requests for a fortune or a throne; you get prayers enough of that sort from other people, and from your habit of convenient deafness I gather that you experience a difficulty in answering them. But there is one thing I should like, which would cost you no trouble to grant.

Zeus. Well, Cyniscus? You shall not be disappointed, if your expectations are as reasonable as you say.

Cyn. I want to ask you a plain question.

Zeus. Such a modest petition is soon granted; ask what you will.

Cyn. Well then: you know your Homer and Hesiod, of course? Is it all true that they sing of Destiny and the Fates—that whatever they spin for a man at his birth must inevitably come about?

Zeus. Unquestionably. Nothing is independent of their control. From their spindle hangs the life of all created things; whose end is predetermined even from the moment of their birth; and that law knows no change.

Cyn. Then when Homer says, for instance, in another place,

Lest unto Hell thou go, *outstripping Fate,*

he is talking nonsense, of course?

Zeus. Absolute nonsense. Such a thing is impossible: the law of the Fates, the thread of Destiny, is over all. No; so long as the poets are under the inspiration of the Muses, they speak truth: but once let those Goddesses leave them to their own devices, and they make blunders and contradict themselves. Nor can we blame them: they are but men; how should they know truth, when the divinity whose mouthpieces they were is departed from them?

Cyn. That point is settled, then. But there is another thing I want to know. There are three Fates, are there not, —Clotho, Lachesis, and Atropus?

Zeus. Quite so.

Cyn. But one also hears a great deal about Destiny and Fortune. Who are they, and what is the extent of their power? Is it equal to that of the Fates? or greater perhaps? People are always talking about the insuperable might of Fortune and Destiny.

Zeus. It is not proper, Cyniscus, that you should know all. But what made you ask me about the Fates?

Cyn. Ah, you must tell me one thing more first. Do the Fates also control you Gods? Do *you* depend from their thread?

Zeus. We do. Why do you smile?

Cyn. I was thinking of that bit in Homer, where he makes you address the Gods in council, and threaten to suspend all the world from a golden cord. You said, you know, that you would let the cord down from Heaven, and all the Gods together, if they liked, might take hold of it and try to pull you down, and they would never do it: whereas you, if you had a mind to it, could easily pull them up,

    And Earth and Sea withal.

I listened to that passage with shuddering reverence; I was much impressed with the idea of your strength. Yet now I understand that you and your cord and your threats all depend from a mere cobweb. It seems to me Clotho should be the one to boast: she has you dangling from her distaff, like a sprat at the end of a fishing- line.

Zeus. I do not catch the drift of your questions.

Cyn. Come, I will speak my mind; and in the name of Destiny and the Fates take not my candour amiss. If the case stands thus, if the Fates are mistresses of all, and their decisions unalterable, then why do men sacrifice to *you*, and bring hecatombs, and pray for good at *your* hands? If our prayers can neither save us from evil nor procure us any boon from Heaven, I fail to see what we get for our trouble.

Zeus. These are nice questions! I see how it is, —you have been with the sophists; accursed race! who would deny us all concern in human affairs. Yes, these are just the points they raise, impiously seeking to pervert mankind from the way of sacrifice and prayer: it is all thrown away, forsooth! the Gods take no thought for mankind; they have no power on the earth. —Ah well; they will be sorry for it some day.

Cyn. Now, by Clotho's own spindle, my questions are free from all sophistic taint. How it has come about, I know not; but one word has brought up another, and the end of it is—there is no use in sacrifice. Let us begin again. I will put you a few more questions; answer me frankly, but think before you speak, this time.

Zeus. Well; if you have the time to waste on such tomfoolery.

Cyn. Everything proceeds from the Fates, you say?

Zeus. Yes.

Cyn. And is it in your power to unspin what they have spun?

Zeus. It is not.

Cyn. Shall I proceed, or is the inference clear?

Zeus. Oh, clear enough. But you seem to think that people sacrifice to us from ulterior motives; that they are driving a bargain with us, *buying* blessings, as it were: not at all; it is a disinterested testimony to our superior merit.

Cyn. There you are, then. As you say, sacrifice answers no useful purpose; it is just our good-natured way of acknowledging your superiority. And mind you, if we had a sophist here, he would want to know all about that superiority. You are our fellow slaves, he would say; if the Fates are our mistresses, they are also yours. Your immortality will not serve you; that only makes things worse. We mortals, after all, are liberated by death: but for you there is no end to the evil; that long thread of yours means eternal servitude.

Zeus. But this eternity is an eternity of happiness; the life of Gods is one round of blessings.

Cyn. Not all Gods' lives. Even in Heaven there are distinctions, not to say mismanagement. *You* are happy, of course: you are king, and you can haul up earth and sea as it were a bucket from the well. But look at Hephaestus: a cripple; a common blacksmith. Look at Prometheus: *he* gets nailed up on Caucasus. And I need not remind you that your own father lies fettered in Tartarus at this hour. It seems, too, that Gods are liable to fall in love; and to receive wounds; nay, they may even have to take service with mortal men; witness your brother Posidon, and Apollo, servants to Laomedon and to Admetus. I see no great happiness in all this; some of you I dare say have a very pleasant time of it, but not so others. I might have added, that you are subject to robbery like the rest of us; your temples get plundered, and the richest of you becomes a pauper in the twinkling of an eye. To more than one of you it has even happened to be melted down, if he was a gold or a silver God. All destiny, of course.

Zeus. Take care, Cyniscus: you are going too far. You will repent of this one day.

Cyn. Spare your threats: you know that nothing can happen to me, except what Fate has settled first. I notice, for instance, that even temple-robbers do not always get punished; most of them, indeed, slip through your hands. Not destined to be caught, I suppose.

Zeus. I knew it! you are one of those who would abolish Providence.

Cyn. You seem to be very much afraid of these gentlemen, for some reason. Not one word can I say, but you must think I picked it up from them. Oblige me by answering another question; I could desire no better authority than yours. What is this Providence? Is she a Fate too? or some greater, a mistress of the Fates?

Zeus. I have already told you that there are things which it is not proper for you to know. You said you were only going to ask me one question, instead of which you go on quibbling without end. I see what it is you are at: you want to make out that we Gods take no thought for human affairs.

Cyn. It is nothing to do with me: it was you who said just now that the Fates ordained everything. Have you thought better of it? Are you going to retract what you said? Are the Gods going to push Destiny aside and make a bid for government?

Zeus. Not at all; but the Fates work *through us.*

Cyn. I see: you are their servants, their underlings. But that comes to the same thing: it is still they who design; you are only their tools, their instruments.

Zeus. How do you make that out?

Cyn. I suppose it is pretty much the same as with a carpenter's adze and drill: they do assist him in his work, but no one would describe them as the workmen; we do not say that a ship has been turned out by such and such an adze, or by such and such a drill; we name the shipwright. In the same way, Destiny and the Fates are the universal shipwrights, and you are their drills and adzes; and it seems to me that instead of paying their respects and their sacrifices to you, men ought to sacrifice to Destiny, and implore *her* favours; though even that would not meet the case, because I take it that things are settled once and for all, and that the Fates themselves are not at liberty to chop and change. If some one gave the spindle a turn in the wrong direction, and undid all Clotho's work, Atropus would have something to say on the subject.

Zeus. So! You would deprive even the Fates of honour? You seem determined to reduce all to one level. Well, we Gods have at least one claim on you: we do prophesy and foretell what the Fates haye disposed.

Cyn. Now even granting that you do, what is the use of knowing what one has to expect, when one can by no possibility take any precautions? Are you going to tell me that a man who finds out that he is to die by a steel point can escape the doom by shutting himself up? Not he. Fate will take him out hunting, and there will be his steel: Adrastus will hurl his spear at the boar, miss the brute, and get Croesus's son; Fate's inflexible law directs his aim. The full absurdity of the thing is seen in the case of Laius:

> Seek not for offspring in the Gods' despite;
> Beget a child, and thou begett'st thy slayer.

Was not this advice superfluous, seeing that the end must come? Accordingly we find that the oracle does not deter Laius from begetting a son, nor that son from being his slayer. On the whole, I cannot see that your prophecies entitle you to reward, even setting aside the obscurity of the oracles, which are generally contrived to cut both ways. You omitted to mention, for instance, whether Croesus—'the Halys crossed'—should destroy his own or Cyrus's mighty realm. ' It might be either, so far as the oracle goes.

Zeus. Apollo was angry with Croesus. When Croesus boiled that lamb and tortoise together in the cauldron, he was making trial of Apollo.

Cyn. Gods ought not to be angry. After all, I suppose it was fated that the Lydian should misinterpret that oracle; his case only serves to illustrate that general ignorance of the future, which Destiny has appointed for mankind. At that rate, your prophetic power too seems to be in her hands.

Zeus. You leave us nothing, then? We exercise no control, we are not entitled to sacrifice, we are very drills and adzes. But you may well despise me: why do I sit here listening to all this, with my thunder-bolt beneath my arm?

Cyn. Nay, smite, if the thunder-bolt is my destiny. I shall think none the worse of you; I shall know it is all Clotho's doing; I will not even blame the bolt that wounds me. And by the way— talking of thunder-bolts—there is one thing I will ask you and Destiny to explain; you can answer for her. Why is it that you leave all the pirates and temple-robbers and ruffians and perjurers to themselves, and direct your shafts (as you are always doing) against an oak-tree or a stone or a harmless mast, or even an honest, God-fearing traveller?... No answer? Is this one of the things it is not proper for me to know?

Zeus. It is, Cyniscus. You are a meddlesome fellow; I don't know where you picked up all these ideas.

Cyn. Well, I suppose I must not ask you all (Providence and Destiny and you) why honest Phocion died in utter poverty and destitution, like Aristides before him, while those two unwhipped puppies, Callias and Alcibiades, and the ruffian Midias, and that Aeginetan libertine Charops, who starved his own mother to death, were all rolling in money? nor again why Socrates was handed over to the Eleven instead of Meletus? nor yet why the effeminate Sardanapalus was a king, and one high-minded Persian after another went to the cross for refusing to countenance his doings? I say nothing of our own days, in which villains and money-grubbers prosper, and honest men are oppressed with want and sickness and a thousand distresses, and can hardly call their souls their own.

Zeus. Surely you know, Cyniscus, what punishments await the evil-doers after death, and how happy will be the lot of the righteous?

Cyn. Ah, to be sure: Hades—Tityus—Tantalus. Whether there is such a place as Hades, I shall be able to satisfy myself when I die. In the meantime, I had rather live a pleasant life here, and have a score or so of vultures at my liver when I am dead, than thirst like Tantalus in this world, on the chance of drinking with the heroes in the Isles of the Blest, and reclining in the fields of Elysium.

Zeus. What! you doubt that there are punishments and rewards to come? You doubt of that judgement-seat before which every soul is arraigned?

Cyn. I *have* heard mention of a judge in that connexion; one Minos, a Cretan. Ah, yes, tell me about him: they say he is your son?

Zeus. And what of him?

Cyn. Whom does he punish in particular?

Zeus. Whom but the wicked? Murderers, for instance, and temple-robbers.

Cyn. And whom does he send to dwell with the heroes?

Zeus. Good men and God-fearing, who have led virtuous lives.

Cyn. Why?

Zeus. Because they deserve punishment and reward respectively.

Cyn. Suppose a man commits a crime accidentally: does he punish him just the same?

Zeus. Certainly not.

Cyn. Similarly, if a man involuntarily performed a good action, he would not reward him?

Zeus. No.

Cyn. Then there is no one for him to reward or punish.

Zeus. How so?

Cyn. Why, we men do nothing of our own free will: we are obeying an irresistible impulse, —that is, if there is any truth in what we settled just now, about Fate's being the cause of everything. Does a man commit a murder? Fate is the murderess. Does he rob a temple? He has her instructions for it. So if there is going to be any justice in Minos's sentences, he will punish Destiny, not Sisyphus; Fate, not Tantalus. What harm did these men do? They only obeyed orders.

Zeus. I am not going to speak to you any more. You are an unscrupulous man; a sophist. I shall go away and leave you to yourself.

Cyn. I wanted to ask you where the Fates lived; and how they managed to attend to all the details of such a vast mass of business, just those three. I do not envy them their lot; they must have a busy time of it, with so much on their hands. Their destiny, apparently, is no better than other people's. I would not exchange with them, if I had the choice; I had rather be poorer than I am, than sit before such a spindleful, watching every thread. —But never mind, if you would rather not answer. Your previous replies have quite cleared up my doubts about Destiny and Providence; and for the rest, I expect I was not destined to hear it.

ZEUS TRAGOEDUS

*Hermes. Hera. Colossus. Heracles. Athene. Posidon. Momus. Hermagoras.
Zeus. Aphrodite. Apollo, Timocles. Damis*

Herm. Wherefore thus brooding, Zeus? wherefore apart,
And palely pacing, as Earth's sages use?
Let me thy counsel know, thy cares partake;
And find thy comfort in a faithful fool.

Ath. Cronides, lord of lords, and all our sire,
I clasp thy knees; grant thou what I require;
A boon the lightning-eyed Tritonia asks:
Speak, rend the veil thy secret thought that masks;
Reveal what care thy mind within thee gnaws,
Blanches thy cheek, and this deep moaning draws.

Zeus. Speech hath no utterance of surpassing fear,
Tragedy holds no misery or woe,
But our divinest essence soon shall taste.

Ath. Alas, how dire a prelude to thy tale!

Zeus. O brood maleficent, teemed from Earth's dark womb!
And thou, Prometheus, how hast thou wrought me woe!

Ath. Possess us; are not we thine own familiars?

Zeus. With a whirr and a crash
Let the levin-bolt dash—
Ah, whither?

Hera. A truce to your passion, Zeus. *We* have not these good people's gift for farce or recitation; *we* have not swallowed Euripides whole, and cannot play up to you. Do you suppose we do not know how to account for your annoyance?

Zeus. Thou knowst not; else thy waitings had been loud.

Hera. Don't tell me; it's a love affair; that's what's the matter with you. However, you won't have any 'wailings' from me; I am too much hardened to neglect. I suppose you have discovered some new

Danae or Semele or Europa whose charms are troubling you; and so you are meditating a transformation into a bull or satyr, or a descent through the roof into your beloved's bosom as a shower of gold; all the symptoms—your groans and your tears and your white face—point to love and nothing else.

Zeus. Happy ignorance, that sees not what perils now forbid love and such toys!

Hera. Is your name Zeus, or not? and, if so, what else can possibly annoy you but love?

Zeus. Hera, our condition is most precarious; it is touch- and-go, as they call it, whether we are still to enjoy reverence and honour from the earth, or be utterly neglected and become of no account.

Hera. Has Earth produced a new brood of giants? Have the Titans broken their chains, overpowered their guards, and taken up arms against us once more?

Zeus. Nay, fear not that; Hell threatens not the Gods.

Hera. What can the matter be, then? To hear you, one might think it was Polus or Aristodemus, not Zeus; and why, pray, if something of that sort is not bothering you?

Zeus. My dear, a discussion somehow arose yesterday between Timocles the Stoic and Damis the Epicurean; there was a numerous and respectable audience (which particularly annoyed me), and they had an argument on the subject of Providence. Damis questioned the existence of the Gods, and utterly denied their interest in or government of events, while Timocles, good man, did his best to champion our cause. A great crowd gathered round; but no conclusion was reached. They broke up with an understanding that the inquiry should be completed another day; and now they are all agog to see which will win and prove his case. You all see how parlous and precarious is our position, depending on a single mortal. These are the alternatives for us: to be dismissed as mere empty names, or (if Timocles prevails) to enjoy our customary honours.

Hera. This is really a serious matter; your ranting was not so uncalled-for, Zeus.

Zeus. You fancied me thinking of some Danae or Antiope; and this was the dread reality. Now, Hermes, Hera, Athene, what is our course? We await your contribution to our plans.

Herm. My opinion is that an assembly be summoned and the community taken into counsel.

Hera. And I concur.

Ath. Sire, I dissent entirely; you should not fill Heaven with apprehensions, nor let your own uneasiness be visible, but take private measures to assure Timocles's victory and Damis's being laughed out of court.

Herm. It cannot be kept quiet, Zeus; the philosophers' debate is public, and you will be accused of despotic methods, if you maintain reserve on a matter of so great and general interest.

Zeus. Make proclamation and summon all, then. I approve your judgement.

Herm. Here, assemble, all ye Gods; don't waste time, come along, here you are; we are going to have an important meeting.

Zeus. What, Hermes? so bald, so plain, so prosy an announcement— on this momentous occasion?

Herm. Why, how would you like it done?

Zeus. Some metre, a little poetic sonority, would make the style impressive, and they would be more likely to come.

Herm. Ah, Zeus, that is work for epic poets or reciters, and I am no good at poetry. I should be sure to put in too many feet, or leave out some, and spoil the thing; they would only laugh at my rude verses. Why, I've known Apollo himself laughed at for some of his oracles; and prophecy has the advantage of obscurity, which gives the hearers something better to do than scanning verses.

Zeus. Well, well, Hermes, you can make lines from Homer the chief ingredient of your composition; summon us in his words; you remember them, of course.

Herm. I cannot say they are exactly on the tip of my tongue; however, I'll do my best:

> Let ne'er a God (tum, tum), nor eke a Goddess,
> Nor yet of Ocean's rivers one be wanting,
> Nor nymphs; but gather to great Zeus's council;
> And all that feast on glorious hecatombs,
> Yea, middle and lower classes of Divinity,
> Or nameless ones that snuff fat altar-fumes

Zeus. Good, Hermes; that is an excellent proclamation: see, here they come pell-mell; now receive and place them in correct precedence, according to their material or workmanship; gold in the front row, silver next, then the ivory ones, then those of stone or bronze. A cross-division will give precedence to the creations of Phidias, Alcamenes, Myron, Euphranor, and artists of that calibre, while the common inartistic jobs can be huddled together in the far corner, hold their tongues, and just make up the rank and file of our assembly.

Herm. All right; they shall have their proper places. But here is a point: suppose one of them is gold, and heavy at that, but not finely finished, quite amateurish and ill proportioned, in fact—is he to take precedence of Myron's and Polyclitus's bronze, or Phidias's and Alcamenes's marble? or is workmanship to count most?

Zeus. It should by rights. Never mind, put the gold first.

Herm. I see; property qualification, comparative wealth, is the test, not merit. —Gold to the front row, please. —Zeus, the front row will be exclusively barbarian, I observe. You see the peculiarity of the Greek contingent: they have grace and beauty and artistic workmanship, but they are all marble or bronze—the most costly of them only ivory with just an occasional gleam of gold, the merest surface-plating; and even those are wood inside, harbouring whole colonies of mice. Whereas Bendis here, Anubis there, Attis next door, and Mithras and Men, are all of solid gold, heavy and intrinsically precious.

Pos. Hermes, is it in order that this dog-faced Egyptian person should sit in front of me, Posidon?

Herm. Certainly. You see, Earth-shaker, the Corinthians had no gold at the time, so Lysippus made you of paltry bronze; Dog- face is a whole gold-mine richer than you. You must put up with being moved back, and not object to the owner of such a golden snout being preferred.

Aph. Then, Hermes, find me a place in the front row; I am golden.

Herm. Not so, Aphrodite, if I can trust my eyes; I am purblind, or you are white marble; you were quarried, I take it, from Pentelicus, turned by Praxiteles's fancy into Aphrodite, and handed over to the Cnidians.

Aph. Wait; my witness is unexceptionable—Homer. 'The Golden Aphrodite' he calls me, up and down his poems.

Herm. Oh, yes, no doubt; *he* called Apollo rich, 'rolling in gold'; but now where will you find Apollo? Somewhere in the third-class seats; his crown has been taken off and his harp pegs stolen by the pirates, you see. So *you* may think yourself lucky with a place above the fourth.

Col. Well, who will dare dispute *my* claim? Am I not the Sun? and look at my height. If the Rhodians had not decided on such grandiose dimensions for me, the same outlay would have furnished forth a round dozen of your golden Gods; I ought to be valued proportionally. And then, besides the size, there is the workmanship and careful finish.

Herm. What shall I do, Zeus? Here is a difficulty again—too much for me. Going by material, he is bronze; but, reckoning the talents his bronze cost, he would be above the first class.

Zeus. What business has he here dwarfing the rest and blocking up all the bench? —Why, my excellent Rhodian, you may be as superior to the golden ones as you will; but how can you possibly go in the front row? Every one would have to get up, to let you sit; half that broad beam of yours would fill the whole House. I must ask you to assist our deliberations standing; you can bend down your head to the meeting.

Herm. Now here is another problem. Both bronze, equal aesthetically, being both from Lysippus's studio, and, to crown all, nothing to choose between them for birth—two sons of yours, Zeus—Dionysus and Heracles. Which is to be first? You can see for yourself, they mean to stand upon their order.

Zeus. We are wasting time, Hermes; the debate should have been in full swing by now. Tell them to sit anyhow, according to taste; we will have an *ad hoc* meeting another day, and then I shall know how to settle the question of precedence.

Herm. My goodness, what a noise! what low vulgar bawling! listen— 'Hurry up with that carving! ' 'Do pass the nectar! ' 'Why no more ambrosia? ' 'When are those hecatombs coming? ' 'Here, shares in that victim! '

Zeus. Call them to order, Hermes; this nonsense must cease, before I can give them the order of the day.

Herm. They do not all know Greek; and I haven't the gift of tongues, to make myself understood by Scythians and Persians and Thracians and Celts. Perhaps I had better hold up my hand and signal for silence.

Zeus. Do.

Herm. Good; they are as quiet as if they were so many teachers of elocution. Now is the time for your speech; see, they are all hanging on your lips.

Zeus. Why—there is something wrong with me—Hermes, my boy — I will be frank with you. You know how confident and impressive I always was as a public speaker?

Herm. I know; I used to be in such a fright; you threatened sometimes to let down your golden cord and heave up earth and sea from their foundations, Gods included.

Zeus. But to-day, my child—it may be this terrible crisis— it may be the size of the audience—there is a vast number of Gods here, isn't there—anyhow, my thoughts are all mixed, I shiver, my tongue seems tied. What is most absurd of all, my exordium is gone clean out of my head; and I had prepared it on purpose to produce a good impression at the start.

Herm. You have spoiled everything, Zeus. They cannot make out your silence; they are expecting to hear of some terrible disaster, to account for your delay.

Zeus. What do you think? Reel off the exordium in Homer?

Herm. Which one?

Zeus. Lend me your ears, Gods all and Goddesses.

Herm. Rubbish! you made quite exhibition enough of yourself in that vein in our cabinet council. However, you might, if you like, drop your metrical fustian, and adapt any one of Demosthenes's Philippics with a few alterations. That is the fashionable method with speakers nowadays.

Zeus. Ah, that is a royal road to eloquence—simplifies matters very much for a man in difficulties.

Herm. Go ahead, then.

Zeus. Men of—Heaven, I presume that you would be willing to pay a great price, if you could know what in the world has occasioned the present summons. Which being so, it is fitting that you should give a ready hearing to my words. Now, whereas the present crisis, Heavenians, may almost be said to lift up a voice and bid us take vigorous hold on opportunity, it seems to me that we are letting it slip from our nerveless grasp. And I wish now (I can't remember any more) to exhibit clearly to you the apprehensions which have led to my summoning you.

As you are all aware, Mnesitheus the ship's-captain yesterday made his votive offering for the narrow escape of his vessel off Caphereus, and those of us whom he had invited attended the banquet in Piraeus. After the libations you went your several ways. I myself, as it was not very late, walked up to town for an afternoon stroll in Ceramicus, reflecting as I went on the parsimony of Mnesitheus. When the ship was driving against the cliff, and already inside the circle of reef, he had vowed whole hecatombs: what he offered in fact, with sixteen Gods to entertain, was a single cock—an old bird afflicted with catarrh—and half a dozen grains of frankincense; these were all mildewed, so that they at once fizzled out on the embers, hardly giving enough smoke to tickle the olfactories. Engaged in these thoughts I reached the Poecile, and there found a great crowd gathered; there were some inside the Portico, a large number outside, and a few seated on the benches vociferating as loud as they could. Guessing correctly that these were philosophers of the militant variety, I had a mind to stop and hear what they were saying. I was enveloped in a good thick cloud, under cover of which I assumed their habit, lengthened my beard, and so made a passable philosopher; then I elbowed my way through the crowd and got in undetected. I found an accomplished scoundrel and a pattern of human virtue at daggers drawn; they were Damis the Epicurean and Timocles the Stoic. The latter was bathed in perspiration, and his voice showed signs of wear, while Damis goaded him on to further exertions with mocking laughter.

The bone of contention was ourselves. Damis—the reptile! — maintained that we did not concern ourselves in thought or act with human affairs, and practically denied our existence; that was what it came to. And he found some support. Timocles was on our side, and loyally, passionately, unshrinkingly did he champion the cause; he extolled our Providence, and illustrated the orderly discerning character of our influence and government. He too had his party; but he was exhausted and quite husky; and the majority were inclining to Damis. I saw how much was at stake, and ordered Night to come on and break up the meeting. They accordingly dispersed, agreeing to conclude the inquiry next day. I kept among the crowd on its way home, heard its commendations of Damis, and found that his views were far the more popular, though some still protested against condemning Timocles out of hand, and preferred to see what he would say for himself to-morrow.

You now know the occasion of this meeting—no light one, ye Gods, if you reflect how entirely our dignity, our revenue, our honour, depend on mankind. If they should accept as true either our absolute non-existence or, short of that, our indifference to them, farewell to our earthly sacrifices, attributes, honours; we shall sit starving and ineffectual in Heaven; our beloved feasts and assemblies, games and sacrifices, vigils and processions—all will be no more. So mighty is the issue; believe me, it behoves us all to search out salvation; and where lies salvation? In the victory and acceptance of Timocles, in laughter that shall drown the voice of Damis. For I doubt the unaided powers of Timocles, if our help be not accorded him.

Hermes, make formal proclamation, and let the debate commence.

Herm. Hear, keep silence, clamour not. Of full and qualified Gods, speak who will. Why, what means this? Doth none rise? Cower ye confounded at these momentous tidings?

Mo.

Away, ye dull as earth, as water weak!

But *I* could find plenty to say, Zeus, if free speech were granted me.

Zeus. Speak, Momus, and fear not. You will use your freedom, surely, for the common good.

Mo. Hear, then, ye Gods; for out of the abundance of the heart the mouth speaketh. You must know, I foresaw all this clearly—our difficulty—the growth of these agitators; it is ourselves who are responsible for their impudence; I swear to you, we need not blame Epicurus nor his friends and successors, for the prevalence of these ideas. Why, what can one expect men to think, when they see all life topsy-turvy—the good neglected, pining in poverty, disease, and slavery, detestable scoundrels honoured, rolling in wealth, and ordering their betters about, temple-robbers undetected and unpunished, the innocent constantly crucified and bastinadoed? With this evidence before them, it is only natural they should conclude against our existence. All the more when they hear the oracles saying that some one

> The Halys crossed, o'erthrows a mighty realm,
> but not specifying whether that realm is his own or his enemy's;

or again

> O sacred Salamis, thou shalt slay
> Full many a mother's son.

The Greeks were mothers' sons as well as the Persians, I suppose. Or again, when they hear the ballads about our loves, our wounds, captivities, thraldoms, quarrels, and endless vicissitudes (mark you, we claim all the while to be blissful and serene), are they not justified in ridiculing and belittling us? And then we say it is outrageous if a few people who are not quite fools expose the absurdity and reject Providence; why, we ought to be glad enough that a few still go on sacrificing to blunderers like us.

And at this point, Zeus—this meeting is private; the human element is not represented among us (except by Heracles, Dionysus, Ganymede, and Asclepius, and they are naturalized)—at this point, answer me a question frankly: did your interest in mankind ever carry you so far as to sift the good from the bad? The answer is in the negative, I know. Very well, then; had not a Theseus, on his way from Troezen to Athens, exterminated the malefactors as an incidental amusement, Sciron and Pityocamptes and Cercyon and the rest of them might have gone on battening on the slaughter of travellers, for all you and your Providence would have done. Had not an old-fashioned thoughtful Eurystheus, benevolently collecting information of local troubles, sent this energetic enterprising servant of his about, the mighty Zeus would never have given a thought to the Hydra or the Stymphalian birds, the Thracian horses and the drunken insolence of Centaurs.

If the truth must out, we sit here with a single eye to one thing— does a man sacrifice and feed the altars fat? Everything else drifts as it may. We get our deserts, and shall continue to get them, when men open their eyes by degrees and find that sacrifices and processions bring them no profit. Before long you will find we are the laughing-stock of people like Epicurus, Metrodorus, Damis, who will have mastered and muzzled our advocates. With whom does it lie to check and remedy this state of things? Why, with you, who have brought it on. As for Momus, what is dishonour to him? He was never among the recipients of honour, while you were still prosperous; your banquetings were too exclusive.

Zeus. He was ever a cross-grained censor; we need not mind his maundering, Gods. We have it from the admirable Demosthenes: imputations, blame, criticism, these are easy things; they tax no one's capacity: what calls for a statesman is the suggesting of a better course; and that is what I rely upon the rest of you for; let us do our best without his help.

Pos. As for me, I live ordinarily under water, as you know, and follow an independent policy in the depths; that policy is to save sailors, set ships on their way, and keep the winds quiet, as best I may. However, I do take an interest in your politics too, and my opinion is that this Damis should be got rid of before the debate; the thunderbolt would do it, or some means could be found; else he might win—you say he is a plausible fellow, Zeus. It would teach them that there is a reckoning for telling such tales about us, too.

Zeus. You must be jesting, Posidon; you cannot have forgotten that we have no say in the matter? It is the Fates that spin a man's thread, whether he be destined to the thunderbolt or the sword, to fever or consumption. If it had depended on me, do you suppose I should have let those temple-robbers get off unblasted from Pisa the other day? —two of my curls shorn off, weighing half a dozen pounds apiece. Would *you* have stood it, when that fisherman from Oreus stole your trident at Geraestus? Moreover, they will think we are sensitive and angry; they will suspect that the reason why we get the man out of the way without waiting to see him matched with Timocles is that we are afraid of his arguments; they will say we are just securing judgement by default.

Pos. Dear, dear! I thought I had hit upon a good short cut to our object.

Zeus. Nonsense, there is something fishy about it, Posidon; and it is a dull notion too, to destroy your adversary beforehand; he dies unvanquished, and leaves his argument behind him still debatable and undecided.

Pos. Then the rest of you must think of something better, if 'fishy' is the best word you have for me.

Apol. If we beardless juniors were competent to address the meeting, *I* might perhaps have contributed usefully to the discussion.

Mo. Oh, Apollo, the inquiry is so important that seniority may be waived, and any one allowed his say; a pretty thing to split hairs about legal competence at a supreme crisis! But *you* are surely qualified by this time; your minority is prehistoric, your name is on the Privy-Council roll, your senatorial rank dates back almost to Cronus. Pray spare us these juvenile airs, and give us your views freely; you need not be bashful about your smooth chin; you have a father's rights in Asclepius's great bush of a beard. Moreover, you never had a better opportunity of showing your wisdom, if your philosophic *seances* with the Muses on Helicon have not been thrown away.

Apol. Why, it does not lie with you to give me leave, Momus; Zeus must do that; and if he bids, I may find words that shall be not all uncultured, but worthy of my Heliconian studies.

Zeus. Speak, son; thou hast my leave.

Apol. This Timocles is a good pious man, and an excellent Stoic scholar; his learning has gained him a wide and paying connexion among young men; in private lessons his manner is indeed very convincing. But in public speaking he is timid, cannot produce his voice, and has a provincial accent; the consequence is, he gets laughed at in company, lacks fluency, stammers and loses his thread—especially when he emphasizes these defects by an attempt at flowers of speech. As far as intelligence goes, he is extremely acute and subtle, so the Stoic experts say; but he spoils it all by the feebleness of his oral explanations; he is confused and unintelligible, deals in paradoxes, and when he is interrogated, explains *ignotum per ignotius*; his audience does not grasp his meaning, and therefore laughs at him. I think lucidity a most important point; there is nothing one should be so careful about as to be comprehensible.

Mo. You praise lucidity, Apollo; your theory is excellent, though your practice does not quite conform; your oracles are crooked and enigmatic, and generally rely upon a safe ambiguity; a second prophet is required to say what they mean. But what is your solution of the problem? How are we to cure Timocles of the impediment in his speech?

Apol. If possible, we should provide him with an able counsel (there are plenty such) to be inspired by him and give adequate expression to his ideas.

Mo. Your sapience is beardless indeed—*in statu pupillari*, one may say. A learned gathering: Timocles with counsel by his side to interpret his ideas, Damis speaking *in propria persona* with his own tongue, his opponent employing a go-between into whose ears he privately pours inspiration, and the go-between producing ornate periods, without, I dare say, understanding what he is told—most entertaining for the listeners! We shall get nothing out of that device.

But, reverend sir, you claim the gift of prophecy, and it has brought you in good pay—golden ingots on one occasion? —why not seize this opportunity of exhibiting your art? You might tell us which of the disputants will win; a prophet knows the future, of course.

Apol. I have no tripod or incense here; no substitute for the divining-well of Castaly.

Mo. Aha! you are caught! you will not come to the scratch.

Zeus. Speak, my son, in spite of all; give not this enemy occasion to blaspheme; let him not flout thy powers with tripod and water and frankincense, as though thine art were lost without them.

Apol. Father, it were better done at Delphi or at Colophon, with all the customary instruments to hand. Yet, bare and unprovided as I am, I will essay to tell whether of them twain shall prevail. —If the metre is a little rough, you must make allowances.

Mo. Go on, then; but remember, Apollo: lucidity; no 'able counsel, ' no solutions that want solving themselves. It is not a question of lamb and tortoise boiling [Footnote: See *Croesus* in Notes.] in Lydia now; you know what we want to get at.

Zeus. What will thine utterance be? How dread, even now, is the making ready! The altered hue, the rolling eyes, the floating locks, the frenzied gesture—all is possession, horror, mystery.

Apol.

> Who lists may hear Apollo's soothfast rede
> Of stiff debate, heroic challenge ringing
> Shrill, and each headpiece lined with fence of proof.
> Alternate clack the strokes in whirling strife;
> Sore buffeted, quakes and shivers heart of oak.
> But when grasshopper feels the vulture's talons,
> Then the storm-boding ravens croak their last,
> Prevail the mules, butts his swift foals the ass.

Zeus. Why that ribald laughter, Momus? It is no laughing matter. Stop, stop, fool; you'll choke yourself.

Mo. Well, such a clear simple oracle puts one in spirits.

Zeus. Indeed? Then perhaps you will kindly expound it.

Mo. No need of a Themistocles this time; it is absolutely plain. The oracle just says in so many words that he is a quack, and we pack-asses (quite true) and mules to believe in him; we have not as much sense, it adds, as a grasshopper.

Herac. Father, I am only an alien, but I am not afraid to give my opinion. Let them begin their debate. Then, if Timocles gets the best of it, we can let the meeting go on, in our own interest; on the other hand, if things look bad, I will give the Portico a shake, if you like, and bring it down on Damis; a confounded fellow like that is not to insult us.

Zeus. Now by Heracles—I can swear by you, I certainly cannot swear by your plan—what a crude—what a shockingly philistine suggestion! What! destroy all those people for one man's wickedness? and the Portico thrown in, with the Miltiades and Cynaegirus on the field of Marathon? Why, if these were ruined, how could the orators ever make another speech, with the best of their stock-in-trade taken from them? Besides, while you were alive, you might possibly have done a thing like that; but now that you are a God, you surely understand that only the Fates are competent, and we cannot interfere?

Herac. Then when I slew the lion or the Hydra, was I only the Fates' instrument?

Zeus. Of course you were.

Herac. And now, suppose any one insults me, or robs my temple, or upsets an image of me, am I not to pulverize him, just because the Fates have not decreed it long ago?

Zeus. Certainly not.

Herac. Then allow me to speak my mind;

I'm a blunt man; I call a spade a spade.

If this is the state of things with you, good-bye for me to your honours and altar-steam and fat of victims; I shall be off to Hades. There, if I show my bow ready for action, the ghosts of the monsters I have slain will be frightened, at least.

Zeus. Oh, splendid! 'Thine own lips testify against thee, ' says the book; you would have saved Damis some trouble by putting this in his mouth.

But who is this breathless messenger? Bronze—a nice clean figure and outline—*chevelure* rather out of date. Ah, he must be your brother, Hermes, who stands in the Market by the Poecile; I see he is all over pitch; that is what comes of having casts taken of you every day. My son, why this haste? Have you important news from Earth?

Hermag. Momentous news, calling for infinite energy.

Zeus. Speak, tarry not, if any peril else hath escaped our vigilance.

Hermag.

> It chanced of late that by the statuaries
> My breast and back were plastered o'er with pitch;
> A mock cuirass tight-clinging hung, to ape
> My bronze, and take the seal of its impression.
> When lo, a crowd! therein a pallid pair
> Sparring amain, vociferating logic;
> 'Twas Damis and —

Zeus. Truce to your iambics, my excellent Hermagoras; I know the pair. But tell me whether the fight has been going on long.

Hermag. Not yet; they were still skirmishing—slinging invective at long range.

Zeus. Then we have only, Gods, to look over and listen. Let the Hours unbar, draw back the clouds, and open the doors of Heaven.

Upon my word, what a vast gathering! And I do not quite like the looks of Timocles; he is trembling; he has lost his head; he will spoil everything; it is perfectly plain, he will not be able to stand up to Damis. Well, there is one thing left us: we can pray for him

> Inwardly, silently, lest Damis hear.

Ti. What, you miscreant, no Gods? no Providence?

Da. No, no; you answer my question first; what makes you believe in them?

Ti. None of that, now; the *onus probandi* is with you, scoundrel.

80

Da. None of that, now; it is with you.

Zeus. At this game ours is much the better man—louder-voiced, rougher-tempered. Good, Timocles; stick to invective; that is your strong point; once you get off that, he will hook and hold you up like a fish.

Ti. I solemnly swear I will not answer first.

Da. Well, put your questions, then; so much you score by your oath. But no abuse, please.

Ti. Done. Tell me, then, and be damned to you, do you deny that the Gods exercise providence?

Da. I do.

Ti. What, are all the events we see uncontrolled, then?

Da. Yes.

Ti. And the regulation of the universe is not under any God's care?

Da. No.

Ti. And everything moves casually, by blind tendency?

Da. Yes.

Ti. Gentlemen, can you tolerate such sentiments? Stone the blasphemer.

Da. What do you mean by hounding them against me? Who are you, that you should protest in the Gods' name? They do not even protest in their own; they have sent no judgement on me, and they have had time enough to hear me, if they have ears.

Ti. They do hear you; they do; and some day their vengeance will find you out.

Da. Pray when are they likely to have time to spare for me? They are far too busy, according to you, with all the infinite concerns of the universe on their hands. That is why they have never punished you for your perjuries and—well, for the rest of your performances, let me say, not to break our compact about abuse. And yet I am at a loss to conceive any more convincing proof they could have given of their Providence, than if they had trounced you as you deserve. But no doubt they are from home—t'other side of Oceanus, possibly, on a visit to 'the blameless Ethiopians. ' We know they have a way of going there to dinner, self-invited sometimes.

Ti. What answer is possible to such ribaldry?

Da. The answer I have been waiting for all this time; you can tell me what made you believe in divine Providence.

Ti. Firstly, the order of nature—the sun running his regular course, the moon the same, the circling seasons, the growth of plants, the generation of living things, the ingenious adaptations in these latter for nutrition, thought, movement, locomotion; look at a carpenter or a shoemaker, for instance; and the thing is infinite. All these effects, and no effecting Providence?

Da. You beg the question; whether the effects are produced by Providence is just what is not yet proved. Your description of nature I accept; it does not follow that there is definite design in it; it is not impossible that things now similar and homogeneous have developed from widely different origins. But you give the name 'order' to mere blind tendency. And you will be very angry if one follows your appreciative catalogue of nature in all its variety, but stops short of accepting it as a proof of detailed Providence. So, as the play says,

Here lurks a fallacy; bring me sounder proof.

Ti. I cannot admit that further proof is required; nevertheless, I will give you one. Will you allow Homer to have been an admirable poet?

Da. Surely.

Ti. Well, *he* maintains Providence, and warrants my belief.

Da. Magnificent! why, every one will grant you Homer's poetic excellence; but not that he, or any other poet for that matter, is good authority on questions of this sort. *Their* object, of course, is not truth, but fascination; they call in the charms of metre, they take tales for the vehicle of what instruction they give, and in short all their efforts are directed to pleasure.

But I should be glad to hear which parts of Homer you pin your faith to. Where he tells how the daughter, the brother, and the wife of Zeus conspired to imprison him? If Thetis had not been moved to compassion and called Briareus, you remember, our excellent Zeus would have been seized and manacled; and his gratitude to her induced him to delude Agamemnon with a lying dream, and bring about the deaths of a number of Greeks. Do you see? The reason was that, if he had struck and blasted Agamemnon's self with a thunderbolt, his double dealing would have come to light. Or perhaps you found the Diomede story most convincing? — Diomede wounded Aphrodite, and afterwards Ares himself, at Athene's instigation; and then the Gods actually fell to blows and went a-tilting—without distinction of sex; Athene overthrew Ares, exhausted no doubt with his previous wound from Diomede; and

> Hermes the stark and stanch 'gainst Leto stood.

Or did you put your trust in Artemis? She was a sensitive lady, who resented not being invited to Oeneus's banquet, and by way of vengeance sent a monstrous irresistible boar to ravage his country. Is it with tales like these that Homer has prevailed on you?

Zeus. Goodness me, what a shout, Gods! they are all cheering Damis. And our man seems posed; he is frightened and trembles; he is going to throw up the sponge, I am certain of it; he looks round for a gap to get away through.

Ti. And will you scout Euripides too, then? Again and again he brings Gods on the stage, and shows them upholding virtue in the Heroes, but chastising wickedness and impiety (like yours).

Da. My noble philosopher, if that is how the tragedians have convinced you, you have only two alternatives: you must suppose that divinity is temporarily lodged either in the actor—a Polus, an Aristodemus, a Satyrus—, or else in the actual masks, buskins, long tunics, cloaks, gloves, stomachers, padding, and ornamental paraphernalia in general of tragedy—a manifest absurdity; for when Euripides can speak his own sentiments unfettered by dramatic necessity, observe the freedom of his remarks:

> Dost see this aether stretching infinite,
> And girdling earth with close yet soft embrace?
> That reckon thou thy Zeus, that name thy God.

And again,

> Zeus, whatever Zeus may be (for, save by hearsay,
> I know not)—;

and there is more of the same sort.

Ti. Well, but all men—ay, all nations—have acknowledged and, feted Gods; was it all delusion?

Da. Thank you; a timely reminder; national observances show better than anything else how vague religious theory is. Confusion is endless, and beliefs as many as believers. Scythia makes offerings to a scimetar, Thrace to the Samian runaway Zamolxis, Phrygia to a Month-God, Ethiopia to a Day-Goddess, Cyllene to Phales, Assyria to a dove, Persia to fire, Egypt to water. In Egypt, though, besides the universal worship of water, Memphis has a private cult of the ox, Pelusium of the onion, other cities of the ibis or the crocodile, others again of baboon, cat, or monkey. Nay, the very villages have their specialities: one deifies the right shoulder, and another across the river the left; one a half skull, another an earthenware bowl or platter. Come, my fine fellow, is it not all ridiculous?

Mo. What did I tell you, Gods? All this was sure to come out and be carefully overhauled.

Zeus. You did, Momus, and your strictures were justified; if once we come safe out of this present peril, I will try to introduce reforms.

Ti. Infidel! where do you find the source of oracles and prophecies, if not in the Gods and their Providence?

Da. About oracles, friend, the less said the better; I shall ask you to choose your instances, you see. Will Apollo's answer to the Lydian suit you? That was as symmetrical as a double-edged knife; or say, it faced both ways, like those Hermae which are made double, alike whether you look at front or back. Consider; will Croesus's passage of the Halys destroy his own realm, or Cyrus's? Tet the wretched Sardian paid a long price for his ambidextrous hexameter.

Mo. The man is realizing just my worst apprehensions. Where is our handsome musician now? Ah, there you are; go down and plead your own cause against him.

Zeus. *Hush, Momus; you are murdering our feelings; it is no time for recrimination.*

Ti. Have a care, Damis; this is sacrilege, no less; what you say amounts to razing the temples and upsetting the altars.

Da. Oh, not *all* the altars; what harm do they do, so long as incense and perfume is the worst of it? As for Artemis's altar at Tauri, though, and her hideous feasts, I should like it overturned from base to cornice.

Zeus. Whence comes this resistless plague among us? There is none of us he spares; he is as free with his tongue as a tub orator,

And grips by turns the innocent and guilty.

Mo. The innocent? You will not find many of those among us, Zeus. He will soon come to laying hands upon some of the great and eminent, I dare say.

Ti. Do you close your ears even to Zeus's thunder, atheist?

Da. I clearly cannot shut out the thunder; whether it is Zeus's thunder, you know better than I perhaps; you may have interviewed the Gods. Travellers from Crete tell another story: there is a tomb there with an inscribed pillar, stating that Zeus is long dead, and not going to thunder any more.

Mo. I could have told you that was coming long ago. What, Zeus? pale? and your teeth chattering? What is the matter? You should cheer up, and treat such manikins with lofty contempt.

Zeus. Contempt? See what a number of them there is—how set against us they are already—and he has them fast by the ears.

Mo. Well, but you have only to choose, and you can let down your golden cord, and then every man of them

With earth and sky and all thou canst draw up.

Ti. Blasphemer, have you ever been a voyage?

Da. Many.

Ti. Well, then, the wind struck the canvas and filled the sails, and it or the oars gave you way, but there was a person responsible for steering and for the safety of the ship?

Da. Certainly.

Ti. Now that ship would not have sailed, without a steersman; and do you suppose that this great universe drifts unsteered and uncontrolled?

Zeus. *Good, this time, Timocles; a cogent illustration, that.*

Da. But, you pattern of piety, the earthly navigator makes his plans, takes his measures, gives his orders, with a single eye to efficiency; there is nothing useless or purposeless on board; everything is to make navigation easy or possible; but as for the navigator for whom you claim the management of this vast ship, he and his crew show no reason or appropriateness in any of their arrangements; the forestays, as likely as not, are made fast to the stern, and both sheets to the bows; the anchor will be gold, the beak lead, decoration below the water-line, and unsightliness above.

As for the men, you will find some lazy awkward coward in second or third command, or a fine swimmer, active as a cat aloft, and a handy man generally, chosen out of all the rest to—pump. It is just the same with the passengers: here is a gaolbird accommodated with a seat next the captain and treated with reverence, there a debauchee or parricide or temple-robber in honourable possession of the best place, while crowds of respectable people are packed together in a corner and hustled by their real inferiors. Consider what sort of a voyage Socrates and Aristides and Phocion had of it, on short rations, not venturing, for the filth, to stretch out their legs on the bare deck; and on the other hand what a comfortable, luxurious, contemptuous life it was for Callias or Midias or Sardanapalus.

That is how things go on board your ship, sir wiseacre; and who shall count the wrecks? If there had been a captain supervising and directing, in the first place he would have known the difference between good and bad passengers, and in the second he would have given them their deserts; the better would have had the better accommodation above by his side, and the worse gone below; with some of the better he would have shared his meals and his counsels. So too for the crew: the keen sailor would have been made look-out man or captain of the watch, or given some sort of precedence, and the lazy shirker have tasted the rope's end half a dozen times a day. The metaphorical ship, your worship, is likely to be capsized by its captain's incompetence.

Mo. He is sweeping on to victory, with wind and tide.

Zeus. Too probable, Momus. And Timocles never gets hold of an effective idea; he can only ladle out trite commonplaces higgledy-piggledy—no sooner heard than refuted.

Ti. Well, well; my ship leaves you unconvinced; I must drop my sheet-anchor, then; that at least is unbreakable.

Zeus. I wonder what it is.

Ti. See whether this is a sound syllogism; can you upset it? —If there are altars, there are Gods: there *are* altars; therefore, there are Gods. Now then.

Da. Ha, ha, ha! I will answer as soon as I can get done with laughing.

Ti. Will you never stop? At least tell me what the joke is.

Da. Why, you don't see that your anchor (sheet-anchor, too) hangs by a mere thread. You defend on connexion between the existence of Gods and the existence of altars, and fancy yourself safe at anchor! As you admit that this was your sheet-anchor, there is nothing further to detain us.

Ti. You retire; you confess yourself beaten, then?

Da. Yes; we have seen you take sanctuary at the altars under persecution. At those altars I am ready (the sheet-anchor be my witness) to swear peace and cease from strife.

Ti. Tou are playing with me, are you, you vile body-snatcher, you loathsome well-whipped scum! As if we didn't know who your father was, how your mother was a harlot! You strangled your own brother, you live in fornication, you debauch the young, you unabashed lecher! Don't be in such a hurry; here is something for you to take with you; this broken pot will serve me to cut your foul throat.

Zeus. Damis makes off with a laugh, and the other after him, calling him names, mad at his insolence. He will get him on the head with that pottery, I know. And now, what are we to do?

Herm. Why, the man in the comedy was not far out:

Put a good face on 't, and thou hast no harm.

It is no such terrible disaster, if a few people go away infected. There are plenty who take the other view—a majority of Greeks, the body and dregs of the people, and the barbarians to a man.

Zeus. Ah, Hermes, but there is a great deal in Darius's remark about Zopyrus—I would rather have had one ally like Damis than be the lord of a thousand Babylons.

THE COCK

Micyllus. A Cock

Mi. Detested bird! May Zeus crunch your every bone! Shrill, envious brute: to wake me from delightful dreams of wealth and magic blessedness with those piercing, deafening notes! Am I not even in sleep to find a refuge from Poverty, Poverty more vile than your vile self? Why, it cannot be midnight yet: all is hushed; numbness—sure messenger of approaching dawn—has not yet performed its morning office upon my limbs: and this wakeful brute (one would think he was guarding the golden fleece) starts crowing before night has fairly begun. But he shall pay for it. —Yes; only wait till daylight comes, and my stick shall avenge me; I am not going to flounder about after you in the dark.

Cock. Why, master, I meant to give you a pleasant surprise: I borrowed what I could from the night, that you might be up early and break the back of your work; think, if you get a shoe done before sunrise, you are so much the nearer to earning your day's bread. However, if you prefer to sleep, I have done; I will be mute as any fish. Only you may find your rich dreams followed by a hungry awakening.

Mi. God of portents! Heracles preserve us from the evil to come! My cock has spoken with a human voice.

Cock. And what if he has? Is that so very portentous?

Mi. I should think it was. All Gods avert the omen!

Cock. Micyllus, I am afraid your education has been sadly neglected. If you had read your Homer, you would know that Achilles's horse Xanthus declined to have anything more to do with neighing, and stood on the field of battle spouting whole hexameters; *he* was not content with plain prose like me; he even took to prophecy, and foretold to Achilles what should befall him. Nor was this considered anything out of the way; Achilles saw nothing portentous about it, nor did he invoke Heracles on the occasion. What a fuss you would have made, if the keel of the Argo had addressed a remark to you, or the leaves of the Dodonaean oak had opened their mouths and prophesied; or if you had seen ox- hides crawling about, and heard the half-cooked flesh of the beasts bellowing on the spit! As for me, considering my connexion with Hermes—most loquacious, most argumentative of Gods—and my familiar intercourse with mankind, it was only to be expected that I should pick up your language pretty quickly. Nay, there is a still better reason for my conversational powers, which I don't mind telling you, if you will promise to keep quiet about it.

Mi. Am I dreaming still, or is this bird really talking to me? —In Hermes' name then, good creature, out with your better reason; I will be mum, never fear; it shall go no further. Why, who would believe the story, when I told him that I had it from a cock?

Cock. Listen. You will doubtless be surprised to learn that not so long ago the cock who stands before you was a man.

Mi. Why, to be sure, I have heard something like this before about a cock. It was the story of a young man called Alectryon [Footnote: Alectryon is the Greek word for a cock.]; he was a friend of Ares, — used to join in his revels and junketings, and give him a hand in his love affairs. Whenever Ares went to pay a sly visit to Aphrodite, he used to take Alectryon with him, and as he was particularly afraid that the Sun would see him, and tell Hephaestus, he would always leave Alectryon at the door, so that he might give him warning when the Sun was up. But one day Alectryon fell asleep, and unwittingly betrayed his trust; the consequence was that the Sun got a peep at the lovers, while Ares was having a comfortable nap, relying on Alectryon to tell him if any one came. Hephaestus heard of it, and caught them in that cage of his, which he had long had waiting for them. When Ares was released, he was so angry with Alectryon that he turned him into a cock, armour and all, as is shown by his crest; and that is what makes you cocks in such a hurry to crow at dawn, to let us know that the Sun is coming up presently; it is your way of apologizing to Ares, though crowing will not mend matters now.

Cock. Yes, there is that story too: but that is nothing to do with mine; I only became a cock quite lately.

Mi. But what I want to know is, how did it happen?

Cock. Did you ever hear of Pythagoras of Samos, son of Mnesarchus?

Mi. What, that sophist quack, who forbade the eating of meat, and would have banished beans from our tables (no beans, indeed! my favourite food!), and who wanted people to go for five years without speaking?

Cock. And who, I may add, was Euphorbus before he was Pythagoras.

Mi. He was a knave and a humbug, that Pythagoras, by all accounts.

Cock. That Pythagoras, my worthy friend, is now before you in person: spare his feelings, especially as you know nothing about his real character.

Mi. Portent upon portent! a cock philosopher! But proceed, son of Mnesarchus: how came you to change from man to bird, from Samos to Tanagra? [Footnote: See Notes.] 'Tis an unconvincing story; I find a difficulty in swallowing it. I have noticed two things about you already, which do not look much like Pythagoras.

Cock. Yes?

Mi. For one thing, you are garrulous; I might say noisy. Now, if I am not mistaken, Pythagoras advocated a course of five years' silence at a stretch. As for the other, it is rank heresy. You will remember that yesterday, not having anything else to give you, I brought you some beans: and you, —you gobbled them up without thinking twice about it! Either you lied when you told me you were Pythagoras, or else you have sinned against your own laws: in eating those beans, you have as good as bolted your own father's head.

Cock. Ah, you don't understand, Micyllus. There is a reason for these things: different diets suit different creatures. I was a philosopher in those days: accordingly I abstained from beans. Now, on the contrary, I propose to eat beans; they are an unexceptionable diet for birds. And now if you like I will tell you how from being Pythagoras I have come to be—what you see me; and all about the other lives I have lived, and what were the good points of each.

Mi. Tell on; there is nothing I should like better. Indeed, if I were given my choice between hearing your story, and having my late dream of riches over again, I don't know which I should decide on.

'Twas a sweet vision, of joys above all price: yet not above the tale of my cock's adventures.

Cock. What, still puzzling over the import of a dream? Still busy with vain phantoms, chasing a visionary happiness through your head, that 'fleeting' joy, as the poet calls it?

Mi. Ah, cock, cock, I shall never forget it. That dream has left its honeyed spell on my eyelids; 'tis all I can do to open them; they would fain close once more in sleep. As a feather tickles the ear, so did that vision tickle my imagination.

Cock. Bless me, you seem to be very hard hit. Dreams are winged, so they say, and their flight circumscribed by sleep: this one seems to have broken bounds, and taken up its abode in wakeful eyes, transferring thither its honeyed spell, its lifelike presence. Tell me this dream of your desire.

Mi. With all my heart; it is a joy to remember it, and to speak of it. But what about your transformations?

Cock. They must wait till you have done dreaming, and wiped the honey from your eyelids. So you begin: I want to see which gates the dream came through, the ivory or the horn.

Mi. Through neither.

Cock. Well, but these are the only two that Homer mentions.

Mi. Homer may go hang: what does a babbling poet know about dreams? Pauper dreams may come through those gates, for all I know; that was the kind that Homer saw, and not over clearly at that, as he was blind. But *my* beauty came through golden gates, golden himself and clothed in gold and bringing gold.

Cock. Enough of gold, most gentle Midas; for to a Midas- prayer it is that I trace your vision; you must have dreamt whole minefuls.

Mi. Gold upon gold was there; picture if you can that glorious lightning-flash! What is it that Pindar says about gold? Can you help me to it? He says water is best, and then very properly proceeds to sing the praises of gold; it comes at the beginning of the book, and a beautiful ode it is.

Cock. What about this?

> Chiefest of all good we hold
> Water: even so doth gold,
> Like a fire that flameth through the night,
> Shine mid lordly wealth most lordly bright.

Mi. The very words; I could fancy that Pindar had seen my vision. And now, my philosophic cock, I will proceed to details. That I did not dine at home last night, you are already aware; the wealthy Eucrates had met me in the morning, and told me to come to dinner after my bath at his usual hour.

Cock. Too well do I know it, after starving all day long. It was quite late before you came home—half-seas over—and gave me those five beans; rather short commons for a cock who has been an athlete in his day, and contended at Olympia, not without distinction.

Mi. Well, so when I got back, and had given you the beans, I went to sleep, and

Through the ambrosial night a dream divine—

ah, divine indeed! —

Cock. Wait: let us have Eucrates first. What sort of a dinner was it? Tell me all about it. Seize the opportunity: dine once more in waking dream; chew the cud of prandial reminiscence.

Mi. I thought all that would bore you; however, if you are curious, all right. I had never dined at a great house in my life before, when yesterday, in a lucky hour for me, I fell in with Eucrates. After saluting him respectfully as usual, I was making off—not to bring discredit on him by walking at his side in my shabby clothes—when he spoke to me: 'Micyllus, ' he said, 'it is my daughter's birthday to-day, and I have invited a number of friends to celebrate it. One of them, I hear, is indisposed, and will not be able to come; you can take his place, always provided that I do not hear from him, for at present I do not know whether to expect him or not. ' I made my bow, and departed, praying that ague, pleurisy, and gout might light upon the invalid whose appetite I had the honour to represent. I thought bath-time would never come; I could not keep my eyes off the dial: where was the shadow now? could I go yet? At last it really was time: I scraped the dirt off, and made myself smart, turning my cloak inside out, so that the clean side might be uppermost. Among the numerous guests assembled at the door, whom should I see but the very man whose understudy I was to be, the invalid, in a litter! He was evidently in a sad way; groaning and coughing and spitting in the most alarmingly emphatic manner; ghostly pale, puffy, and not much less, I reckoned, than sixty years old. He was a philosopher, so they said, —one of those who fill boys' heads with nonsensical ideas. Certainly his beard was well adapted to the part he played; it cried aloud for the barber. Archibius the doctor asked him what induced him to venture out in that state of health. 'Oh, ' says he, 'a man must not shirk his duties, least of all a philosopher; no matter if a thousand ailments stand in his way. Eucrates would have taken it as a slight. ' 'You're out there, ' I cried; 'Eucrates would be only too glad if you would cough out your soul at home instead of doing it at his table. ' He made as if he had not heard my jest; he was above such things. Presently in came Eucrates from his bath, and seeing Thesmopolis (the philosopher), 'Ah, Professor, ' says he, 'I am glad to see you here; not that it would have made any difference, even if you had stayed at home; I should have had everything sent over to you. ' And with that he took the philosopher's hand, and with the help of the slaves, conducted him in. I thought it was time for me to be going about my business: however, Eucrates turned round to me, and seeing how glum I looked, 'Micyllus, ' says he, after a good deal of humming and ha'ing, 'you must join us; we shall find room for you; I can send my boy to dine with his mother and the women. ' It had very nearly turned out a wild-goose chase, but not quite: I walked in, feeling rather ashamed of myself for having done the boy out of his dinner. We were now to take our places. Thesmopolis was first hoisted into his, with some difficulty, by five stalwart youths, who propped him up on every side with cushions to keep him in his place and enable him to hold out to the end. As no one else was disposed to have him for a neighbour, that privilege was assigned to me without ceremony. And then dinner was brought in: such dainties, Pythagoras, such variety! and everything served on gold or silver. Golden cups, smart servants, musicians, jesters, — altogether, it was delightful. Thesmopolis, though, annoyed me a good deal: he kept on worrying about virtue, and explaining how two negatives make one positive, and how when it is day it is not night [Footnote: See *Puzzles* in Notes.]; among other things, he would have it that I had horns [Footnote: See *Puzzles* in Notes.]. I wanted none of his philosophy, but on he went, quite spoiling my pleasure; it was impossible to listen to the music and singing. So that is what the dinner was like.

Cock. Not much of a one, especially with that old fool for your neighbour.

Mi. And now for the dream, which was about no other than Eucrates. How it came about I don't know, but Eucrates was childless, and was on his death-bed; he sent for me and made his will, leaving everything to me, and soon after died. I now came into the property, and ladled out gold and silver by the bucketful from springs that never dried; furniture and plate, clothes and servants, all were mine. I drove abroad, the admiration of all eyes and the envy of all hearts, lolling in my carriage behind a pair of creams, with a crowd of attendants on horseback and on foot in front of me, and a larger crowd behind. Dressed in Eucrates's splendid clothes, my fingers loaded with a score or so of rings, I ordered a magnificent feast to be prepared for the entertainment of my friends. The next moment they were there, —it happens so in dreams; dinner was brought in, the wine splashed in the cups. I was pledging each of my friends in turn in beakers of gold, and the biscuits were just being brought in, when that unlucky crow of yours spoilt all: over went the tables, and away flew my visionary wealth to all the quarters of Heaven. Had I not some reason to be annoyed with you? I could have gone on with that dream for three nights on end.

Cock. Is the love of gold so absorbing a passion? Gold the only thing you can find to admire? The possession of gold the sole happiness?

Mi. I am not the only one, Pythagoras. Why, you yourself (when you were Euphorbus) used to go to battle with your hair adorned with gold and silver, though iron would have been more to the point than gold under the circumstances; however, you thought differently, and fought with a golden circlet about your brow; which I suppose is why Homer compares your hair to that of the Graces

in gold and silver clasped.

No doubt its charm would be greatly enhanced by the glitter of the interwoven gold. After all, though, you, my golden-haired friend, were but the son of Panthus; one can understand your respect for gold. But the father of Gods and men, the son of Cronus and Rhea himself, could find no surer way to the heart of his Argive enchantress [Footnote: Danae.]—or to those of her gaolers—than this same metal; you know the story, how he turned himself into gold, and came showering down through the roof into the presence of his beloved? Need I say more? Need I point out the useful purposes that gold serves? the beauty and wisdom and strength, the honour and glory it confers on its possessors, at a moment's notice turning obscurity and infamy into world-wide fame? You know my neighbour and fellow craftsman, Simon, who supped with me not long since? 'Twas at the Saturnalia, the day I made that pease-pudding, with the two slices of sausage in it?

Cock. I know: the little snub-nosed fellow, who went off with our pudding-basin under his arm, —the only one we had; I saw him with these eyes.

Mi. So it was he who stole that basin! and he swore by all his Gods that he knew nothing of it! But you should have called out, and told me how we were being plundered.

Cock. I did crow; it was all I could do just then. But what were you going to say about Simon?

Mi. He had a cousin, Drimylus, who was tremendously rich. During his lifetime, Drimylus never gave him a penny; and no wonder, for he never laid a finger on his money himself. But the other day he died, and Simon has come in for everything. No more dirty rags for him now, no more trencher-licking: he drives abroad clothed in purple and scarlet; slaves and horses are his, golden cups and ivory-footed tables, and men prostrate themselves before him. As for me, he will not so much as look at me: it was only the other day that I met him, and said, 'Good day, Simon': he flew into a rage: 'Tell that beggar, ' he said, 'not to cut down my name; it is Simonides, not Simon. ' And that is not all, —the women are in love with him too, and Simon is coy and cold: some he receives graciously, but the neglected ones declare they will hang themselves. See what gold can do! It is like Aphrodite's girdle, transforming the unsightly and making them lovely to behold. What say the poets?

Happy the hand that grasps thee, Gold!

and again,

Gold hath dominion over mortal men.

But what are you laughing at?

Cock. Ah, Micyllus, I see that you are no wiser than your neighbours; you have the usual mistaken notions about the rich, whose life, I assure you, is far more miserable than your own. I ought to know: I have tried everything, and been poor man and rich man times out of number. You will find out all about it before long.

Mi. Ah, to be sure, it is your turn now. Tell me how you came to be changed into a cock, and what each of your lives was like.

Cock. Very well; and I may remark, by way of preface, that of all the lives I have ever known none was happier than yours.

Mi. Than mine? Exasperating fowl! All I say is, may you have one like it! Now then: begin from Euphorbus, and tell me how you came to be Pythagoras, and so on, down to the cock. I'll warrant you have not been through all those different lives without seeing some strange sights, and having your adventures.

Cock. How my spirit first proceeded from Apollo, and took flight to earth, and entered into a human form, and what was the nature of the crime thus expiated, —all this would take too long to tell; nor is it fitting either for me to speak of such matters or for you to hear of them. I pass to the time when I became Euphorbus, —

Mi. Wait a minute: have I ever been changed in this way?

Cock. You have.

Mi. Then who was I, do you know? I am curious about that.

Cock. Why, you were an Indian ant, of the gold-digging species.

Mi. What could induce me, misguided insect that I was, to leave that life without so much as a grain of gold-dust to supply my needs in this one? And what am I going to be next? I suppose you can tell me. If it is anything good, I'll hang myself this moment from the very perch on which you stand.

Cock. That I can on no account divulge. To resume. When I was Euphorbus, I fought at Troy, and was slain by Menelaus. Some time then elapsed before I entered into the body of Pythagoras. During this interval, I remained without a habitation, waiting till Mnesarchus had prepared one for me.

Mi. What, without meat or drink?

Cock. Oh yes; these are mere bodily requirements.

Mi. Well, first I will have about the Trojan war. Did it all happen as Homer describes?

Cock. Homer! What should he know of the matter? He was a camel in Bactria all the time. I may tell you that things were not on such a tremendous scale in those days as is commonly supposed: Ajax was not so very tall, nor Helen so very beautiful. I saw her: she had a fair complexion, to be sure, and her neck was long enough to suggest her swan parentage [Footnote: See *Helen* in Notes.]: but then she was such an age—as old as Hecuba, almost. You see, Theseus had carried her off first, and she had lived with him at Aphidnae: now Theseus was a contemporary of Heracles, and the former capture of Troy, by Heracles, had taken place in the generation before mine; my father, who told me all this, remembered seeing Heracles when he was himself a boy.

Mi. Well, and Achilles: was he so much better than other people, or is that all stuff and nonsense?

Cock. Ah, I never came across Achilles; I am not very strong on the Greeks; I was on the other side, of course. There is one thing, though: I made pretty short work of his friend Patroclus— ran him clean through with my spear.

Mi. After which Menelaus settled you with still greater facility. Well, that will do for Troy. And when you were Pythagoras?

Cock. When I was Pythagoras, I was—not to deceive you—a sophist; that is the long and short of it. At the same time, I was not uncultured, not unversed in polite learning. I travelled in Egypt, cultivated the acquaintance of the priests, and learnt wisdom from their mouths; I penetrated into their temples and mastered the sacred books of Orus and Isis; finally, I took ship to Italy, where I made such an impression on the Greeks that they reckoned me among the Gods.

Mi. I have heard all about that; and also how you were supposed to have risen from the dead, and how you had a golden thigh, and favoured the public with a sight of it on occasion. But what put it into your head to make that law about meat and beans?

Cock. Ah, don't ask me that, Micyllus.

Mi. But why not?

Cock. I am ashamed to answer you.

Mi. Come, out with it! I am your friend and fellow lodger; we will drop the 'master' now.

Cock. There was neither common sense nor philosophy in that law. The fact is, I saw that if I did just the same as other people, I should draw very few admirers; my prestige, I considered, would be in proportion to my originality. Hence these innovations, the motive of which I wrapped up in mystery; each man was left to make his own conjecture, that all might be equally impressed by my oracular obscurity. There now! you are laughing at me; it is your turn this time.

Mi. I am laughing much more at the folk of Cortona and Metapontum and Tarentum, and the rest of those mute disciples who worshipped the ground you trod on. And in what form was your spirit next clothed, after it had put off Pythagoras?

Cock. In that of Aspasia, the Milesian courtesan.

Mi. Dear, dear! And your versatility has even changed sexes? My gallant cock has positively laid eggs in his time? Pythagoras has carded and spun? Pythagoras the mistress—and the mother—of a Pericles? My Pythagoras no better than he should be?

Cock. I do not stand alone. I had the example of Tiresias and of Caeneus; your gibes touch them as well as me.

Mi. And did you like being a man best, or receiving the addresses of Pericles?

Cock. Ha! the question that Tiresias paid so dearly for answering!

Mi. Never mind, then, —Euripides has settled the point; he says he would

> rather bear the shock of battle thrice
> Than once the pangs of labour.

Cock. Ah, just a word in your ear: those pangs will shortly be your own; more than once, in the course of a lengthy career, you will be a woman.

Mi. Strangulation on the bird! Does he think we all hail from Miletus or Samos? Yes, I said Samos; Pythagoras has had his admirers, by all accounts, as well as Aspasia. However; —what was your sex next time?

Cock. I was the Cynic Crates.

Mi. Castor and Pollux! What a change was there!

Cock. Then it was a king; then a pauper, and presently a satrap, and after that came horse, jackdaw, frog, and I know not how many more; there is no reckoning them up in detail. Latterly, I have been a cock several times. I liked the life; many is the king, many the pauper and millionaire, with whom I took service in that capacity before I came to you. In your lamentations about poverty, and your admiration of the rich, I find an unfailing source of entertainment; little do you know what those rich have to put up with! If you had any idea of their anxieties, you would laugh to think how you had been deceived as to the blessedness of wealth.

Mi. Well, Pythagoras, —or is there any other name you prefer? I shall throw you out, perhaps, if I keep on calling you different things?

Cock. Euphorbus or Pythagoras, Aspasia or Crates, it is all the same to me; one is as much my name as another. Or stay: not to be wanting in respect to a bird whose humble exterior contains so many souls, you had better use the evidence of your own eyes and call me Cock.

Mi. Then, cock, as you have tried wellnigh every kind of life, you can next give me a clear description of the lives of rich and poor respectively; we will see if there was any truth in your assertion, that I was better off than the rich.

Cock. Well now, look at it this way. To begin with, you are very little troubled with military matters. Suppose there is talk of an invasion: *you* are under no uneasiness about the destruction of your crops, or the cutting-up of your gardens, or the ruin of your vines; at the first sound of the trumpet (if you even hear it), all you have to think of is, how to convey your own person out of harm's way. Well, the rich have got to provide for that too, and they have the mortification into the bargain of looking on while their lands are being ravaged. Is a war-tax to be levied? It all falls on them. When you take the field, theirs are the posts of honour—and danger: whereas you, with no worse encumbrance than your wicker shield, are in the best of trim for taking care of yourself; and when the time comes for the general to offer up a sacrifice of thanksgiving for his victory, your presence may be relied on at the festive scene.

Then again, in time of peace, you, as one of the commons, march up to the Assembly to lord it over the rich, who tremble and crouch before you, and seek to propitiate you with grants. They must labour, that you may be supplied with baths and games and spectacles and the like to your satisfaction; you are their censor and critic, their stern taskmaster, who will not always hear before condemning; nay, you may give them a smart shower of stones, if the fancy takes you, or confiscate their property. The informer's tongue has no terrors for you; no burglar will scale or undermine *your* walls in search of gold; you are not troubled with book-keeping or debt-collecting; you have no rascally steward to wrangle with; none of the thousand worries of the rich distract you. No, you patch your shoe, and you take your tenpence; and at dusk up you jump from your bench, get a bath if you are in the humour for it, buy yourself a haddock or some sprats or a few heads of garlic, and make merry therewith; Poverty, best of philosophers, is your companion, and you are seldom at a loss for a song. And what is the result? Health and strength, and a hardiness that sets cold at defiance. Your work keeps you keen-set; the ills that seem insuperable to other men find a tough customer in you. Why, no serious sickness ever comes near you: fever, perhaps, lays a light hand on you now and again; you let him have his way for a day or two, and then you are up again, and shake the pest off; he beats a hasty retreat, not liking the look of a man who drinks cold water at that rate, and has such a short way with the doctors. But look at the rich: name the disease to which these creatures are not subjected by their intemperance; gout, consumption, pneumonia, dropsy, —they all come of high feeding. Some of these men are like Icarus: they fly too high, they get near the sun, not realizing that their wings are fastened with wax; and then some day there is a great splash, and they have disappeared headlong into the deep. Others there are who follow Daedalus's example; such minds eschew the upper air, and keep their wax within splashing distance of the sea; these generally get safely to their journey's end.

Mi. Shrewd, sensible fellows.

Cock. Yes, but among the others you may see some ugly shipwrecks. Croesus is plucked of his feathers, and mounts a pyre for the amusement of the Persians. A tyranny capsizes, and the lordly Dionysius is discovered teaching Corinthian children their alphabet.

Mi. You tell me, cock, that you have been a king yourself: now how did *you* find the life? I expect you had a pleasant time of it, living on the very fat of the land?

Cock. Do not remind me of that miserable existence. A pleasant time! So people thought, no doubt: I knew better; it was vexation upon vexation.

Mi. You surprise me. How should that be? It sounds unlikely.

Cock. The country over which I ruled was both extensive and fertile. Its population and the beauty of its cities alike entitled it to the highest consideration. It possessed navigable rivers and excellent harbours. My army was large, my pike-men numerous, my cavalry in a high state of efficiency; it was the same with my fleet; and my wealth was beyond calculation. No circumstance of kingly pomp was wanting; gold plate in abundance, everything on the most magnificent scale. I could not leave my palace without receiving the reverential greetings of the public, who looked on me as a God, and crowded together to see me pass; some enthusiasts would even betake themselves to the roofs of the houses, lest any detail of my equipage, clothes, crown or attendants should escape them. I could make allowance for the ignorance of my subjects, but this did not prevent me from pitying myself, when I reflected on the vexations and worries of my position. I was like those colossal statues, the work of Phidias, Myron or Praxiteles: they too look extremely well from outside: 'tis Posidon with his trident, Zeus with his thunderbolt, all ivory and gold: but take a peep inside, and what have we? One tangle of bars, bolts, nails, planks, wedges, with pitch and mortar and everything that is unsightly; not to mention a possible colony of rats or mice. There you have royalty.

Mi. But you have not told me what is the mortar, what the bolts and bars and other unsightlinesses that lurk behind a throne. Admiration, dominion, divine honours, —these no doubt fit your simile; there is a touch of the godlike about them. But now let me have the inside of your colossus.

Cock. And where shall I begin? With fear and suspicion? The resentments of courtiers and the machinations of conspirators? Scant and broken sleep, troubled dreams, perplexities, forebodings? Or again with the hurry of business—fiscal—legal—military? Orders to be issued, treaties to be drawn up, estimates to be formed? As for pleasure, such a thing is not to be dreamt of; no, one man must think for all, toil incessantly for all. The Achaean host is snoring to a man:

> But sweet sleep came not nigh to Atreus' son,
> Who pondered many things within his heart.

Lydian Croesus is troubled because his son is dumb; Persian Artaxerxes, because Clearchus is raising a host for Cyrus; Dionysius, because Dion whispers in Syracusan ears; Alexander, because Parmenio is praised. Perdiccas has no peace for Ptolemy, Ptolemy none for Seleucus. And there are other griefs than these: his favourite is cold; his concubine loves another; there is talk of a rebellion; there has been muttering among a half-dozen of his guards. And the bitterness of it is, that his nearest and dearest are those whom he is most called on to distrust; from them he must ever look for harm. One we see poisoned by his son, another by his own favourite; and a third will probably fare no better.

Mi. Whew! I like not this, my cock. Methinks there is safety in bent backs and leather-cutting, and none in golden loving-cups; I will pledge no man in hemlock or in aconite. All *I* have to fear is that my knife may slip out of the line, and draw a drop or two from my fingers: but your kings would seem to sit down to dinner with Death, and to lead dogs' lives into the bargain. They go at last; and then they are more like play-actors than anything else—like such a one as you may see taking the part of Cecrops or Sisyphus or Telephus. He has his diadem and his ivory-hilted sword, his waving hair and spangled cloak: but accidents will happen, — suppose he makes a false step: down he comes on the middle of the stage, and the audience roars with laughter. For there is his mask, crumpled up, diadem and all, and his own bloody coxcomb showing underneath it; his legs are laid bare to the knees, and you see the dirty rags inside his fine robe, and the great lumbering buskins. Ha, ha, friend cock, have I learnt to turn a simile already? Well, there are my views on tyranny. Now for the horses and dogs and frogs and fishes: how did you like that kind of thing?

Cock. Your question would take a long time to answer; more time than we can spare. But—to sum up my experience in two words—every one of these creatures has an easier life of it than man. Their aims, their wants, are all confined to the body: such a thing as a tax-farming horse or a litigant frog, a jackdaw sophist, a gnat confectioner, or a cock pander, is unknown; they leave such things to humanity.

Mi. It may be as you say. But, cock (I don't mind making a clean breast of it to you), I have had a fancy all my life for being rich, and I am as bad as ever; nay, worse, for there is the dream, still flaunting its gold before my eyes; and that confounded Simon, too, —it chokes me to think of him rolling in luxury.

Cock. I'll put that right. It is still dark, get up and come with me. You shall pay a visit to Simon and other rich men, and see how things stand with them.

Mi. But the doors are locked. Would you have me break in?

Cock. Oh no; but I have a certain privilege from Hermes, my patron: you see my longest tail-feather, the curling one that hangs down, —

Mi. There are two curling ones that hang down.

Cock. The one on the right. By allowing any one to pluck out that feather and carry it, I give him the power, for as long as I like, of opening all doors and seeing everything, himself unseen.

Mi. Cock, you are a positive conjurer. Only give me the feather, and it shall not be long before Simon's wealth shifts its quarters; I'll slip in and make a clean sweep. His teeth shall tug leather again.

Cock. That must not be. I have my instructions from Hermes, and if my feather is put to any such purpose, I am to call out and expose the offender.

Mi. Hermes, of all people, grudge a man a little thievery? I'll not believe it of him. However, let us start; I promise not to touch the gold... if I can help it.

Cock. You must pluck out the feather first.... What's this? You have taken both!

Mi. Better to be on the safe side. And it would look so bad to have one half of your tail gone and not the other.

Cock. Well. Where shall we go first? To Simon's?

Mi. Yes, yes, Simon first. Simonides it is, nowadays; two syllables is not enough for him since he has come into money.... Here we are; what do I do next?

Cock. Apply the feather to the bolt.

Mi. So. Heracles! it might be a key; the door flies open.

Cock. Walk in; you go first. Do you see him? He is sitting up over his accounts.

Mi. See him! I should think I did. What a light! That lamp wants a drink. And what makes Simon so pale? He is shrivelled up to nothing. That comes of his worries; there is nothing else the matter with him, that I have heard of.

Cock. Listen, and you will understand.

Si. That seventeen thousand in the hole under my bed is safe enough; not a soul saw me that time. But I believe Sosylus caught me hiding the four thousand under the manger: he is not the most industrious of grooms, he was never too fond of work; but he *lives* in that stable now. And I expect that is not all that has gone, by a long way. What was Tibius doing with those fine great kippers yesterday? And they tell me he paid no less a sum than four shillings for a pair of earrings for his wife. God help me, it's *my* money they're flinging about. I'm not easy about all that plate either: what if some one should knock a hole in the wall, and make off with it? Many is the one that envies me, and has an eye on my gold; my neighbour Micyllus is as bad as any of them.

Mi. Hear, hear! He is as bad as Simon; he walks off with other people's pudding-basins under his arm.

Cock. Hush! we shall be caught.

Si. There's nothing like sitting up, and having everything under one's own eye. I'll jump up and go my rounds.... You there! you burglar! I see you.... Ah, it is but a post; all is well. I'll pull up the gold and count it again; I may have missed something just now.... Hark! a step! I knew it; he is upon me! I am beset with enemies. The world conspires against me. Where is my dagger? Only let me catch... —I'll put the gold back.

Cock. There: now you have seen Simon at home. Let us go on to another house, while there is still some of the night left.

Mi. The worm! what a life! I wish all my enemies such wealth as his. I'll just lend him a box on the ear, and then I am ready.

Si. Who was that? Some one struck me! Ah! I am robbed!

Mi. Whine away, Simon, and sit up of nights till you are as yellow as the gold you clutch. —I should like to go to Gniphon the usurer's next; it is quite close.... Again the door opens to us.

Cock. He is sitting up too, look. It is an anxious time with him; he is reckoning his interest. His fingers are worn to the bone. Presently he will have to leave all this, and become a cockroach, or a gnat, or a bluebottle.

Mi. Senseless brute! it will hardly be a change for the worse. He, like Simon, is pretty well thinned down by his calculations. Let us try some one else.

Cock. What about your friend Eucrates? See, the door stands open; let us go in.

Mi. An hour ago, all this was mine!

Cock. Still the golden dream! —Look at the hoary old reprobate: with one of his own slaves!

Mi. Monstrous! And his wife is not much better; she takes her paramour from the kitchen.

Cock. Well? Is the inheritance to your liking? Will you have it all?

Mi. I will starve first. Good-bye to gold and high living. Preserve me from my own servants, and I will call myself rich on twopence-halfpenny.

Cock. Well, well, we must be getting home; see, it is just dawn. The rest must wait for another day.

ICAROMENIPPUS, AN AERIAL EXPEDITION

Menippus and a Friend

Me. Let me see, now. First stage, Earth to Moon, 350 miles. Second stage, up to the Sun, 500 leagues. Then the third, to the actual Heaven and Zeus's citadel, might be put at a day's journey for an eagle in light marching order.

Fr. In the name of goodness, Menippus, what are these astronomical sums you are doing under your breath? I have been dogging yon for some time, listening to your suns and moons, queerly mixed up with common earthly stages and leagues.

Me. Ah, you must not be surprised if my talk is rather exalted and ethereal; I was making out the mileage of my journey.

Fr. Oh, I see; using stars to steer by, like the Phoenicians?

Me. Oh no, travelling among them.

Fr. Well, to be sure, it must have been a longish dream, if you lost yourself in it for whole leagues.

Me. Dream, my good man? I am just come straight from Zeus. Dream, indeed!

Fr. How? What? Our Menippus a literal godsend from Heaven?

Me. 'Tis even so; from very Zeus I come this day, eyes and ears yet full of wonders. Oh, doubt, if you will. That my fortune should pass belief makes it only the more gratifying.

Fr. Nay, my worshipful Olympian, how should I, 'a man begotten, treading this poor earth, ' doubt him who transcends the clouds, a 'denizen of Heaven, ' as Homer says? But vouchsafe to tell me how you were uplifted, and where you got your mighty tall ladder. There is hardly enough of Ganymede in your looks to suggest that you were carried off by the eagle for a cupbearer.

Me. I see you are bent on making a jest of it. Well, it *is* extraordinary; you could not be expected to see that it is not a romance. The fact is, I needed neither ladder nor amorous eagle; I had wings of my own.

Fr. Stranger and stranger! this beats Daedalus. What, you turned into a hawk or a crow on the sly?

Me. Now that is not a bad shot; it was Daedalus's wing trick that I tried.

Fr. Well, talk of foolhardiness! did you like the idea of falling into the sea, and giving us a *Mare Menippeum* after the precedent of the *Icarium*?

Me. No fear. Icarus's feathers were fastened with wax, and of course, directly the sun warmed this, he moulted and fell. No wax for me, thank you.

Fr. How did you manage, then? I declare I shall be believing you soon, if you go on like this.

Me. Well, I caught a fine eagle, and also a particularly powerful vulture, and cut off their wings above the shoulder- joint.... But no; if you are not in a hurry, I may as well give you the enterprise from the beginning.

Fr. Do, do; I am rapt aloft by your words already, my mouth open for your *bonne bouche*; as you love me, leave me not in those upper regions hung up by the ears!

Me. Listen, then; it would be a sorry sight, a friend deserted, with his mouth open, and *sus. per aures.* —Well, a very short survey of life had convinced me of the absurdity and meanness and insecurity that pervade all human objects, such as wealth, office, power. I was filled with contempt for them, realized that to care for them was to lose all chance of what deserved care, and determined to grovel no more, but fix my gaze upon the great All. Here I found my first problem in what wise men call the universal order; I could not tell how it came into being, who made it, what was its beginning, or what its end. But my next step, which was the examination of details, landed me in yet worse perplexity. I found the stars dotted quite casually about the sky, and I wanted to know what the sun was. Especially the phenomena of the moon struck me as extraordinary, and quite passed my comprehension; there must be some mystery to account for those many phases, I conjectured. Nor could I feel any greater certainty about such things as the passage of lightning, the roll of thunder, the descent of rain and snow and hail.

In this state of mind, the best I could think of was to get at the truth of it all from the people called philosophers; they of course would be able to give it me. So I selected the best of them, if solemnity of visage, pallor of complexion and length of beard are any criterion— for there could not be a moment's doubt of their soaring words and heaven-high thoughts—and in their hands I placed myself. For a considerable sum down, and more to be paid when they should have perfected me in wisdom, I was to be made an airy metaphysician and instructed in the order of the universe. Unfortunately, so far from dispelling my previous ignorance, they perplexed me more and more, with their daily drenches of beginnings and ends, atoms and voids, matters and forms. My greatest difficulty was that, though they differed among themselves, and all they said was full of inconsistency and contradiction, they expected me to believe them, each pulling me in his own direction.

Fr. How absurd that wise men should quarrel about facts, and hold different opinions on the same things!

Me. Ah, but keep your laughter till you have heard something of their pretentious mystifications. To begin with, their feet are on the ground; they are no taller than the rest of us 'men that walk the earth'; they are no sharper-sighted than their neighbours, some of them purblind, indeed, with age or indolence; and yet they say they can distinguish the limits of the sky, they measure the sun's circumference, take their walks in the supra-lunar regions, and specify the sizes and shapes of the stars as though they had fallen from them; often one of them could not tell you correctly the number of miles from Megara to Athens, but has no hesitation about the distance in feet from the sun to the moon. How high the atmosphere is, how deep the sea, how far it is round the earth— they have the figures for all that; and moreover, they have only to draw some circles, arrange a few triangles and squares, add certain complicated spheres, and lo, they have the cubic contents of Heaven.

Then, how reasonable and modest of them, dealing with subjects so debatable, to issue their views without a hint of uncertainty; thus it must be and it shall be; *contra gentes* they will have it so; they will tell you on oath the sun is a molten mass, the moon inhabited, and the stars water-drinkers, moisture being drawn up by the sun's rope and bucket and equitably distributed among them.

How their theories conflict is soon apparent; next-door neighbours? no, they are miles apart. In the first place, their views of the world differ. Some say it had no beginning, and cannot end; others boldly talk of its creator and his procedure; what particularly entertained me was that these latter set up a contriver of the universe, but fail to mention where he came from, or what he stood on while about his elaborate task, though it is by no means obvious how there could be place or time before the universe came into being.

Fr. You really do make them out very audacious conjurers.

Me. My dear fellow, I wish I could give you their lucubrations on ideas and incorporeals, on finite and infinite. Over that point, now, there is fierce battle; some circumscribe the All, others will have it unlimited. At the same time they declare for a plurality of worlds, and speak scornfully of others who make only one. And there is a bellicose person who maintains that war is the father of the universe. [Footnote: Variously attributed to Heraclitus, who denies the possibility of repose, and insists that all things are in a state of flux; and to Empedocles, who makes all change and becoming depend on the interaction of the two principles, attraction and repulsion.]

As to Gods, I need hardly deal with that question. For some of them God is a number; some swear by dogs and geese and plane-trees. [Footnote: Socrates made a practice of substituting these for the names of Gods in his oaths.] Some again banish all other Gods, and attribute the control of the universe to a single one; I got rather depressed on learning how small the supply of divinity was. But I was comforted by the lavish souls who not only make many, but classify; there was a First God, and second and third classes of divinity. Yet again, some regard the divine nature as unsubstantial and without form, while others conceive it as a substance. Then they were not all disposed to recognize a Providence; some relieve the Gods of all care, as we relieve the superannuated of their civic duties; in fact, they treat them exactly like supernumeraries on the stage. The last step is also taken, of saying that Gods do not exist at all, and leaving the world to drift along without a master or a guiding hand.

Well, when I heard all this, I dared not disbelieve people whose voices and beards were equally suggestive of Zeus. But I knew not where to turn for a theory that was not open to exception, nor combated by one as soon as propounded by another. I found myself in the state Homer has described; many a time I would vigorously start believing one of these gentlemen;

But then came second thoughts.

So in my distress I began to despair of ever getting any knowledge about these things on earth; the only possible escape from perplexity would be to take to myself wings and go up to Heaven. Partly the wish was father to the thought; but it was confirmed by Aesop's Fables, from which it appears that Heaven is accessible to eagles, beetles, and sometimes camels. It was pretty clear that I could not possibly develop feathers of my own. But if I were to wear vulture's or eagle's wings—the only kinds equal to a man's weight—I might perhaps succeed. I caught the birds, and effectually amputated the eagle's right, and the vulture's left wing. These I fastened together, attached them to my shoulders with broad thick straps, and provided grips for my hands near the end of the quill-feathers. Then I made experiments, first jumping up and helping the jump by flapping my hands, or imitating the way a goose raises itself without leaving the ground and combines running with flight. Finding the machine obedient, I next made a bolder venture, went up the Acropolis, and launched myself from the cliff right over the theatre.

Getting safely to the bottom that time, my aspirations shot up aloft. I took to starting from Parnes or Hymettus, flying to Geranea, thence to the top of the Acrocorinthus, and over Pholoe and Erymanthus to Taygetus. The training for my venture was now complete; my powers were developed, and equal to a lofty flight; no more fledgeling essays for me. I went up Olympus, provisioning myself as lightly as possible. The moment was come; I soared skywards, giddy at first with that great void below, but soon conquering this difficulty. When I approached the Moon, long after parting from the clouds, I was conscious of fatigue, especially in the left or vulture's wing. So I alighted and sat down to rest, having a bird's-eye view of the Earth, like the Homeric Zeus,

Surveying now the Thracian horsemen's land,
Now Mysia,

and again, as the fancy took me, Greece or Persia or India. From all which I drew a manifold delight.

Fr. Oh well, Menippus, tell me all about it. I do not want to miss a single one of your travel experiences; if you picked up any stray information, let me have that too. I promise myself a great many facts about the shape of the Earth, and how everything on it looked to you from your point of vantage.

Me. And you will not be disappointed there, friend. So do your best to get up to the Moon, with my story for travelling companion and showman of the terrestrial scene.

Imagine yourself first descrying a tiny Earth, far smaller than the Moon looks; on turning my eyes down, I could not think for some time what had become of our mighty mountains and vast sea. If I had not caught sight of the Colossus of Rhodes and the Pharus tower, I assure you I should never have made out the Earth at all. But their height and projection, with the faint shimmer of Ocean in the sun, showed me it must be the Earth I was looking at. Then, when once I had got my sight properly focused, the whole human race was clear to me, not merely in the shape of nations and cities, but the individuals, sailing, fighting, ploughing, going to law; the women, the beasts, and in short every breed 'that feedeth on earth's foison. '

Fr. Most unconvincing and contradictory. Just now you were searching for the Earth, it was so diminished by distance, and if the Colossus had not betrayed it, you would have taken it for something else; and now you develop suddenly into a Lynceus, and distinguish everything upon it, the men, the beasts, one might almost say the gnat-swarms. Explain, please.

Me. Why, to be sure! how did I come to leave out so essential a particular? I had made out the Earth, you see, but could not distinguish any details; the distance was so great, quite beyond the scope of my vision; so I was much chagrined and baffled. At this moment of depression—I was very near tears—who should come up behind me but Empedocles the physicist? His complexion was like charcoal variegated with ashes, as if he had been baked. I will not deny that I felt some tremors at the sight of him, taking him for some lunar spirit. But he said: 'Do not be afraid, Menippus;

A mortal I, no God; how vain thy dreams.

I am Empedocles the physicist. When I threw myself into the crater in such a hurry, the smoke of Etna whirled me off up here; and now I live in the Moon, doing a good deal of high thinking on a diet of dew. So I have come to help you out of your difficulty; you are distressed, I take it, at not being able to see everything on the Earth. ' 'Thank you so much, you good Empedocles, ' I said; 'as soon as my wings have brought me back to Greece, I will remember to pour libations to you up the chimney, and salute you on the first of every month with three moonward yawns. ' 'Endymion be my witness, ' he replied, 'I had no thought of such a bargain; I was touched by the sight of your distress. Now, what do you think is the way to sharpen your sight? '

'I have no idea, unless you were to remove the mist from my eyes for me; the sight seems quite bleared. ' 'Oh, you can do without me; the thing that gives sharp sight you have brought with you from Earth. ' 'Unconsciously, then; what is it? ' 'Why, you know that you have on an eagle's right wing? ' 'Of course I do; but what have wings and eyes to do with one another? ' 'Only this, ' he said; 'the eagle is far the strongest-eyed of all living things, the only one that can look straight at the sun; the test of the true royal eagle is, his meeting its rays without blinking. ' 'So I have heard; I wish I had taken out my own eyes when I was starting, and substituted the eagle's. I am an imperfect specimen now I am here, not up to the royal standard at all, but like the rejected bastards. ' 'Well, you can very soon acquire one royal eye. If you will stand up for a minute, keep the vulture wing still, and work the other, your right eye, corresponding to that wing, will gain strength. As for the other, its dimness cannot possibly be obviated, as it belongs to the inferior member. ' 'Oh, I shall be quite content with aquiline vision for the right eye only, ' I said; 'I have often observed that carpenters in ruling their wood find one better than two. ' So saying, I proceeded to carry out my instructions at once. Empedocles began gradually to disappear, and at last vanished in smoke.

I had no sooner flapped the wing than a flood of light enveloped me, and things that before I had not even been aware of became perfectly clear. I turned my eyes down earthwards, and with ease discerned cities, men, and all that was going on, not merely in the open, but in the fancied security of houses. There was Ptolemy in his sister's arms, the son of Lysimachus plotting against his father, Seleucus's son Antiochus making signs to his step-mother Stratonice, Alexander of Pherae being murdered by his wife, Antigonus corrupting his daughter-in-law, the son of Attalus putting the poison in his cup; Arsaces was in the act of slaying his mistress, while the eunuch Arbaces drew his sword upon him; the guards were dragging Spatinus the Mede out from the banquet by the foot, with the lump on his brow from the golden cup. Similar sights were to be seen in the palaces of Libya and Scythia and Thrace— adulteries, murders, treasons, robberies, perjuries, suspicions, and monstrous betrayals.

Such was the entertainment afforded me by royalty; private life was much more amusing; for I could make that out too. I saw Hermodorus the Epicurean perjuring himself for 40 pounds, Agathocles the Stoic suing a pupil for his fees, lawyer Clinias stealing a bowl from the temple of Asclepius, and Herophilus the cynic sleeping in a brothel. Not to mention the multitude of burglars, litigants, usurers, duns; oh, it was a fine representative show!

Fr. I must say, Menippus, I should have liked the details here too; it all seems to have been very much to your taste.

Me. I could not go through the whole of it, even to please you; to take it in with the eyes kept one busy. But the main divisions were very much what Homer gives from the shield of Achilles: here junketings and marriages, there courts and councils, in another compartment a sacrifice, and hard by a mourning. If I glanced at Getica, I would see the Getae at war; at Scythia, there were the Scythians wandering about on their waggons; half a turn in another direction gave me Egyptians at the plough, or Phoenicians chaffering, Cilician pirates, Spartan flagellants, Athenians at law.

All this was simultaneous, you understand; and you must try to conceive what a queer jumble it all made. It was as if a man were to collect a number of choristers, or rather of choruses, [Footnote: The Greek chorus combined singing with dancing.] and then tell each individual to disregard the others and start a strain of his own; if each did his best, went his own way, and tried to drown his neighbour, can you imagine what the musical effect would be?

Fr. A very ridiculous confusion.

Me. Well, friend, such are the earthly dancers; the life of man is just such a discordant performance; not only are the voices jangled, but the steps are not uniform, the motions not concerted, the objects not agreed upon—until the impresario dismisses them one by one from the stage, with a 'not wanted. ' Then they are all alike, and quiet enough, confounding no longer their undisciplined rival strains. But as long as the show lasts in its marvellous diversity, there is plenty of food for laughter in its vagaries.

The people who most amused me, however, were those who dispute about boundaries, or pride themselves on cultivating the plain of Sicyon, or holding the Oenoe side of Marathon, or a thousand acres at Acharnae. The whole of Greece, as I then saw it, might measure some four inches; how much smaller Athens on the same scale. So I realized what sort of sized basis for their pride remains to our rich men. The widest-acred of them all, methought, was the proud cultivator of an Epicurean atom. Then I looked at the Peloponnese, my eyes fell on the Cynurian district, and the thought occurred that it was for this little plot, no broader than an Egyptian lentil, that all those Argives and Spartans fell in a single day. Or if I saw a man puffed up by the possession of seven or eight gold rings and half as many gold cups, again my lungs would begin to crow; why, Pangaeus with all its mines was about the size of a grain of millet.

Fr. You lucky man! what a rare sight you had! And how big, now, did the towns and the people look from there?

Me. You must often have seen a community of ants, some of them a seething mass, some going abroad, others coming back to town. One is a scavenger, another a bustling porter loaded with a bit of bean-pod or half a wheat grain. They no doubt have, on their modest myrmecic scale, their architects and politicians, their magistrates and composers and philosophers. At any rate, what men and cities suggested to me was just so many ant-hills. If you think the similitude too disparaging, look into the Thessalian legends, and you will find that the most warlike tribe there was the Myrmidons, or ants turned men. Well, when I had had enough of contemplation and laughter, I roused myself and soared

To join the Gods, where dwells the Lord of storms.

I had only flown a couple of hundred yards, when Selene's feminine voice reached me: 'Menippus, do me an errand to Zeus, and I will wish you a pleasant journey. ' 'You have only to name it, ' I said, 'provided it is not something to carry. ' 'It is a simple message of entreaty to Zeus. I am tired to death, you must know, of being slandered by these philosophers; they have no better occupation than impertinent curiosity about me—What am I? how big am I? why am I halved? why am I gibbous? I am inhabited; I am just a mirror hung over the sea; I am—whatever their latest fancy suggests. It is the last straw when they say my light is stolen, sham, imported from the sun, and keep on doing their best to get up jealousy and ill feeling between brother and sister. They might have been contented with making *him* out a stone or a red-hot lump.

'These gentry who in the day look so stern and manly, dress so gravely, and are so revered by common men, would be surprised to learn how much I know of their vile nightly abominations. I see them all, though I never tell; it would be too indecent to make revelations, and show up the contrast between their nightly doings and their public performances; so, if I catch one of them in adultery or theft or other nocturnal adventure, I pull my cloud veil over me; I do not want the vulgar to see old men disgracing their long beards and their virtuous calling. But they go on giving tongue and worrying me all the same, and, so help me Night, I have thought many a time of going a long, long way off, out of reach of their impertinent tongues. Will you remember to tell Zeus all this? and you may add that I cannot remain at my post unless he will pulverize the physicists, muzzle the logicians, raze the Porch, burn the Academy, and put an end to strolling in the Lyceum. That might secure me a little peace from these daily mensurations. '

'I will remember, ' said I, and resumed my upward flight to Heaven, through

> A region where nor ox nor man had wrought.

For the Moon was soon but a small object, with the Earth entirely hidden behind it. Three days' flight through the stars, with the Sun on my right hand, brought me close to Heaven; and my first idea was to go straight in as I was; I should easily pass unobserved in virtue of my half-eagleship; for of course the eagle was Zeus's familiar; on second thoughts, though, my vulture wing would very soon betray me. So, thinking it better not to run any risks, I went up to the door and knocked. Hermes opened, took my name, and hurried off to inform Zeus. After a brief wait I was asked to step in; I was now trembling with apprehension, and I found that the Gods, who were all seated together, were not quite easy themselves. The unexpected nature of the visit was slightly disturbing to them, and they had visions of all mankind arriving at my heels by the same conveyance.

But Zeus bent upon me a Titanic glance, awful, penetrating, and spoke:

Who art thou? where thy city? who thy kin?

At the sound, I nearly died of fear, but remained upright, though mute and paralysed by that thunderous voice. I gradually recovered, began at the beginning, and gave a clear account of myself—how I had been possessed with curiosity about the heavens, had gone to the philosophers, found their accounts conflicting, and grown tired of being logically rent in twain; so I came to my great idea, my wings, and ultimately to Heaven; I added Selene's message. Zeus smiled and slightly unbent his brow. 'What of Otus and Ephialtes now? ' he said; 'here is Menippus scaling Heaven! Well, well, for to-day consider yourself our guest. To-morrow we will treat with you of your business, and send you on your way. ' And therewith he rose and walked to the acoustic centre of Heaven, it being prayer time.

As he went, he put questions to me about earthly affairs, beginning with, What was wheat a quarter in Greece? had we suffered much from cold last winter? and did the vegetables want more rain? Then he wished to know whether any of Phidias's kin were alive, why there had been no Diasia at Athens all these years, whether his Olympieum was ever going to be completed, and had the robbers of his temple at Dodona been caught? I answered all these questions, and he proceeded: —'Tell me, Menippus, what are men's feelings towards me? ' 'What should they be, Lord, but those of absolute reverence, as to the King of all Gods? ' 'Now, now, chaffing as usual, ' he said; 'I know their fickleness very well, for all your dissimulation. There was a time when I was their prophet, their healer, and their all,

And Zeus filled every street and gathering-place.

In those days Dodona and Pisa were glorious and far-famed, and I could not get a view for the clouds of sacrificial steam. But now Apollo has set up his oracle at Delphi, Asclepius his temple of health at Pergamum, Bendis and Anubis and Artemis their shrines in Thrace, Egypt, Ephesus; and to these all run; theirs the festal gatherings and the hecatombs. As for me, I am superannuated; they think themselves very generous if they offer me a victim at Olympia at four-year intervals. My altars are cold as Plato's *Laws* or Chrysippus's *Syllogisms*. '

So talking, we reached the spot where he was to sit and listen to the prayers. There was a row of openings with lids like well- covers, and a chair of gold by each. Zeus took his seat at the first, lifted off the lid and inclined his ear. From every quarter of Earth were coming the most various and contradictory petitions; for I too bent down my head and listened. Here are specimens. 'O Zeus, that I might be king!' 'O Zeus, that my onions and garlic might thrive! ' 'Ye Gods, a speedy death for my father! ' Or again, 'Would that I might succeed to my wife's property! ' 'Grant that my plot against my brother be not detected. ' 'Let me win my suit. ' 'Give me an Olympic garland. ' Of those at sea, one prayed for a north, another for a south wind; the farmer asked for rain, the fuller for sun. Zeus listened, and gave each prayer careful consideration, but without promising to grant them all;

> Our Father this bestowed, and that withheld.

Righteous prayers he allowed to come up through the hole, received and laid them down at his right, while he sent the unholy ones packing with a downward puff of breath, that Heaven might not be defiled by their entrance. In one case I saw him puzzled; two men praying for opposite things and promising the same sacrifices, he could not tell which of them to favour, and experienced a truly Academic suspense of judgement, showing a reserve and equilibrium worthy of Pyrrho himself.

The prayers disposed of, he went on to the next chair and opening, and attended to oaths and their takers. These done with, and Hermodorus the Epicurean annihilated, he proceeded to the next chair to deal with omens, prophetic voices, and auguries. Then came the turn of the sacrifice aperture, through which the smoke came up and communicated to Zeus the name of the devotee it represented. After that, he was free to give his wind and weather orders: —Rain for Scythia to-day, a thunderstorm for Libya, snow for Greece. The north wind he instructed to blow in Lydia, the west to raise a storm in the Adriatic, the south to take a rest; a thousand bushels of hail to be distributed over Cappadocia.

His work was now pretty well completed, and as it was just dinner time, we went to the banquet hall. Hermes received me, and gave me my place next to a group of Gods whose alien origin left them in a rather doubtful position—Pan, the Corybants, Attis, and Sabazius. I was supplied with bread by Demeter, wine by Dionysus, meat by Heracles, myrtle-blossoms by Aphrodite, and sprats by Posidon. But I also got a sly taste of ambrosia and nectar; good-natured Ganymede, as often as he saw that Zeus's attention was engaged elsewhere, brought round the nectar and indulged me with a half-pint or so. The Gods, as Homer (who I think must have had the same opportunities of observation as myself) somewhere says, neither eat bread nor drink the ruddy wine; they heap their plates with ambrosia, and are nectar-bibbers; but their choicest dainties are the smoke of sacrifice ascending with rich fumes, and the blood of victims poured by their worshippers round the altars. During dinner, Apollo harped, Silenus danced his wild measures, the Muses uprose and sang to us from Hesiod's *Birth of Gods*, and the first of Pindar's odes. When we had our fill and had well drunken, we slumbered, each where he was.

> Slept all the Gods, and men with plumed helms,
> That livelong night; but me kind sleep forsook;

for I had much upon my mind; most of all, how came it that Apollo, in all that time, had never grown a beard? and how was night possible in Heaven, with the sun always there taking his share of the good cheer? So I had but a short nap of it. And in the morning Zeus arose, and bade summon an assembly.

When all were gathered, he thus commenced: —'The immediate occasion of my summoning you is the arrival of this stranger yesterday. But I have long intended to take counsel with you regarding the philosophers, and now, urged by Selene and her complaints, I have determined to defer the consideration of the question no longer. There is a class which has recently become conspicuous among men; they are idle, quarrelsome, vain, irritable, lickerish, silly, puffed up, arrogant, and, in Homeric phrase, vain cumberers of the earth. These men have divided themselves into bands, each dwelling in a separate word-maze of its own construction, and call themselves Stoics, Epicureans, Peripatetics, and more farcical names yet. Then they take to themselves the holy name of Virtue, and with uplifted brows and flowing beards exhibit the deceitful semblance that hides immoral lives; their model is the tragic actor, from whom if you strip off the mask and the gold-spangled robe, there is nothing left but a paltry fellow hired for a few shillings to play a part.

'Nevertheless, quite undeterred by their own characters, they scorn the human and travesty the divine; they gather a company of guileless youths, and feed them with solemn chatter upon Virtue and quibbling verbal puzzles; in their pupils' presence they are all for fortitude and temperance, and have no words bad enough for wealth and pleasure: when they are by themselves, there is no limit to their gluttony, their lechery, their licking of dirty pence. But the head and front of their offending is this: they neither work themselves nor help others' work; they are useless drones,

> Of no avail in council nor in war;

which notwithstanding, they censure others; they store up poisoned words, they con invectives, they heap their neighbours with reproaches; their highest honours are for him who shall be loudest and most overbearing and boldest in abuse.

'Ask one of these brawling bawling censors, And what do *you* do? in God's name, what shall we call *your* contribution to progress? and he would reply, if conscience and truth were anything to him: I consider it superfluous to sail the sea or till the earth or fight for my country or follow a trade; but I have a loud voice and a dirty body; I eschew warm water and go barefoot through the winter; I am a Momus who can always pick holes in other people's coats; if a rich man keeps a costly table or a mistress, I make it my business to be properly horrified; but if my familiar friend is lying sick, in need of help and care, I am not aware of it. Such, your Godheads, is the nature of this vermin.

'There is a special insolence in those who call themselves Epicureans; these go so far as to lay their hands on our character; we take no interest in human affairs, they say, and in fact have nothing to do with the course of events. And this is a serious question for you; if once they infect their generation with this view, you will learn what hunger means. Who will sacrifice to you, if he does not expect to profit by it? As to Selene's complaints, you all heard them yesterday from this stranger's lips. And now decide upon such measures as shall advantage mankind and secure your own safety. '

Zeus had no sooner closed his speech than clamour prevailed, all crying at once: Blast! burn! annihilate! to the pit with them! to Tartarus! to the Giants! Zeus ordered silence again, and then, 'Your wishes, ' he said, 'shall be executed; they shall all be annihilated, and their logic with them. But just at present chastisement is not lawful; you are aware that we are now in the four months of the long vacation; the formal notice has lately been issued. In the spring of next year, the baleful levin-bolt shall give them the fate they deserve.'

He spake, and sealed his word with lowering brows.

'As to Menippus, ' he added, 'my pleasure is this. He shall be deprived of his wings, and so incapacitated for repeating his visit, but shall to-day be conveyed back to Earth by Hermes. ' So saying, he dismissed the assembly. The Cyllenian accordingly lifted me up by the right ear, and yesterday evening deposited me in the Ceramicus. And now, friend, you have all the latest from Heaven. I must be off to the Poecile, to let the philosophers loitering there know the luck they are in.

THE DOUBLE INDICTMENT

Zeus. Hermes. Justice. Pan. Several Athenians. The Academy. The Porch. Epicurus. Virtue. Luxury. Diogenes. Rhetoric. A Syrian. Dialogue

Zeus. A curse on all those philosophers who will have it that none but the Gods are happy! If they could but know what we have to put up with on men's account, they would not envy us our nectar and our ambrosia. They take Homer's word for it all, —the word of a blind quack; 'tis he who pronounces us blessed, and expatiates on heavenly glories, he who could not see in front of his own nose. Look at the Sun, now. He yokes that chariot, and is riding through the heavens from morn till night, clothed in his garment of fire, and dispensing his rays abroad; not so much breathing-space as goes to the scratching of an ear; once let his horses catch him napping, and they have the bit between their teeth and are off 'cross country, with the result that the Earth is scorched to a cinder. The Moon is no better off: she is kept up into the small hours to light the reveller and the diner-out upon their homeward path. And then Apollo, —*he* has his work cut out for him: with such a press of oracular business, it is much if he has any ears left to hear with: he is wanted at Delphi; the next minute, he must be off to Colophon; then away to Xanthus; then back at a trot to Clarus; then it is Delos, then Branchidae; —in short, he is at the beck of every priestess who has taken her draught of holy water, munched her laurel-leaf, and made the tripod rock; it is now or never; if he is not there that minute to reel off the required oracle, his credit is gone. The traps they set for him too! He must have a dog's nose for lamb and tortoise in the pot, or his Lydian customer [Footnote: See *Croesus* in Notes.] departs, laughing him to scorn. As for Asclepius, he has no peace for his patients: his eyes are acquainted with horror, and his hands with loathsomeness; another's sickness is his pain. To say nothing of the work that the Winds have to get through, what with sowing and winnowing and getting the ships along; or of Sleep, always on the wing, with Dream at his side all night giving a helping hand. Men have to thank us for all this: every one of us contributes his share to their well-being. And the others have an easy time of it, compared to me, to me the King and Father of all. The annoyances I have to put up with! the worry of thinking of all these things at once! I must keep an eye on all the rest, to begin with, or they would be making some silly mistake; and as for the work I have to do with my own hands, there is no end to it; such complications! it is all I can do to get through with it. It is not as if I had only the main issues to attend to, the rain and hail and wind and lightning, and as soon as I had arranged them could sit down, feeling that my own particular work was over: no, besides all that, I must be looking every way at once, Argus-eyed for theft and perjury, as for sacrifice; the moment a libation has been poured, it is for me to locate the savoury smoke that rises; for me it is to hear the cry of the sick man and of the sailor; at one and the same moment, a hecatomb demands my presence at Olympia, a battle in the plain of Babylon; hail is due in Thrace, dinner in Ethiopia; 'tis too much! And do what I may, it is hard to give satisfaction. Many is the time that all besides, both Gods and men of plumed helm, have slept the long night through, while unto Zeus sweet slumber has not come nigh. If I nod for a moment, behold, Epicurus is justified, and our indifference to the affairs of Earth made manifest; and if once men lend an ear to that doctrine, the consequences will be serious: our temples will go ungarlanded; the streets will be redolent no longer of roast meat, the bowl no longer yield us libation; our altars will be cold, sacrifice and oblation will be at an end, and utter starvation must ensue. Hence like a pilot I stand up at the helm all alone, tiller in hand, while every soul on board is asleep, and probably drunk; no rest, no food for me, while I ponder in my mind and breast on the common safety; and my reward? to be called the Lord of all! I should like to ask those philosophers who assign us the monopoly of blessedness, when they suppose we find time for nectar and ambrosia among our ceaseless occupations. Look at the mildewed, cob-webbed stack of petitions mouldering on their files in our chancery, for want of time to attend to them: look only at the cases pending between men and the various Arts and Sciences; venerable relics, some of them! Angry protests against the delays of the law reach me from all quarters; men cannot understand that it is from no neglect of ours that these judgements have been postponed; it is simply pressure of business—pressure of blessedness, if they will have it so.

Her. I myself, father, have heard a great deal of dissatisfaction expressed on Earth, only I did not like to mention it to you. However, as you have introduced the subject yourself, I may say that the discontent is general: men do not venture to express their resentment openly, but there are mutterings in corners about the delay. It is high time they were all put out of their suspense, for better or for worse.

Zeus. And what would you have me do, my boy? hold a session at once? or shall we say next year?

124

Her. Oh, at once, by all means.

Zeus. To work, then: fly down, and make proclamation in the following terms: All litigant parties to assemble this day on Areopagus: Justice to assign them their juries from the whole body of the Athenians, the number of the jury to be in proportion to the amount of damages claimed; any party doubting the justice of his sentence to have the right of appeal to me. And you, my daughter, take your seat by the side of the Dread Goddesses [Footnote: See *Erinnyes* in Notes.], cast lots for the order of the trials, and superintend the formation of juries.

Just. You would have me return to Earth, once more to be driven thence in ignominious flight by the intolerable taunts of Injustice?

Zeus. Hope for better things. The philosophers have quite convinced every one by this time of your superiority. The son of Sophroniscus was particularly strong on your merits: he laid it down that Justice was the highest Good.

Just. Yes; and very serviceable his dissertations on Justice were to him, were they not, when he was handed over to the Eleven, and thrown into prison, and drank the hemlock? Poor man, he had not even time to sacrifice the cock he owed to Asclepius. His accusers were too much for him altogether, and *their* philosophy had Injustice for its object.

Zeus. But in those days philosophy was not generally known, and had but few exponents; it is not surprising that the scale turned in favour of Anytus and Meletus. But now it is different: look at the number of cloaks and sticks and wallets that are about; everywhere philosophers, long-bearded, book in hand, maintain your cause; the public walks are filled with their contending hosts, and every man of them calls Virtue his nurse. Numbers have abandoned their former professions to pounce upon wallet and cloak; these ready-made philosophers, carpenters once or cobblers, now duly tanned to the true Ethiopian hue, are singing your praises high and low. 'He that falls on shipboard strikes wood, ' says the proverb; and the eye, wheresoever it fall, will light on philosophers.

Just. Yes, father, but they frighten me: they quarrel so among themselves; and when they talk about me, they only expose their own little minds. And, from what I hear, most of those who make so free with my name show no inclination at all to put my principles into practice. I may count upon finding their doors closed to *me*: Injustice has been beforehand with me.

Zeus. Come, child, they are not all so bad, and if you can find a few honest men it will be something. Now, off with you both, and see if you can't get a few cases settled up to-day.

Her. Well, Justice: yonder is our road: straight in the line for Sunium, to the foot of Hymettus, taking Parnes on our right; you see those two hills? You have quite forgotten the way, I suppose, in all this time? Now, now: weeping? why so vexed? There is nothing to fear. Things are quite different in these days: the Scirons and Pityocampteses and Busirises and Phalarises who used to frighten you so are all dead: Wisdom, the Academy, the Porch, now hold sway everywhere. They are all your admirers; their talk is all of you; they yearn to see you descend to them once more.

Just. Tell me, Hermes, —you if any one must know the truth; you are generally busy either in the Gymnasium or else in the Market, making proclamation to the Assembly, —what are the Athenians like now? shall I be able to live with them?

Her. We are brother and sister, it is only right that I should tell you the truth. Well then, Philosophy has made a considerable change for the better in most of them; at the worst, their respect for the cloth is some check on their misdeeds. At the same time—not to conceal anything—you will find villains amongst them; and you will find some who are neither quite philosophers nor quite knaves. The fact is, Philosophy's dyeing process is still going on. Some have absorbed the full quantity of dye; these are perfect specimens of her art, and show no admixture of other colours; with them you will find a ready reception. But others, owing to their original impurities, are not yet completely saturated; they are better than the generality of mankind, but they are not all they should be; they are piebald or spotted or dappled. Others again there are who have contented themselves with merely rubbing a fingertip in the soot on the outside of the cauldron, and smearing themselves with that; after which they consider the dyeing process complete. But you, of course, will only live with the best. Meanwhile, here we are, close to Attica; we must now leave Sunium on our right, and diverge towards the Acropolis. Good: *terra firma*. You had better sit down somewhere here on the Areopagus, in the direction of the Pnyx, and wait whilst I make

Zeus's proclamation. I shall go up into the Acropolis; that will be the easiest way of making every one hear the summons.

Just. Before you go, Hermes, tell me who this is coming along; a man with horns and a pipe and shaggy legs.

Her. Why, you must know Pan, most festive of all Dionysus's followers? He used to live on Mount Parthenius: but at the time of the Persian expedition under Datis, when the barbarians landed at Marathon, he volunteered in the Athenian service; and ever since then he has had the cave yonder at the foot of the Acropolis, a little past the Pelasgicum, and pays his taxes like any other naturalized foreigner. Seeing us so near at hand, I suppose he is coming up to make his compliments.

Pan. Hail, Justice and Hermes!

Just. Hail, Pan; chief of Satyrs in dance and song, and most gallant of Athens' soldiers!

Pan. But what brings you here, Hermes?

Her. Justice will explain; I must be off to the Acropolis on my errand.

Just. Zeus has sent me down, Pan, to preside in the law- court. — And how do you like Athens?

Pan. Well, the fact is, I am a good deal disappointed: they do not treat me with the consideration to which I am entitled, after repelling that tremendous barbarian invasion. All they do is to come up to my cave two or three times a year with a particularly high-scented goat, and sacrifice him: I am permitted to look on whilst they enjoy the feast, and am complimented with a perfunctory dance. However, there is some joking and merrymaking on the occasion, and that I find rather fun.

Just. And, Pan, —have they become more virtuous under the hands of the philosophers?

Pan. Philosophers? Oh! people with beards just like mine; sepulchral beings, who are always getting together and jabbering?

Just. Those are they.

Pan. I can't understand a word they say; their philosophy is too much for me. I am mountain-bred; smart city-language is not in my line; sophists and philosophers are not known in Arcadia. I am a good hand at flute or pipe; I can mind goats, I can dance, I can fight at a pinch, and that is all. But I hear them all day long, bawling out a string of hard words about virtue, and nature, and ideas, and things incorporeal. They are good enough friends when the argument begins, but their voices mount higher and higher as they go on, and end in a scream; they get more and more excited, and all try to speak at once; they grow red in the face, their necks swell, and their veins stand out, for all the world like a flute-player on a high note. The argument is turned upside down, they forget what they are trying to prove, and finally go off abusing one another and brushing the sweat from their brows; victory rests with him who can show the boldest front and the loudest voice, and hold his ground the longest. The people, especially those who have nothing better to do, adore them, and stand spellbound under their confident bawlings. For all that I could see, they were no better than humbugs, and I was none too pleased at their copying my beard. If there were any use in their noise, if the talking did any good to the public, I should not have a word to say against them: but, to tell you the plain unvarnished truth, I have more than once looked out from my peep-hole yonder and seen them—

Just. Hush, Pan: was not that Hermes making the proclamation?

Pan. I thought so.

Her. Be it known to all men that we purpose on this seventh day of March to hold a court of justice, and Fortune defend the right! All litigant parties to assemble on Areopagus, where Justice will assign the juries and preside over the trials in person. The juries to be taken from the whole Athenian people; the pay to be sixpence for each case; the number of jurors to vary with the nature of the accusation. Any parties who had commenced legal proceedings and have died in the interim to be sent up by Aeacus. Any party doubting the justice of his sentence may appeal; the appeal to he heard by Zeus.

Pan. Talk about noise! how they shout! And what a hurry they are in to get here! See how one hales another up the hill! Here comes Hermes himself. Well, I leave you to your juries and your evidence; you are accustomed to it. I will return to my cave, and there play over one of those amorous ditties with which I love to upbraid Echo.

As to rhetoric and law-pleadings, I hear enough of those every day in this very court of Areopagus.

Her. We had better summon the parties, Justice.

Just. True. Only look at the crowd, bustling and buzzing about the hilltop like a swarm of wasps!

First Ath. I've got you, curse you.

Second Ath. Pooh! a trumped-up charge.

Third Ath. At last! you shall get your deserts this time.

Fourth Ath. Your villany shall be unmasked.

Fifth Ath. My jury first, Hermes.

Sixth Ath. Come along: into court with you, rascal.

Seventh Ath. You needn't throttle me.

Just. Do you know what I think we had better do, Hermes? Put off all the other cases for to-morrow, and only take to-day the charges brought by Arts, Professions, and Philosophies. Pick me out all of that kind.

Her. Drink *v.* the Academy, *re* Polemon, kidnapped.

Just. Seven jurors.

Her. Porch *v.* Pleasure. Defendant is charged with seducing Dionysius, plaintiff's admirer.

Just. Five will do for that.

Her. Luxury *v.* Virtue, *re* Aristippus.

Just. Five again.

Her. Bank *v.* Diogenes, alleged to have run away from plaintiff's service.

Just. Three only.

Her. Painting *v.* Pyrrho. Desertion from the ranks.

Just. That will want nine.

Her. What about these two charges just brought against a rhetorician?

Just. No, those can stand over; we must work off the arrears first.

Her. Well, these cases are of just the same kind. They are not old ones, it is true, but they are very like those you have taken, and might fairly be heard with them.

Just. That looks rather like favouritism, Hermes. However, as you like; only these must be the last; we have got quite enough. What are they?

Her. Rhetoric *v.* a Syrian [Footnote: i.e. Lucian. See Volume I, Introduction, Section I, Life.], for neglect; Dialogue *v.* the same, for assault.

Just. And who is this Syrian? There is no name given.

Her. That is all: the Syrian rhetorician; he can have a jury without having a name.

Just. So! here on Areopagus I am to give juries to outsiders, who ought to be tried on the other side of the Euphrates? Well, give him eleven, and they can hear both cases.

Her. That's right; it will save a lot of expense.

Just. First case: the Academy *versus* Drink. Let the jury take their seats. Mark the time, ' Hermes. Drink, open the case.... Not a word? can you do nothing but nod? —Hermes, go and see what is the matter with her.

Her. She says she cannot plead, she would only be laughed at; wine has tied her tongue. As you see, she can hardly stand.

Just. Well, there are plenty of able counsel present, ready to shout themselves hoarse for sixpence; let her employ one of them.

Her. No one will have anything to do with such a client in open court. But she makes a very reasonable proposal.

Just. Yes?

Her. The Academy is always ready to take both sides; she makes a point of contradicting herself plausibly. 'Let her speak first on my behalf, ' says Drink, 'and then on her own. '

Just. A novel form of procedure. However, go on, Academy; speak on both sides, if you find it so easy.

Acad. First, gentlemen of the jury, let me state the case for 16 Drink, as her time is now being taken.

My unfortunate client, gentlemen, has been cruelly wronged: I have torn from her the one slave on whose loyalty and affection she could rely, the only one who saw nothing censurable in her conduct. I allude to Polemon, whose days, from morning to night, were spent in revel; who in broad daylight sought the publicity of the Market in the company of music—girls and singers; ever drunk, ever headachy, ever garlanded. In support of my statements, I appeal to every man in Athens to say whether he had ever seen Polemon sober. But in an evil hour for him, his revels, which had brought him to so many other doors, brought him at length to my own. I laid hands on him, tore him away by brute force from the plaintiff, and made him my own; giving him water to drink, teaching him sobriety, and stripping him of his garlands. He, who should have been sitting over his wine, now became acquainted with the perverse, the harassing, the pernicious quibbles of philosophy. Alas! the ruddy glow has departed from his cheek; he is pale and wasted; his songs are all forgotten; there are times when he will sit far on into the night, tasting neither meat nor drink, while he reels out the meaningless platitudes with which I have so abundantly supplied him. I have even incited him to attack the character of my client, and to utter a thousand base insinuations against her good fame.

The case of Drink is now complete. I proceed to state my own. Let my time be taken.

Just. What will the defendant have to say to that, I wonder? Give her the same time allowance.

Acad. Nothing, gentlemen of the jury, could sound more plausible than the arguments advanced by my learned friend on her client's behalf. And yet, if you will give me your favourable attention, I shall convince you that the plaintiff has suffered no wrong at my hands. This Polemon, whom plaintiff claims as her servant, so far from having any natural connexion with her, is one whose excellent parts entitle him to claim kinship and affinity with myself. He was still a boy, his powers were yet unformed, when plaintiff, aided and abetted by Pleasure—ever her partner in crime—seized upon him, and delivered him over into the clutches of debauchery and dissipation, under whose corrupt influence the unfortunate young man utterly lost all sense of shame. Those very facts that plaintiff supposed to be so many arguments in her favour will be found, on the contrary, to make for my own case. From early morning (as my learned friend has just observed) did the misguided Polemon, with aching head and garlanded, stagger through the open market to the noise of flutes, never sober, brawling with all he met; a reproach to his ancestors and his city, a laughing-stock to foreigners. One day he reached my door. He found it open: I was discoursing to a company of my disciples, as is my wont, upon virtue and temperance. He stood there, with the flute-girl at his side and the garlands on his head, and sought at first to drown our conversation with his noisy outcry. But we paid no heed to him, and little by little our words produced a sobering effect, for Drink had not entire possession of him: he bade the flute-girl cease, tore off his garlands, and looked with shame at his luxurious dress. Like one waking from deep sleep, he saw himself as he was, and repented of his past life; the flush of drunkenness faded and vanished from his cheek, and was succeeded by a blush of shame; at last, not (as plaintiff would have you believe) in response to any invitation of mine, nor under any compulsion, but of his own free will, and in the conviction of my superiority, he renounced his former mistress there and then, and entered my service. Bring him into court. You shall see for yourselves, gentlemen, what he has become under my treatment. Behold that Polemon whom I found drunk, unable to speak or stand upright, an object of ridicule: I turned him from his evil ways; I taught him sobriety; and I present him to you, no longer a slave, but a decent and orderly citizen, a credit to his nation. In conclusion let me say that the change I have wrought in him has won me the gratitude not only of Polemon himself but of all his friends. Which of us has been the more profitable companion for him, it is now for the jury to decide.

Her. Come, gentlemen, get up and give your votes. There is no time to be lost; we have other cases coming on.

Just. Academy wins, by six votes to one.

Her. I am not surprised to find that Drink has one adherent. Jurors in the case of Porch *v.* Pleasure *re* Dionysius take their seats! The lady of the frescoes [Footnote: See *Poecile* in Notes.] may begin; her time is noted.

Porch. I am not ignorant, gentlemen, of the attractions of my adversary. I see how your eyes turn in her direction; she has your smiles, I your contempt, because my hair is close-cropped, and my expression stern and masculine. Yet if you will give me a fair hearing, I fear her not; for justice is on my side. Nay, it is with these same meretricious attractions of hers that my accusation is concerned: it was by her specious appearance that she beguiled the virtuous Dionysius, my lover, and drew him to herself. The present case is in fact closely allied with that of Drink and the Academy, with which your colleagues have just dealt. The question now before you is this: are men to live the lives of swine, wallowing in voluptuousness, with never a high or noble thought: or are they to set virtue above enjoyment, and follow the dictates of freedom and philosophy, fearing not to grapple with pain, nor seeking the degrading service of pleasure, as though happiness were to be found in a pot of honey or a cake of figs? These are the baits my adversary throws out for fools, and toil the bugbear with which she frightens them: her artifices seldom fail; and among her victims is this unfortunate whom she has constrained to rebel against my authority. She had to wait till she found him on a sick-bed; never while he was himself would he have listened to her proposals. Yet what right have *I* to complain? She spares not even the Gods; she impugns the wisdom of Providence; she is guilty of blasphemy; you have a double penalty to impose, if you would be wise. I hear that she has not even been at the pains of preparing a defence: Epicurus is to speak for her! She does not stand upon ceremony with you, gentlemen. —Ask her what Heracles would have been, what your own Theseus would have been, if they had listened to the voice of pleasure, and shrunk back from toil: their toils were the only check upon wickedness, which else must have overrun the whole Earth.

And now I have done; I am no lover of long speeches. Yet if my adversary would consent to answer a few questions, her worthlessness would soon appear. Let me remind you, gentlemen, of your oath: give your votes in accordance with that oath, and believe not Epicurus, when he tells you that the Gods take no thought for the things of Earth.

Her. Stand down, madam. Epicurus will now speak on behalf of pleasure.

Epi. I shall not detain you long, gentlemen of the jury; there is no occasion for me to do so. If it were true, as the plaintiff asserts, that Dionysius was her lover, and that my client by means of drugs or incantations had constrained him to withdraw his affections from the plaintiff and transfer them to herself, —if this were true, then my client might fairly be accused of witchcraft, nor could her wicked practices upon her rival's admirers escape condemnation. On the other hand, if a free citizen of a free state, deciding for himself in a matter where the law is silent, takes a violent aversion to this lady's person, concludes that the blessedness with which she promises to crown his labours is neither more nor less than moonshine, and accordingly makes the best of his way out of her labyrinthine maze of argument into the attractive arms of Pleasure, bursts the bonds of verbal subtlety, exchanges credulity for common sense, and pronounces, with great justice, that toil is toilsome, and that pleasure is pleasant, —I ask, is this shipwrecked mariner to be excluded from the calm haven of his desire, and hurled back headlong into a sea of toil? is this poor suppliant at the altar of Mercy—in other words of Pleasure— is he to be delivered over into the power of perplexity, — and all on the chance that his hot climb up the steep hill of Virtue may be rewarded with a glimpse of that celebrated lady on the top, and his life of toil followed by a hereafter of happiness? We could scarcely ask for a better judge of the matter than Dionysius himself. He was as familiar with the Stoic doctrines as any man, and held at one time that virtue was the only Good: but he presently discovered that toil was an evil: he then chose what seemed to him the better course. He would no doubt observe that those philosophers who had so much to say on the subject of patience and endurance under toil were secretly the servants of Pleasure, carefully abiding by her laws in their own homes, though they made so free with her name in their discourses. They cannot bear to be detected in any relaxation, or any departure from their principles: but, poor men, they lead a Tantalus life of it in consequence, and when they *do* get a chance of sinning without being found out, they drink down pleasure by the bucketful. Depend on it, if some one would make them a present of Gyges's ring of invisibility, or Hades's cap, they would cut the acquaintance of toil without further ceremony, and elbow their way into the presence of Pleasure; they would all be Dionysiuses then. As long as Dionysius was well, he thought that there was some good in all this talk about endurance; but when he fell ill, and found out what pain really was, he perceived that his body was of another school than the Porch, and held quite other tenets: he was converted, realized that he was flesh and blood, and from that day ceased to behave as if he were made of marble; he knew now that the man who talks nonsense about the iniquity of pleasure

But toys with words: his thoughts are bent elsewhither.

And now, gentlemen, I leave you to your vote.

Porch. Not yet! Let me ask him a few questions.

Epi. Yes? I am ready.

Porch. You hold toil to be an evil?

Epi. I do.

Porch. And pleasure a good?

Epi. Unquestionably.

Porch. Do you recognize the distinction between *differentia* and *indifferentia*? between *praeposita* and *rejecta*?

Epi. Why, certainly.

Her. Madam, this discussion must cease; the jury say they do not understand word-chopping. They will now give their votes.

Porch. Ah; I should have won, if I could have tried him with my third figure of *self-evidents*.

Just. Who wins?

Her. Unanimous verdict for Pleasure.

Porch. I appeal to Zeus.

Just. By all means. Next case, Hermes.

Her. Luxury *v.* Virtue, *re* Aristippus; Aristippus must appear 23 in person.

Vir. I ought to speak first. Aristippus is mine; his words and his deeds alike proclaim him mine.

Lux. On the contrary, any one who will observe his garlands and his purple robes and his perfumes will agree that he is mine.

Just. Peace! This suit must stand over, until Zeus has decided the appeal *re* Dionysius. The cases are similar. If Porch wins her appeal, Aristippus shall be adjudged to Virtue: if not, Luxury must have him. Bring the next case. By the way, those jurors must not have their fee; they have not earned it.

Her. So the poor old gentlemen have climbed up all this way for nothing!

Just. Well, they must be content with a third. Now go away, all of you, and don't be cross; you shall have another chance.

Her. Diogenes of Sinope wanted! Bank, it is for you to speak. 24

Diog. Look here, Madam Justice, if she doesn't stop bothering, I shall have assault and battery to answer for before long, instead of desertion; my stick is ready.

Just. What is the meaning of this? Bank has run away, and Diogenes after her, with his stick raised. Poor Bank! I am afraid she will be roughly handled. Call Pyrrho.

Her. Here is Painting, but Pyrrho has never come up. 25 I knew how it would be.

Just. And what was his reason?

Her. He holds that there is no such thing as a true decision.

Just. Then judgement goes against him by default. Now for the Syrian advocate. The indictments were only filed a day or two ago; there was no such hurry. However—. We will first take the case in which Rhetoric is plaintiff. How people crowd in to hear it!

Her. Just so: the case has not had time to get stale, you see; it has the charm of novelty, the indictment, as you say, having only been filed yesterday. The prospect, too, of hearing the Syrian defend himself against two such plaintiffs as Rhetoric and Dialogue, one after the other, is a great attraction. Well, Rhetoric, when are you going to begin?

Rhet. Before all things, men of Athens, I pray the Gods that you may listen to me throughout this trial with feelings not less warm than those that I have ever entertained towards my country and towards each one of you, my countrymen. And if, further, I pray them so to dispose your hearts that you will suffer me to conduct my case in accordance with my original intention and design, without interruption from my adversary, I shall be asking no more than justice. When I listen to the defendant's words, and then reflect upon the treatment I have received from him, I know not how I am to reconcile the two. You will presently find him holding a language scarcely distinguishable from my own: yet examine into his conduct, and you will see, from the lengths to which he has already gone, that I am justified in taking steps to prevent his going yet further. But enough of preamble: I am wasting time that might be better employed in accusing my adversary.

Gentlemen, the defendant was no more than a boy—he still spoke with his native accent, and might at any moment have exhibited himself in the garb of an Assyrian—when I found him wandering up and down Ionia, at a loss for employment. I took him in hand; I gave him an education; and, convinced of his capabilities and of his devotion to me (for he was my very humble servant in those days, and had no admiration to spare for any one else), I turned my back upon the many suitors who sought my hand, upon the wealthy, the brilliant and the high-born, and betrothed myself to this monster of ingratitude; upon this obscure pauper boy I bestowed the rich dowry of my surpassing eloquence, brought him to be enrolled among my own people, and made him my fellow citizen, to the bitter mortification of his unsuccessful rivals. When he formed the resolution of travelling, in order to make his good fortune known to the world, I did not remain behind: I accompanied him everywhere, from city to city, shedding my lustre upon him, and clothing him in honour and renown. Of our travels in Greece and Ionia, I say nothing: he expressed a wish to visit Italy: I sailed the Ionian Sea with him, and attended him even as far as Gaul, scattering plenty in his path.

For a long time he consulted my wishes in everything, was unfailing in his attendance upon me, and never passed a night away from my side. But no sooner had he secured an adequate provision, no sooner did he consider his reputation established, than his countenance changed towards me: he assumed a haughty air, and neglected, nay, utterly abandoned me; having conceived a violent affection for the bearded old person yonder, whom you may know from his dress to be Dialogue, and who passes for a son of Philosophy. With this Dialogue, in spite of the disparity of age, he is now living; and is not ashamed to clip the wings of free, high-soaring eloquence, and submit himself to the comedian's fetters of bald question and answer. He, whose thoughts should have found utterance in thundering oratory, is content to weave a puny network of conversation. Such things may draw a smile from his audience, a nod, an unimpassioned wave of the hand, a murmur of approbation: they can never hope to evoke the deafening uproar of universal applause. And this, gentlemen, is the fascination under which he looks coldly upon me; I commend his taste! They say, indeed, that he is not on the best of terms even with his beloved Dialogue; apparently I am not the only victim of his overweening pride. Does not such ingratitude as this render him liable to the penalties imposed by the marriage-laws? He leaves me, his lawful wife, to whom he is indebted alike for wealth and reputation, leaves me to neglect, and goes off in pursuit of novelty; and that, at a time when all eyes are turned upon me, when all men write me their protectress. I hold out against the entreaties of countless suitors: they knock, and my doors remain closed to them; they call loudly upon my name, but I scorn their empty clamours, and answer them not. All is in vain: he will not return to me, nor withdraw his eyes from this new love. In Heaven's name, what does he expect to get from him? what has Dialogue but his cloak?

In conclusion, gentlemen: should he attempt to employ my art in his defence, suffer him not thus unscrupulously to sharpen my own sword against me; bid him defend himself, if he can, with the weapons of his adored Dialogue.

Her. Now there, madam, you are unreasonable: how can he possibly make a dialogue of it all by himself? No, no; let him deliver a regular speech, just the same as other people.

Syrian. In view, gentlemen, of the indignation that plaintiff has expressed at the idea of my employing her gift of eloquence in order to maintain my cause at large, I shall confine myself to a brief and summary refutation of her charges, and shall then leave the whole matter to your discernment.

Gentlemen, all that the plaintiff has said is true. She educated me; she bore me company in my travels; she made a Greek of me. She has each of these claims to a husband's gratitude. I have now to give my reasons for abandoning her, and cultivating the acquaintance of Dialogue: and, believe me, no motive of self- interest shall induce me to misrepresent the facts. I found, then, that the discreet bearing, the seemly dress, which had distinguished her in the days of her union with the illustrious demesman of Paeania [Footnote: Demosthenes.], were now thrown aside: I saw her tricked out and bedizened, rouged and painted like a courtesan. My suspicions were aroused, and I began to watch the direction of her eyes. To make a long story short, our street was nightly infested with the serenades of her tipsy gallants, some of whom, not content with knocking at our doors, threw aside all restraint, and forced their way into the house. These attentions amused and delighted my wife: she was commonly to be seen leaning over the parapet and listening to the loose ditties that were bawled up from below; and when she thought she was unobserved, she would even open the door, and admit the gallant to her shameless embraces. Such things were not to be endured: I was loth to bring her into the divorce-court, and accordingly sought the hospitality of Dialogue, who was my near neighbour.

Such, gentlemen, are the grievous wrongs that plaintiff has suffered at my hands. Even had the provocation I have described been wanting, my age (I was then nearly forty years old) called upon me to withdraw from the turmoil of the law-courts, and suffer the 'gentlemen of the jury' to rest in peace. Tyrants enough had been arraigned, princes enough been eulogized: it was time to retreat to the walks of Academy or the Lyceum, there to enjoy, in the delightful society of Dialogue, that tranquil discourse which aims not at noisy acclamations. I might say much more, but I forbear: you, gentlemen, will give your votes in accordance with the dictates of conscience. *Just.* Who wins?

Her. The Syrian has all votes but one.

Just. And that one a rhetorician's, I suppose. Dialogue will now address the same jury. Gentlemen, you will remain and hear this second case, and will receive a double fee.

Dia. If I had had my choice, gentlemen, I should have addressed you in the conversational style to which I am accustomed, instead of delivering a long harangue. However, I must conform to the custom of the law-courts, though I have neither skill nor experience in such matters. So much by way of exordium: and now for the outrage committed on me by the defendant. In former days, gentlemen, I was a person of exalted character: my speculations turned upon the Gods, and Nature, and the *Annus Magnus*; I trod those aerial plains wherein Zeus on winged car is borne along through the heights. My flight had actually brought me to the heavenly vault; I was just setting foot upon the upper surface of that dome, when this Syrian took it upon himself to drag me down, break my wings, and reduce me to the common level of humanity. Whisking off the seemly tragic mask I then wore, he clapped on in its place a comic one that was little short of ludicrous: his next step was to huddle me into a corner with Jest, Lampoon, Cynicism, and the comedians Eupolis and Aristophanes, persons with a horrible knack of making light of sacred things, and girding at all that is as it should be. But the climax was reached when he unearthed a barking, snarling old Cynic, Menippus by name, and thrust *his* company upon me; a grim bulldog, if ever there was one; a treacherous brute that will snap at you while his tail is yet wagging. Could any man be more abominably misused? Stripped of my proper attire, I am made to play the buffoon, and to give expression to every whimsical absurdity that his caprice dictates. And, as if that were not preposterous enough, he has forbidden me either to walk on my feet or to rise on the wings of poesy: I am a ridiculous cross between prose and verse; a monster of incongruity; a literary Centaur.

Her. Now, Syrian: what do you say to that?

Syrian. Gentlemen of the jury, I am surprised. Nothing could be more unexpected than the charge Dialogue has brought against me. When I first took him in hand, he was regarded by the world at large as one whose interminable discussions had soured his temper and exhausted his vitality. His labours entitled him to respect, but he had none of the attractive qualities that could secure him popularity. My first step was to accustom him to walk upon the common ground like the rest of mankind; my next, to make him presentable, by giving him a good bath and teaching him to smile. Finally, I assigned him Comedy as his yokefellow, thus gaining him the confidence of his hearers, who until then would as soon have thought of picking up a hedgehog as of venturing into the thorny presence of Dialogue.

But I know what the grievance is: he wants me to sit and discourse subtle nothings with him about the immortality of the soul, and the exact number of pints of pure homogeneous essence that went to the making of the universe, and the claims of rhetoric to be called a shadow of a fraction of statecraft, or a fourth part of flattery. He takes a curious pleasure in refinements of this kind; it tickles his vanity most deliciously to be told that not every man can see so far into the ideal as he. Evidently he expects *me* to conform to his taste in this respect; he is still hankering after those lost wings; his eyes are turned upwards; he cannot see the things that lie before his feet. I think there is nothing else he can complain of. He cannot say that I, who pass for a barbarian, have torn off his Greek dress, and replaced it with one like my own: that would have been another matter; to deprive him of his native garb were indeed a crime.

Gentlemen, I have made my defence, as far as in me lies: I trust that your present verdict will confirm the former one.

Her. Well I never! All ten are for you again. Only one dissentient, and he the same one as before. True to his envious principles, he must ever give his vote against his betters. The jurors may now leave the court. The remaining cases will come on to-morrow.

THE PARASITE, A DEMONSTRATION THAT SPONGING IS A PROFESSION

Tychiades. Simon

Tyc. I am curious about you, Simon. Ordinary people, free and slaves alike, have some trade or profession that enables them to benefit themselves and others; you seem to be an exception.

Si. I do not quite see what you mean, Tychiades; put it a little clearer.

Tyc. I want to know whether you have a profession of any sort; for instance, are you a musician?

Si. Certainly not.

Tyc. A doctor?

Si. No.

Tyc. A mathematician?

Si. No.

Tyc. Do you teach rhetoric, then? I need not ask about philosophy; you have about as much to do with that as sin has.

Si. Less, if possible. Do not imagine that you are enlightening me upon my failings. I acknowledge myself a sinner—worse than you take me for.

Tyc. Very well. But possibly you have abstained from these professions because nothing great is easy. Perhaps a trade is more in your way; are you a carpenter or cobbler? Your circumstances are hardly such as to make a trade superfluous.

Si. Quite true. Well, I have no skill in any of these.

Tye. But in——?

Si. An excellent one, in my opinion; if you were acquainted with it you would agree, I am sure. I can claim to be a practical master in the art by this time; whether I can give an account of my faith is another question.

Tyc. What is it?

Si. No, I do not think I have got up the theory of it sufficiently. For the present, rest assured that I have a profession, and cease your strictures on that head. Its nature you shall know another time.

Tyc. No, no; I will not be put off like that.

Si. Well, I am afraid my profession would be rather a shock to you.

Tyc. I like shocks.

Si. Well, I will tell you some day.

Tyc. Now, I say; or else I shall know you are ashamed of it.

Si. Well, then, I sponge.

Tyc. Why, what sane man would call sponging a profession?

Si. I, for one. And if you think I am not sane, put down my innocence of other professions to insanity, and let that be my sufficient excuse. My lady Insanity, they say, is unkind to her votaries in most respects; but at least she excuses their offences, which she makes herself responsible for, like a schoolmaster or tutor.

Tyc. So sponging is an art, eh?

Si. It is; and I profess it.

Tyc. So you are a sponger?

Si. What an awful reproach!

Tyc. What! you do not blush to call yourself a sponger?

Si. On the contrary, I should be ashamed of not calling myself so.

Tyc. And when we want to distinguish you for the benefit of any one who does not know you, but has occasion to find you out, we must say 'the sponger, ' naturally?

Si. The name will be more welcome to me than 'statuary' to Phidias; I am as proud of my profession as Phidias of his Zeus.

Tyc. Ha, ha, ha! Excuse me—just a particular that occurred to me.

Si. Namely——?

Tyc. Think of the address of your letters—Simon the Sponger!

Si. Simon the Sponger, Dion the Philosopher. I shall like mine as well as he his.

Tyc. Well, well, your taste in titles concerns me very little. Come now to the next absurdity.

Si. Which is——?

Tyc. The getting it entered on the list of arts. When any one asks what the art is, how do we describe it? Letters we know, Medicine we know; Sponging?

Si. My own opinion is, that it has an exceptionally good right to the name of art. If you care to listen, I will explain, though I have not got this properly into shape, as I remarked before.

Tyc. Oh, a brief exposition will do, provided it is true.

Si. I think, if you agree, we had better examine Art generically first; that will enable us to go into the question whether the specific arts really belong under it.

Tyc. Well, what is Art? Of course you know that?

Si. Quite well.

Tyc. Out with it, then, as you know.

Si. An art, as I once heard a wise man say, is a body of perceptions regularly employed for some useful purpose in human life.

Tyc. And he was quite right.

Si. So, if sponging has all these marks, it must be an art?

Tyc. If, yes.

Si. Well, now we will bring to bear on sponging each of these essential elements of Art, and see whether its character rings true, or returns a cracked note like bad pottery when it is tapped. It has got to be, like all art, a body of perceptions. Well, we find at once that our artist has to distinguish critically the man who will entertain him satisfactorily and not give him reason to wish that he had sponged elsewhere. Now, in as much as assaying—which is no more than the power of distinguishing between false and true coin—is a recognized profession, you will hardly refuse the same status to that which distinguishes between false and true *men*; the genuineness of men is more obscure than that of coins; this indeed is the gist of the wise Euripides's complaint:

> But among men how tell the base apart?
> Virtue and vice stamp not the outward flesh.

So much the greater the sponger's art, which beats prophecy in the certainty of its conclusions upon problems so difficult.

Next, there is the faculty of so directing your words and actions as to effect intimacy and convince your patron of your devotion: is that consistent with weak understanding or perception?

Tyc. Certainly not.

Si. Then at table one has to outshine other people, and show the difference between amateur and professional: is that to be done without thought and ingenuity?

Tyc. No, indeed.

Si. Or perhaps you fancy that any outsider who will take the trouble can tell a good dinner from a bad one. Well, the mighty Plato says, if the guest is not versed in cookery, the dressing of the banquet will be but unworthily judged.

The next point to be established is, that sponging depends not merely on perceptions, but on perceptions regularly employed. Nothing simpler. The perceptions on which other arts are based frequently remain unemployed by their owner for days, nights, months, or years, without his art's perishing; whereas, if those of the sponger were to miss their daily exercise, not merely his art would perish, but he with it.

There remains the 'useful purpose in human life'; it would take a madman to question that here. I find nothing that serves a more useful purpose in human life than eating and drinking; without them you cannot live.

Tyc. That is true.

Si. Moreover, sponging is not to be classed with beauty and strength, and so called a quality instead of an art?

Tyc. No.

Si. And, in the sphere of art, it does not denote the negative condition, of unskilfulness. That never brings its owner prosperity. Take an instance: if a man who did not understand navigation took charge of a ship in a stormy sea, would he be safe?

Tyc. Not he.

Si. Why, now? Because he wants the art which would enable him to save his life?

Tyc. Exactly.

Si. It follows that, if sponging was the negative of art, the sponger would not save his life by its means?

Tyc. Yes.

Si. A man is saved by art, not by the absence of it?

Tyc. Quite so.

Si. So sponging is an art?

Tyc. Apparently.

Si. Let me add that I have often known even good navigators and skilful drivers come to grief, resulting with the latter in bruises and with the former in death but no one will tell you of a sponger who ever made shipwreck. Very well, then, sponging is neither the negative of art, nor is it a quality; but it is a body of perceptions regularly employed. So it emerges from the present discussion an art.

Tyc. That seems to be the upshot. But now proceed to give us a good definition of your art.

Si. Well thought of. And I fancy this will about do: Sponging is the art of eating and drinking, and of the talk by which these may be secured; its end is Pleasure.

Tyc. A very good definition, I think. But I warn you that your end will bring you into conflict with some of the philosophers.

St. Ah well, if sponging agrees with Happiness about the end, we may be content.

And that it does I will soon show you. The wise Homer, admiring the sponger's life as the only blissful enviable one, has this:

> I say no fairer end may be attained
> Than when the people is attuned to mirth,
> . . . .. and groans the festal board
> With meat and bread, and the cup-bearer's ladle
> From flowing bowl to cup the sweet wine dips.

As if this had not made his admiration quite clear enough, he lays a little more emphasis, good man, on his personal opinion:

This in my heart I count the highest bliss.

Moreover, the character to whom he entrusts these words is not just any one; it is the wisest of the Greeks. Well now, if Odysseus had cared to say a word for the end approved by the Stoics, he had plenty of chances—when he brought back Philoctetes from Lemnos, when he sacked Troy, when he stopped the Greeks from giving up, or when he made his way into Troy by scourging himself and putting on rags bad enough for any Stoic. But no; he never said theirs was a fairer end. And again, when he was living an Epicurean life with Calypso, when he could spend idle luxurious days, enjoying the daughter of Atlas and giving the rein to every soft emotion, even then he had not his fairer end; that was still the life of the sponger. Banqueter was the word used for sponger in his day; what does he say? I must quote the lines again; nothing like repetition: 'The banqueters in order set'; and 'groans the festal board With meat and bread. '

It was a remarkable piece of impudence on Epicurus's part to appropriate the end that belongs to sponging for his system of Happiness. That it *was* a bit of larceny—Epicurus having nothing, and the sponger much, to do with Pleasure—I will soon show you. I take it that Pleasure means, first, bodily tranquillity, and secondly, an untroubled soul. Well, the sponger attains both, Epicurus neither. A man who is busy inquiring into the earth's shape, the infinity of worlds, the sun's size, astronomic distances, the elements, the existence or non-existence of Gods, and who is engaged in incessant controversies about the end—he is a prey not merely to human, but to cosmic perturbations. Whereas the sponger, convinced that all is for the best in the best of all possible worlds, living secure and calm with no such perplexities to trouble him, eats and sleeps and lies on his back, letting his hands and feet look after themselves, like Odysseus on his passage home from Scheria.

But here is an independent refutation of Epicurus's pretensions to Pleasure. Our Epicurus, whoever his Wisdom may be, either is, or is not, supplied with victuals. If he is not, so far from having a pleasurable life, he will have no life at all. If he is, does he get them out of his own means, or from some one else? If the latter, he is a sponger, and not what he says he is; if the former, he will not have a pleasurable life.

Tyc. How so?

Si. Why, if his food is provided out of his own means, that way of life has many consequences; reckon them up. You will admit that, if the principle of your life is to be pleasure, all your appetites have to be satisfied?

Tyc. I agree.

Si. Well, a large income may possibly meet that requirement, a scanty one certainly not; consequently, a poor man cannot be a philosopher, or in other words attain the end, which is Pleasure. But neither will the rich, who lavishes his substance on his desires, attain it. And why? Because spending has many worries inseparably attached to it; your cook disappoints you, and you must either have strained relations with him, or else purchase peace and quiet by feeding badly and missing your pleasure. Then similar difficulties attend your steward's management of the house. You must admit all this.

Tyc. Oh, certainly, I agree.

Si. In fact, something or other is sure to happen and cut off Epicurus from his end. Now the sponger has no cook to be angry with, no farm, steward or money to be annoyed at the loss of; at the same time he lives on the fat of the land, and is the one person who can eat and drink without the worries from which others cannot escape.

That sponging is an art, has now been abundantly proved; it remains to show its superiority; and this I shall take in two divisions: first, it has a general superiority to all the arts; and, secondly, it is superior to each of them separately. The general superiority is this: the arts have to be instilled by dint of toil, threats and blows—regrettable necessities, all of them; my own art, of which the acquisition costs no toil, is perhaps the only exception. Who ever came away from dinner in tears? with the schoolroom it is different; or who ever went out to dinner with the dismal expression characteristic of going to school? No, the sponger needs no pressing to get him to table; he is devoted to his profession; it is the other apprentices who hate theirs, to the point of running away, sometimes. And it is worth your notice that a parent's usual reward for a child who makes progress in the ordinary arts is just the thing that the sponger gets regularly. The lad has done his writing well, they say; let him have something nice: what vile writing! let him go without. Oh, the mouth is very useful for reward and punishment.

Again, with the other arts the result comes only after the learning is done; their fruits alone are agreeable; 'long and steep the road thereto.' Sponging is once more an exception, in that profit and learning here go hand in hand; you grasp your end as soon as you begin. And whereas all other arts are practised solely for the sustenance they will ultimately bring, the sponger has his sustenance from the day he starts. You realize, of course, that the farmer's object in farming is something else than farming, the carpenter's something different from abstract carpentering; but the sponger has no ulterior object; occupation and pre-occupation are for him one and the same.

Then it is no news to any one that other professions slave habitually, and get just one or two holidays a month; States keep some monthly and some yearly festivals; these are their times of enjoyment. But the sponger has thirty festivals a month; every day is a red-letter day with him.

Once more, success in the other arts presupposes a diet as abstemious as any invalid's; eat and drink to your heart's content, and you make no progress in your studies.

Other arts, again, are useless to their professor unless he has his plant; you cannot play the flute if you have not one to play; lyrical music requires a lyre, horsemanship a horse. But of ours one of the excellences and conveniences is that no instrument is required for its exercise.

Other arts we pay, this we are paid, to learn.

Further, while the rest have their teachers, no one teaches sponging; it is a gift from Heaven, as Socrates said of poetry.

Then do not forget that, while the others have to be suspended during a journey or a voyage, this may be in full swing under those circumstances too.

Tyc. No doubt about that.

Si. Another point that strikes me is that other arts feel the need of this one, but not vice versa.

Tyc. Well, but is the appropriation of what belongs to others no offence?

Si. Of course it is.

Tyc. Well, the sponger does that; why is he privileged to offend?

Si. Ah, I know nothing about that. But now look here: you know how common and mean are the beginnings of the other arts; that of sponging, on the contrary, is noble. Friendship, that theme of the encomiast, is neither more nor less, you will find, than the beginning of sponging.

Tyc. How do you make that out?

Si. Well, no one asks an enemy, a stranger, or even a mere acquaintance, to dinner; the man must be his friend before he will share bit and sup with him, and admit him to initiation in these sacred mysteries. I know I have often heard people say, Friend, indeed! by what right? he has never eaten or drunk with us. You see; only the man who has done that is a friend to be trusted.

Next take a sound proof, though not the only one, that it is the most royal of the arts: at the rest of them men have to work (not to mention toil and sweat) in the sitting or standing posture, which marks them for the absolute slaves of their art, whereas the sponger is free to recline like a king.

As to his happy condition, I need no more than allude to the wise Homer's words; he it is, and he alone, that 'planteth not, nor ploughs'; he 'reapeth where he hath not ploughed nor sown. '

Again, while knavery and folly are no bar to rhetoric, mathematics, or copper-working, no knave or fool can get on as a sponger.

Tyc. Dear, dear, what an amazing profession! I am almost tempted to exchange my own for it.

Si. I consider I have now established its superiority to art in general; let us next show how it excels individual arts. And it would be silly to compare it with the trades; I leave that to its detractors, and undertake to prove it superior to the greatest and most honourable professions. Such by universal acknowledgement are Rhetoric and Philosophy; indeed, some people insist that no name but science is grand enough for them; so if I prove sponging to be far above even these, *a fortiori* it will excel the others as Nausicaa her maids.

Now, its first superiority it enjoys over Philosophy and Rhetoric alike, and this is in the matter of real existence; it can claim that, they cannot. Instead of our having a single consistent notion of Rhetoric, some of us consider it an art, some the negation of art, some a mere artfulness, and so on. Similarly there is no unity in Philosophy's subject, or in its relation to it; Epicurus takes one view, the Stoics another, the Academy, the Peripatetics, others; in fact Philosophy has as many definitions as definers. So far at least victory wavers between them, and their profession cannot be called *one*. The conclusion is obvious; I utterly deny that what has no real existence can be an art. To illustrate: there is one and only one Arithmetic; twice two is four whether here or in Persia; Greeks and barbarians have no quarrel over that; but philosophies are many and various, agreed neither upon their beginnings nor their ends.

Tyc. Perfectly true; they call Philosophy one, but they make it many.

Si. Well, such a want of harmony might be excused in other arts, they being of a contingent nature, and the perceptions on which they are based not being immutable. But that *Philosophy* should lack unity, and even conflict with itself like instruments out of tune—how can that be tolerated? Philosophy, then, is not one, for I find its diversity infinite. And it cannot be many, because it is Philosophy, not philosophies.

The real existence of Rhetoric must incur the same criticism. That with the same subject-matter all professors should not agree, but maintain conflicting opinions, amounts to a demonstration: that which is differently apprehended cannot exist. The inquiry whether a thing is this or that, in place of agreement that it is one, is tantamount to a negation of its existence.

How different is the case of Sponging! for Greeks or barbarians, *one* in nature and subject and method. No one will tell you that these sponge this way, and those that; there are no spongers with peculiar principles, to match those of Stoics and Epicureans, that I know of; they are all agreed; their conduct and their end alike harmonious. Sponging, I take it on this showing, is just Wisdom itself.

Tyc. Yes, I think you have dealt with that point sufficiently; apart from that, how do you show the inferiority of Philosophy to your art?

Si. I must first mention that no sponger was ever in love with Philosophy; but many philosophers are recorded to have set their hearts on Sponging, to which they still remain constant.

Tyc. Philosophers caring to sponge? Names, please.

Si. Names? You know them well enough; you only play at not knowing because you regard it as a slur on their characters, instead of as the credit it is.

Tyc. Simon, I solemnly assure you I cannot think where you will find your instances.

Si. Honour bright? Then I conclude you never patronize their biographers, or you could not hesitate about my reference.

Tyc. Seriously, I long to hear their names.

Si. Oh, I will give you a list; not bad names either; the *elite*, if I am correctly informed; they will rather surprise you. Aeschines the Socratic, now, author of dialogues as witty as they are long, brought them with him to Sicily in the hope that they would gain him the royal notice of Dionysius; having given a reading of the *Miltiades*, and found himself famous, he settled down in Sicily to sponge on Dionysius and forget Socratic composition.

Again, I suppose you will pass Aristippus of Cyrene as a distinguished philosopher?

Tyc. Assuredly.

Si. Well, he was living there too at the same time and on the same terms. Dionysius reckoned him the best of all spongers; he had indeed a special gift that way; the prince used to send his cooks to him daily for instruction. He, I think, was really an ornament to the profession.

Well then, Plato, the noblest of you all, came to Sicily with the same view; he did a few days' sponging, but found himself incompetent and had to leave. He went back to Athens, took considerable pains with himself, and then had another try, with exactly the same result, however. Plato's Sicilian disaster seems to me to bear comparison with that of Nicias.

Tyc. Your authority for all this, pray?

Si. Oh, there are plenty of authorities; but I will specify Aristoxenus the musician, a weighty one enough, and himself attached as a sponger to Neleus. Then you of course know that Euripides held this relation to Archelaus till the day of his death, and Anaxarchus to Alexander.

As for Aristotle, that tiro in all arts was a tiro here too.

I have shown you, then, and without exaggeration, the philosophic passion for sponging. On the other hand, no one can point to a sponger who ever cared to philosophize.

But of course, if never to be hungry, thirsty, or cold, is to be happy, the sponger is the man who is in that position. Cold hungry philosophers you may see any day, but never a cold hungry sponger; the man would not be a sponger, that is all, but a wretched pauper, no better than a philosopher.

Tyc. Well, let that pass. And now what about those many points in which your art is superior to Rhetoric and Philosophy?

Si. Human life, my dear sir, has its times and seasons; there is peace time and there is war time. These provide unfailing tests for the character of arts and their professors. Shall we take war time first, and see who will do best for himself and for his city under those conditions?

Tyc. Ah, now comes the tug of war. It tickles me, this queer match between sponger and philosopher.

Si. Well, to make the thing more natural, and enable you to take it seriously, let us picture the circumstances. Sudden news has come of a hostile invasion; it has to be met; we are not going to sit still while our outlying territory is laid waste; the commander-in-chief issues orders for a general muster of all liable to serve; the troops gather, including philosophers, rhetoricians, and spongers. We had better strip them first, as the proper preliminary to arming. Now, my dear sir, have a look at them individually and see how they shape. Some of them you will find thin and white with underfeeding—all goose-flesh, as if they were lying wounded already. Now, when you think of a hard day, a stand- up fight with press and dust and wounds, what is it but a sorry jest to talk of such starvelings' being able to stand it?

154

Now go and inspect the sponger. Full-bodied, flesh a nice colour, neither white like a woman's nor tanned like a slave's; you can see his spirit; he has a keen look, as a gentleman should, and a high, full-blooded one to boot; none of your shrinking feminine glances when you are going to war! A noble pike-man that, and a noble corpse, for that matter, if a noble death is his fate.

But why deal in conjecture when there are facts to hand? I make the simple statement that in war, of all the rhetoricians and philosophers who ever lived, most never ventured outside the city walls, and the few who did, under compulsion, take their places in the ranks left their posts and went home.

Tyc. A bold extravagant assertion. Well, prove it.

Si. Rhetoricians, then. Of these, Isocrates, so far from serving in war, never even ventured into a law-court; he was afraid, because his voice was weak, I understand. Well, then Demades, Aeschines, and Philocrates, directly the Macedonian war broke out, were frightened into betraying their country and themselves to Philip. They simply espoused his interests in Athenian politics; and any other Athenian who took the same side was their friend. As for Hyperides, Demosthenes, and Lycurgus, supposed to be bolder spirits, and always raising scenes in the assembly with their abuse of Philip, how did they ever show their prowess in the war? Hyperides and Lycurgus never went out, did not so much as dare show their noses beyond the gates; they sat snug inside in a domestic state of siege, composing poor little decrees and resolutions. And their great chieftain, who had no gentler words for Philip in the assembly than 'the brute from Macedon, which cannot produce even a slave worth buying'—well, he did take heart of grace and go to Boeotia the day before; but battle had not been joined when he threw away his shield and made off. You must have heard this before; it was common talk not only at Athens, but in Thrace and Scythia, whence the creature was derived.

Tyc. Yes, I know all that. But then these are orators, trained to speak, not to fight. But the philosophers; you cannot say the same of them.

Si. Oh, yes; they discuss manliness every day, and do a great deal more towards wearing out the word Virtue than the orators; but you will find them still greater cowards and shirkers. —How do I know? —In the first place, can any one name a philosopher killed in battle?

No, they either do not serve, or else run away. Antisthenes, Diogenes, Crates, Zeno, Plato, Aeschines, Aristotle, and all their company, never set eyes on a battle array. Their wise Socrates was the solitary one who dared to go out; and in the battle of Delium he ran away from Mount Parnes and got safe to the gymnasium of Taureas. It was a far more civilized proceeding, according to his ideas, to sit there talking soft nonsense to handsome striplings and posing the company with quibbles, than to cross spears with a grown Spartan.

Tyc. Well, I have heard these stories before, and from people who had no satirical intent. So I acquit you of slandering them by way of magnifying your own profession.

But come now, if you don't mind, to the sponger's military behaviour; and also tell me whether there is any sponging recorded of the ancients.

Si. My dear fellow, the most uneducated of us has surely heard enough of Homer to know that he makes the best of his heroes spongers. The great Nestor, whose tongue distilled honeyed speech, sponged on the King; Achilles was, and was known for, the most upright of the Greeks in form and in mind; but neither for him, for Ajax, nor for Diomede, has Agamemnon such admiring praise as for Nestor. It is not for ten Ajaxes or Achilleses that he prays; no, Troy would have been taken long ago, if he had had in his host ten men like—that old sponger. Idomeneus, of Zeus's own kindred, is also represented in the same relation to Agamemnon.

Tyc. I know the passages; but I do not feel sure of the sense in which they were spongers.

Si. Well, recall the lines in which Agamemnon addresses Idomeneus.

Tyc. How do they go?

Si.

> For thee the cup stands ever full,
> Even as for me, whene'er it lists thee drink.

When he speaks of the cup ever full, he means not that it is perpetually ready (when Idomeneus is fighting or sleeping, for instance), but that he has had the peculiar privilege all through his life of sharing the King's table without that special invitation which is necessary for his other followers. Ajax, after a glorious single combat with Hector, 'they brought to lordly Agamemnon, ' we are told; he, you see, is admitted to the royal table (and high time too) as an honour; whereas Idomeneus and Nestor were the King's regular table companions; at least that is my idea. Nestor I take to have been an exceedingly good and skilful sponger on royalty; Agamemnon was not his first patron; he had served his apprenticeship under Caeneus and Exadius. And but for Agamemnon's death I imagine he would never have relinquished the profession.

Tyc. Yes, that was a first-class sponger. Can you give me any more?

Si. Why, Tychiades, what else was Patroclus's relation to Achilles? and he was as fine a fellow, all round, as any Greek of them all. Judging by his actions, I cannot make out that he was inferior to Achilles himself. When Hector had forced the gates and was fighting inside by the ships, it was Patroclus who repelled him and extinguished the flames which had got a hold on Protesilaus's ship; yet one would not have said the people aboard her were inefficient— Ajax and Teucer they were, one as good in the *melee* as the other with his bow. A great number of the barbarians, including Sarpedon the son of Zeus, fell to this sponger. His own death was no common one. It took only one man, Achilles, to slay Hector; Paris was enough for Achilles himself; but two men and a God went to the killing of the sponger. And his last words bore no resemblance to those of the mighty Hector, who prostrated himself before Achilles and besought him to let his relations have his body; no, they were such as might be expected from one of his profession. Here they are: —

> But of thy like I would have faced a score,
> And all the score my spear had given to death.

Tyc. Yes, you have proved him a good man; but can you show him to have been not Achilles's friend, but a sponger?

Si. I will produce you his own statement to that effect.

Tyc. What a miracle-worker you are!

Si. Listen to the lines, then:

Achilles, lay my bones not far from thine;
Thou and thine fed me; let me lie by thee.

And a little further on he says:

Peleus me received,
And nurtured gently, and thy henchman named,

that is, gave him the right of sponging; if he had meant to allude to Patroclus as his son's friend, he would not have used the word henchman; for he was a free man. What is a henchman, slaves and friends being excluded? Why, obviously a sponger. Accordingly Homer uses the same word of Meriones's relation to Idomeneus. And by the way it is not Idomeneus, though he was son of Zeus, that he describes as 'peer of Ares'; it is the sponger Meriones.

Again, did not Aristogiton, poor and of mean extraction, as Thucydides describes him, sponge on Harmodius? He was also, of course, in love with him—a quite natural relation between the two classes. This sponger it was, then, who delivered Athens from tyranny, and now adorns the marketplace in bronze, side by side with the object of his passion. And now I have given you an example or two of the profession.

But what sort of a guess do you make at the sponger's behaviour in war? In the first place, he will fight on a full belly, as Odysseus advises. You must feed the man who is to fight, he says, however early in the morning it may happen to be. The time that others spend in fitting on helmet or breastplate with nervous care, or in anticipating the horrors of battle, he will devote to putting away his food with a cheerful countenance, and as soon as business begins you will find him in front. His patron will take his place behind him, sheltering under his shield as Teucer under Ajax's; when missiles begin to fly the sponger will expose himself for his patron, whose safety he values more than his own.

Should he fall in battle, neither officer nor comrade need feel ashamed of that great body, which now reclines as appropriate an ornament of the battle-field as it once was of the dining-room. A pretty sight is a philosopher's body by its side, withered, squalid, and bearded; he was dead before the fight began, poor weakling. Who would not despise the city whose guards are such miserable creatures? Who would not suppose, seeing these pallid, hairy manikins scattered on the ground, that it had none to fight for it, and so had turned out its gaol-birds to fill the ranks? That is how the spongers differ from the rhetoricians and philosophers in war.

Then in peace time, sponging seems to me as much better than philosophy as peace itself than war. Be kind enough to glance first at the scenes of peace.

Tyc. I do not quite know what they are; but let us glance at them, by all means.

Si. Well, you will let me describe as civil scenes the market, the courts, the wrestling-schools and gymnasia, the hunting field and the dining-room?

Tyc. Certainly.

Si. To market and courts the sponger gives a wide berth they are the haunts of chicanery; there is no satisfaction to be got out of them. But at wrestling-school and gymnasium he is in his element; he is their chief glory. Show me a philosopher or orator who is in the same class with him when he strips in the wrestling- school; look at them in the gymnasium; they shame instead of adorning it. And in a lonely place none of them would face the onset of a wild beast; the sponger will, though, and find no difficulty in disposing of it; his table familiarity with it has bred contempt. A stag or a wild boar may put up its bristles; he will not mind; the boar may whet its tusks against him; he only returns the compliment. As for hares, he is more deadly to them than a greyhound. And then in the dining-room, where is his match, to jest or to eat? Who will contribute most to entertainment, he with his song and his joke, or a person who has not a laugh in him, sits in a threadbare cloak, and keeps his eyes on the ground as if he was at a funeral and not a dinner? If you ask me, I think a philosopher has about as much business in a dining-room as a bull in a china-shop.

But enough of this. What impression does one get of the sponger's actual life, when one compares it with the other? First it will be found that he is indifferent to reputation, and does not care a jot what people think about him, whereas all rhetoricians and philosophers without exception are the slaves of vanity, reputation, and what is worse, of money. No one could be more careless of the pebbles on the shore than the sponger is of money; he would as soon touch fire as gold. But the rhetoricians and, as if that were not bad enough, the professed philosophers, are beneath contempt in this respect. No need to illustrate in the case of the rhetoricians; but of the philosophers whose repute stands highest at present, one was lately convicted of taking a bribe for his verdict in a law-suit, and another expects a salary for giving a prince his company, and counts it no shame to go into exile in his old age, and hire himself out for pay like some Indian or Scythian captive. The very name his conduct has earned him calls no blush to his cheek.

But their susceptibilities are by no means limited to these; pain, temper, jealousy, and all sorts of desires, must be added; all of which the sponger is beyond the reach of; he does not yield to temper because on the one hand he has fortitude, and on the other hand he has no one to irritate him. Or if he is by any chance moved to wrath, there is nothing disagreeable or sullen about it; it entertains and amuses merely. As to pain, he has less of that to endure than anybody, one of his profession's recommendations and privileges being just that immunity. He has neither money, house, slave, wife, nor children—those hostages to Fortune. He desires neither fame, wealth, nor beauty.

Tyc. He will feel pain if the supplies run short, I presume.

Si. Ah, but you see, he is not a sponger if that happens. A courageous man is not courageous if he has no courage, a sensible one not sensible if he has no sense. He could not be a sponger under those conditions. We are discussing the sponger, not the non- sponger. If the courageous is so in virtue of his courage, the sensible sensible in virtue of his sense, then the sponger is a sponger in virtue of sponging. Take that away, and we shall be dealing with something else, and not with a sponger at all.

Tyc. So his supplies will never run short?

Si. Manifestly. So he is as free from that sort of pain as from others.

Then all philosophers and rhetoricians are timorous creatures together. You may generally see them carrying sticks on their walks; well, of course they would not go armed if they were not afraid. And they bar their doors elaborately, for fear of night attacks. Now our man just latches his room door, so that the wind may not blow it open; if there is a noise in the night, it is all the same to him as if there were none; he will travel a lonely road and wear no sword; he does not know what fear is. But I am always seeing philosophers, though there is nothing to be afraid of, carrying bows and arrows; as for their sticks, they take them to bath or breakfast with them.

Again, no one can accuse a sponger of adultery, violence, rape, or in fact of any crime whatsoever. One guilty of such offences will not be sponging, but ruining himself. If he is caught in adultery, his style thenceforth is taken from his offence. Just as a piece of cowardice brings a man not repute, but disrepute, so, I take it, the sponger who commits an offence loses his previous title and gets in exchange that proper to the offence. Of such offences on the part of rhetoricians and philosophers, on the other hand, we have not only abundant examples in our own time, but records against the ancients in their own writings. There is an Apology of Socrates, of Aeschines, of Hyperides, of Demosthenes, and indeed of most of their kind. There is no sponger's apology extant, and you will never hear of anybody's bringing a suit against one.

Now I suppose you will tell me that the sponger's life may be better than theirs, but his death is worse. Not a bit of it; it is a far happier one. We know very well that all or most philosophers have had the wretched fate they deserved, some by poison after condemnation for heinous crimes, some by burning alive, some by strangury, some in exile. No one can adduce a sponger's death to match these; he eats and drinks, and dies a blissful death. If you are told that any died a violent one, be sure it was nothing worse than indigestion.

Tyc. I must say, you have done well for your kind against the philosophers. And now look at it from the patron's point of view; does he get his money's worth? It strikes me the rich man does the kindness, confers the favour, finds the food, and it is all a little discreditable to the man who takes them.

Si. Now, really, Tychiades, that is rather silly of you. Can you not see that a rich man, if he had the gold of Gyges, is yet poor as long as he dines alone, and no better than a tramp if he goes abroad unattended? A soldier without his arms, a dress without its purple, a horse without its trappings, are poor things; and a rich man without his sponger is a mean, cheap spectacle. The sponger gives lustre to the patron, never the patron to the other.

Moreover, none of the reproach that you imagine attaches to sponging; you refer, of course, to the difference in their degrees; but then it is an advantage to the rich man to keep the other; apart from his ornamental use, he is a most valuable bodyguard. In battle no one will be over ready to undertake the rich man with such a comrade at his side; and you can hardly, having him, die by poison. Who would dare attempt such a thing, with him tasting your food and drink? So he brings you not only credit, but insurance. His affection is such that he will run all risks; he would never leave his patron to face the dangers of the table alone; no, he would rather eat and die with him.

Tyc. You have stated your case without missing a point, Simon. Do not tell me you were unprepared again; you have been trained in a good school, man. But one thing more I should like to know. There is a nasty sound about the word sponger, don't you think?

Si. See whether I have a satisfactory answer to that. Oblige me by giving what you consider the right answers to my questions. Sponging is an old word; what does it really mean?

Tyc. Getting your dinner at some one else's expense.

Si. Dining out, in fact?

Tyc. Yes.

Si. And we may call a sponger an out-diner?

Tyc. The gravamen's in that; he should dine at home.

Si. A few more answers, please. Of these pairs, which do you consider the best? Which would you take, if you had the choice? -To sail, or to out-sail?

Tyc. The latter.

Si. To run or out-run?

Tyc. The latter.

Si. Ride or out-ride, shoot or out-shoot?

Tyc. Still the same.

Si. So I presume an out-diner is better than a diner?

Tyc. Indisputable. Henceforward I shall come to you morning and afternoon like a schoolboy for lessons. And I am sure you ought to do your very best for me, as your first pupil. The first child is always the mother's joy, you know. [Footnote: It has been necessary, in Section 60, to tamper a little with the Greek in order to get the point, such as it is; but it has not been seriously misrepresented.]

ANACHARSIS, A DISCUSSION OF PHYSICAL TRAINING

Anacharsis. Solon

An. Why do your young men behave like this, Solon? Some of them grappling and tripping each other, some throttling, struggling, intertwining in the clay like so many pigs wallowing. And yet their first proceeding after they have stripped-I noticed that-is to oil and scrape each other quite amicably; but then I do not know what comes over them—they put down their heads and begin to push, and crash their foreheads together like a pair of rival rams. There, look! that one has lifted the other right off his legs, and dropped him on the ground; now he has fallen on top, and will not let him get his head up, but presses it down into the clay; and to finish him off he twines his legs tight round his belly, thrusts his elbow hard against his throat, and throttles the wretched victim, who meanwhile is patting his shoulder; that will be a form of supplication; he is asking not to be quite choked to death. Regardless of their fresh oil, they get all filthy, smother themselves in mud and sweat till they might as well not have been anointed, and present, to me at least, the most ludicrous resemblance to eels slipping through a man's hands.

Then here in the open court are others doing just the same, except that, instead of the clay, they have for floor a depression filled with deep sand, with which they sprinkle one another, scraping up the dust on purpose, like fowls; I suppose they want their interfacings to be tighter; the sand is to neutralize the slipperiness of the oil, and by drying it up to give a firmer grip.

And here are others, sanded too, but on their legs, going at each other with blows and kicks. We shall surely see this poor fellow spit out his teeth in a minute; his mouth is all full of blood and sand; he has had a blow on the jaw from the other's fist, you see. Why does not the official there separate them and put an end to it? I guess that he is an official from his purple; but no, he encourages them, and commends the one who gave that blow.

Wherever you look, every one busy-rising on his toes, jumping up and kicking the air, or something.

Now I want to know what is the good of it all. To me it looks more like madness than anything else. It will not be very easy to convince me that people who behave like this are not wrong in their heads.

So. It is quite natural it should strike you that way, being so novel, and so utterly contrary to Scythian customs. Similarly you have no doubt many methods and habits that would seem extraordinary enough to us Greeks, v if we were spectators of them as you now are of ours. But be reassured, my dear sir; these proceedings are not madness; it is no spirit of violence that sets them hitting each other, wallowing in clay, and sprinkling dust. The thing has its use, and its delight too, resulting in admirable physical condition. If you make some stay, as I imagine you will, in Greece, you are bound to be either a clay-bob or a dust-bob before long; you will be so taken with the pleasure and profit of the pursuit.

An. Hands off, please. No, I wish you all joy of your pleasures and your profits; but if any of you treats me like that, he will find out that we do not wear scimetars for ornament.

But would you mind giving a name to all this? What are we to say they are doing?

So. The place is called a gymnasium, and is dedicated to the Lycean Apollo. You see his statue there; the one leaning on the pillar, with a bow in the left hand. The right arm bent over the head indicates that the God is resting after some great exertion.

Of the exercises here, that in the clay is called wrestling; the youths in the dust are also called wrestlers, and those who strike each other standing are engaged in what we call the pancratium. But we have other gymnasiums for boxing, quoit-throwing, and high- jumping; and in all these we hold contests, the winner in which is honoured above all his contemporaries, and receives prizes.

An. Ah, and what are the prizes, now?

So. At Olympia a wreath of wild olive, at the Isthmus one of pine, at Nemea of parsley, at Pytho some of the God's sacred apples, and at our Panathenaea oil pressed from the temple olives. What are you laughing at, Anacharsis? Are the prizes too small?

An. Oh dear no; your prize-list is most imposing; the givers may well plume themselves on their munificence, and the competitors be monstrous keen on winning. Who would not go through this amount of preparatory toil, and take his chance of a choking or a dislocation, for apples or parsley? It is obviously impossible for any one who has a fancy to a supply of apples, or a wreath of parsley or pine, to get them without a mud plaster on his face, or a kick in the stomach from his competitor. O *So.* My dear sir, it is not the things' intrinsic value that we look at. They are the symbols of victory, labels of the winners; it is the fame attaching to them that is worth any price to their holders; that is why the man whose quest of honour leads through toil is content to take his kicks. No toil, no honour; he who covets that must start with enduring hardship; when he has done that, he may begin to look for the pleasure and profit his labours are to bring.

An. Which pleasure and profit consists in their being seen in their wreaths by every one, and congratulated on their victory by those who before commiserated their pain; their happiness lies in their exchange of apples and parsley for toil.

So. Ah, you certainly do not understand our ways yet. You will revise your opinions before long, when you go to the great festivals and see the crowds gathering to look on, the stands filling up, the competitors receiving their ovations, and the victor being idolized.

An. Why, Solon, that is just where the humiliation comes in; they are treated like this not in something like privacy, but with all these spectators to watch the affronts they endure—who, I am to believe, count them happy when they see them dripping with blood or being throttled; for such are the happy concomitants of victory. In my country, if a man strikes a citizen, knocks him down, or tears his clothes, our elders punish him severely, even though there were only one or two witnesses, not like your vast Olympic or Isthmian gatherings. However, though I cannot help pitying the competitors, I am still more astonished at the spectators; you tell me the chief people from all over Greece attend; how can they leave their serious concerns and waste time on such things? How they can like it passes my comprehension—to look on at people being struck and knocked about, dashed to the ground and pounded by one another.

So. If the Olympia, Isthmia, or Panathenaea were only on now, those object-lessons might have been enough to convince you that our keenness is not thrown away. I cannot make you apprehend the delights of them by description; you should be there sitting in the middle of the spectators, looking at the men's courage and physical beauty, their marvellous condition, effective skill and invincible strength, their enterprise, their emulation, their unconquerable spirit, and their unwearied pursuit of victory. Oh, I know very well, you would never have been tired of talking about your favourites, backing them with voice and hand.

An. I dare say, and with laugh and flout too. All the fine things in your list, your courages and conditions, your beauties and enterprises, I see you wasting in no high cause; your country is not in danger, your land not being ravaged, your friends or relations not being haled away. The more ridiculous that such patterns of perfection as you make them out should endure the misery all for nothing, and spoil their beauty and their fine figures with sand and black eyes, just for the triumphant possession of an apple or a sprig of wild olive. Oh, how I love to think of those prizes! By the way, do all who enter get them?

So. No, indeed. There is only one winner.

An. And do you mean to say such a number can be found to toil for a remote uncertainty of success, knowing that the winner cannot be more than one, and the failures must be many, with their bruises, or their wounds very likely, for sole reward?

So. Dear me; you have no idea yet of what is a good political constitution, or you would never depreciate the best of our customs. If you ever take the trouble to inquire how a State may best be organized, and its citizens best developed, you will find yourself commending these practices and the earnestness with which we cultivate them; then you will realize what good effects are inseparable from those toils which seem for the moment to tax our energies to no purpose.

An. Well, Solon, why did I come all the way from Scythia, why did I make the long stormy passage of the Euxine, but to learn the laws of Greece, observe your customs, and work out the best constitution? That was why I chose you of all Athenians for my friend and host; I had heard of you; I had been told you were a legislator, you had devised the most admirable customs, introduced institutions of great excellence, and in fact built up what you call a constitution. Before all things, then, teach me; make me your pupil. Nothing would please me more than to sit by your side without bit or sup for as long as you could hold out, and listen open-mouthed to what you have to say of constitution and laws.

So. The whole thing can hardly be so shortly disposed of, friend. You must take the different departments, one by one, and find out our views upon the Gods, then upon parents, upon marriage, and so for the rest. But I will let you know at once what we think about the young, and how we treat them when higher things begin to dawn upon their intelligence, when their frames begin to set and to be capable of endurance. Then you will grasp our purpose in imposing these exercises upon them and insisting on physical effort; our view is not bounded by the contests, and directed to their carrying off prizes there—of course only a small proportion of them ever reach that point; no; the indirect benefit that we secure for their city and themselves is of more importance. There is another contest in which all good citizens get prizes, and its wreaths are not of pine or wild olive or parsley, but of complete human happiness, including individual freedom and political independence, wealth and repute, enjoyment of our ancient ritual, security of our dear ones, and all the choicest boons a man might ask of Heaven. It is of these materials that the wreath I tell you of is woven; and they are provided by that contest for which this training and these toils are the preparation.

An. You strange man! you had all these grand prizes up your sleeve, and you told me a tale of apples and parsley and tufts of wild olive and pine.

So. Ah, you will not think those such trifles either, when you take my meaning. They are manifestations of the same spirit, all small parts of that greater contest, and of the wreath of happiness I told you of. But it is true that instead of beginning at the beginning I was carried away to the meetings at the Isthmus and Olympia and Nemea. However, we have plenty of time, and you profess curiosity; it is a simple matter to go back to the beginning, to that many-prized contest which I tell you is the real end of all.

An. That will be better; we are more likely to prosper on the high road; perhaps I shall even be cured of my inclination to laugh at any one I see priding himself on his olive or parsley wreath. But I propose that we go into the shade over there and sit down on the benches, not to be interrupted by these rounds of cheering. And indeed I must confess I have had enough of this sun; how it scorches one's bare head! I did not want to look like a foreigner, so I left my hat at home. But the year is at its hottest; the dog-star, as you call it, is burning everything up, and not leaving a drop of moisture in the air; and the noonday sun right overhead gives an absolutely intolerable heat. I cannot make out how you at your age, so far from dripping like me, never turn a hair; instead of looking about for some hospitable shade, you take your sunning quite kindly.

So. Ah, Anacharsis, these useless toils, these perpetual clay-baths, these miseries in the sand and the open air, are prophylactics against the sun's rays; *we* need no hats to ward off his shafts. But come along.

And you are not to regard me as an authority whose statements are to be accepted as matter of faith; wherever you think I have not made out my case, you are to contradict me at once and get the thing straight. So we shall stand to win; either you, after relieving your mind of all objections that strike you, will reach a firm conviction, or, failing that, I shall have found out my mistake. And in the latter case, Athens will owe you a debt that she cannot be too quick to acknowledge; for your instructions and corrections of my ideas will redound to her advantage. I shall keep nothing back; I shall produce it all in public, stand up in the assembly and say: *Men of Athens, I drew up for you such laws as I thought would most advantage you; but this stranger*—and at that word I point to you, Anacharsis—*this stranger from Scythia has been wise enough to show me my mistake and teach me better ways. Let his name be inscribed as your benefactor's; set him up in bronze beside your name-Gods, or by Athene on the citadel.* And be assured that Athens will not be ashamed to learn what is for her good from a barbarian and an alien.

An. Ah, now I have a specimen of that Attic irony which I have so often heard of. I am an unsettled wanderer who lives on his cart and goes from land to land, who has never dwelt in a city, nor even seen one till now; how should I lay down a constitution, or give lessons to a people that is one with the soil it lives on [Footnote: See *Athenians* in Notes.], and for all these ages has enjoyed the blessings of perfect order in this ancient city? How, above all, instruct that Solon whose native gift all men say it is to know how a state may best be governed, and what laws will bring it happiness? Nevertheless, you shall be my legislator too; I will contradict you, where I think you wrong, for my own better instruction. And here we are, safely covered from the sun's pursuit, and this cool stone invites us to take our ease. Start now and give me your reasons. Why seize upon the rising generation so young, and subject them to such toils? How do you develop perfect virtue out of clay and training? What is the exact contribution to it of dust and summersaults? That and that only is my first curiosity. All the rest you shall give me by degrees as occasion rises later. But, Solon, one thing you must bear in mind: you are talking to a barbarian. What I mean is, you must be simple, and brief; I am afraid I shall forget the beginning, if a very abundant flow follows.

So. Why, you had better work the sluice yourself, whenever the word-stream is either turbid or diverging into a wrong channel. As for mere continuance, you can cut that up by questions. However, so long as what I have to say is not irrelevant, I do not know that length matters. There is an ancient procedure in the Areopagus, our murder court. When the members have ascended the hill, and taken their seats to decide a case of murder or deliberate maiming or arson, each side is allowed to address the court in turn, prosecution and defence being conducted either by the principals or by counsel. As long as they speak to the matter in hand, the court listens silently and patiently. But if either prefaces his speech with an appeal to its benevolence, or attempts to stir its compassion or indignation by irrelevant considerations —and the legal profession have numberless ways of playing upon juries—, the usher at once comes up and silences him. The court is not to be trifled with or have its food disguised with condiments, but to be shown the bare facts. Now, Anacharsis, I hereby create you a temporary Areopagite; you shall hear me according to that court's practice, and silence me if you find me cajoling you; but as long as I keep to the point, I may speak at large. For there is no sun here to make length a burden to you; we have plenty of shade and plenty of time.

An. That sounds reasonable. And I take it very kindly that you should have given me this incidental view of the proceedings on the Areopagus; they are very remarkable, quite a pattern of the way a judicial decision should be arrived at. Let your speech be regulated accordingly, and the Areopagite of your appointment shall listen as his office requires.

So. Well, I must start with a brief preliminary statement of our views upon city and citizens. A city in our conception is not the buildings—walls, temples, docks, and so forth; these are no more than the local habitation that provides the members of the community with shelter and safety; it is in the citizens that we find the root of the matter; they it is that replenish and organize and achieve and guard, corresponding in the city to the soul in man. Holding this view, we are not indifferent, as you see, to our city's body; that we adorn with all the beauty we can impart to it; it is provided with internal buildings, and fenced as securely as may be with external walls. But our first, our engrossing preoccupation is to make our citizens noble of spirit and strong of body. So they will in peace time make the most of themselves and their political unity, while in war they will bring their city through safe with its freedom and well-being unimpaired. Their early breeding we leave to their mothers, nurses, and tutors, who are to rear them in the elements of a liberal education. But as soon as they attain to a knowledge of good and evil, when reverence and shame and fear and ambition spring up in them, when their bodies begin to set and strengthen and be equal to toil, then we take them over, and appoint them both a course of mental instruction and discipline, and one of bodily endurance. We are not satisfied with mere spontaneous development either for body or soul; we think that the addition of systematic teaching will improve the gifted and reform the inferior. We conform our practice to that of the farmer, who shelters and fences his plants while they are yet small and tender, to protect them from the winds, but, as soon as the shoot has gathered substance, prunes it and lets the winds beat upon it and knock it about, and makes it thereby the more fruitful.

We first kindle their minds with music and arithmetic, teach them to write and to read with expression. Then, as they get on, we versify, for the better impressing their memories, the sayings of wise men, the deeds of old time, or moral tales. And as they hear of worship won and works that live in song, they yearn ever more, and are fired to emulation, that they too may be sung and marvelled at by them that come after, and have their Hesiod and their Homer. And when they attain their civil rights, and it is time for them to take their share in governing—but all this, it may be, is irrelevant. My subject was not how we train their souls, but why we think fit to subject them to the toils we do. I will silence myself without waiting for the usher, or for you, my Areopagite, who have been too considerate, methinks, in letting me maunder on out of bounds all this way.

An. Another point of Areopagite procedure, please, Solon. When a speaker passes over essential matters in silence, has the court no penalty for him?

So. Why? I do not take you.

An. Why, you propose to pass by the question of the soul, which is the noblest and the most attractive to me, and discuss the less essential matters of gymnasiums and physical exercise.

So. You see, my dear sir, I have my eye on our original conditions; I do not want to divert the word-stream; it might confuse your memory with its irregular flow. However, I will do what I can in the way of a mere summary for this branch of the subject; as for a detailed examination of it, that must be deferred.

Well, we regulate their sentiments partly by teaching them the laws of the land, which are inscribed in large letters and exposed at the public expense for all to read, enjoining certain acts and forbidding others, and partly by making them attend good men, who teach them to speak with propriety, act with justice, content themselves with political equality, eschew evil, ensue good, and abstain from violence; sophist and philosopher are the names by which these teachers are known. Moreover, we pay for their admission to the theatre, where the contemplation of ancient heroes and villains in tragedy or comedy has its educational effect of warning or encouragement. To the comic writers we further give the licence of mockery and invective against any of their fellow citizens whose conduct they find discreditable; such exposure may act both directly upon the culprits, and upon others by way of example.

An. Ah, I have seen the tragedians and comedians you speak of, at least if the former are men in heavy stilted shoes, and clothes all picked out with gold bands; they have absurd head- pieces with vast open mouths, from inside which comes an enormous voice, while they take great strides which it seems to me must be dangerous in those shoes. I think there was a festival to Dionysus going on at the time. Then the comedians are shorter, go on their own feet, are more human, and smaller-voiced; but their head-pieces are still more ridiculous, so much so that the audience was laughing at them like one man. But to the others, the tall ones, every one listened with a dismal face; I suppose they were sorry for them, having to drag about those great clogs.

So. Oh no, it was not for the actors that they were sorry. The poet was probably setting forth some sad tale of long ago, with fine speeches that appealed to the audience's feelings and drew tears from them. I dare say you observed also some flute-players, with other persons who stood in a circle and sang in chorus. These too are things that have their uses. Well, our youths' souls are made susceptible and developed by these and similar influences.

Then their bodily training, to which your curiosity was especially directed, is as follows. When their first pithless tenderness is past, we strip them and aim at hardening them to the temperature of the various seasons, till heat does not incommode nor frost paralyse them. Then we anoint them with oil by way of softening them into suppleness. It would be absurd that leather, dead stuff as it is, should be made tougher and more lasting by being softened with oil, and the living body get no advantage from the same process. Accordingly we devise elaborate gymnastic exercises, appoint instructors of each variety, and teach one boxing, another the pancratium. They are to be habituated to endurance, to meet blows half way, and never shrink from a wound. This method works two admirable effects in them: makes them spirited and heedless of bodily danger, and at the same time strong and enduring. Those whom you saw lowering their heads and wrestling learn to fall safely and pick themselves up lightly, to shove and grapple and twist, to endure throttling, and to heave an adversary off his legs. *Their* acquirements are not unserviceable either; the one great thing they gain is beyond dispute; their bodies are hardened and strengthened by this rough treatment. Add another advantage of some importance: it is all so much practice against the day of battle. Obviously a man thus trained, when he meets a real enemy, will grapple and throw him the quicker, or if he falls will know better how to get up again. All through we are reckoning with that real test in arms; we expect much better results from our material if we supple and exercise their bodies before the armour goes on, so increasing their strength and efficiency, making them light and wiry in themselves (though the enemy will rather be impressed with their weight).

You see how it will act. Something may surely be expected from those in arms who even without them would be considered awkward customers; they show no inert pasty masses of flesh, no cadaverous skinniness, they are not shade-blighted women; they do not quiver and run with sweat at the least exertion, and pant under their helmets as soon as a midday sun like this adds to the burden. What would be the use of creatures who should be overpowered by thirst and dust, unnerved at sight of blood, and as good as dead before they came within bow-shot or spear-thrust of the enemy? But our fellows are ruddy and sunburnt and steady-eyed, there is spirit and fire and virility in their looks, they are in prime condition, neither shrunken and withered nor running to corpulence, but well and truly proportioned; the waste superfluity of their tissues they have sweated out; the stuff that gives strength and activity, purged from all inferior admixture, remains part of their substance. The winnowing fan has its counterpart in our gymnastics, which blow away chaff and husks, and sift and collect the clean grain.

The inevitable result is sound health and great capacity of enduring fatigue. A man like this does not sweat for a trifle, and seldom shows signs of distress. Returning to my winnowing simile— if you were to set fire on the one hand to pure wheat grain, and on the other to its chaff and straw, the latter would surely blaze up much the quicker; the grain would burn only gradually, without a blaze and not all at once; it would smoulder slowly and take much longer to consume. Well, disease or fatigue being similarly applied to this sort of body will not easily find weak spots, nor get the mastery of it lightly. Its interior is in good order, its exterior strongly fortified against such assaults, so that it gives neither admission nor entertainment to the destroying agencies of sun or frost. To any place that begins to weaken under toil comes an accession from the abundant internal heat collected and stored up against the day of need; it fills the vacancy, restores the vital force, and lengthens endurance to the utmost. Past exertion means not dissipation but increase of force, which can be fanned into fresh life.

Further, we accustom them to running, both of the long distance and of the sprinting kind. And they have to run not on hard ground with a good footing, but in deep sand on which you can neither tread firmly nor get a good push off, the foot sinking in. Then, to fit them to leap a trench or other obstacle, we make them practise with leaden dumb-bells in their hands. And again there are distance matches with the javelin. Yes, and you saw in the gymnasium a bronze disk like a small buckler, but without handle or straps; you tried it as it lay there, and found it heavy and, owing to its smooth surface, hard to handle. Well, that they hurl upwards and forwards, trying who can get furthest and outdo his competitors—an exercise that strengthens the shoulders and braces the fingers and toes.

As to the clay and dust that first moved your laughter, I will tell you now why they are provided. In the first place, that a fall may be not on a hard surface, but soft and safe. Secondly, greater slipperiness is secured by sweat and clay combined (you compared them to eels, you remember); now this is neither useless nor absurd, but contributes appreciably to strength and activity. An adversary in that condition must be gripped tightly enough to baffle his attempts at escape. To lift up a man who is all over clay, sweat, and oil, and who is doing his very best to get away and slip through your fingers, is no light task, I assure you. And I repeat that all these things have their military uses too: you may want to take up a wounded friend and convey him out of danger; you may want to heave an enemy over your head and make off with him. So we give them still harder tasks in training, that they may be abundantly equal to the less.

The function we assign to dust is just the reverse, to prevent one who is gripped from getting loose. After learning in the clay to retain their hold on the elusive, they are accustomed in turn to escape themselves even from a firm grasp. Also, we believe the dust forms a plaster that keeps in excessive sweat, prevents waste of power, and obviates the ill effects of the wind playing upon a body when its pores are all relaxed and open. Besides which, it cleanses the skin and makes it glossy. I should like to put side by side one of the white creatures who live sheltered lives and, after washing off his dust and clay, any of the Lyceum frequenters you should select, and then ask you which you would rather resemble. I know you would make your choice at the first glance, without waiting to see what they could do; you would rather be solid and well-knit than delicate and soft and white for want of the blood that had hidden itself away out of sight.

Such are the exercises we prescribe to our young men, Anacharsis; we look to find them good guardians of their country and bulwarks of our freedom; thus we defeat our enemies if they invade us, and so far overawe our immediate neighbours that they mostly acknowledge our supremacy and pay us tribute. During peace also we find our account in their being free from vulgar ambitions and from the insolence generated by idleness; they have these things to fill their lives and occupy their leisure. I told you of a prize that all may win and of a supreme political happiness; these are attained when we find our youth in the highest condition alike for peace and war, intent upon all that is noblest.

An. I see, Solon; when an enemy invades, you anoint yourselves with oil, dust yourselves over, and go forth sparring at them; then they of course cower before you and run away, afraid of getting a handful of your sand in their open mouths, or of your dancing round to get behind them, twining your legs tight round their bellies, and throttling them with your elbows rammed well in under their chinpieces. It is true they will try the effect of arrows and javelins; but you are so sunburnt and full-blooded, the missiles will hurt you no more than if you were statues; you are not chaff and husks; you will not be readily disposed of by the blows you get; much time and attention will be required before you at last, cut to pieces with deep wounds, have a few drops of blood extracted from you. Have I misunderstood your figure, or is this a fair deduction from it?

But perhaps you will take the equipment of your tragedians and comedians, and when you get your marching orders put on those wide- mouthed headpieces, to scare the foe with their appalling terrors; of course, and you can put the stilted things on your feet; they will be light for running away (if that should be advisable), or, if you are in pursuit, the strides they lend themselves to will make your enemy's escape impossible. Seriously now, are not these refinements of yours all child's play—something for your idle, slack youngsters to do? If you really want to be free and happy, you must have other exercises than these; your training must be a genuine martial one; no toy contests with friends, but real ones with enemies; danger must be an element in your character- development. Never mind dust and oil; teach them to use bow and javelin; and none of your light darts diverted by a puff of wind; let it be a ponderous spear that whistles as it flies; to which add stones, a handful each, the axe, the shield, the breastplate, and the helmet.

On your present system, I cannot help thinking you should be very grateful to some God for not having allowed you to perish under the attack of any half-armed band. Why, if I were to draw this little dagger at my girdle and run amuck at your collective youth, I could take the gymnasium without more ado; they would all run away and not dare face the cold steel; they would skip round the statues, hide behind pillars, and whimper and quake till I laughed again. We should have no more of the ruddy frames they now display; they would be another colour then, all white with terror. That is the temper that deep peace has infused into you; you could not endure the sight of a single plume on an enemy's crest.

So. Ah, Anacharsis, the Thracians who invaded us with Eumolpus told another tale; so did your women who assailed Athens with Hippolyta; so every one who has met us in the field. My dear sir, it does not follow from our exercising our youths without arms that we expose them in the same condition to the real thing; the independent bodily development once complete, training in arms follows; and to this they come much the fitter for their previous work.

An. Where is your military gymnasium, then? I have been all over Athens, and seen no sign of it.

So. But if you stay longer you will find that every man has arms enough, for use at the proper time; you will see our plumes and horse-trappings, our horses and horsemen; these last amounting to a quarter of our citizens. But to carry arms and be girded with scimetars we consider unnecessary in peace time; indeed there is a fine for going armed in town without due cause, or producing weapons in public. *You* of course may be pardoned for living in arms. The want of walls gives conspiracy its chance; you have many enemies; you never know when somebody may come upon you in your sleep, pull you out of your cart, and dispatch you. And then, in the mutual distrust inseparable from an independence that recognizes no law or constitution, the sword must be always at hand to repel violence.

An. Oho, you think the wearing of arms, except on occasion, unnecessary; you are careful of your weapons, avoid wear and tear for them, and put them away for use when the time comes; but the bodies of your youth you keep at work even when no danger presses; you knock them about and dissolve them in sweat; instead of husbanding their strength for the day of need, you expend it idly on clay and dust. How is that?

So. I fancy you conceive of force as something similar to wine or water or liquid of some sort. You are afraid of its dribbling away in exercise as those might from an earthenware jar, and by its disappearance leaving the body, which is supposed to have no internal reserves, empty and dry. That is not the case; the greater the drain upon it in the course of exercise, the greater the supply; did you ever hear a story about the Hydra? cut off one of its heads, and two immediately sprang up in its place. No, it is the unexercised and fibreless, in whom no adequate store of material has ever been laid up, that will peak and pine under toil. There is a similar difference between a fire and a lamp; the same breath that kindles the former and soon excites it to greater heat will put out the latter, which is but ill provided to resist the blast; it has a precarious tenure, you see.

An. Ah, I cannot get hold of all that, Solon; it is too subtle for me— wants exact thought and keen intelligence. But I wish you would tell me—at the Olympic, Isthmian, Pythian, and other Games, attended, you tell me, by crowds to see your youth contend, why do you have no martial events? Instead, you put them in a conspicuous place and exhibit them kicking and cuffing one another, and when they win give them apples or wild olive. Now your reason for that would be worth hearing.

So. Well, we think it will increase their keenness for exercise to see the champions at it honoured and proclaimed by name among the assembled Greeks. It is the thought of having to strip before such a crowd that makes them take pains with their condition; they do not want to be a shameful spectacle, so each does his best to deserve success. And the prizes, as I said before, are not small things—to be applauded by the spectators, to be the mark of all eyes and fingers as the best of one's contemporaries. Accordingly, numbers of spectators, not too old for training, depart with a passion thus engendered for toilsome excellence. Ah, Anacharsis, if the love of fair fame were to be wiped out of our lives, what good would remain? Who would care to do a glorious deed? But as things are you may form your conclusions from what you see. These who are so keen for victory when they have no weapons and only a sprig of wild olive or an apple to contend for, how would they behave in martial array, with country and wives and children and altars at stake?

I wonder what your feelings would be if you saw our quail and cock fights, and the excitement they raise. You would laugh, no doubt, especially when you were told that they are enjoined by law, and that all of military age must attend and watch how the birds spar till they are utterly exhausted. And yet it is not a thing to laugh at either; a spirit of contempt for danger is thus instilled into men's souls; shall they yield to cocks in nobility and courage? shall they let wounds or weariness or discomfort incapacitate them before there is need? But as for testing our men in arms and looking on while they gash one another, no, thank you! that would be brutality and savagery, besides the bad policy of butchering our bravest, who would serve us best against our enemies.

You say you are going to visit the rest of Greece also. Well, if you go to Sparta, remember not to laugh at them either, nor think their labour is all in vain, when they charge and strike one another over a ball in the theatre; or perhaps they will go into a place enclosed by water, divide into two troops, and handle one another as severely as enemies (except that they too have no arms), until the Lycurgites drive the Heraclids, or vice versa, out of the enclosure and into the water; it is all over then; not another blow breaks the peace. Still worse, you may see them being scourged at the altar, streaming with blood, while their parents look on—the mothers, far from being distressed by the sight, actually making them hold out with threats, imploring them to endure pain to the last extremity and not be unmanned by suffering. There are many instances of their dying under the trial; while they had life and their people's eyes were on them, they would not give up, nor concede anything to bodily pain; and you will find their statues there, set up *honoris causa* by the Spartan state. Seeing these things, never take them for madmen, nor say that, since it is neither a tyrant's bidding nor a conqueror's ordinance, they victimize themselves for no good reason. Lycurgus their lawgiver would have many reasonable remarks to make to you on the subject, and give you his grounds for thus afflicting them; he was not moved by enmity or hatred; he was not wasting the state's young blood for nothing; he only thought it proper that defenders of their country should have endurance in the highest degree and be entirely superior to fear. However, you need no Lycurgus to tell you; you can surely see for yourself that, if one of these men were captured in war, no tortures would wring a Spartan secret out of him; he would take his scourging with a smile, and try whether the scourger would not be tired sooner than the scourged.

An. Solon, did Lycurgus take his whippings at the fighting age, or did he make these spirited regulations on the safe basis of superannuation?

So. It was in his old age, after returning from Crete, that he legislated. He had been attracted to Crete by hearing that their laws were the best possible, devised by Minos, son of Zeus.

An. Well, and why did you not copy Lycurgus and whip your young men? It is a fine institution quite worthy of yourselves.

So. Oh, we were content with our native exercises; we are not much given to imitating other nations.

An. No, no; you realize what a thing it is to be stripped and scourged with one's hands up, without benefit to oneself or one's country. If I do happen to be at Sparta when this performance is on, I shall expect a public stoning at their hands for laughing at it all, when I see them being whipped like robbers or thieves or such malefactors. Really, I think a state that submits to such ridiculous treatment at its own hands wants a dose of hellebore.

So. Friend, do not plume yourself on winning an undefended case where you have it all your own way in the absence of your opponents. In Sparta you will find some one to plead properly for their customs. But now, as I have described ours to you, not apparently to your satisfaction, I may fairly ask you to take your turn and tell me how you train your youth in Scythia; what exercises do you bring them up in? how do you make good men of them?

An. Quite a fair demand, Solon; I will give you the Scythian customs; there is no grandeur about them; they are not much like yours; for we would never take a single box on the ears, we are such cowards; but such as they are, you shall have them. We must put off our talk till to-morrow, though, if you do not mind; I want to think quietly over what you have said, and collect materials for what I am to say myself. On that understanding let us go home; for it is getting late.

OF MOURNING

The behaviour of the average man in a time of bereavement, his own language and the remarks offered him by way of consolation, are things that will reward the attention of a curious observer. The mourner takes it for granted that a terrible blow has fallen both upon himself and upon the object of his lamentations: yet for all he knows to the contrary (and here I appeal to Pluto and Persephone) the departed one, so far from being entitled to commiseration, may find himself in improved circumstances. The feelings of the bereaved party are in fact guided solely by custom and convention. The procedure in such cases—but no: let me first state the popular beliefs on the subject of death itself; we shall then understand the motives for the elaborate ceremonial with which it is attended.

The vulgar (as philosophers call the generality of mankind), implicitly taking as their text-book the fictions of Homer and Hesiod and other poets, assume the existence of a deep subterranean hole called Hades; spacious, murky, and sunless, but by some mysterious means sufficiently lighted to render all its details visible. Its king is a brother of Zeus, one Pluto; whose name—so an able philologer assures me—contains a complimentary allusion to his ghostly wealth. As to the nature of his government, and the condition of his subjects, the authority allotted to him extends over all the dead, who, from the moment that they come under his control, are kept in unbreakable fetters; Shades are on no account permitted to return to Earth; to this rule there have been only two or three exceptions since the beginning of the world, and these were made for very urgent reasons. His realm is encompassed by vast rivers, whose very names inspire awe: Cocytus, Pyriphlegethon, and the like. Most formidable of all, and first to arrest the progress of the new-comer, is Acheron, that lake which none may pass save by the ferryman's boat; it is too deep to be waded, too broad for the swimmer, and even defies the flight of birds deceased. At the very beginning of the descent is a gate of adamant: here Aeacus, a nephew of the king, stands on guard. By his side is a three-headed dog, a grim brute; to new arrivals, however, he is friendly enough, reserving his bark, and the yawning horror of his jaws, for the would-be runaway. On the inner shore of the lake is a meadow, wherein grows asphodel; here, too, is the fountain that makes war on memory, and is hence called Lethe. All these particulars the ancients would doubtless obtain from the Thessalian queen Alcestis and her fellow-countryman Protesilaus, from Theseus the son of Aegeus, and from the hero of the Odyssey. These witnesses (whose evidence is entitled to our most respectful acceptance) did not, as I gather, drink of the waters of Lethe; because then they would not have remembered. According to them, the supreme power is entirely in the hands of Pluto and Persephone, who, however, are assisted in the labours of government by a host of underlings: such are the Furies, the Pains, the Fears; such too is Hermes, though he is not always in attendance. Judicial powers are vested in two satraps or viceroys, Minos and Rhadamanthus, both Cretans, and both sons of Zeus. By them all good and just men who have followed the precepts of virtue are sent off in large detachments to form colonies, as it were, in the Elysian Plain, and there to lead the perfect life. Evil-doers, on the contrary, are handed over to the Furies, who conduct them to the place of the wicked, where they are punished in due proportion to their iniquities. What a variety of torments is there presented! The rack, the fire, the gnawing vulture; here Ixion spins upon his wheel, there Sisyphus rolls his stone. I have not forgotten Tantalus; but he stands elsewhere, stands parched on the Lake's very brink, like to die of thirst, poor wretch! Then there is the numerous class of neutral characters; these wander about the meadow; formless phantoms, that evade the touch like smoke. It seems that they depend for their nourishment upon the libations and victims offered by us upon their tombs; accordingly, a Shade who has no surviving friends or relations passes a hungry time of it in the lower world.

So profoundly have the common people been impressed with these doctrines that, when a man dies, the first act of his relations is to put a penny into his mouth, that he may have wherewithal to pay the ferryman: they do not stop to inquire what is the local currency, whether Attic or Macedonian or Aeginetan; nor does it occur to them how much better it would be for the departed one if the fare were not forthcoming, —because then the ferryman would decline to take him, and he would be sent back into the living world. Lest the Stygian Lake should prove inadequate to the requirements of ghostly toilets, the corpse is next washed, anointed with the choicest unguents to arrest the progress of decay, crowned with fresh flowers, and laid out in sumptuous raiment; an obvious precaution, this last; it would not do for the deceased to take a chill on the journey, nor to exhibit himself to Cerberus with nothing on. Lamentation follows. The women wail; men and women alike weep and beat their breasts and rend their hair and lacerate their cheeks; clothes are also torn on the occasion, and dust sprinkled on the head.

The survivors are thus reduced to a more pitiable condition than the deceased: while they in all probability are rolling about and dashing their heads on the ground, he, bravely attired and gloriously garlanded, reposes gracefully upon his lofty bier, adorned as it were for some pageant. The mother—nay, it is the father, as likely as not, —now advances from among the relatives, falls upon the bier (to heighten the dramatic effect, we will suppose its occupant to be young and handsome), and utters wild and meaningless ejaculations; the corpse cannot speak, otherwise it might have something to say in reply. His son—the father exclaims, with a mournful emphasis on every word, —his beloved son is no more; he is gone; torn away before his hour was come, leaving him alone to mourn; he has never married, never begotten children, never been on the field of battle, never laid hand to the plough, never reached old age; never again will he make merry, never again know the joys of love, never, alas! tipple at the convivial board among his comrades. And so on, and so on. He imagines his son to be still coveting these things, and coveting them in vain. But this is nothing: time after time men have been known to slaughter horses upon the tomb, and concubines and pages; to burn clothes and other finery, or bury it, in the idea that the deceased will find a profitable use for such things in the lower world. Now the afflicted senior, in delivering the tragic utterances I have suggested above, and others of the same kind, is not, as I understand it, consulting the interests of his son (who he knows will not hear him, though he shout louder than Stentor), nor yet his own; he is perfectly aware of his sentiments, and has no occasion to bellow them into his own ear. The natural conclusion is, that this tomfoolery is for the benefit of the spectators; and all the time he has not an idea where his son is, or what may be his condition; he cannot even have reflected upon human life generally, or he would know that the loss of it is no such great matter. Let us imagine that the son has obtained leave from Aeacus and Pluto to take a peep into the daylight, and put a stop to these parental maunderings. 'Confound it, sir, ' he might exclaim, 'what is the noise about? You bore me. Enough of hair-plucking and face- scratching. When you call me an ill-fated wretch, you abuse a better man than yourself, and a more fortunate. Why are you so sorry for me? Is it because I am not a bald, bent, wrinkled old cripple like yourself? Is it because I have not lived to be a battered wreck, nor seen a thousand moons wax and wane, only to make a fool of myself at the last before a crowd? Can your sapience point to any single convenience of life, of which we are deprived in the lower world? I know what you will say: clothes and good dinners, wine and women, without which you think I shall be inconsolable. Are you now to learn that freedom from hunger and thirst is better than meat and drink, and insensibility to cold better than plenty of clothes? Come, I see you need enlightenment; I will show you how lamentation ought to be done. Make a fresh start, thus: Alas, my son! Hunger and thirst and cold are his no longer! He is gone, gone beyond the reach of sickness; he fears not fever any more, nor enemies nor tyrants. Never again, my son, shall love disturb your peace, impair your health, make hourly inroads on your purse; oh, heavy change! Never can you reach contemptible old age, never be an eyesore to your juniors! —Confess, now, that my lamentation has the advantage of yours, in veracity, as in absurdity.

'Perhaps it is the pitchy darkness of the infernal regions that runs in your head? is that the trouble? Are you afraid I shall be suffocated in the confinement of the tomb? You should reflect that my eyes will presently decay, or (if such is your good pleasure) be consumed with fire; after which I shall have no occasion to notice either light or darkness. However, let that pass. But all this lamentation, now; this fluting and beating of breasts; these wholly disproportionate wailings: how am I the better for it all? And what do I want with a garlanded column over my grave? And what good do you suppose you are going to do by pouring wine on it? do you expect it to filter through all the way to Hades? As to the victims, you must surely see for yourselves that all the solid nutriment is whisked away heavenwards in the form of smoke, leaving us Shades precisely as we were; the residue, being dust, is useless; or is it your theory that Shades batten on ashes? Pluto's realm is not so barren, nor asphodel so scarce with us, that we must apply to you for provisions. —What with this winding-sheet and these woollen bandages, my jaws have been effectually sealed up, or, by Tisiphone, I should have burst out laughing long before this at the stuff you talk and the things you do.'

And at the word Death sealed his lips for ever.

Thus far our corpse, leaning on one side, supported on an elbow. Can we doubt that he is in the right of it? And yet these simpletons, not content with their own noise, must call in professional assistance: an artist in grief, with a fine repertoire of cut-and-dried sorrows at his command, assumes the direction of this inane choir, and supplies a theme for their woful acclamations. So far, all men are fools alike: but at this point national peculiarities make their appearance. The Greeks burn their dead, the Persians bury them; the Indian glazes the body, the Scythian eats it, the Egyptian embalms it. In Egypt, indeed, the corpse, duly dried, is actually placed at table, —I have seen it done; and it is quite a common thing for an Egyptian to relieve himself from pecuniary embarrassment by a timely visit to the pawnbroker, with his brother or father deceased. The childish futility of pyramids and mounds and columns, with their short-lived inscriptions, is obvious. But some people go further, and attempt to plead the cause of the deceased with his infernal judges, or testify to his merits, by means of funeral games and laudatory epitaphs. The final absurdity is the funeral feast, at which the assembled relatives strive to console the parents, and to prevail upon them to take food; and, Heaven knows, they are willing enough to be persuaded, being almost prostrated by a three days' fast. 'How long is this to go on? ' some one expostulates. 'Suffer the spirit of your departed saint to rest in peace. Or if mourn you will, then for that very reason you must eat, that your strength may be proportioned to your grief. ' At this point, a couple of lines of Homer go the round of the company:

Ev'n fair-haired Niobe forgat not food,

and

Not fasting mourn th' Achaeans for their dead.

The parents are persuaded, though they go to work at first in a somewhat shamefaced manner; they do not want it to be thought that after their bereavement they are still subject to the infirmities of the flesh.

Such are some of the absurdities that may be observed in mourners; for I have by no means exhausted the list. And all springs from the vulgar error, that Death is the worst thing that can befall a man.

THE RHETORICIAN'S VADE MECUM

See note at end of piece.

You ask, young man, how you may become a rhetorician, and win yourself the imposing and reverend style of Professor. You tell me life is for you not worth living, if you cannot clothe yourself in that power of the word which shall make you invincible and irresistible, the cynosure of all men's admiration, the desired of all Grecian ears. Your one wish is to be shown the way to that goal. And small blame, youngster, to one who in the days of his youth sets his gaze upon the things that are highest, and knowing not how he shall attain, comes as you now come to me with the privileged demand for counsel. Take then the best of it that I can give, doubting nothing but you shall speedily be a man accomplished to see the right and to give it expression, if you will henceforth abide by what you now hear from me, practise it with assiduity, and go confidently on your way till it brings you to the desired end.

The object of your pursuit is no poor one, worth but a moderate endeavour; to grasp it you might be content to toil and watch and endure to the utmost; mark how many they are who once were but cyphers, but whom words have raised to fame and opulence, ay, and to noble lineage.

Yet fear not, nor be appalled, when you contemplate the greatness of your aim, by thought of the thousand toils first to be accomplished. It is by no rough mountainous perspiring track that I shall lead you; else were I no better than those other guides who point you to the common way, long, steep, toilsome, nay, for the most part desperate. What should commend my counsel to you is even this: a road most pleasant and most brief, a carriage road of downward slope, shall bring you in all delight and ease, at what leisurely effortless pace you will, through flowery meadows and plenteous shade, to that summit which you shall mount and hold untired and there lie feasting, the while you survey from your height those panting ones who took the other track; they are yet in the first stage of their climb, forcing their slow way amid rough or slippery crags, with many a headlong fall and many a wound from those sharp rocks. But you will long have been up, and garlanded and blest; you have slept, and waked to find that Rhetoric has lavished upon you all her gifts at once.

Fine promises, these, are they not? But pray let it not stir your doubts, that I offer to make most easy that which is most sweet. It was but plucking a few leaves from Helicon, and the shepherd Hesiod was a poet, possessed of the Muses and singing the birth of Gods and Heroes; and may not a rhetorician ('tis no such proud title as that of poet) be quickly made, if one but knows the speediest way?

Let me tell you of an idea that came to nothing for want of faith, and brought no profit to the man it was offered to. Alexander had fought Arbela, deposed Darius, and was lord of Persia; his orders had to be conveyed to every part of his empire by dispatch-runners. Now from Persia to Egypt was a long journey; to make the necessary circuit round the mountains, cross Babylonia into Arabia, traverse a great desert, and so finally reach Egypt, took at the best full twenty days. And as Alexander had intelligence of disturbances in Egypt, it was an inconvenience not to be able to send instructions rapidly to his lieutenants there. A Sidonian trader came to him and offered to shorten the distance: if a man cut straight across the mountains, which could be done in three days, he would be in Egypt without more ado. This was a fact; but Alexander took the man for an impostor, and would have nothing to say to him. That is the reception any surprisingly good offer may expect from most men.

Be not like them. A trial will soon show you that you may fly over the mountains from Persia to Egypt, and in a day, in part of a day, take rank as rhetorician. But first I will be your Cebes and give you word-pictures of the two different ways leading to that Rhetoric, with which I see you so in love. Imagine her seated on a height, fair and comely; her right hand holds an Amalthea's horn heaped high with all fruits, and at her other side you are to see Wealth standing in all his golden glamour. In attendance too are Repute and Might; and all about your lady's person flutter and cling embodied Praises like tiny Loves. Or you may have seen a painted Nilus; he reclines himself upon a crocodile or hippopotamus, with which his stream abounds, and round him play the tiny children they call in Egypt his *Cubits*; so play the Praises about Rhetoric. Add yourself, the lover, who long to be straightway at the top, that you may wed her, and all that is hers be yours; for him that weds her she must endow with her worldly goods.

When you have reached the mountain, you at first despair of scaling it; you seem to have set yourself the task that Aornus [Footnote: i.e., birdless.] presented to the Macedonians; how sheer it was on every side! it was true, they thought, even a bird could hardly soar that height; to take it would be work for a Dionysus or Heracles. Then in a little while you discern two roads; or no, one is no more than a track, narrow, thorny, rough, promising thirst and sweat. But I need say no more of it; Hesiod has described it long ago The other is broad, and fringed with flowers and well watered and—not to keep you back with vain repetitions from the prize even now within your grasp—such a road as I told you of but now.

This much, however, I must add: that rough steep way shows not many steps of travellers; a few there are, but of ancient date. It was my own ill fortune to go up by it, expending needless toil; but I could see from far off how level and direct was that other, though I did not use it; in my young days I was perverse, and put trust in the poet who told me that the Good is won by toil. He was in error; I see that the many who toil not are more richly rewarded for their fortunate choice of route and method. But the question is now of you; I know that when you come to the parting of the ways you will doubt—you doubt even now—which turn to take. What you must do, then, to find the easiest ascent, and blessedness, and your bride, and universal fame, I will tell you. Enough that *I* have been cheated into toil; for you let all grow unsown and unploughed as in the age of gold.

A strong severe-looking man will at once come up to you; he has a firm step, a deeply sunburnt body, a decided eye and wide-awake air; it is the guide of the rough track. This absurd person makes foolish suggestions that you should employ him, and points you out the footmarks of Demosthenes, Plato, and others; they are larger than what we make, but mostly half obliterated by time; he tells you you will attain bliss and have Rhetoric to your lawful wife, if you stick as closely to these as a rope-walker to his rope; but diverge for a moment, make a false step, or incline your weight too much either way, and farewell to your path and your bride. He will exhort you to imitate these ancients, and offer you antiquated models that lend themselves as little to imitation as old sculpture, say the clean-cut, sinewy, hard, firmly outlined productions of Hegesias, or the school of Critius and Nesiotes; and he will tell you that toil and vigilance, abstinence and perseverance, are indispensable, if you would accomplish your journey. Most mortifying of all, the time he will stipulate for is immense, years upon years; he does not so much as mention days or months; whole Olympiads are his units; you feel tired at the mere sound of them, and ready to relinquish the happiness you had set your heart upon. And as if this was not enough, he wishes to be paid handsomely for your trouble, and must have a good sum down before he will even put you in the way.

So he will talk—a conceited primitive old-world personage; for models he offers you old masters long dead and done with, and expects you to exhume rusty speeches as if they were buried treasures; you are to copy a certain cutler's son [Footnote: Demosthenes.] or one who called the clerk Atrometus father [Footnote: Aeschines.]; he forgets that we are at peace now, with no invading Philip or hectoring Alexander to give a temporary value to that sort of eloquence; and he has never heard of our new road to Rhetoric, short, easy, and direct. Let him not prevail with you; heed not him at all; in his charge, if you do not first break your neck, you will wear yourself into a premature old age. If you are really in love, and would enjoy Rhetoric before your prime is past, and be made much of by her, dismiss this hairy specimen of ultra- virility, and leave him to climb by himself or with what dupes he can make, panting and perspiring to his heart's content.

Go you to the other road, where you will find much good company, but in especial one man. Is he clever? is he engaging? Mark the negligent ease of his gait, his neck's willowy curve, his languishing glance; these words are honey, that breath perfume; was ever head scratched with so graceful a forefinger? and those locks —were there but more of them left—how hyacinthine their wavy order! he is tender as Sardanapalus or Cinyras; 'tis Agathon's self, loveliest of tragedy-makers. Take these traits, that seeing you may know him; I would not have you miss so divine an apparition, the darling of Aphrodite and the Graces. Yet how needless! were he to come near while your eyes were closed, and unbar those Hymettian lips to the voice that dwells within, you could not want the thought that this was none of us who munch the fruits of earth, but some spirit from afar that on honeydew hath fed, and drunk the milk of Paradise. Him seek; trust yourself to him, and you shall be in a trice rhetorician and man of note, and in his own great phrase, King of Words, mounted without an effort of your own upon the chariot of discourse. For here is the lore he shall impart to his disciple.

But let him describe it himself. For one so eloquent it is absurd that I should speak; my histrionic talent is not equal to so mighty a task; I might trip, and break the heroic mask in my fall. He thus addresses you, then, with a touch of the hand to those scanty curls, and the usual charming delicate smile; you might take him— so engaging is his utterance—for a Glycera, a Malthace, or her comic and meretricious majesty, Thais herself. What has a refined bewitching orator to do with the vulgar masculine?

Listen now to his modest remarks. Dear sir, was it Apollo sent you here? did he call me best of rhetoricians, as when Chaerephon asked and was told who was wisest of his generation? If it has not been so, if you have come directed only by the amazement and applause, the wonder and despair, that attend my achievements, then shall you soon learn whether there is divinity or no in him whom you have sought. Look not for a greatness that may find its parallel in this man or that; a Tityus, an Otus, an Ephialtes there may have been; but here is a portent and a marvel greater far than they. You are to hear a voice that puts to silence all others, as the trumpet the flute, as the cicala the bee, as the choir the tuning-fork.

But you wish to be a rhetorician yourself; well, you could have applied in no better quarter; my dear young friend, you have only to follow my instructions and example, and keep carefully in mind the rules I lay down for your guidance. Indeed you may start this moment without a tremor; never let it disturb you that you have not been through the laborious preliminaries with which the ordinary system besets the path of fools; they are quite unnecessary. Stay not to find your slippers, as the song has it; your naked feet will do as well; writing is a not uncommon accomplishment, but I do not insist upon it; it is one thing, and rhetoric is another.

I will first give you a list of the equipment and supplies for your journey that you must bring with you from home, with a view to making your way rapidly. After that, I will show you as we go along some practical illustrations, add a few verbal precepts, and before set of sun you shall be as superior a rhetorician as myself, the absolute microcosm of your profession. Bring then above all ignorance, to which add confidence, audacity, and effrontery; as for diffidence, equity, moderation, and shame, you will please leave them at home; they are not merely needless, they are encumbrances. The loudest voice you can come by, please, a ready falsetto, and a gait modelled on my own. That exhausts the real necessaries; very often there would be no occasion for anything further. But I recommend bright colours or white for your clothes; the Tarentine stuff that lets the body show through is best; for shoes, wear either the Attic woman's shape with the open network, or else the Sicyonians that show white lining. Always have a train of attendants, and a book in your hand.

The rest you will take in with your eyes and ears as we go. I will tell you the rules you must observe, if Rhetoric is to recognize and admit you; otherwise she will turn from you and drive you away as an uninitiated intruder upon her mysteries. You must first be exceedingly careful about your appearance; your clothes must be quite the thing. Next, you must scrape up some fifteen old Attic words—say twenty for an outside estimate; and these you must rehearse diligently till you have them at the tip of your tongue; let us say *sundry, whereupon, say you so, in some wise, my masters;* that is the sort of thing; these are for general garnish, you understand; and you need not concern yourself about any little dissimilarity, repulsion, discord, between them and the rest; so long as your upper garment is fair and bright, what matter if there is coarse serge beneath it?

Next, fill your quiver with queer mysterious words used once or twice by the ancients, ready to be discharged at a moment's notice in conversation. This will attract the attention of the common herd, who will take you for a wonder, so much better educated than themselves. Put on your clothes? of course not; *invest yourself.* Will you sit in the porch, when there is a *parvys* to hand? No earnest-money for us; let it be an *arles-penny.* And no breakfast-time, pray, but *undern.* You may also do a little word-formation of your own on occasion, and enact that a person good, at exposition shall be known as a *clarifier,* a sensible one as a *cogitant,* or a pantomime as a *manuactor.* If you commit a blunder or provincialism, you have only to carry it off boldly with an instant reference to the authority of some poet or historian, who need not exist or ever have existed; your phrase has his approval, and he was a wise man and a past master in language. As for your reading, leave the ancients alone; never mind a foolish Isocrates, a tasteless Demosthenes, a frigid Plato; study the works of the last generation; you will find the declamations, as they call them, a plenteous store on which to draw at need.

When the time comes for you to perform, and the audience have proposed subjects and invented cases for discussion, you should get rid of the difficult ones by calling them trivial, and complain that there is nothing in this selection that can really test a man's powers. When they have chosen, do not hesitate a moment, but start; the tongue is an unruly member; do not attempt to rule it; never care whether your firstly is logics firstly, or your secondly and thirdly in the right order; just say what comes; you may greave your head and helmet your legs, but whatever you do, move, keep going, never pause. If your subject is assault or adultery in Athens, cite the Indians and Medes. Always have your Marathon and your Cynaegirus handy; they are indispensable. Hardly less so are a fleet crossing Mount Athos, an army treading the Hellespont, a sun eclipsed by Persian arrows, a flying Xerxes, an admired Leonidas, an inscriptive Othryades. Salamis, Artemisium, and Plataea, should also be in constant use. All this dressed as usual with our seasoning-garnish aforesaid—that persuasive flavour of *sundry* and *methinks*; do not wait till these seem to be called for; they are pretty words, quite apart from their relevancy.

If a fancy for impassioned *recitative* comes over you, indulge it as long as you will, and air your falsetto. If your matter is not of the right poetic sort, you may consider yourself to have met the requirements if you run over the names of the jury in a rhythmic manner. Appeal constantly to the pathetic instinct, smite your thigh, mouth your words well, punctuate with loud sighs, and let your very back be eloquent as you pace to and fro. If the audience fails to applaud, take offence, and give your offence words; if they get up and prepare to go out in disgust, tell them to sit down again; discipline must be maintained.

It will win you credit for copiousness, if you start with the Trojan War—you may if you like go right hack to the nuptials of Deucalion and Pyrrha—and thence trace your subject down to to-day. People of sense, remember, are rare, and they will probably hold their tongues out of charity; or if they do comment, it will be put down to jealousy. The rest are awed by your costume, your voice, gait, motions, falsetto, shoes, and *sundry*; when they see how you perspire and pant, they cannot admit a moment's doubt of your being a very fine rhetorical performer. With them, your mere rapidity is a miracle quite sufficient to establish your character. Never prepare notes, then, nor think out a subject beforehand; that shows one up at once.

Your friends' feet will be loud on the floor, in payment for the dinners you give them; if they observe you in difficulties, they will come to the rescue, and give you a chance, in the relief afforded by rounds of applause, of thinking how to go on. A devoted *claque* of your own, by the way, is among your requirements. Its use while you are performing I have given; and as you walk home afterwards, discussing the points you made, you should be absolutely surrounded by them as a bodyguard. If you meet acquaintances on the way, talk very big about yourself, put a good value on your merits, and never mind about their feelings. Ask them, Where is Demosthenes now? Or wonder *which* of the ancients comes nearest you.

But dear me, I had very nearly passed over the most important and effectual of all aids to reputation: the pouring of ridicule upon your rivals. If a man has a fine style, its beauties are borrowed; if a sober one, it is bad altogether. When you go to a recitation, arrive late, which makes you conspicuous; and when all are listening intently, interject some inappropriate commendation that will distract and annoy the audience; they will be so sickened with your offensive words that they cannot listen. And then do not wave your hand too much—warm approval is rather low; and as to jumping up, never do it more than once or twice. A slight smile is your best expression; make it clear that you do not think much of the thing. Only let your ears be critical, and you are sure of finding plenty to condemn. In fact, all the qualities needed are easily come by—audacity, effrontery, ready lying, indifference to perjury, impartial jealousy, hatred, abuse, and skilful slander— that is all you want to win you speedy credit and renown. So much for your visible public life.

And in private you need draw the line at nothing, gambling, drink, fornication, nor adultery; the last you should boast of, whether truly or not; make no secret of it, but exhibit your notes from real or imaginary frail ones. One of your aims should be to pass for a pretty fellow, in much favour with the ladies; the report will be professionally useful to you, your influence with the sex being accounted for by your rhetorical eminence.

Master these instructions, young man—they are surely simple enough not to overtax your powers—, and I confidently promise that you shall soon be a first-class rhetorician like myself; after which I need not tell you what great and what rapid advancement Rhetoric will put in your way. You have but to look at me. My father was an obscure person barely above a slave; he had in fact been one south of Xois and Thmuis; my mother a common sempstress. I was myself not without pretensions to beauty in my youth, which earned me a bare living from a miserly ill-conditioned admirer; but I discovered this easy short-cut, made my way to the top—for I had, if I may be bold to say it, all the qualifications I told you of, confidence, ignorance, and effrontery—, and at once found myself in a position to change my name of Pothinus to one that levels me with the children of Zeus and Leda. I then established myself in an old dame's house, where I earned my keep by professing a passion for her seventy years and her half-dozen remaining teeth, dentist's gold and all. However, poverty reconciled me to my task; even for those cold coffin kisses, *fames* was *condimentum optimum*. And it was by the merest ill luck that I missed inheriting her wealth—that damned slave who peached about the poison I had bought!

I was turned out neck and crop, but even so I did not starve. I have my professional position and am well known in the courts— especially for collusion and the corruption-agency which I keep for credulous litigants. My cases generally go against me; but the palms at my door [Transcriber's Note: Lengthy footnote relocated to chapter end.] are fresh and flower-crowned—springes to catch woodcocks, you know. Then, to be the object of universal detestation, to be distinguished only less for the badness of one's character than for that of one's speeches, to be pointed at by every finger as the famous champion of all-round villany—this seems to me no inconsiderable attainment. And now you have my advice; take it with the blessing of the great Goddess Lubricity. It is the same that I gave myself long ago; and very thankful I have been to myself for it.

Ah! our admirable friend seems to have done. If you decide to take his advice, you may regard yourself as practically arrived at your goal. Keep his rules, and your path is clear; you may dominate the courts, triumph in the lecture-room, be smiled on by the fair; your bride shall be not, like your lawgiver and teacher's, an old woman off the comic stage, but lovely dame Rhetoric. Plato told of Zeus sweeping on in his winged car; you shall use the figure as fitly of yourself. And I? why, I lack spirit and courage; I will stand out of your way. I will resign—nay, I have resigned—my high place about our lady's person to you; for I cannot pay my court to her like the new school. Do your walk over, then, hear your name announced, take your plaudits; I ask you only to remember that you owe the victory not to your speed, but to your discovery of the easy down-hill route.

[Note at end of piece: It is apparent from the later half of this piece that the satire is aimed at an individual. He is generally identified with Julius Pollux. This Pollux (1) was contemporary (floruit A. D. 183) with Lucian. (2) Explains by his name the reference to Leda's children (Castor and Pollux) in Section 24. (3) Published an Onomasticon, or classified vocabulary; cf. Sections 16, 17. (4) Published a collection of declamations, or school rhetorical exercises on set themes; cf. Section 17. (5) Came from Egypt; cf. Section 24; Xois and Thmuis were in that country. (6) Is said to have been appointed professor of rhetoric at Athens by Commodus purely on account of his mellifluous voice; cf. Section 19.

It is supposed that *Lexiphanes* (in the dialogue of that name, which has much in common with the present satire) is also Julius Pollux.]

[Relocated Footnote:

Now stretch your throat, unhappy man! now raise
Your clamours, that, when hoarse, a bunch of bays,
Stuck in your garret window, may declare,
That some victorious pleader nestles there.

Juvenal, vii. 118 (Gifford).]

THE LIAR

Tychiades. Philocles

Tyc. Philocles, what *is* it that makes most men so fond of a lie? Can you explain it? Their delight in romancing themselves is only equalled by the earnest attention with which they receive other people's efforts in the same direction.

Phi. Why, in some cases there is no lack of motives for lying, — motives of self-interest.

Tyc. Ah, but that is neither here nor there. I am not speaking of men who lie with an object. There is some excuse for that: indeed, it is sometimes to their credit, when they deceive their country's enemies, for instance, or when mendacity is but the medicine to heal their sickness. Odysseus, seeking to preserve his life and bring his companions safe home, was a liar of that kind. The men I mean are innocent of any ulterior motive: they prefer a lie to truth, simply on its own merits; they like lying, it is their favourite occupation; there is no necessity in the case. Now what good can they get out of it?

Phi. Why, have you ever known any one with such a strong natural turn for lying?

Tyc. Any number of them.

Phi. Then I can only say they must be fools, if they really prefer evil to good.

Tyc. Oh, that is not it. I could point you out plenty of men of first-rate ability, sensible enough in all other respects, who have somehow picked up this vice of romancing. It makes me quite angry: what satisfaction can there be to men of their good qualities in deceiving themselves and their neighbours? There are instances among the ancients with which you must be more familiar than I. Look at Herodotus, or Ctesias of Cnidus; or, to go further back, take the poets—Homer himself: here are men of world-wide celebrity, perpetuating their mendacity in black and white; not content with deceiving their hearers, they must send their lies down to posterity, under the protection of the most admirable verse. Many a time I have blushed for them, as I read of the mutilation of Uranus, the fetters of Prometheus, the revolt of the Giants, the torments of Hell; enamoured Zeus taking the shape of bull or swan; women turning into birds and bears; Pegasuses, Chimaeras, Gorgons, Cyclopes, and the rest of it; monstrous medley! fit only to charm the imaginations of children for whom Mormo and Lamia have still their terrors. However, poets, I suppose, will be poets. But when it comes to national lies, when one finds whole cities bouncing collectively like one man, how is one to keep one's countenance? A Cretan will look you in the face, and tell you that yonder is Zeus's tomb. In Athens, you are informed that Erichthonius sprang out of the Earth, and that the first Athenians grew up from the soil like so many cabbages; and this story assumes quite a sober aspect when compared with that of the Sparti, for whom the Thebans claim descent from a dragon's teeth. If you presume to doubt these stories, if you choose to exert your common sense, and leave Triptolemus's winged aerial car, and Pan's Marathonian exploits, and Orithyia's mishap, to the stronger digestions of a Coroebus and a Margites, you are a fool and a blasphemer, for questioning such palpable truths. Such is the power of lies!

Phi. I must say I think there is some excuse, Tychiades, both for your national liars and for the poets. The latter are quite right in throwing in a little mythology: it has a very pleasing effect, and is just the thing to secure the attention of their hearers. On the other hand, the Athenians and the Thebans and the rest are only trying to add to the lustre of their respective cities. Take away the legendary treasures of Greece, and you condemn the whole race of ciceroni to starvation: sightseers do not want the truth; they would not take it at a gift. However, I surrender to your ridicule any one who has no such motive, and yet rejoices in lies.

Tyc. Very well: now I have just been with the great Eucrates, who treated me to a whole string of old wives' tales. I came away in the middle of it; he was too much for me altogether; Furies could not have driven me out more effectually than his marvel-working tongue.

Phi. What, Eucrates, of all credible witnesses? That venerably bearded sexagenarian, with his philosophic leanings? I could never have believed that he would lend his countenance to other people's lies, much less that *he* was capable of such things himself

Tyc. My dear sir, you should have heard the stuff he told me; the way in which he vouched for the truth of it all too, solemnly staking the lives of his children on his veracity! I stared at him in amazement, not knowing what to make of it: one moment I thought he must be out of his mind; the next I concluded he had been a humbug all along, an ape in a lion's skin. Oh, it was monstrous.

Phi. Do tell me all about it; I am curious to see the quackery that shelters beneath so long a beard.

Tyc. I often look in on Eucrates when I have time on my hands, but to-day I had gone there to see Leontichus; he is a friend of mine, you know, and I understood from his boy that he had gone off early to inquire after Eucrates's health, I had not heard that there was anything the matter with him, but this was an additional reason for paying him a visit. When I got there, Leontichus had just gone away, so Eucrates said; but he had a number of other visitors. There was Cleodemus the Peripatetic and Dinomachus the Stoic, and Ion. You know Ion? he is the man who fancies himself so much on his knowledge of Plato; if you take his word for it, he is the only man who has ever really got to the bottom of that philosopher's meaning, or is qualified to act as his interpreter. There is a company for you; Wisdom and Virtue personified, the *elite* of every school, most reverend gentlemen all of them; it almost frightened one. Then there was Antigonus the doctor, who I suppose attended in his professional capacity. Eucrates seemed to be better already: he had come to an understanding with the gout, which had now settled down in his feet again. He motioned me to a seat on the couch beside him. His voice sank to the proper invalid level when he saw me coming, but on my way in I had overheard him bellowing away most lustily. I made him the usual compliments—explained that this was the first I had heard of his illness, and that I had come to him post-haste—and sat down at his side, in very gingerly fashion, lest I should touch his feet. There had been a good deal of talk already about gout, and this was still going on; each man had his pet prescription to offer. Cleodemus was giving his. 'In the left hand take up the tooth of a field-mouse, which has been killed in the manner described, and attach it to the skin of a freshly flayed lion; then bind the skin about your legs, and the pain will instantly cease. ' 'A lion's skin? ' says Dinomachus; 'I understood it was an uncovered hind's. That sounds more likely: a hind has more pace, you see, and is particularly strong in the feet. A lion is a brave beast, I grant you; his fat, his right fore-paw, and his beard-bristles, are all very efficacious, if you know the proper incantation to use with each; but they would hardly be much use for gout. ' 'Ah, yes; that is what I used to think for a long time: a hind was fast, so her skin must be the one for the purpose. But I know better now: a Libyan, who understands these things, tells me that lions are faster than stags; they must be, he says, because how else could they catch them? 'All agreed that the Libyan's argument was convincing. When I asked what good incantations could do, and how an internal complaint could be cured by external attachments, I only got laughed at for my pains; evidently they set me down as a simpleton, ignorant of the merest truisms, that no one in his senses would think of disputing. However, I thought doctor Antigonus seemed rather pleased at my question. I expect his professional advice had been slighted: he wanted to lower Eucrates's tone, —cut down his wine, and put him on a vegetable diet. 'What, Tychiades, ' says Cleodemus, with a faint grin, ' you don't believe these remedies are good for anything? ' 'I should have to be pretty far gone, ' I replied, 'before I could admit that external things, which have no communication with the internal causes of disease, are going to work by means of incantations and stuff, and effect a cure merely by being hung on. You might take the skin of the Nemean lion himself, with a dozen of field-mice tacked on, and you would do no good. Why, I have seen a live lion limping before now, hide and all complete. ' 'Ah, you have a great deal to learn, ' cried Dinomachus; 'you have never taken the trouble to inquire into the operation of these valuable remedies. It would not surprise me to hear you disputing the most palpable facts, such as the curing of tumours and intermittent fevers, the charming of reptiles, and so on; things that every old woman can effect in these days. And this being so, why should not the same principles be extended further? ' 'Nail drives out nail, ' I replied; 'you argue in a circle. How do I know that these cures are brought about by the means to which you attribute them? You have first to show inductively that it is in the course of nature for a fever or a tumour to take fright and bolt at the sound of holy names and foreign incantations; till then, your instances are no better than old wives' tales. ' 'In other words, you do not believe in the existence of the Gods, since you maintain that cures cannot be wrought by the use of holy names? ' 'Nay, say not so, my dear Dinomachus, ' I answered; 'the Gods may exist, and these things may yet be lies. I respect the Gods: I see the cures performed by them, I see their beneficence at work in restoring the sick through the medium of the medical faculty and their drugs. Asclepius, and his sons after him, compounded soothing medicines and healed the sick, —without the lion's-skin-and-field-mouse process. '

'Never mind Asclepius, ' cried Ion. 'I will tell you of a strange thing that happened when I was a boy of fourteen or so. Some one came and told my father that Midas, his gardener, a sturdy fellow and a good workman, had been bitten that morning by an adder, and was now lying prostrate, mortification having set in the leg. He had been tying the vine-branches to the trellis-work, when the reptile crept up and bit him on the great toe, getting off to its hole before he could catch it; and he was now in a terrible way. Before our informant had finished speaking, we saw Midas being carried up by his fellow servants on a stretcher: his whole body was swollen, livid and mortifying, and life appeared to be almost extinct. My father was very much troubled about it; but a friend of his who was there assured him there was no cause for uneasiness. 'I know of a Babylonian, ' he said, 'what they call a Chaldaean; I will go and fetch him at once, and he will put the man right. ' To make a long story short, the Babylonian came, and by means of an incantation expelled the venom from the body, and restored Midas to health; besides the incantation, however, he used a splinter of stone chipped from the monument of a virgin; this he applied to Midas's foot. And as if that were not enough (Midas, I may mention, actually picked up the stretcher on which he had been brought, and took it off with him into the vineyard! and it was all done by an incantation and a bit of stone), the Chaldaean followed it up with an exhibition nothing short of miraculous. Early in the morning he went into the field, pronounced seven names of sacred import, taken from an old book, purified the ground by going thrice round it with sulphur and burning torches, and thereby drove every single reptile off the estate! They came as if drawn by a spell: venomous toads and snakes of every description, asp and adder, cerastes and acontias; only one old serpent, disabled apparently by age, ignored the summons. The Chaldaean declared that the number was not complete, appointed the youngest of the snakes as his ambassador, and sent him to fetch the old serpent who presently arrived. Having got them all together, he blew upon them; and imagine our astonishment when every one of them was immediately consumed! '

'Ion, ' said I, 'about that one who was so old: did the ambassador snake give him an arm, or had he a stick to lean on? ' 'Ah, you will have your joke, ' Cleodemus put in; 'I was an unbeliever myself once—worse than you; in fact I considered it absolutely impossible to give credit to such things. I held out for a long time, but all my scruples were overcome the first time I saw the Flying Stranger; a Hyperborean, he was; I have his own word for it. There was no more to be said after that: there was he travelling through the air in broad daylight, walking on the water, or strolling through fire, perfectly at his ease! ' 'What, ' I exclaimed, ' you saw this Hyperborean actually flying and walking on water? ' 'I did; he wore brogues, as the Hyperboreans usually do. I need not detain you with the everyday manifestations of his power: how he would make people fall in love, call up spirits, resuscitate corpses, bring down the Moon, and show you Hecate herself, as large as life. But I will just tell you of a thing I saw him do at Glaucias's. It was not long after Glaucias's father, Alexicles, had died. Glaucias, on coming into the property, had fallen in love with Chrysis, Demaenetus's daughter. I was teaching him philosophy at the time, and if it had not been for this love-affair he would have thoroughly mastered the Peripatetic doctrines: at eighteen years old that boy had been through his physics, and begun analysis. Well, he was in a dreadful way, and told me all about his love troubles. It was clearly my duty to introduce him to this Hyperborean wizard, which I accordingly did; his preliminary fee, to cover the expenses of sacrifice, was to be 15 pounds, and he was to have another 60 pounds if Glaucias succeeded with Chrysis. Well, as soon as the moon was full, that being the time usually chosen for these enchantments, he dug a trench in the courtyard of the house, and commenced operations, at about midnight, by summoning Glaucias's father, who had now been dead for seven months. The old man did not approve of his son's passion, and was very angry at first; however, he was prevailed on to give his consent. Hecate was next ordered to appear, with Cerberus in her train, and the Moon was brought down, and went through a variety of transformations; she appeared first in the form of a woman, but presently she turned into a most magnificent ox, and after that into a puppy. At length the Hyperborean moulded a clay Eros, and ordered it to *go and fetch Chrysis*. Off went the image, and before long there was a knock at the door, and there stood Chrysis. She came in and threw her arms about Glaucias's neck; you would have said she was dying for love of him; and she stayed on till at last we heard cocks crowing. Away flew the Moon into Heaven, Hecate disappeared under ground, all the apparitions vanished, and we saw Chrysis out of the house just about dawn. —Now, Tychiades, if you had seen that, it would have been enough to convince you that there was something in incantations. '

'Exactly, ' I replied. 'If I had seen it, I should have been convinced: as it is, you must bear with me if I have not your eyes for the miraculous. But as to Chrysis, I know her for a most inflammable lady. I do not see what occasion there was for the clay ambassador and the Moon, or for a wizard all the way from the land of the Hyperboreans; why, Chrysis would go that distance herself for the sum of twenty shillings; 'tis a form of incantation she cannot resist. She is the exact opposite of an apparition: apparitions, you tell me, take flight at the clash of brass or iron, whereas if Chrysis hears the chink of silver, she flies to the spot. By the way, I like your wizard: instead of making all the wealthiest women in love with himself, and getting thousands out of them, he condescends to pick up 15 pounds by rendering Glaucias irresistible. '

'This is sheer folly, ' said Ion; 'you are determined not to believe any one. I shall be glad, now, to hear your views on the subject of those who cure demoniacal possession; the effect of *their* exorcisms is clear enough, and they have spirits to deal with. I need not enlarge on the subject: look at that Syrian adept from Palestine: every one knows how time after time he has found a man thrown down on the ground in a lunatic fit, foaming at the mouth and rolling his eyes; and how he has got him on to his feet again and sent him away in his right mind; and a handsome fee he takes for freeing men from such horrors. He stands over them as they lie, and asks the spirit whence it is. The patient says not a word, but the spirit in him makes answer, in Greek or in some foreign tongue as the case may be, stating where it comes from, and how it entered into him. Then with adjurations, and if need be with threats, the Syrian constrains it to come out of the man. I myself once saw one coming out: it was of a dark, smoky complexion. ' 'Ah, that is nothing for you, ' I replied; 'your eyes can discern those *ideas* which are set forth in the works of Plato, the founder of your school: now they make a very faint impression on the dull optics of us ordinary men. '

'Do you suppose, ' asked Eucrates, 'that he is the only man who has seen such things? Plenty of people besides Ion have met with spirits, by night and by day. As for me, if I have seen one apparition, I have seen a thousand. I used not to like them at first, but I am accustomed to them now, and think nothing of it; especially since the Arab gave me my ring of gallows-iron, and taught me the incantation with all those names in it. But perhaps you will doubt my word too? ' 'Doubt the word of Eucrates, the learned son of Dino? Never! least of all when he unbosoms himself in the liberty of his own house. ' 'Well, what I am going to tell you about the statue was witnessed night after night by all my household, from the eldest to the youngest, and any one of them could tell you the story as well as myself. ' 'What statue is this? ' 'Have you never noticed as you came in that beautiful one in the court, by Demetrius the portrait-sculptor? ' 'Is that the one with the quoit, —leaning forward for the throw, with his face turned back towards the hand that holds the quoit, and one knee bent, ready to rise as he lets it go? ' 'Ah, that is a fine piece of work, too, —a Myron; but I don't mean that, nor the beautiful Polyclitus next it, the Youth tying on the Fillet. No, forget all you pass on your right as you come in; the Tyrannicides [Footnote: Harmodius and Aristogiton.] of Critius and Nesiotes are on that side too: — but did you never notice one just by the fountain? — bald, pot- bellied, half-naked; beard partly caught by the wind; protruding veins? that is the one I mean; it looks as if it must be a portrait, and is thought to be Pelichus, the Corinthian general. ' 'Ah, to be sure, I have seen it, ' I replied; 'it is to the right of the Cronus; the head is crowned with fillets and withered garlands, and the breast gilded. ' 'Yes, I had that done, when he cured me of the tertian ague; I had been at Death's door with it. ' 'Bravo, Pelichus! ' I exclaimed; 'so he was a doctor too? ' 'Not was, but is. Beware of trifling with him, or he may pay you a visit before long. Well do I know what virtue is in that statue with which you make so merry. Can you doubt that he who cures the ague may also inflict it at will? ' 'I implore his favour, ' I cried; 'may he be as merciful as he is mighty! And what are his other doings, to which all your household are witnesses? ' 'At nightfall, ' said Eucrates, 'he descends from his pedestal, and walks all round the house; one or other of us is continually meeting with him; sometimes he is singing. He has never done any harm to any one: all we have to do when we see him is to step aside, and he passes on his way without molesting us. He is fond of taking a bath; you may hear him splashing about in the water all night long. ' 'Perhaps, ' I suggested, 'it is not Pelichus at all, but Talos the Cretan, the son of Minos? He was of bronze, and used to walk all round the island. Or if only he were made of wood instead of bronze, he might quite well be one of Daedalus's ingenious mechanisms—you say he plays truant from his pedestal just like them—and not the work of Demetrius at all. ' 'Take care, Tychiades; you will be sorry for this some day. I have not forgotten what happened to the thief who stole his monthly pennies. ' 'The sacrilegious villain! ' cried Ion; 'I hope he got a lesson. How was he punished? Do tell me: never mind Tychiades; he can be as incredulous as he likes. ' 'At the feet of the statue a number of pence were laid, and other coins were attached to his thigh by means of wax; some of these were silver, and there were also silver plates, all being the thank-offerings of those whom he had cured of fever. Now we had a scamp of a Libyan groom, who took it into his head to filch all this coin under cover of night. He waited till the statue had descended from his pedestal, and then put his plan into effect. Pelichus detected the robbery as soon as he got back; and this is how he found the offender out and punished him. He caused the wretch to wander about in the court all night long, unable to find his way out, just as if he had been in a maze; till at daybreak he was caught with the stolen property in his possession. His guilt was clear, and he received a sound flogging there and then; and before long he died a villain's death. It seems from his own confession that he was scourged every night; and each succeeding morning the weals were to be seen on his body. —*Now*, Tychiades, let me hear you laugh at Pelichus: I am a dotard, am I not? a relic from the time of Minos? '

'My dear Eucrates, ' said I, 'if bronze is bronze, and if that statue was cast by Demetrius of Alopece, who dealt not in Gods but in men, then I cannot anticipate any danger from a statue of Pelichus; even the menaces of the original would not have alarmed me particularly.'

Here Antigonus, the doctor, put in a word. 'I myself, ' he informed his host, 'have a Hippocrates in bronze, some eighteen inches high. Now the moment my candle is out, he goes clattering about all over the house, slamming the door, turning all my boxes upside down, and mixing up all my drugs; especially when his annual sacrifice is overdue. ' 'What are we coming to? ' I cried; 'Hippocrates must have sacrifices, must he? he must be feasted with all pomp and circumstance, and punctually to the day, or his leechship is angry? Why, he ought to be only too pleased to be complimented with a cup of mead or a garland, like other dead men. '

'Now here, ' Eucrates went on, 'is a thing that I saw happen five years ago, in the presence of witnesses. It was during the vintage. I had left the labourers busy in the vineyard at midday, and was walking off into the wood, occupied with my own thoughts. I had already got under the shade of the trees, when I heard dogs barking, and supposed that my boy Mnason was amusing himself in the chase as usual, and had penetrated into the copse with his friends. However, that was not it: presently there was an earthquake; I heard a voice like a thunderclap, and saw a terrible woman approaching, not much less than three hundred feet high. She carried a torch in her left hand, and a sword in her right; the sword might be thirty feet long. Her lower extremities were those of a dragon; but the upper half was like Medusa—as to the eyes, I mean; they were quite awful in their expression. Instead of hair, she had clusters of snakes writhing about her neck, and curling over her shoulders. See here: it makes my flesh creep, only to speak of it! ' And he showed us all his arm, with the hair standing on end.

Ion and Dinomachus and Cleodemus and the rest of them drank down every word. The narrator led them by their venerable noses, and this least convincing of colossal bogies, this hundred-yarder, was the object of their mute adorations. And these (I was reflecting all the time)—these are the admired teachers from whom our youth are to learn wisdom! Two circumstances distinguish them from babies: they have white hair, and they have beards: but when it comes to swallowing a lie, they are babes and more than babes.

Dinomachus, for instance, wanted to know 'how big were the Goddess's dogs? ' 'They were taller than Indian elephants, ' he was assured, 'and as black, with coarse, matted coats. At the sight of her, I stood stock still, and turned the seal of my Arab's ring inwards; whereupon Hecate smote upon the ground with her dragon's foot, and caused a vast chasm to open, wide as the mouth of Hell. Into this she presently leaped, and was lost to sight. I began to pluck up courage, and looked over the edge; but first I took hold of a tree that grew near, for fear I should be giddy, and fall in. And then I saw the whole of Hades: there was Pyriphlegethon, the Lake of Acheron, Cerberus, the Shades. I even recognized some of them: I made out my father quite distinctly; he was still wearing the same clothes in which we buried him. ' 'And what were the spirits doing? ' asked Ion. 'Doing? Oh, they were just lying about on the asphodel, among their friends and kinsmen, all arranged according to their clans and tribes. ' 'There now! ' exclaimed Ion; 'after that I should like to hear the Epicureans say another word against the divine Plato and his account of the spiritual world. I suppose you did not happen to see Socrates or Plato among the Shades? ' 'Yes, I did; I saw Socrates; not very plainly, though; I only went by the bald head and corpulent figure. Plato I did *not* make out; I will speak the plain truth; we are all friends here. I had just had a good look at everything, when the chasm began to close up; some of the servants who came to look for me (Pyrrhias here was among them) arrived while the gap was still visible. —Pyrrhias, is that the fact? ' 'Indeed it is, ' says Pyrrhias; 'what is more, I heard a dog barking in the hole, and if I am not

mistaken I caught a glimmer of torchlight. ' I could not help a smile;
it was handsome in Pyrrhias, this of the bark and the torchlight.

'Your experience, ' observed Cleodemus, 'is by no means without
precedent. In fact I saw something of the same kind myself, not long
ago. I had been ill, and Antigonus here was attending me. The fever
had been on me for seven days, and was now aggravated by the
excessive heat. All my attendants were outside, having closed the
door and left me to myself; those were your orders, you know,
Antigonus; I was to get some sleep if I could. Well, I woke up to find
a handsome young man standing at my side, in a white cloak. He
raised me up from the bed, and conducted me through a sort of
chasm into Hades; I knew where I was at once, because I saw
Tantalus and Tityus and Sisyphus. Not to go into details, I came to
the Judgement-hall, and there were Aeacus and Charon and the
Fates and the Furies. One person of a majestic appearance—Pluto, I
suppose it was—sat reading out the names of those who were due to
die, their term of life having lapsed. The young man took me and set
me before him, but Pluto flew into a rage: "Away with him, " he said
to my conductor; "his thread is not yet out; go and fetch Demylus the
smith; *he* has had his spindleful and more. " I ran off home, nothing
loath. My fever had now disappeared, and I told everybody that
Demylus was as good as dead. He lived close by, and was said to
have some illness, and it was not long before we heard the voices of
mourners in his house. '

'This need not surprise us, ' remarked Antigonus; 'I know of a man
who rose from the dead twenty days after he had been buried; I
attended him both before his death and after his resurrection. ' 'I
should have thought, ' said I, 'that the body must have putrefied in
all that time, or if not that, that he must have collapsed for want of
nourishment. Was your patient a second Epimenides? '

At this point in the conversation, Eucrates's sons came in from the
gymnasium, one of them quite a young man, the other a boy of
fifteen or so. After saluting the company, they took their seats on the
couch at their father's side, and a chair was brought for me. The
appearance of the boys seemed to remind Eucrates of something:
laying a hand upon each of them, he addressed me as follows.
'Tychiades, if what I am now about to tell you is anything but the
truth, then may I never have joy of these lads. It is well known to
every one how fond I was of my sainted wife, their mother; and I
showed it in my treatment of her, not only in her lifetime, but even

after her death; for I ordered all the jewels and clothes that she had valued to be burnt upon her pyre. Now on the seventh day after her death, I was sitting here on this very couch, as it might be now, trying to find comfort for my affliction in Plato's book about the soul. I was quietly reading this, when Demaenete herself appeared, and sat down at my side exactly as Eucratides is doing now. ' Here he pointed to the younger boy, who had turned quite pale during this narrative, and now shuddered in childish terror. 'The moment I saw her, ' he continued, 'I threw my arms about her neck and wept aloud. She bade me cease; and complained that though I had consulted her wishes in everything else, I had neglected to burn one of her golden sandals, which she said had fallen under a chest. We had been unable to find this sandal, and had only burnt the fellow to it. While we were still conversing, a hateful little Maltese terrier that lay under the couch started barking, and my wife immediately vanished. The sandal, however, was found beneath the chest, and was eventually burnt. —Do you still doubt, Tychiades, in the face of one convincing piece of evidence after another? ' 'God forbid! ' I cried; 'the doubter who should presume, thus to brazen it out in the face of Truth would deserve to have a golden sandal applied to him after the nursery fashion. '

Arignotus the Pythagorean now came in—the 'divine' Arignotus, as he is called; the philosopher of the long hair and the solemn countenance, you know, of whose wisdom we hear so much. I breathed again when I saw him. 'Ah! ' thought I, 'the very man we want! here is the axe to hew their lies asunder. The sage will soon pull them up when he hears their cock-and-bull stories. Fortune has brought a *deus ex machina* upon the scene. ' He sat down (Cleodemus rising to make room for him) and inquired after Eucrates's health. Eucrates replied that he was better. 'And what, ' Arignotus next asked, 'is the subject of your learned conversation? I overheard your voices as I came in, and doubt not that your time will prove to have been profitably employed. ' Eucrates pointed to me. 'We were only trying, ' he said, 'to convince this man of adamant that there are such things as supernatural beings and ghosts, and that the spirits of the dead walk the earth and manifest themselves to whomsoever they will. ' Moved by the august presence of Arignotus, I blushed, and hung my head. 'Ah, but, Eucrates, ' said he, 'perhaps all that Tychiades means is, that a spirit only walks if its owner met with a violent end, if he was strangled, for instance, or beheaded or crucified, and not if he died a natural death. If that is what he means, there is great justice in his contention. ' 'No, no, ' says Dinomachus, 'he maintains that there is absolutely no such thing as an apparition. ' 'What is this I hear? ' asked Arignotus, scowling upon me; 'you deny the existence of the supernatural, when there is scarcely a man who has not seen some evidence of it? ' 'Therein lies my exculpation, ' I replied: 'I do not believe in the supernatural, because, unlike the rest of mankind, I do not see it: if I saw, I should doubtless believe, just as you all do. ' 'Well, ' said he, 'next time you are in Corinth, ask for the house of Eubatides, near the Craneum; and when you have found it, go up to Tibius the door-keeper, and tell him you would like to see the spot on which Arignotus the Pythagorean unearthed the demon, whose expulsion rendered the house habitable again. ' 'What was that about, Arignotus? ' asked Eucrates.

'The house, ' replied the other, 'was haunted, and had been uninhabited for years: each intending occupant had been at once driven out of it in abject terror by a most grim and formidable apparition. Finally it had fallen into a ruinous state, the roof was giving way, and in short no one would have thought of entering it. Well, when I heard about this, I got my books together (I have a considerable number of Egyptian works on these subjects) and went off to the house about bed-time, undeterred by the remonstrances of my host, who considered that I was walking into the jaws of Death, and would almost have detained me by force when he learnt my destination. I took a lamp and entered alone, and putting down my light in the principal room, I sat on the floor quietly reading. The spirit now made his appearance, thinking that he had to do with an ordinary person, and that he would frighten me as he had frightened so many others. He was pitch-black, with a tangled mass of hair. He drew near, and assailed me from all quarters, trying every means to get the better of me, and changing in a moment from dog to bull, from bull to lion. Armed with my most appalling adjuration, uttered in the Egyptian tongue, I drove him spell-bound into the corner of a dark room, marked the spot at which he disappeared, and passed the rest of the night in peace. In the morning, to the amazement of all beholders (for every one had given me up for lost, and expected to find me lying dead like former occupants), I issued from the house, and carried to Eubatides the welcome news that it was now cleared of its grim visitant, and fit to serve as a human habitation. He and a number of others, whom curiosity had prompted to join us, followed me to the spot at which I had seen the demon vanish. I instructed them to take spades and pick-axes and dig: they did so; and at about a fathom's depth we discovered a mouldering corpse, of which nothing but the bones remained entire. We took the skeleton up, and placed it in a grave; and from that day to this the house has never been troubled with apparitions. '

After such a story as this-coming as it did from Arignotus, who was generally looked up to as a man of inspired wisdom—my incredulous attitude towards the supernatural was loudly condemned on all hands. However, I was not frightened by his long hair, nor by his reputation. 'Dear, dear! ' I exclaimed, 'so Arignotus, the sole mainstay of Truth, is as bad as the rest of them, as full of windy imaginings! Our treasure proves to be but ashes. ' 'Now look here, Tychiades, ' said Arignotus, 'you will not believe me, nor Dinomachus, nor Cleodemus here, nor yet Eucrates: we shall be glad to know who is your great authority on the other side, who is to outweigh us all? ' 'No less a person, ' I replied, 'than the sage of Abdera, the wondrous Democritus himself. *His* disbelief in apparitions is sufficiently clear. When he had shut himself up in that tomb outside the city gates, there to spend his days and nights in literary labours, certain young fellows, who had a mind to play their pranks on the philosopher and give him a fright, got themselves up in black palls and skull-masks, formed a ring round him, and treated him to a brisk dance. Was Democritus alarmed at the ghosts? Not he: "Come, enough of that nonsense, " was all he had to say to them; and that without so much as looking up, or taking pen from paper. Evidently *he* had quite made up his mind about disembodied spirits. ' 'Which simply proves, ' retorted Eucrates, 'that Democritus was no wiser than yourself. Now I am going to tell you of another thing that happened to me personally; I did not get the story second-hand. Even you, Tychiades, will scarcely hold out against so convincing a narrative.

'When I was a young man, I passed some time in Egypt, my father having sent me to that country for my education. I took it into my head to sail up the Nile to Coptus, and thence pay a visit to the statue of Memnon, and hear the curious sound that proceeds from it at sunrise. In this respect, I was more fortunate than most people, who hear nothing but an indistinct voice: Memnon actually opened his lips, and delivered me an oracle in seven hexameters; it is foreign to my present purpose, or I would quote you the very lines. Well now, one of my fellow passengers on the way up was a scribe of Memphis, an extraordinarily able man, versed in all the lore of the Egyptians. He was said to have passed twenty-three years of his life underground in the tombs, studying occult sciences under the instruction of Isis herself. ' 'You must mean the divine Pancrates, my teacher, ' exclaimed Arignotus; 'tall, clean-shaven, snub-nosed, protruding lips, rather thin in the legs; dresses entirely in linen, has a thoughtful expression, and speaks Greek with a slight accent? ' 'Yes, it was Pancrates himself. I knew nothing about him at first, but whenever we anchored I used to see him doing the most marvellous things, —for instance, he would actually ride on the crocodiles' backs, and swim about among the brutes, and they would fawn upon him and wag their tails; and then I realized that he was no common man. I made some advances, and by imperceptible degrees came to be on quite a friendly footing with him, and was admitted to a share in his mysterious arts. The end of it was, that he prevailed on me to leave all my servants behind at Memphis, and accompany him alone; assuring me that we should not want for attendance. This plan we accordingly followed from that time onwards. Whenever we came to an inn, he used to take up the bar of the door, or a broom, or perhaps a pestle, dress it up in clothes, and utter a certain incantation; whereupon the thing would begin to walk about, so that every one took it for a man. It would go off and draw water, buy and cook provisions, and make itself generally useful. When we had no further occasion for its services, there was another incantation, after which the broom was a broom once more, or the pestle a pestle. I could never get him to teach me this incantation, though it was not for want of trying; open as he was about everything else, he guarded this one secret jealously. At last one day I hid in a dark corner, and overheard the magic syllables; they were three in number. The Egyptian gave the pestle its instructions, and then went off to the market. Well, next day he was again busy in the market: so I took the pestle, dressed it, pronounced the three syllables exactly as he had done, and ordered it to become a water-carrier. It brought me the pitcher full; and then I said: *Stop: be water-carrier no longer, but pestle as heretofore.* But the thing would take no notice of me: it went on drawing water the whole time, until at last the house was full of it. This was awkward: if Pancrates came back, he would be angry, I thought (and so indeed it turned out). I took an axe, and cut the pestle in two. The result was that both halves took pitchers and fetched water; I had two water-carriers instead of one. This was still going on, when Pancrates appeared. He saw how things stood, and turned the water-carriers back into wood; and then he withdrew himself from me, and went away, whither I knew not. '

'And you can actually make a man out of a pestle to this day? ' asked Dinomachus. 'Yes, I can do *that,* but that is only half the process: I cannot turn it back again into its original form; if once it became a water-carrier, its activity would swamp the house. '

'Oh, stop! ' I cried: 'if the thought that you are old men is not enough to deter you from talking this trash, at least remember who is present: if you do not want to fill these boys' heads with ghosts and hobgoblins, postpone your grotesque horrors for a more suitable occasion. Have some mercy on the lads: do not accustom them to listen to a tangle of superstitious stuff that will cling to them for the rest of their lives, and make them start at their own shadows. '

'Ah, talking of superstition, now, ' says Eucrates, 'that reminds me: what do you make of oracles, for instance, and omens? of inspired utterances, of voices from the shrine, of the priestess's prophetic lines? You will deny all that too, of course? If I were to tell you of a certain magic ring in my possession, the seal of which is a portrait of the Pythian Apollo, and actually *speaks* to me, I suppose you would decline to believe it, you would think I was bragging? But I must tell you all of what I heard in the temple of Amphilochus at Mallus, when that hero appeared to me in person and gave me counsel, and of what I saw with my own eyes on that occasion; and again of all I saw at Pergamum and heard at Patara. It was on my way home from Egypt that the oracle of Mallus was mentioned to me as a particularly intelligible and veracious one: I was told that any question, duly written down on a tablet and handed to the priest, would receive a plain, definite answer. I thought it would be a good thing to take the oracle on my way home, and consult the God as to my future. '

I saw what was coming: this was but the prologue to a whole tragedy of the oracular. It was clear enough that I was not wanted, and as I did not feel called upon to pose as the sole champion of the cause of Truth among so many, I took my leave there and then, while Eucrates was still upon the high seas between Egypt and Mallus. 'I must go and find Leontichus, ' I explained; 'I have to see him about something. Meanwhile, you gentlemen, to whom human affairs are not sufficient occupation, may solicit the insertion of divine fingers into your mythologic pie. ' And with that I went out. Relieved of my presence, I doubt not that they fell to with a will on their banquet of mendacity.

That is what I got by going to Eucrates's; and, upon my word, Philocles, my overloaded stomach needs an emetic as much as if I had been drinking new wine. I would pay something for the drug that should work oblivion in me: I fear the effects of haunting reminiscence; monsters, demons, Hecates, seem to pass before my eyes.

Phi. I am not much better off. They tell us it is not only the mad dog that inflicts hydrophobia: his human victim's bite is as deadly as his own, and communicates the evil as surely. You, it seems, have been bitten with many bites by the liar Eucrates, and have passed it on to me; no otherwise can I explain the demoniacal poison that runs in my veins.

Tyc. What matter, friend? Truth and good sense: these are the drugs for our ailment; let us employ them, and that empty thing, a lie, need have no terrors for us. F.

DIONYSUS, AN INTRODUCTORY LECTURE

When Dionysus invaded India—for I may tell you a Bacchic legend, may I not? —it is recorded that the natives so underrated him that his approach only amused them at first; or rather, his rashness filled them with compassion; he would so soon be trampled to death by their elephants, if he took the field against them. Their scouts had doubtless given them amazing details about his army: the rank and file were frantic mad women crowned with ivy, clad in fawn- skins, with little pikes that had no steel about them, but were ivy-wreathed like themselves, and toy bucklers that tinkled at a touch; they took the tambourines for shields, you see; and then there were a few bumpkins among them, stark naked, who danced wildly, and had tails, and horns like a new-born kid's.

Their general, who rode on a car drawn by panthers, was quite beardless, with not even a vestige of fluff on his face, had horns, was crowned with grape-clusters, his hair tied with a fillet, his cloak purple, and his shoes of gold. Of his lieutenants, one was short, thick-set, paunchy, and flat-nosed, with great upright ears; he trembled perpetually, leant upon a narthex-wand, rode mostly upon an ass, wore saffron to his superior's purple, and was a very suitable general of division for him. The other was a half-human hybrid, with hairy legs, horns, and flowing beard, passionate and quick-tempered; with a reed-pipe in his left hand, and waving a crooked staff in his right, he skipped round and round the host, a terror to the women, who let their dishevelled tresses fly abroad as he came, with cries of Evoe—the name of their lord, guessed the scouts. Their flocks had suffered, they added, the young had been seized alive and torn piecemeal by the women; they ate raw flesh, it seemed.

All this was food for laughter, as well it might be, to the Indians and their king: Take the field? array their hosts against him? no, indeed; at worst they might match their women with his, if he still came on; for themselves such a victory would be a disgrace; a set of mad women, a general in a snood, a little old drunkard, a half- soldier, and a few naked dancers; why should they murder such a droll crew? However, when they heard how the God was wasting their land with fire, giving cities and citizens to the flames, burning their forests, and making one great conflagration of all India—for fire is the Bacchic instrument, Dionysus's very birthright—, then they lost no more time, but armed; they girthed, bitted, and castled their

213

elephants, and out they marched; not that they had ceased to scorn; but now they were angry too, and in a hurry to crush this beardless warrior with all his host.

When the two armies came to sight of one another, the Indians drew up their elephants in front and advanced their phalanx; on the other side, Dionysus held the centre, Silenus led his right, and Pan his left wing; his colonels and captains were the satyrs, and the word for the day *evoe*. Straightway tambourines clattered, cymbals sounded to battle, a satyr blew the war-note on his horn, Silenus's ass sent forth a martial bray, and the maenads leapt shrill-voiced on the foe, girt with serpents and baring now the steel of their thyrsus-heads. In a moment Indians and elephants turned and fled disordered, before even a missile could carry across; and the end was that they were smitten and led captive by the objects of their laughter; they had learnt the lesson that it is not safe to take the first report, and scorn an enemy of whom nothing is known.

But you wonder what all this is about—suspect me, possibly, of being only too fresh from the company of Bacchus. Perhaps the explanation, involving a comparison of myself with Gods, will only more convince you of my exalted or my drunken mood; it is, that ordinary people are affected by literary novelties (my own productions, for instance) much as the Indians were by that experience. They have an idea that literary satyr-dances, absurdities, pure farce, are to be expected from me, and, however they reach their conception of me, they incline to one of two attitudes. Some of them avoid my readings altogether, seeing no reason for climbing down from their elephants and paying attention to revelling women and skipping satyrs; others come with their preconceived idea, and when they find that the thyrsus-head has a steel point under it, they are too much startled by the surprise to venture approval. I confidently promise them, however, that if they will attend the rite repeatedly now as in days of yore, if my old boon-companions will call to mind the revels that once we shared, not be too shy of satyrs and Silenuses, and drink deep of the bowl I bring, the frenzy shall take hold upon them too, till their *evoes* vie with mine.

Well, they are free to listen or not; let them take their choice. Meanwhile, we are still in India, and I should like to give you another fact from that country, again a link between Dionysus and our business. In the territory of the Machlaeans, who occupy the left bank of the Indus right down to the sea, there is a grove, of no great size, but enclosed both round about and overhead, light being almost excluded by the profusion of ivy and vine. In it are three springs of fair pellucid water, called, one of them the satyrs' well, the second Pan's, and the other that of Silenus. The Indians enter this grove once a year at the festival of Dionysus, and taste the wells, not promiscuously, however, but according to age; the satyrs' well is for the young, Pan's for the middle-aged, and Silenus's for those at my time of life.

What effect their draught produces on the children, what doings the men are spurred to, Pan-ridden, must not detain us; but the behaviour of the old under their water intoxication has its interest. As soon as one of them has drunk, and Silenus has possessed him, he falls dumb for a space like one in vinous lethargy; then on a sudden his voice is strong, his articulation clear, his intonation musical; from dead silence issues a stream of talk; the gag would scarce restrain him from incessant chatter; tale upon tale he reels you off. Yet all is sense and order withal; his words are as many, and find their place as well, as those 'winter snowflakes' of Homer's orator. You may talk of his swan- song if you will, mindful of his years; but you must add that his chirping is quick and lively as the grasshopper's, till evening comes; then the fit is past; he falls silent, and is his common self again. But the greatest wonder I have yet to tell: if he leave unfinished the tale he was upon, and the setting sun cut him short, then at his next year's draught he will resume it where the inspiration of this year deserted him.

Gentlemen, I have been pointing Momus-like at my own foibles; I need not trouble you with the application; you can make out the resemblance for yourselves. But if you find me babbling, you know now what has loosed my tongue; and if there is shrewdness in any of my words, then to Silenus be the thanks.

HERACLES, AN INTRODUCTORY LECTURE

Our Heracles is known among the Gauls under the local name of Ogmius; and the appearance he presents in their pictures is truly grotesque. They make him out as old as old can be: the few hairs he has left (he is quite bald in front) are dead white, and his skin is wrinkled and tanned as black as any old salt's. You would take him for some infernal deity, for Charon or Iapetus, —any one rather than Heracles. Such as he is, however, he has all the proper attributes of that God: the lion's-skin hangs over his shoulders, his right hand grasps the club, his left the strung bow, and a quiver is slung at his side; nothing is wanting to the Heraclean equipment.

Now I thought at first that this was just a cut at the Greek Gods; that in taking these liberties with the personal appearance of Heracles, the Gauls were merely exacting pictorial vengeance for his invasion of their territory; for in his search after the herds of Geryon he had overrun and plundered most of the peoples of the West. However, I have yet to mention the most remarkable feature in the portrait. This ancient Heracles drags after him a vast crowd of men, all of whom are fastened by the ears with thin chains composed of gold and amber, and looking more like beautiful necklaces than anything else. From this flimsy bondage they make no attempt to escape, though escape must be easy. There is not the slightest show of resistance: instead of planting their heels in the ground and dragging back, they follow with joyful alacrity, singing their captor's praises the while; and from the eagerness with which they hurry after him to prevent the chains from tightening, one would say that release is the last thing they desire. Nor will I conceal from you what struck me as the most curious circumstance of all. Heracles's right hand is occupied with the club, and his left with the bow: how is he to hold the ends of the chains? The painter solves the difficulty by boring a hole in the tip of the God's tongue, and making that the means of attachment; his head is turned round, and he regards his followers with a smiling countenance.

For a long time I stood staring at this in amazement: I knew not what to make of it, and was beginning to feel somewhat nettled, when I was addressed in admirable Greek by a Gaul who stood at my side, and who besides possessing a scholarly acquaintance with the Gallic mythology, proved to be not unfamiliar with our own. 'Sir, ' he said, 'I see this picture puzzles you: let me solve the riddle. We Gauls connect eloquence not with Hermes, as you do, but with the mightier Heracles. Nor need it surprise you to see him represented as an old man. It is the prerogative of eloquence, that it reaches perfection in old age; at least if we may believe your poets, who tell us that

Youth is the sport of every random gust,

whereas old age

Hath that to say that passes youthful wit.

Thus we find that from Nestor's lips honey is distilled; and that the words of the Trojan counsellors are compared to the lily, which, if I have not forgotten my Greek, is the name of a flower. Hence, if you will consider the relation that exists between tongue and ear, you will find nothing more natural than the way in which our Heracles, who is Eloquence personified, draws men along with their ears tied to his tongue. Nor is any slight intended by the hole bored through that member: I recollect a passage in one of your comic poets in which we are told that

There is a hole in every glib tongue's tip.

Indeed, we refer the achievements of the original Heracles, from first to last, to his wisdom and persuasive eloquence. His shafts, as I take it, are no other than his words; swift, keen-pointed, true-aimed to do deadly execution on the soul. ' And in conclusion he reminded me of our own phrase, 'winged words. '

Now while I was debating within myself the advisability of appearing before you, and of submitting myself for a second time to the verdict of this enormous jury, old as I am, and long unused to lecturing, the thought of this Heracles portrait came to my relief. I had been afraid that some of you would consider it a piece of youthful audacity inexcusable in one of my years. 'Thy force, ' some Homeric youth might remark with crushing effect, 'is spent; dull age hath borne thee down'; and he might add, in playful allusion to my gouty toes,

Slow are thy steeds, and weakness waits upon thee.

But the thought of having that venerable hero to keep me in countenance emboldens me to risk everything: I am no older than he.

Good-bye, then, to bodily perfections, to strength and speed and beauty; Love, when he sees my grey beard, is welcome to fly past, as the poet of Teos [Footnote: Anacreon.] has it, with rush of gilded wings; 'tis all one to Hippoclides. Old age is Wisdom's youth, the day of her glorious flower: let her draw whom she can by the ears; let her shoot her bolts freely; no fear now lest the supply run short. There is the old man's comfort, on the strength of which he ventures to drag down his boat, which has long lain high and dry, provision her as best he may, and once more put out to sea.

Never did I stand in more need of a generous breeze, to fill my sails and speed me on my way: may the Gods dispose you to contribute thereto; so shall I not be found wanting, and of me, as of Odysseus, it shall be said

How stout a thigh lurked 'neath the old man's rags!

SWANS AND AMBER

You have no doubt a proper faith in the amber legend—how it is the tears shed by poplars on the Eridanus for Phaethon, the said poplars being his sisters, who were changed to trees in the course of their mourning, and continue to distil their lacrimal amber. That was what the poets taught me, and I looked forward, if ever fortune should bring me to the Eridanus, to standing under a poplar, catching a few tears in a fold of my dress, and having a supply of the commodity.

Sure enough, I found myself there not long ago upon another errand, and had occasion to go up the Eridanus; but, though I was all eyes, I saw neither poplars nor amber, and the natives had not so much as heard of Phaethon. I started my inquiries by asking when we should come to the amber poplars; the boatmen only laughed, and requested explanations. I told them the story: Phaethon was a son of Helius, and when he grew up came to his father and asked if he might drive his car, and be the day-maker just that once. His father consented, but he was thrown out and killed, and his mourning sisters 'in this land of yours, ' I said, 'where he fell on the Eridanus, turned into poplars, and still weep amber for him. '

'What liar took you in like that, sir? ' they said; 'we never saw a coachman spilt; and where are the poplars? why, do you suppose, if it was true, we would row or tow up stream for sixpences? we should only have to collect poplar-tears to be rich men. ' This truth impressed me a good deal; I said no more, and was painfully conscious of my childishness in trusting the poets; they deal in such extravagant fictions, they come to scorn sober fact. Here was one hope gone; I had set my heart upon it, and was as much chagrined as if I had dropped the amber out of my hands; I had had all my plans ready for the various uses to which it was to be put.

However, there was one thing I still thought I really should find there, and that was flocks of swans singing on the banks. We were still on the way up, and I applied to the boatmen again: 'About what time do the swans take post for their famous musical entertainment? —Apollo's fellow craftsmen, you know, who were changed here from men to birds, and still sing in memory of their ancient art. '

But they only jeered at me: 'Are you going to lie all day about our country and our river, pray? We are always on the water; we have worked all our lives on the Eridanus; well, we do see a swan now and again in the marshes; and a harsh feeble croak their note is; crows or jackdaws are sirens to them; as for sweet singing such as you tell of, not a ghost of it. We cannot make out where you folk get all these tales about us. '

Such disappointments are the natural consequence of trusting picturesque reporters. Well now, I am afraid the newcomers among you, who hear me for the first time, may have been expecting swans and amber from me, and may presently depart laughing at the people who encouraged them to look for such literary treasures. But I solemnly aver that no one has ever heard or ever shall hear me making any such claims. Other persons in plenty you may find who are Eridanuses, rich not in amber, but in very gold, and more melodious far than the poets' swans. But you see how plain and unromantic is my material; song is not in me. Any one who expects great things from me will be like a man looking at an object in water. Its image is magnified by an optical effect; he takes the reality to correspond to the appearance, and when he fishes it up is disgusted to find it so small. So I pour out the water, exhibit my wares, and warn you not to hope for a large haul; if you do, you have only yourselves to blame. H.

THE FLY, AN APPRECIATION

The fly is not the smallest of winged things, on a level with gnats, midges, and still tinier creatures; it is as much larger than they as smaller than the bee. It has not feathers of the usual sort, is not fledged all over like some, nor provided with quill- feathers like other birds, but resembles locusts, grasshoppers, and bees in being gauze-winged, this sort of wing being as much more delicate than the ordinary as Indian fabrics are lighter and softer than Greek. Moreover, close inspection of them when spread out and moving in the sun will show them to be peacock-hued.

Its flight is accompanied neither by the incessant wing-beat of the bat, the jump of the locust, nor the buzz of the wasp, but carries it easily in any direction. It has the further merit of a music neither sullen as with the gnat kind, deep as with the bee, nor grim and threatening as with the wasp; it is as much more tuneful than they as the flute is sweeter than trumpet or cymbals.

As for the rest of its person, the head is very slenderly attached by the neck, easily turned, and not all of one piece with the body as in the locust; the eyes are projecting and horny; the chest strong, with the legs springing freely from it instead of lying close like a wasp's. The belly also is well fortified, and looks like a breastplate, with its broad bands and scales. Its weapons are not in the tail as with wasp and bee, but in its mouth and proboscis; with the latter, in which it is like the elephant, it forages, takes hold of things, and by means of a sucker at its tip attaches itself firmly to them. This proboscis is also supplied with a projecting tooth, with which the fly makes a puncture, and so drinks blood. It does drink milk, but also likes blood, which it gets without hurting its prey much. Of its six legs, four only are for walking, and the front pair serves for hands; you may see it standing on four legs and holding up a morsel in these hands, which it consumes in very human fashion.

It does not come into being in its ultimate shape, but starts as a worm in the dead body of man or animal; then it gradually develops legs, puts forth wings and becomes a flying instead of a creeping thing, which generates in turn and produces a little worm, one day to be a fly. Living with man, sharing his food and his table, it tastes everything except his oil, to drink which is death to it. In any case it soon perishes, having but a short span of life allotted to it, but while it lives it loves the light, and is active only under its influence; at night it rests, neither flying nor buzzing, but retiring and keeping quiet.

I am able to record its considerable wisdom, shown in evading the plots of its enemy the spider. It is always on the look-out for his ambushes, and in the most circumspect way dodges about, that it may not be caught, netted, and entangled in his meshes. Its valour and spirit require no mention of mine; Homer, mightiest-voiced of poets, seeking a compliment for the greatest of heroes, likens his spirit not to a lion's, a panther's, a boar's, but to the courage of the fly, to its unshrinking and persistent assault; mark, it is not mere audacity, but courage, that he attributes to it. Though you drive it off, he says, it will not leave you; it will have its bite. He is so earnest an admirer of the fly that he alludes to it not once nor twice, but constantly; a mention of it is felt to be a poetic ornament. Now it is its multitudinous descent upon the milk that he celebrates; now he is in want of an illustration for Athene as she wards off a spear from the vitals of Menelaus; so he makes her a mother caring for her sleeping child, and in comes the fly again. Moreover he gives them that pretty epithet, 'thick- clust'ring'; and 'nations' is his dignified word for a swarm of them.

The fly's force is shown by the fact that its bite pierces not merely the human skin, but that of cattle and horses; it annoys the elephant by getting into the folds of its hide, and letting it know the efficiency of even a tiny trunk. There is much ease and freedom about their love affairs, which are not disposed of so expeditiously as by the domestic fowl; the act of union is prolonged, and is found quite compatible with flight. A fly will live and breathe for some time after its head is cut off.

The most remarkable point about its natural history is that which I am now to mention. It is the one fact that Plato seems to me to have overlooked in his discourse of the soul and its immortality. If a little ashes be sprinkled on a dead fly, it gets up, experiences a second birth, and starts life afresh, which is recognized as a convincing proof that its soul is immortal, inasmuch as after it has departed it returns, recognizes and reanimates the body, and enables it to fly; so is confirmed the tale about Hermotimus of Clazomenae—how his soul frequently left him and went off on its own account, and afterwards returning occupied the body again and restored the man to life.

It toils not, but lives at its case, profiting by the labours of others, and finding everywhere a table spread for it. For it the goats are milked, for its behoof and man's the honey is stored, to its palate the *chef* adapts his sauces; it tastes before the king himself, walks upon his table, shares his meal, and has the use of all that is his.

Nest, home, local habitation, it has none; like the Scythians, it elects to lead a wandering life, and where night finds it, there is its hearth and its chamber. But as I said, it works no deeds of darkness; 'live openly' is its motto; its principle is to do no villany that, done in the face of day, would dishonour it.

Legend tells how Myia (the fly's ancient name) was once a maiden, exceeding fair, but over-given to talk and chatter and song, Selene's rival for the love of Endymion. When the young man slept, she was for ever waking him with her gossip and tunes and merriment, till he lost patience, and Selene in wrath turned her to what she now is. And therefore it is that she still, in memory of Endymion, grudges all sleepers their rest, and most of all the young and tender. Her very bite and blood-thirst tell not of savagery, but of love and human kindness; she is but enjoying mankind as she may, and sipping beauty.

In ancient times there was a woman of her name, a poetess wise and beautiful, and another a famous Attic courtesan, of whom the comic poet wrote:

As deep as to his heart fair Myia bit him.

The comic Muse, we see, disdained not the name, nor refused it the hospitality of the boards; and parents took no shame to give it to their daughters. Tragedy goes further and speaks of the fly in high terms of praise, as witness the following:

Foul shame the little fly, with might courageous,
Should leap upon men's limbs, athirst for blood,
But men-at-arms shrink from the foeman's steel!

I might add many details about Pythagoras's daughter Myia, were not her story too well known.

There are also flies of very large size, called generally soldier- flies, or dog-flies; these have a hoarse buzz, a very rapid flight, and quite long lives; they last the winter through without food, mostly in sheltered nooks below the roof; the most remarkable fact about these is that they are hermaphrodites.

But I must break off; not that my subject is exhausted; only that to exhaust such a subject is too like breaking a butterfly on the wheel.

REMARKS ADDRESSED TO AN ILLITERATE BOOK-FANCIER

Let me tell you, that you are choosing the worst way to attain your object. You think that by buying up all the best books you can lay your hands on, you will pass for a man of literary tastes: not a bit of it; you are merely exposing thereby your own ignorance of literature. Why, you cannot even buy the right things: any casual recommendation is enough to guide your choice; you are as clay in the hands of the unscrupulous amateur, and as good as cash down to any dealer. How are you to know the difference between genuine old books that are worth money, and trash whose only merit is that it is falling to pieces? You are reduced to taking the worms and moths into your confidence; their activity is your sole clue to the value of a book; as to the accuracy and fidelity of the copyist, that is quite beyond you.

And supposing even that you had managed to pick out such veritable treasures as the exquisite editions of Callinus, or those of the far-famed Atticus, most conscientious of publishers, —what does it profit you? Their beauty means nothing to you, my poor friend; you will get precisely as much enjoyment out of them as a blind lover would derive from the possession of a handsome mistress. Your eyes, to be sure, are open; you do see your books, goodness knows, see them till you must be sick of the sight; you even read a bit here and there, in a scrambling fashion, your lips still busy with one sentence while your eyes are on the next. But what is the use of that? You cannot tell good from bad: you miss the writer's general drift, you miss his subtle arrangements of words: the chaste elegance of a pure style, the false ring of the counterfeit, —'tis all one to you.

Are we to understand that you possess literary discernment without the assistance of any study? And how should that be? perhaps, like Hesiod, you received a laurel-branch from the Muses? As to that, I doubt whether you have so much as heard of Helicon, the reputed haunt of those Goddesses; your youthful pursuits were not those of a Hesiod; take not the Muses' names in vain. They might not have any scruples about appearing to a hardy, hairy, sunburnt shepherd: but as for coming near such a one as you (you will excuse my particularizing further just now, when I appeal to you in the name of the Goddess of Lebanon?) they would scorn the thought; instead of laurel, you would have tamarisk and mallow-leaves about your back; the waters of Olmeum and Hippocrene are for thirsty sheep and stainless shepherds, they must not be polluted by unclean lips. I grant you a very creditable stock of effrontery: but you will scarcely have the assurance to call yourself an educated man; you will scarcely pretend that your acquaintance with literature is more than skin-deep, or give us the names of your teacher and your fellow students?

No; you think you are going to work off all arrears by the simple expedient of buying a number of books. But there again: you may get together the works of Demosthenes, and his eight beautiful copies of Thucydides, all in the orator's own handwriting, and all the manuscripts that Sulla sent away from Athens to Italy, —and you will be no nearer to culture at the end of it, though you should sleep with them under your pillow, or paste them together and wear them as a garment; an ape is still an ape, says the proverb, though his trappings be of gold. So it is with you: you have always a book in your hand, you are always reading; but what it is all about, you have not an idea; you do but prick up asinine ears at the lyre's sound. Books would be precious things indeed, if the mere possession of them guaranteed culture to their owner. You rich men would have it all your own way then; we paupers could not stand against you, if learning were a marketable commodity; and as for the dealers, no one would presume to contest the point of culture with men who have whole shopfuls of books at their disposal. However, you will find on examination that these privileged persons are scarcely less ignorant than yourself. They have just your vile accent, and are as deficient in intelligence as one would expect men to be who have never learnt to distinguish good from bad. Now you see, *you* have merely bought a few odd volumes from them: they are at the fountain-head, and are handling books day and night. Judge from this how much good your purchases are likely to do you; unless you think that your very book-cases acquire a tincture of learning, from the bare fact of their housing so many ancient manuscripts.

Oblige me by answering some questions; or rather, as circumstances will not admit of your answering, just nod or shake your head. If the flute of Timotheus, or that of Ismenias, which its owner sold in Corinth for a couple of thousand pounds, were to fall into the hands of a person who did not know how to play the instrument, would that make him a flute-player? would his acquisition leave him any wiser than it found him? You very properly shake your head. A man might possess the instrument of a Marsyas or an Olympus, and still he would not be able to play it if he had never learnt. Take another case: a man gets hold of Heracles's bow and arrows: but he is no Philoctetes; he has neither that marksman's strength nor his eye. What do you say? will he acquit himself creditably? Again you shake your head. The same will be the case with the ignorant pilot who is entrusted with a ship, or with the unpractised rider on horseback. Nothing is wanting to the beauty and efficiency of the vessel, and the horse may be a Median or a Thessalian or a Koppa [Footnote: The brand of the obsolete letter Koppa is supposed to have denoted the Corinthian breed.]: yet I take it that the incompetence of their respective owners will be made clear; am I right? And now let me ask your assent to one more proposition: if an illiterate person like yourself goes in for buying books, he is thereby laying himself open to ridicule. You hesitate? Yet surely nothing could be clearer: who could observe such a man at work, and abstain from the inevitable allusion to pearls and swine?

There was a wealthy man in Asia, not many years ago, who was so unfortunate as to lose both his feet; I think he had been travelling through snow-drifts, and had got them frost-bitten. Well, of course, it was a very hard case; and in ordering a pair of wooden feet, by means of which he contrived to get along with the assistance of servants, he was no doubt only making the best of a bad job. But the absurd thing was, that he would always make a point of having the smartest and newest of shoes to set off his stumps—feet, I mean. Now are you any wiser than he, when for the adornment of that hobbling, wooden understanding of yours you go to the expense of such golden shoes as would tax the agility of a sound-limbed intellect?

Among your other purchases are several copies of Homer. Get some one to turn up the second book of the Iliad, and read to you. There is only one part you need trouble about; the rest does not apply to your case. I refer to the harangue of a certain ludicrous, maimed, distorted creature called Thersites. Now imagine this Thersites, such as he is there depicted, to have clothed himself in the armour of Achilles. What will be the result? Will he be converted there and then into a stalwart, comely warrior, clearing the river at a bound, and staining its waters with Phrygian blood? Will he prove a slayer of Asteropaeuses and Lycaons, and finally of Hectors, he who cannot so much as bear Achilles's spear upon his shoulders? Of course not. He will simply be ridiculous: the weight of the shield will cause him to stagger, and will presently bring him on to his nose; beneath the helmet, as often as he looks up, will be seen that squint; the

Achillean greaves will be a sad drag to his progress, and the rise and fall of the breast-plate will tell a tale of a humped-back; in short, neither the armourer nor the owner of the arms will have much to boast of. You are just like Thersites, if only you could see it. When you take in hand your fine volume, purple-cased, gilt-bossed, and begin reading with that accent of yours, maiming and murdering its contents, you make yourself ridiculous to all educated men: your own toadies commend you, but they generally get in a chuckle too, as they catch one another's eye.

Let me tell you a story of what happened once at Delphi. A native of Tarentum, Evangelus by name, a person of some note in his own city, conceived the ambition of winning a prize in the Pythian Games. Well, he saw at once that the athletic contests were quite out of the question; he had neither the strength nor the agility required. A musical victory, on the other hand, would be an easy matter; so at least he was persuaded by his vile parasites, who used to burst into a roar of applause the moment he touched the strings of his lyre. He arrived at Delphi in great style: among other things, he had provided himself with gold-bespangled garments, and a beautiful golden laurel-wreath, with full-size emerald berries. As for his lyre, that was a most gorgeous and costly affair—solid gold throughout, and ornamented with all kinds of gems, and with figures of Apollo and Orpheus and the Muses, a wonder to all beholders. The eventful day at length arrived. There were three competitors, of whom Evangelus was to come second. Thespis the Theban performed first, and acquitted himself creditably; and then Evangelus appeared, resplendent in gold and emeralds, beryls and jacinths, the effect being heightened by his purple robe, which made a background to the gold; the house was all excitement and wondering anticipation. As singing and playing were an essential part of the competition, Evangelus now struck up with a few meaningless, disconnected notes, assaulting his lyre with such needless violence that he broke three strings at the start; and when he began to sing with his discordant pipe of a voice the whole audience was convulsed with laughter, and the stewards, enraged at his presumption, scourged him out of the theatre. Our golden Evangelus now presented a very queer spectacle, as the floggers drove him across the stage, weeping and bloody- limbed, and stooping to pick up the gems that had fallen from the lyre; for that instrument had come in for its share of the castigation. His place was presently taken by one Eumelus of Elis: his lyre was an old one, with wooden pegs, and his clothes and crown would scarcely have fetched ten shillings between them. But for all that his well-managed voice and admirable execution caused him to be proclaimed the victor; and he was very merry over the unavailing splendours of his rival's gem-studded instrument. 'Evangelus, ' he is reported to have said to him, 'yours is the golden laurel—you can afford it: I am a pauper, and must put up with the Delphian wreath. No one will be sorry for your defeat; your arrogance and incompetence have made you an object of detestation; that is all your equipment has done for you. ' Here again the application is obvious; Evangelus differing from you only in his sensibility to public ridicule.

I have also an old Lesbian story which is very much to the point. It is said that after Orpheus had been torn to pieces by the Thracian women, his head and his lyre were carried down the Hebrus into the sea; the head, it seems, floated down upon the lyre, singing Orpheus's dirge as it went, while the winds blew an accompaniment upon the strings. In this manner they reached the coast of Lesbos; the head was then taken up and buried on the site of the present temple of Bacchus, and the lyre was long preserved as a relic in the temple of Apollo. Later on, however, Neanthus, son of the tyrant Pittacus, hearing how the lyre had charmed beasts and trees and stones, and how after Orpheus's destruction it had played of its own accord, conceived a violent fancy for the instrument, and by means of a considerable bribe prevailed upon the priest to give him the genuine lyre, and replace it with one of similar appearance. Not thinking it advisable to display his acquisition in the city in broad daylight, he waited till night, and then, putting it under his cloak, walked off into the outskirts; and there this youth, who had not a note of music in him, produced his instrument and began jangling on the strings, expecting such divine strains to issue therefrom as would subdue all souls, and prove him the fortunate heir to Orpheus's power. He went on till a number of dogs collected at the sound and tore him limb from limb; thus far, at least, his fate resembled that of Orpheus, though his power of attraction extended only to hostile dogs. It was abundantly proved that the charm lay not in the lyre, but solely in those peculiar gifts of song and music that had been bestowed upon Orpheus by his mother; as to the lyre, it was just like other lyres.

But there: what need to go back to Orpheus and Neanthus? We have instances in our own days: I believe the man is still alive who paid 120 pounds for the earthenware lamp of Epictetus the Stoic. I suppose he thought he had only to read by the light of that lamp, and the wisdom of Epictetus would be communicated to him in his dreams, and he himself assume the likeness of that venerable sage. And it was only a day or two ago that another enthusiast paid down 250 pounds for the staff dropped by the Cynic Proteus [Footnote: See *Peregrine* in Notes.] when he leaped upon the pyre. He treasures this relic, and shows it off just as the people of Tegea do the hide of the Calydonian boar [Footnote: See *Oeneus* in Notes.], or the Thebans the bones of Geryon, or the Memphians Isis' hair. Now the original owner of this precious staff was one who for ignorance and vulgarity would have borne away the palm from yourself. —My friend, you are in a bad way: a stick across the head is what you want.

They say that when Dionysius took to tragedy-writing he made such sad stuff of it that Philoxenus was more than once thrown into the quarries because he could not control his laughter. Finding that his efforts only made him ridiculous, Dionysius was at some pains to procure the tablets on which Aeschylus had been wont to write. He looked to draw divine inspiration from them: as it turned out, however, he now wrote considerably worse rubbish than before. Among the contents of the tablets I may quote:

'Twas Dionysius' wife, Doridion.

Here is another:

Most serviceable woman! thou art gone!

Genuine tablet that, and the next:

Men that are fools are their own folly's butt.

Taken with reference to yourself, by the way, nothing could be more to the point than this last line; Dionysius's tablets deserved gilding, if only for that.

What is your idea, now, in all this rolling and unrolling of scrolls? To what end the gluing and the trimming, the cedar-oil and saffron, the leather cases and the bosses? Much good your purchases have been to you; one sees that already: why, your language—no, I am wrong there, you are as dumb as a fish-but your life, your unmentionable vices, make every one hate the sight of you; if that is what books do, one cannot keep too clear of them. There are two ways in which a man may derive benefit from the study of the ancients: he may learn to express himself, or he may improve his morals by their example and warning; when it is clear that he has not profited in either of these respects, what are his books but a habitation for mice and vermin, and a source of castigation to negligent servants?

And how very foolish you must look when any one finds you with a book in your hand (and you are never to be seen without) and asks you who is your orator, your poet, or your historian: you have seen the title, of course, and can answer that question pat: but then one word brings up another, and some criticism, favourable or the reverse, is passed upon the contents of your volume: you are dumb and helpless; you pray for the earth to open and swallow you; you stand like Bellerophon with the warrant for your own execution in your hand.

Once in Corinth Demetrius the Cynic found some illiterate person reading aloud from a very handsome volume, the Bacchae of Euripides, I think it was. He had got to the place where the messenger is relating the destruction of Pentheus by Agave, when Demetrius snatched the book from him and tore it in two: 'Better, ' he exclaimed, 'that Pentheus should suffer one rending at my hands than many at yours. '

I have often wondered, though I have never been able to satisfy myself, what it is that makes you such an ardent buyer of books. The idea of your making any profitable use of them is one that nobody who has the slightest acquaintance with you would entertain for a moment: does the bald man buy a comb, the blind a mirror, the deaf a flute-player? the eunuch a concubine, the landsman an oar, the pilot a plough? Are you merely seizing an opportunity of displaying your wealth? Is it just your way of showing the public that you can afford to spend money even on things that are of no use to you? Why, even a Syrian like myself knows that if you had not got your name foisted into that old man's will, you would have been starving by this time, and all your books must have been put up to sale.

Only one possible explanation remains: your toadies have made you believe that in addition to your charms of person you have an extraordinary gift for rhetoric, history, and philosophy; and you buy books merely to countenance their flatteries. It seems that you actually hold forth to them at table; and they, poor thirsty frogs, must croak dry-throated applause till they burst, or there is no drink for them. You are a most curiously gullible person: you take in every word they say to you. You were made to believe at one time that your features resembled those of a certain Emperor. We had had a pseudo-Alexander, and a pseudo-Philip, the fuller, and there was a pseudo-Nero as recently as our own grandfathers' times: you were for adding one more to the noble army of pseudos. After all, it was nothing for an illiterate fool like you to take such a fancy into his head, and walk about with his chin in the air, aping the gait and dress and expression of his supposed model: even the Epirot king Pyrrhus, remarkable man that he was in other respects, had the same foible, and was persuaded by his flatterers that he was like Alexander, Alexander the Great, that is. In point of fact, I have seen Pyrrhus's portrait, and the two—to borrow a musical phrase— are about as much like one another as bass and treble; and yet he was convinced he was the image of Alexander. However, if that were all, it would be rather too bad of me to insult Pyrrhus by the comparison: but I am justified by the sequel; it suits your case so exactly. When once Pyrrhus had got this fancy into his head, every one else ran mad for company, till at last an old woman of Larissa, who did not know Pyrrhus, told him the plain truth, and cured his delusion. After showing her portraits of Philip, Perdiccas, Alexander, Casander, and other kings, Pyrrhus finally asked her which of these he resembled, taking it as a matter of course that she would fix upon Alexander: however, she considered for some time, and at length informed him that he was most like Batrachion the cook, there being a cook of that name in Larissa who *was* very like Pyrrhus. What particular theatrical pander *you* most resemble I will not pretend to decide: all I can state with certainty is that to this day you pass for a raving madman on the strength of this fancy.. After such an instance of your critical discernment, we need not be surprised to find that your flatterers have inspired you with the further ambition of being taken for a scholar.

But I am talking nonsense. The cause of your bibliomania is clear enough; I must have been dozing, or I should have seen it long ago. This is your idea of strategy: you know the Emperor's scholarly tastes, and his respect for culture, and you think it will be worth something to you if he hears of your literary pursuits. Once let your name be mentioned to him as a great buyer and collector of books, and you reckon that your fortune is made. Vile creature! and is the Emperor drugged with mandragora that he should hear of this and never know the rest, your daylight iniquities, your tipplings, your monstrous nightly debauches? Know you not that an Emperor has many eyes and many ears? Yet *your* deeds are such as cannot be concealed from the blind or the deaf. I may tell you at once, as you seem not to know it, that a man's hopes of the Imperial favour depend not on his book-bills, but on his character and daily life. Are you counting upon Atticus and Callinus, the copyists, to put in a good word for you? Then you are deceived: those relentless gentlemen propose, with the Gods' good leave, to grind you down and reduce you to utter destitution. Come to your senses while there is yet time: sell your library to some scholar, and whilst you are about it sell your new house too, and wipe off part of your debt to the slave-dealers.

You see, you will ride both these hobbies at once; there is the trouble: besides your expensive books you must have your superannuated minions; you are insatiable in these pursuits, and you cannot follow both without money. Now observe how precious a thing is counsel. I recommend you to dispense with the superfluous, and confine your attention to your other foible; in other words, keep your money for the slave-dealers, or your private supplies will run short, and you will be reduced to calling in the services of freemen, who will want every penny you possess; otherwise there is nothing to prevent them from telling how your time is spent when you are in liquor. Only the other day I heard some very ugly stories about you—backed, too, by ocular evidence: the bystanders on that occasion are my witnesses how angry I was on your account; I was in two minds about giving the fellow a thrashing; and the annoying part of it was that he appealed to more than one witness who had had the same experience and told just the same tale. Let this be a warning to you to economize, so that you may be able to have your enjoyments at home in all security. I do not suggest that you should give up these practices: that is quite hopeless; the dog that has gnawed leather once will gnaw leather always.

On the other hand, you can easily do without books. Your education is complete; you have nothing more to learn; you have the ancients as it were on the tip of your tongue; all history is known to you; you are a master of the choice and management of words, you have got the true Attic vocabulary; the multitude of your books has made a ripe scholar of you. (You love flattery, and there is no reason why I should not indulge you as well as another.)

But I am rather curious on one point: what are your favourite books among so many? Plato? Antisthenes? Archilochus? Hipponax? Or are they passed over in favour of the orators? Do you ever read the speech of Aeschines against Timarchus? All that sort of thing I suppose you have by heart. And have you grappled with Aristophanes and Eupolis? Did you ever go through the *Baptae* [Footnote: See Cotytto in Notes.]? Well then, you must surely have come on some embarrassing home-truths in that play? It is difficult to imagine that mind of yours bent upon literary studies, and those hands turning over the pages. When do you do your reading? In the daytime, or at night? If the former, you must do it when no one is looking: and if the latter, is it done in the midst of more engrossing pursuits, or do you work it in before your rhetorical outpourings? As you reverence Cotytto, venture not again into the paths of literature; have done with books, and keep to your own peculiar business. If you had any sense of shame, to be sure, you would abandon that too: think of Phaedra's indignant protest against her sex:

> Darkness is their accomplice, yet they fear not,
> Fear not the chamber-walls, their confidants.

But no: you are determined not to be cured. Very well: buy book upon book, shut them safely up, and reap the glory that comes of possession: only, let that be enough; presume not to touch nor read; pollute not with that tongue the poetry and eloquence of the ancients; what harm have they ever done to you?

All this advice is thrown away, I know that. Shall an Ethiopian change his skin? You will go on buying books that you cannot use — to the amusement of educated men, who derive profit not from the price of a book, nor from its handsome appearance, but from the sense and sound of its contents. You think by the multitude of books to supply the deficiencies of your education, and to throw dust in our eyes. Did you but know it, you are exactly like the quack doctors, who provide themselves with silver cupping-glasses, gold-handled lancets, and ivory cases for their instruments; they are quite incapable of using them when the time comes, and have to give place to some properly qualified surgeon, who produces a lancet with a keen edge and a rusty handle, and affords immediate relief to the sufferer. Or here is a better parallel: take the case of the barbers: you will find that the skilled practitioners have just the razor, scissors, and mirror that their work requires: the impostors' razors are numerous, and their mirrors magnificent. However, that does not serve to conceal their incompetence, and the result is most amusing: the average man gets his hair cut by one of their more capable neighbours, and then goes and arranges it before *their* glasses. That is just what your books are good for — to lend to other people; you are quite incapable of using them yourself. Not that you ever have lent any one a single volume; true to your dog-in-the-manger principles, you neither eat the corn yourself, nor give the horse a chance.

There you have my candid opinion about your books: I shall find other opportunities of dealing with your disreputable conduct in general.

Lightning Source UK Ltd.
Milton Keynes UK
UKOW02f0340110816

280439UK00001B/167/P